New York Times ...
Shirley Jump spe... her shoe addiction ... cleverly finds writi... allowing them to dress in the clothes they find on the floor and encouraging the dogs to double as vacuum cleaners. Chat with her via Facebook: www.facebook.com/shirleyjump.author or her website: www.shirleyjump.com

Brenda Harlen is a former lawyer who once had the privilege of appearing before the Supreme Court of Canada. The practice of law taught her a lot about the world and reinforced her determination to become a writer – because in fiction, she could promise a happy ending! Now she is an award-winning, RITA® Award-nominated nationally bestselling author of more than thirty titles for Mills & Boon. You can keep up to date with Brenda on Facebook and Twitter, or through her website, brendaharlen.com

Sarah M. Anderson is happiest when writing. Her book *A Man of Privilege* won the 2012 RT Reviewers' Choice Best Book Award. *The Nanny Plan* won the 2016 RITA® Award for Contemporary Romance: Short. Find out more about Sarah's conversations with imaginary cowboys and billionaires at sarahmanderson.com and sign up for the new-release newsletter at eepurl.com/nv39b

After Hours

After Hours: Falling for the Nanny

SHIRLEY JUMP

BRENDA HARLEN

SARAH M. ANDERSON

MILLS & BOON

First Published in Great Britain 2021
By Mills & Boon, an imprint of HarperCollins*Publishers* Ltd
1 London Bridge Street, London, SE1 9GF

www.harpercollins.co.uk

HarperCollins*Publishers*
1st Floor, Watermarque Building,
Ringsend Road, Dublin 4, Ireland

AFTER HOURS: FALLING FOR THE NANNY © 2021 Harlequin Books S.A.

Winning the Nanny's Heart © 2017 Shirley Kawa-Jump, LLC
Prince Daddy & the Nanny © 2011 Brenda Harlen
The Nanny Plan © 2015 Sarah M. Anderson

ISBN: 978-0-263-30022-2

MIX
Paper from
responsible sources
FSC™ C007454

This book is produced from independently certified FSC™ paper to ensure responsible forest management.

For more information visit: www.harpercollins.co.uk/green

Printed and bound in Spain
by CPI, Barcelona

WINNING THE NANNY'S HEART

SHIRLEY JUMP

To my awesome, super-smart editor Susan Litman,
who has made every one of the Barlow Brothers
books better and stronger. Working with her has
been an honor and a pleasure.

Chapter One

The first time Katie Williams ran away from home, she was eight years old.

She packed her Barbie backpack with a clean T-shirt, a handful of granola bars and three stuffed animals (because she couldn't possibly choose between Rabbit, Harvey and Willard), then set out into the world. Well, not the world, really, just the end of Seventh Street, where the alley met the back of the park. She'd settled into the dark, tight space under the stairs for the slide, and told herself she wasn't scared.

Her brother, Colton, found her an hour later, hungry and weepy and cold. "I was gonna make pancakes for breakfast tomorrow, Piglet," he'd said, as if it were just another ordinary Tuesday. "And nobody wants to miss out on pancakes." He wrapped her in the thick fleeced comfort of his sweatshirt, then carried her home piggyback. While he walked, his back hunched under her weight, he told her a story about a brave princess who lived in a castle high on a hill, with an ogre for a friend. Colton had carried her straight to her room, deposited Katie in her squeaky twin bed and bundled her under the thin blankets. He paused, then let out a sigh.

She did it again, Colton had said.

It wasn't even a question. Katie nodded, afraid to say the words out loud. To tell her brother how their mother had lashed out at Katie again, for a sin no more egregious than asking if there was anything for supper. In those days, their mother drank more than she ate, and for whatever reason, had taken her anger out on Katie more than Colton.

Colton had given her a nod of understanding, a hug and a whisper in her ear, *You're a good kid. Don't ever forget that*. He'd talked to her until her tears dried up and then he'd tucked her into her bed, and left her with a sandwich he'd sneaked out of the kitchen.

She supposed it was kind of ironic that almost twenty years later, she was running away from home again, but this time *toward* her brother. And once again, he didn't ask a single question when she showed up on his doorstep late in the afternoon in a tiny quaint town in North Carolina.

"Hey," she said, when she walked into the Stone Gap Fire Department and found Colton standing by Engine No. 1, polishing the chrome. "I'm here."

He stopped working, tossed the rag onto the counter and grinned at her. "Hey yourself, Piglet." She'd never escaped his childhood nickname for her, but that was okay. "'Bout time you showed up."

She propped a fist on her hip and gave her six-foot-two brother a well-practiced look of annoyance. He was seven inches taller than her and looked ten times stronger in his dark blue uniform. But that didn't stop her from teasing him. "Just because you call and invite me to come visit you doesn't mean I'm going to rush on down here."

"I don't know why not. Seeing as how I'm your favorite person and all." His grin widened and he stepped forward, opening his arms and dragging her into a hug before she could protest. "Even if you are my annoying little sister."

Katie drew back and squared her shoulders. She could have leaned into Colton's hug forever, but if she did that, she was afraid the fragile hold she had on her emotions would crumble, and then she'd be a sobbing mess. If there was one thing Katie didn't do, it was cave to emotions. She hadn't gotten to be a partner at one of the largest accounting firms in Atlanta by acting weak. And she wasn't going to get through the next couple weeks without staying strong.

After that, she should be fine. Or at least that was what she had told herself the whole way here. Two weeks, she'd decided, was long enough to find a new job, a new life, a new everything. And maybe, just maybe, stop hurting.

"All right, so now I'm here," she said, brushing her bangs off her forehead, as if that action could brush the worry away from her mind, too. "You want to show me around this town you've raved so much about?"

Truth be told, Colton had done far more raving about Rachel Morris, the girl he was engaged to. He was clearly head over heels for the wedding planner he'd met a few months ago. He'd taken a job at the local fire department, and from what Katie could tell from his texts and phone calls, settled right into Stone Gap like he was born here. She shouldn't have been surprised—

Colton was the kind of guy who fit in anywhere, even with the half brothers he'd recently met. Katie, on the other hand, had never had the same kind of ease around people. Maybe it was from doing such a left-brained job, or maybe it was just that Colton had enough charm for the two of them combined.

"I can't leave now, sis, sorry. I just started my shift and I'm on the clock for a full twenty-four," he said. "But why don't you head over to the Stone Gap Inn, and I'll meet you there tomorrow night at suppertime? Tell Della I sent you. I stayed there until I rented a house in town. It's awesome. If anyone knows how to be a hostess, it's Della. She's my dad's wife, and I guarantee she's going to make you feel like a long lost member of the family."

Katie wasn't so sure about that. Right now, all she wanted was a room to herself and some time to think. "Sounds like a plan. Say…six o'clock?"

"On the dot." Then he winked. "More or less. You know you have to give me a ten-minute window, in either direction."

She rolled your eyes at him. "I swear, you do that on purpose."

Colton draped an arm over her shoulders and started walking her back to her car. "You are just a tiny bit too uptight, Piglet. Learn to loosen up. Run late once in a while. Get messy. Your life will be ten times more fun that way."

"And your life would be ten times easier if you just got a little more organized and on time."

Colton chuckled. "See you tomorrow, sis."

Katie climbed into her car and started the engine. She waved goodbye to her brother, then drove two miles away from downtown Stone Gap before turning on a pretty side street lined with trees. She'd been in town only for an hour and already knew her way around—such a difference from the crazy congestion of Atlanta. Okay, so she'd also studied a Google map of the town before making the drive from Atlanta, and written down the directions to the B and B after Colton had referred her to it when she'd broached the idea of visiting. But overall, Stone Gap was easy—easy to drive through, easy to enjoy.

This was what she wanted and needed, she told herself. A quiet, picturesque seaside town where she could…forget. Move on. *Take some time to process this*, the doctor had told her. *Don't expect to bounce right back into your normal life. You've had a loss, and you need time to deal with it.*

But how did one "process" a miscarriage? Katie's hand strayed to her belly, as if touching the place where the baby had been would change anything. Everything about her life was different now, had been for two months. Two months where she had buried her feelings and told herself she was okay. Then had a major meltdown at work, and lost the firm's two biggest clients. All in one day. The next day, her boss had sat her down and told her maybe it would be best for all involved if she moved on, a pretty little euphemism for being fired. Except Katie wasn't sure what to do next. How to move forward or move on.

For one brief moment—a handful of weeks, really—Katie had dared to consider a different life from the one she'd been living. She'd dreamed of detouring from the careful career path she'd been on. Quitting her job, because working eighty hours a week didn't jibe with being a mom, and maybe going out on her own or working at a smaller firm. She'd flipped through baby mag-

azines and surfed nursery design websites. She'd even
set up a Pinterest account, thinking she'd want a way to
organize and save all the things she had found.

And then one morning she'd woken up in pain, her
stomach curling in against her like a fist, and she'd
known, in that innate way a woman reads the whispers
of her body. Later that day, the doctor had confirmed
the wrenching truth Katie already knew.

The baby, the different life, the dream, were all gone.
She laid a hand on her stomach and could almost hear
it echoing inside. Katie had wanted to roll into a ball
in that hospital bed and cry, but instead, she'd gotten
dressed, checked out and gone to work.

Because she thought that would help her forget.

It hadn't.

And now, here she was, in a town not much bigger
than a postage stamp, looking for…peace. A direction.
She'd start, she decided, small. At the Stone Gap Inn.

She pulled into the driveway of the address Colton
had given her and looked up at the two-story white
antebellum-style house before her. A long, columned
front porch greeted visitors like a smile, anchored by
a swing on one end and two comfy rocking chairs on
the other. A rainbow of flowers flanked the walkway,
leading a happy march up to a bright red front door.
Katie half expected a girl in a corset and hoopskirt to
step onto the porch and offer visitors some sweet tea.

Just as she rang the bell, the front door opened and
a curvy red-haired woman in a floral apron greeted her
with a wide smile. "Why, hello! You must be Colton's
sister. He called me and told me you were on your way.
I'm Della." She put out her hand and shook with Katie.
"Della Barlow. I own this bed-and-breakfast, and run
it with my best friend, Mavis."

It was a fast, breathless, friendly introduction that rushed over Katie like a wave. "Uh, hi. Yes, I'm Colton's younger sister and he said he made a reservation for me?"

"He did indeed. Come right in." Della waved her in, and waited a beat while Katie stood in the foyer, mouth agape, and took in the grand staircase that zippered up the middle of the house.

It was like walking into the pages of *Gone with the Wind*. The staircase curved in at the center, with white risers marrying the wood treads and a carved railing that formed a graceful swoop up to the second floor. On the main floor, a formal parlor sat to the left, with a pair of vanilla love seats sitting on either side of an upright piano. Long, satiny cream drapes framed the floor-to-ceiling windows and a small rolltop desk against the far wall. The dining room was on the right, dominated by a long mahogany table with a wide spray of bright pink and white flowers at its center. The coffered ceiling provided the perfect backdrop to an elaborate chandelier filled with teardrop crystals. Shades of whites, creams and soft pastels filled every room, as inviting as sinking into a cloud. Katie loved it immediately.

"Welcome to the Stone Gap Inn," Della said, as she walked up the stairs with Katie right behind. "We just opened a few months ago, so we might still have a hiccup or two. The house was abandoned for years before Mavis and I bought it. It still had strong bones, though, being pre–Civil War, one of the few that survived those years. My husband and sons helped renovate it, along with some help from my wonderful soon-to-be daughter-in-law, who restores old houses. They all worked on it, top to bottom, but we kept as many period details as we could. Don't worry, though, we made sure all the plumbing and electricity is modern, along with Wi-Fi and satellite TV in each of the rooms."

Katie laughed. "It sounds perfect. In fact, it looks perfect. The house is stunning."

"Thank you. We love it, and so far, our guests have, too. They've all been so grateful to have a place to stay, ever since the original hotel in town closed up. The owner retired, moved to Minnesota to be near his grandkids, but was gracious enough to send all his customers to us. He said a B and B fits Stone Gap better, and I might be biased, but I happen to agree."

"I do, too," Katie said. "This place seems perfect for a small seaside town."

"Thank you. Mavis and I were looking for something to keep us busy in our golden years, and the way business has been going, we got our wish." Della laughed. "Anyway, I put you in the Charlotte Room," she said, opening a door as she spoke. "I hope you like it."

If Katie could have dreamed up a perfect bedroom, this would have been it. Pale green, bright white and accents of butter yellow made the room feel like a garden. A canopy bed dominated the space, looking more like a cloud than a place to sleep. Piles of pillows cascaded down the center of a thick white comforter. A low bench sat at the foot of the bed, with a basket filled with fluffy towels and soaps and bath salts on one end, a tray with mini bottles of water and a bowl of fresh fruit on the other. A ceiling-high armoire sat between the windows, and a thick white terry-cloth robe hung inside, just begging someone to slip it on, curl up in the armchair in the corner and read one of the books piled in the small bookcase.

Katie gasped. "Wow. It's gorgeous."

"I'm so glad you like the room. I'll give you some

time to get settled. If you want to join me in the kitchen for some coffee and fresh-baked cookies, come on downstairs." Della placed a room key in Katie's palm. "Welcome to Stone Gap."

Katie sank onto the bed after Della was gone, and thought yes, this was exactly what she needed. Maybe, just maybe, here in this town that seemed to wrap around her like a warm blanket, she could find a way to move forward again.

The scent of chocolate chip cookies drew Katie out of her nap and back downstairs an hour later. She'd slept better in that hour than she had in the last two months. It had to be the bed, or the total quiet that surrounded her, so unlike the constant hum of Atlanta.

In the kitchen, Della was at the stove, stirring something that smelled amazing. She turned when Katie entered the kitchen. "Coffee?"

"Do you have decaf?"

"I do indeed. Have a seat and—"

Katie waved off Della's instructions. She felt useless just relaxing like this. "Please, let me help."

"I'll do no such thing. Bed-and-breakfast means you get a place to sleep and breakfast served to you. But an inn means you get all that and more." Della grabbed a coffee mug and filled it with steaming brew. She placed it before Katie, along with cream and sugar in cute little cow-shaped containers. "Now, sit down and enjoy yourself. This is your vacation, dear."

"Will you please sit with me?" Katie said. For some reason, she didn't want to be alone. Maybe because when she was alone she tended to think, and that just brought everything back to the surface again. "Please."

Della glanced at the stove, then at the small table's

empty chair. "I think I will. My feet are barking at me to take a few minutes to sit on my duff. Besides, that crab chowder is done enough to cook all by itself." Della slipped out of the apron and hung it over the back of a chair, then poured herself a cup of coffee and added a splash of cream. "So, tell me, what brings you to Stone Gap?"

"Like you said, vacation. And..." Katie toyed with the mug. There was something friendly and open about Della Barlow that warmed the air between them and made Katie want to confide, a little, about all that was going on in her life. "And maybe find a job. I'm sort of between things and not sure where I want to go next. Colton raves about this town, and I thought I'd give it a couple weeks to see if it grows on me, too."

"If you're not careful, this town will wrap around your heart like ivy on an oak tree, pretty and strong. That's what it did to me, more than thirty-five years ago, when I moved here with my Bobby. 'Course, it helped that the man himself was also wrapped around my heart." Della smiled, clearly proud of her town and the man she'd married.

A man who had had an affair more than thirty years ago with Katie's mother, an affair that had produced Colton. Katie had seen pictures of her mother from those years, before her drinking took its toll. Vanessa Williams had been beautiful, with long dark hair, deep green eyes and a wide smile. In the years since Colton and Katie had been born, she'd morphed into a sullen, resentful woman who considered both her children as unwanted burdens.

But Della Barlow—she was obviously the kind of mother everyone wished they could have. It was clear she loved her sons and her husband, despite the brief bump their marriage had hit more than three decades ago. Katie had no doubt staying here would be like coming home.

"So, Katie, what do you do?" Della asked. "Or, a better question, what do you *want* to do, since not all of us work at our first-love jobs when we're young."

It had been a long time since Katie had thought about her ideal career. She felt like she was in middle school again, lying on her bed and looking up at the cracks in the ceiling. When she was eleven, she'd imagined they were paths, creeping like a spider out in different directions. If she took this path, she'd end up there, by that missing chunk of plaster. That path, and she'd connect with that path and that one, and end up fading into the window frame. The world had seemed open and endless back then, filled with crazy ideas like becoming a veterinarian and an actress and a chef, all at the same time. "I… I don't know. I've been an accountant for so long, I don't know anything else."

"Was that your dream, working with numbers?"

Katie scoffed. "No. I sort of fell into it. I was good at math, and I got a scholarship to college, as long as I enrolled in the accounting program. I've been doing this job so long, I don't know if I can do anything else."

Della waved that off. "Honey, you are as young as a baby bird. You still have time to go after whatever dream you want. Heck, I'm in my fifties and just now embarking on my dream." She gestured at the sunny yellow kitchen, the off-white cabinets, the wide plank floors. "Dare to do something different, while you aren't tied down to a family and a dog."

Dare to do something different. That was part of why Katie was here, because she didn't know what else to do with herself, except for something different. She couldn't stay one more second in Atlanta, where everything she looked at reminded her of what she had lost. "I don't even know where to start."

Della's hand covered hers. "Start with cookies."

"Cookies?"

"Of course. Everything's better with cookies." Della grinned. "And then, if you're interested in something temporary, I know someone who needs some help for the next few weeks. It's not a glamorous job, but I guarantee it'll be fun and not at all like accounting."

Katie took a bite out of a chewy chocolate chip cookie that melted against her tongue. Like the rest of the house and the owner herself, the cookies were the best ever. "What kind of job are you talking about?"

"Well…" Della took a sip of coffee, then wrapped her hands around the mug, "Sam Millwright is in need of a tutor. If you ask me, he needs a good nanny, too. I've met Charity Jacobs, the one working for him now, and she's a dear girl, but in over her head."

A tutor maybe, but a nanny? As in someone who watched kids all day? Katie had zero experience with children, unless one counted the couple summers she'd spent as a camp counselor. But that had been a team experience—never one where she was on her own, in charge of everything from sunup to sundown for a kid. She'd never had a younger sibling, never really babysat (okay, so she had watched her neighbor's Pomeranians twice, and commandeered her cousins almost every holiday meal, but that wasn't the same thing), never even watched a friend's child, let alone helped anyone with homework. And the thought of being with a baby…

"Sam's kids are just the cutest little things you ever did see. Libby just turned eight, and Henry is three," Della said. "You'd love them."

Three and eight. So not babies. Maybe doable. Maybe. But still, a nanny? Della was right, that was about as far removed from accountant as Katie could get. Except she had no desire to be a nanny, and not enough experience to even consider the job.

"Wait...did you say he needed a tutor, too?"

Della nodded. "Libby's struggling in school. Ever since her mom passed away, she's been having a hard time keeping up, poor thing. Sam's doing the best he can, but it's tough, being breadwinner and everything else at the same time. His regular babysitter up and quit a month ago, and Sam's been struggling ever since to find someone to watch the kids. He's got Charity filling in part of the time, but she's..." Della made a little face. "Anyway, I had the kids over here yesterday, trying to take the load off Sam, but you know, it's hard to run a business and watch two kids." She smiled. "Even if they're truly the nicest kids ever."

Couple of nice, sweet kids. How hard could it be? Katie would have to tutor only one of them, it seemed. And the extra money would be a godsend while she was debating her next move. Not to mention, as Della had said, it wasn't accounting. It wouldn't be a job that would require her to remember a million details or figure out complicated tax structures. It would be almost as easy as just staying home all day, except she'd hopefully be too busy to think. If the girl was eight, it wasn't like Katie was going to need a master's in English to tutor her. What was that, third grade? She could handle third grade homework help. And surely the math would be a breeze for her. As much as Katie said she wanted time to think, to breathe, just the thought of all that time in her head...

She'd rather be working. Doing something that

wasn't difficult, but still kept her mind from spinning. "Sure. I'll talk to him."

"Lovely!" Della grinned. "I'll give him a call quicker than a bunny running through a pepper patch."

Della did as she'd promised, calling up Sam Millwright a second later. Katie caught only half the conversation, but it was full of "you're going to love her" and "she's delightful" endorsements of Katie. Della dropped Colton's name into the conversation and that seemed to be the clincher. Della hung up the phone, then scribbled an address on a piece of paper. "Here's his address," she said. "He said to be there at eight thirty tomorrow morning and he'll give you an interview."

"Sounds like a plan," Katie said, taking the paper. It wasn't moving on or moving forward, but it wasn't standing still, either, and for now, that was enough.

Chapter Two

It was only a little after eight in the morning and already Sam had resorted to bribery. "If you eat your breakfast, Libby Bear, I'll let you have a cookie."

Probably not the healthiest bribe, but at this point, after dealing with the kids for two hours—thanks to Henry waking up at the crack of way-too-early—Sam was desperate. Hell, most days he was desperate. Between the kids and an overly eager one-year-old golden retriever, Sam felt outnumbered, outmaneuvered and out of ideas.

"Miss Della's cookies?" Libby asked with a wary look. "Because your cookies smell weird."

As in *eau de burned*. Della Barlow had taken one look at the snack Sam had packed for the kids yesterday and baked them three dozen chocolate chip pity cookies. Thank God, because Sam couldn't cook his way out of a paper bag. He wasn't much good at housework or doing ponytails or answering tough questions from a still-grieving three- and eight-year-old. What he was good at was corporate real estate. Or at least he had been, until the agency he worked for went belly-up. All the profits on million-dollar deals he'd brought into the agency had been frittered away by the owner, leaving the coffers dry when it came to making the payments on their own building. Sam had walked into work last Monday and found a for-sale sign on the door, and the locks changed, most likely by the bank. All his pending deals went up in smoke as panicked clients ran off to other agents, and the commission check Sam had been counting on to pay the bills had bounced higher than a new tennis ball.

It was partly his own fault. All the signs of a business in trouble had been there, but he'd been too distracted, trying to run a household and keep the kids fed and clothed and going to bed on time, to pay attention. He'd done the one thing he couldn't afford to do—turned his focus away from his job—and it had nearly cost him everything.

He had an interview with the agency's biggest competitor later this morning. The problem? He had yet to find regular child care. One would think it wouldn't be hard, but the three nannies he had met so far had been like the Three Stooges: incompetent, irresponsible and insane. He'd hired Charity Jacobs a couple weeks ago. She was okay, but not exactly Nanny of the Year, nor was she interested in taking on the job full-time. She kept saying something about needing to see her boyfriend. Half the time, Charity looked terrified to be left alone with the kids. But so far she'd kept them fed and clean, and that was more than the others had done.

On top of that, there was Libby and the constant

worry about her falling behind. Third grade was a pivotal year for math skills, her teacher had said, with the kind of impending doom in her voice that suggested Libby would end up a panhandler if she didn't grasp the basics this year. She needed a tutor and Sam needed a miracle.

Thank God Della had called yesterday and promised the perfect candidate in Colton's little sister.

Sam liked Colton. Liked all the Barlows, in fact. He'd met Colton, half brother to Mac, Luke and Jack, at a town picnic a couple months ago. There'd been a rousing and surprisingly competitive game of cornhole, which Colton was close to winning until Sam made his final shot. The two men had laughed, then shared a couple beers and found a common ground in fishing, something Colton had done a lot of recently with his future father-in-law and his fiancée. Sam and he had hung out a few times since, now that Colton had moved to Stone Gap on a permanent basis.

Libby hopped down off the chair and started twirling. Her skirt swung out around her in a rising bell. "I want ballet lessons. Can I have ballet lessons?"

Ballet lessons. Another thing he'd have to schedule and run to. Libby made a constant argument in favor of the lessons by wearing an old, tattered ballerina dress, a Halloween costume from years ago, pretty much every day. He'd wanted Libby to wear jeans and a T-shirt to school today. Libby had thrown a fit, pitching herself onto the floor and sobbing, saying that Mommy had bought her the ballerina dress and she really wanted to wear it—

And Sam caved. He'd also caved on letting the kids watch cartoons while they ate, though Bugs Bunny and friends hadn't exactly inspired anyone to take a single bite yet.

He glanced at the still untouched waffle on Libby's plate. "Libby, you need to eat your breakfast so we can get to school and I can get Henry over to the community center." He had just enough time to give the tutor a quick interview, drop the kids at school by nine and get to his interview at nine fifteen.

Libby let out a sigh that sounded way too grown-up. "We don't have school today."

"Of course you have school today. It's Tuesday."

Libby shook her head. "Miss McCarthy said we didn't. There's some big meeting for the teachers or something."

Sam crossed to the fridge, moving menus and notes and drawings around until he finally found the school calendar, tacked in place by a thick magnet. He ran his finger down to today's date—

No School. In-Service Teacher Day.

He started to curse, then stopped himself. Now what was he supposed to do? He pulled out his phone and texted Charity. No school today. Need you ASAP.

"And Uncle Ty said the community center is closed today. 'Cuz he had to fix the bathroom or something."

"There's no storytime today?" What else could go wrong this morning?

Libby shrugged. "Can I go play?"

"Eat your breakfast first." *While I come up with a miracle.* He had forty-five minutes until his interview. Forty-five minutes to get Charity over here and interview this new girl for the tutor job.

Libby shook her head. "I don't like those waffles. I like the ones…"

Her voice trailed off, but Sam could fill in the blank

himself. She liked the ones her mommy had made, before Mommy had been killed by a drunk driver. The year and a half since then had passed in a blur, with Sam juggling a job and the kids and babysitters and his grief. He'd thought he was doing a good job, until he lost first Mrs. Rey, the best nanny in the world, who had moved to Florida to be with her grandkids, then a few weeks later, his job. He'd tried to step in and do it all, but he wasn't much good at being two parents in one. Time, he told himself, time fixed everything.

Except when he was running late. "Libby, you need to eat because I need to—"

She stopped spinning and crossed her arms over her chest. "No."

Lately, Libby had mastered defiance. She wasn't outright disobedient, just enough to add another stress to Sam's day.

From his booster seat at the other end of the kitchen table, Henry let out a shriek of support. Sam turned to his son. "Hey, buddy, want to eat breakfast?"

Henry shook his head.

"Do you want something else? Just say it, buddy, and I'll get you whatever you want."

Henry stared at his father for one long moment. Sam waited, his heart in his throat. Maybe this time…

Instead, Henry picked up his waffle and flung it on the floor. Before Sam could react, the golden retriever dashed in and stole a bonus meal.

That made Libby laugh, while she tossed her waffle at the dog, too. "Get it, Bandit. Get it!"

"Libby—"

But she was already gone, tearing off to the living room to snatch up the TV remote and raise the volume to deafening levels. Henry saw his own opportunity for escape, and clambered down from the chair and over to the giant box of Legos that Sam had forgotten to put up on the top shelf. Before Sam could say "don't touch that," Henry had knocked it onto the floor, releasing a cavalcade of miniature bricks.

And then the doorbell rang.

The dog started barking. Libby started peppering her father with questions about who was there, was it Miss Della, was it the mailman, was it Barney the dinosaur. Sam closed his eyes for a too-brief second, then strode down the hall and pulled open the door.

One of the most beautiful women Sam had ever seen stared back at him, with big brown doe-like eyes peeking out from under long dark wavy hair. She wore a pencil skirt that hugged her curves, a satiny pink blouse and dark pumps that raised her from what he guessed was a normal height of about five foot three. "Uh, I'm Katie Williams," she said, while he continued to stare. "I'm here to interview for the tutor position? I'm sorry I'm a few minutes early."

The tutor. Of course. Already, he'd forgotten about her appointment. Maybe he was the one who should have eaten his breakfast. Or, for that matter, had a cup of coffee. Thus far, Sam was lucky he'd had enough time to throw on some clothes and brush his teeth. And given that Charity hadn't responded to his text yet, that meant he still didn't have anyone to watch Libby, and his interview was in less than forty-five minutes… "Oh, yes, I'm sorry. I—" He threw up his hands and gave up trying to formulate any kind of excuse. How did he encapsulate months of feeling overwhelmed into one sentence? "It's been a morning and a half. Katie Williams—Colton's little sister, right?"

"Yes."

Which made her probably only a couple years younger than Sam. He didn't know why that mattered so much, but it suddenly did. "Colton's a great guy."

"Who's here?" Libby skidded to a stop beside him and poked her head around the door. "Hi. I'm Libby."

Katie bent down. "Hi, Libby. I'm Katie." She raised her gaze and peered at the space behind Sam. "And who's that?"

Libby turned. "Oh, that's my little brother, Henry. He's shy."

Katie wiggled her fingers in Henry's direction. "Hi, Henry. I'm Katie."

Henry stood at the corner for a second longer, then dashed back into the living room. He never uttered a peep. Not that Sam had expected him to. Henry had almost completely stopped talking after his mother died. Sam had taken his son to doctor after doctor, spent hours searching the internet, but the conclusion was the same—Henry would talk when he was ready.

Lord, how Sam missed the sound of Henry's voice. The curiosity in the lilting questions he used to ask. Sam's heart ached, literally ached, for the things he had lost. The things he couldn't change.

Libby, the more outgoing of the two kids, just kept looking up at Katie with obvious curiosity. "Do you like dogs?" Libby asked.

Katie smiled. "I love dogs."

One point in favor of Katie Williams. Hopefully, she liked dogs with plenty of puppy energy, because he could feel Bandit nudging past him. Just as Sam reached for the dog's collar, Bandit leaped, paws landing on Katie's chest. She stumbled back, and for a long, heart-stopping second, Sam thought she was going to fall down his porch stairs. Visions of hospitals and lawsuits popped into his mind. He reached for her, caught her hand, just as she recovered her balance and swayed forward. But then she overcorrected, and swayed straight into his chest.

"Oh, God. I'm… I'm sorry," she said, jerking away from him.

He knew he should say the same, but for one long second there he hadn't been sorry at all that she had touched him. Maybe it was because he'd been alone for so long, or maybe it was because she was one of the most beautiful women he'd ever seen, but either way, a little frisson of electricity had run through Sam when Katie touched his chest. It was chased by a wave of guilt. Wendy had been dead for only a year and a half. What was he doing, reacting to another woman like that?

"I'm the one who needs to apologize. My, uh, dog is still learning his manners," Sam said, and thought it would be a good thing if his owner remembered his. "But please come in, have a seat while we talk. I can lock Bandit up if you want."

"Oh, no, the dog is fine. I love dogs, remember? Really." Katie started to follow Sam into the house, with Bandit hot on her heels.

"You can come with me," Libby said. She put her hand in Katie's and tugged her down the hall. "My father says I gotta be nice to people who come over to the house."

My father. Not Daddy. He hadn't heard Daddy, or even Dad in a long time. He bit back another sigh.

"And he's supposed to be nice, too," Libby added, giving Sam a pointed glare.

Katie looked up at Sam and smiled. She had a nice smile. A really nice smile. "Is that so?"

"Yup. 'Cuz sometimes he's grumpy," Libby added, thumbing in the direction of Sam.

Sam groaned. That was the problem with kids. They said too much and always at the wrong time. "I'm not grumpy. Just…stressed."

"How come?" Libby asked.

He ruffled his daughter's hair. She stiffened, an almost imperceptible amount, but the distance was there. The easy relationship he'd had with his eldest had also disappeared in the last year and a half. Sam put on a bright face, pretending, as he always did, that he didn't notice. That they were all just fine. "Because *some people* feed their breakfast to the dog."

Katie bit back a laugh. "My brother used to do that."

"Not you?"

"Of course not. I was the good one." Katie smiled when she said that, which sent his mind spiraling down a couple paths that were not appropriate for interviewing the tutor. Yeah, he definitely had been alone too long. That was all it was.

Sam cleared his throat and gestured toward the dining room table. The kitchen was a mess—as was typical pretty much every day of the week—with dirty dishes piled in the sink, breakfast crumbs scattered across the table and countertops, and a set of muddy paw prints running circles around the table. They never used the dining room, which meant it was relatively clean, if he ignored the light coating of dust on everything. "Libby, go watch cartoons with Henry."

"But I wanna—"

"Go watch cartoons with Henry. Please." He prayed Libby wouldn't argue, that she would just do what he said.

Libby stood her ground a moment longer, but then

the sounds of Bugs Bunny and Daffy Duck drew her into the other room. Sam had a brief moment of peace in his house, which meant he'd better get this interview done fast, before Katie realized things here were actually more like a zoo, and she ran out the door, like more than one nanny he'd interviewed.

"Is there any chance you also want to be a nanny?" he asked, only half joking. Still no text back from Charity.

"I've never been a nanny, or a tutor," she said. "I'm a CPA, but I'm…looking for a new direction for now. I'm in town for a couple weeks while I think about my career options."

A CPA? What had Della been thinking? Talk about overqualified for the job.

"Do you have *any* experience with kids?" He should have realized that when she showed up on his doorstep. Any tutor in her right mind wouldn't be wearing heels and a figure-hugging pencil skirt.

He glanced at his phone again. Nothing from Charity. Damn. The last thing he wanted to do was take the kids with him. He'd had to do that a few times with client appointments and the results had been…disastrous to say the least. He was still paying for the marker decorations that Henry had drawn on a custom-made leather sofa in one client's office. It was almost impossible to carry on a conversation of any kind of substance with the kids in the room. And for him to show up at an interview with them…

He might as well kiss the job goodbye. "You know, maybe we should reschedule. This is a crazy busy morning for me. If you could come back—"

"No!" Libby's shriek cut through the air like a knife. "No!"

Sam bolted out of the chair and charged down the hall, his heart a tight ball in his throat. He never should have left the kids alone in the living room. This was how awful things happened, and if there was one thing that would break Sam, it would be one of his kids getting hurt. Or worse. *Please be okay, please be okay.*

It was probably only ten yards from the dining room to the living room, but to Sam, it felt like ten thousand. "Libby? You okay?"

"Henry took my bear when I was playing with it! He's hurting him! Tell him to stop!"

It took Sam a second to process the fact that Libby and Henry were both fine. Just engaged in a tug-of-war over a stuffed bear. Libby's voice was at decibels usually reserved for rock concerts, the sound nearly outpaced by Henry's screams. No words, just the frustrated screams that Sam had heard too much of in the last year and a half.

"Henry, give Libby back her bear."

But Henry didn't listen. Instead, he tugged harder, at the same time that Libby tugged in the opposite direction. There was a horrible tearing sound, and then an explosion of fiberfill in the air. The kids tumbled onto the carpet, each holding half a bear, like some kind of biblical division of property.

The sobs multiplied in volume. Libby was screaming at Henry and Henry was screaming back, and Sam just wanted to quit. Quit being a terrible father. Quit being the chief everything when he didn't know what the hell he was doing. Just run away somewhere that was quiet and peaceful and clean.

His wife would have known what to do. Wendy had had a way with the kids, a calming presence that seemed to bring everyone back to earth in seconds. God, he

missed her, and how she could handle all these things
that he sucked at. Wendy would have known whose
bear that was, but Sam—Sam couldn't even remember buying the bear.

"No!" Libby screamed again. "Look what you did,
Henry! You ruined him!"

While Sam stood there, at a loss, with two kids in
the throes of tantrums, Bandit ran into the fray and
grabbed a chunk of bear, then darted into the corner like
he'd scored a new chew toy. And Libby started to sob.

Great, just great. Now how was he supposed to fix
this?

He stayed immobile, frozen with indecision, afraid of
doing the wrong thing, making it worse. Katie brushed
past him. "Don't cry, Libby. I can sew this," she said,
bending down in the space between the kids. "Fix him
up as good as new."

Libby swiped at her nose with the back of her arm.
"You can?"

Katie nodded while she gathered up the fiberfill and
began stuffing it into the bear's belly. Henry quieted,
too, and just watched, eyes wide. "I learned how to sew
when I was your age. If you want, I can teach you how."

"*He* doesn't know how to sew," Libby said, jabbing
another thumb in her father's direction.

Katie shot Sam a grin. "Some daddies don't and
some mommies don't. But if I teach you, then you'll
know and next time you can fix—" she tapped the bear's
decapitated head, then turned to Henry "—what's his
name?"

Henry just stared at her. His fist clenched around
the puff of stuffing.

"A bear's gotta have a name." Katie smiled at Henry,
then inched closer. Sam started to go in there, to stop

her, to tell her Henry was just going to run from her, but Katie kept talking, her voice calm and soft. Mesmerizing. "When I was a little girl, I had a bear like this one. I used to get scared a lot when it was dark, and my big brother, Colton, would find my bear and bring it to me. He would tuck me in and tell me stories until I stopped being scared and I fell asleep. I shared my bear with my brother sometimes, too, and Colton even gave Willard his own nicknames. My bear was my bestest friend when I was little, and I bet this guy is your friend, huh?"

Henry nodded.

"My bear's name was Willard, but my brother nicknamed him Patch, because he was fixed so many times he had a patch over his belly. He wasn't near as nice as your bear. So," Katie said, giving the bodyless bear a little tap on the nose, "what's his name? I gotta know his name so I can fix him, and tell him it's all going to be okay."

Henry shifted from foot to foot. Even though Libby knew the answer, she stood silently behind Katie, staring, waiting, just like Sam was. Katie just gave Henry a patient smile.

Then, very slowly, Henry held out his hand and uncurled his tight fist. A pouf of fiberfill sprang up like a daisy in his palm. "Henry help fix George?"

Henry's little voice rang like a bell in the quiet of the living room. Libby turned to her father, mouth agape. Sam put a hand on his chest, sure he was hearing things.

Henry had *spoken*. A handful of words, but to Sam, it might as well have been the Gettysburg Address. *Henry had spoken*—and Sam's heart was so full, he was sure it would burst just like the bear.

Katie nodded. "Of course Henry can help. And for the record, I think George is a terrific name for a bear."

"T'ank you," Henry said quietly, then he dropped the puff of stuffing into Katie's lap.

Sam swallowed the lump in his throat. He didn't give a damn that Katie Williams had come in here looking like she was walking into court. He didn't give a damn that she didn't have much, if any, experience. If she could get through to Henry, he had little doubt that she could get through to Libby, too, and restore his daughter's love for school. Katie had brought about a miracle that no one else had. She'd shifted the tides in a family too long on a rolling ocean, and for Sam, that was résumé enough. "You're hired."

Chapter Three

Katie wasn't so sure she'd heard Sam right. She was hired? Just like that?

And did she even really want the job?

She'd be with these two kids for at least an hour at a time if she became Libby's tutor. Small children with winsome faces and those little-kid voices. The very thing she had been looking forward to, before—

Could she do it? Or would it be too painful?

Katie was still kneeling on the floor between Henry and Libby, holding the tattered remains of George the teddy bear. Libby, who seemed ten times older than her age, came over and stood in front of her. She propped her fists on her tiny hips and cocked her brown curls to one side. "Are you gonna stay?" Libby's eyes, so like her father's, clouded. "Just 'cuz, you know, 'cuz our mommy died and…and… I really wanna fix George."

The naked honesty and pain in Libby's face was almost too much to bear. Katie could see the yearning for a mother, the way that loss had impacted the little girl in a thousand ways, in the empty shadows in Libby's eyes. Katie's heart broke for Libby, and for little Henry, standing there silently, his thumb in his mouth, just watching her. Katie had no doubt Sam loved his kids, but he was clearly overwhelmed, and these two little ones needed someone. Being a tutor wouldn't be all that tough, she figured, and she could help people who clearly needed help.

And given the way the two kids were staring at her, with a mix of hope and wary trust in their faces, she knew they wanted that someone to be her. It felt nice to be needed, even if only for this little while. Katie knew what it was like to crave a parent who engaged. Who cared. Katie wasn't going to be their parent, but maybe she could help fill some of the gaps.

"Okay," Katie said to Libby. "I'll stay. We can fix George, if you have some thread and a needle?"

Sam put out his hands. "If we do, I have no idea where."

"No problem. I'll pick some up this week." She bent down to Henry's level again. "George is gonna need some special thread to be fixed. Can you wait for me to bring that over?"

Henry gave her a reluctant nod.

Libby ran into the other room, then hurried back. She thrust a stuffed dog into Henry's arms. "Here. You can play with Puppy until then. But don't break him."

Henry grinned, then clutched the stuffed animal close to his chest.

"That was very nice, Libby," Katie said.

"Thanks." A slow smile spread across Libby's face, then she turned and grabbed Henry's hand. "Come on, Henry. Let's watch *SpongeBob*." The two of them plopped on the sofa, with Libby working the remote to switch to the underwater cartoon.

Katie rose and turned toward Sam. She'd accepted a job she wasn't sure she wanted, without knowing a single thing about the hours, the pay, anything. That was as far outside the realm of how she normally operated as she could get. "So, maybe we should discuss the details."

He grinned. She liked his smile. It was warm, friendly, like the way brownies made you feel when you first pulled them out of the oven. He was a handsome man, six foot two, trim and muscular, with close-cropped medium brown hair and dark brown eyes. He was wearing a T-shirt that seemed molded to his chest—not that she was complaining—and a pair of jeans that hung low on his hips. His feet were bare, and there was just something about the intimacy of that that made Katie feel like she was intruding in his space. From the moment she'd seen him, standing at the door, annoyed and flustered, she'd felt this warmth in her gut that rippled through her veins.

His phone buzzed and he glanced down. "My appointment was just moved to nine thirty, which means I have time to finally have a cup of coffee. Do you want one?"

"Coffee would be great." And maybe with a mug in her hands she'd stop staring at the hot widower's body. She followed him out to the kitchen, which looked pretty much like the tornado from *The Wizard of Oz* had just blown through. Dirty dishes teetered in the sink, a stack of newspapers lay scattered across the counter, crumbs littered the floor and the space around

the toaster, and there was a pile of dirty laundry bulg-
ing out from the laundry room door like an impending
avalanche.

Yup, Sam was clearly stressed. A lot stressed.

"Uh, sorry, I think I have a second clean cup here."
He opened a cabinet door, another, then finally un-
earthed two mugs from the back of the third cabinet
he looked in. Sam poured her a cup of coffee, then
held it out. "I don't have any cream, but I do have milk
and sugar."

"Black is fine. Thank you." She sipped the coffee, a
surprisingly rich and good brew, and kept her back to
the counter rather than taking the only free chair at the
kitchen table. The others had stacks of mail and toys
piled on them, as if the rest of the house was coming
for lunch.

"Uh, sorry." Sam rushed forward and scooped a pile
of things off one of the chairs. He started to put it on
the table, then thought better of that and pivoted to the
left, depositing the toys and books onto the floor by a
drooping and browning potted plant. "It's, uh, been hard
to work and watch the kids and...well, my last nanny
quit a few weeks ago and the new one isn't as good as
the other one, and..." He let out a breath. "Mostly, I'm
just not good at this juggling thing."

She laughed. "It's fine, really. And made all that
much better by a man who admits he can't do it all."

"I definitely can't do it all." Sam gestured toward the
empty seat and waited for her to take it before he sat
opposite her. "At work, I can juggle multiple clients and
deals, but here, I'm bested regularly by a three-year-old
and a third-grader."

"You seem to be doing fine." Okay, so maybe she was generously stretching the definition of the word *fine*.

He ran a hand through his hair, a move that made him seem more vulnerable somehow. "I'm not, but thanks for saying that. I really need some help, at least until Libby gets caught up. It's a short-term job, if that's okay. Feel free to say no. You are incredibly overqualified to teach math to a third-grader."

She didn't want to get into the reasons why an over-qualified CPA would take on a tutoring job. "That works for me. I wasn't really looking for anything permanent, so I'm flexible with whatever schedule you want." It shouldn't be too hard, right? Though the thirtyish man across from her didn't seem to have it under control, so why would she think she could do it better?

"Aren't you here on vacation?" Sam asked. "I'd hate to take up whatever free time you have. You said two weeks, which, if you can work with Libby regularly, should give her a good head start on getting caught up. I'll worry about a more permanent solution once I find one." He sighed. "Anyway, I really don't want to monopolize your time off."

"It's only sort of a vacation." How did she begin to explain the meltdown in the office, the clear signs that she needed to get away, to leave town, to start over? How once she'd arrived here and had more than five minutes of quiet, all those thoughts and memories and emotions she'd been avoiding washed over her like a tidal wave? And how the one thing she was banking on with being Sam's tutor was that it would leave her too busy to think? "This job works perfectly with my plans."

"Well, I am glad to hear that." Relief washed over her at his words. He mentioned a decent hourly rate, and she agreed. His phone buzzed and he pulled it out of his pocket, then read the text on the screen. "Thank God. Charity is on her way over. Normally, I bring Henry to storytime at the community center my uncle runs, and Charity picks him up from there. But since Libby doesn't have school today, it's easiest if I just leave Henry here. She can watch him while you work with Libby. If it's at all possible, do you think you could start with Libby today?"

"Today?"

"If you can't, well, I understand, but Charity is still new and though she's great, she gets overwhelmed when she has both kids. With you here, that should help her out. I'd take them, but I have this job interview and I can't take the kids because I'm still paying for Henry's 'creativity'—" Sam rolled his eyes and made air quotes "—at the last place I interviewed at."

She bit back a laugh. Sam was so clearly out of his depth with these kids that she couldn't help but want to make it easier on him. Plus, if she started today, she wouldn't have a long, endless day stretching ahead of her with nothing to fill the hours. Colton was sleeping, after getting off his shift at the fire station, and wouldn't be available until dinnertime. "Today sounds perfect."

"Great. Thank you." He glanced over at the sofa. "The kids are quiet right now, so if it's okay, I'm going to run upstairs, take a shower and get ready. Charity should be here in ten minutes, but I have to leave in… eleven. If you don't mind waiting, I'd appreciate it. Give me five minutes. Ten, tops. Okay?"

"I think I can handle this for ten minutes." She gave him a soft smile, and tried to pretend a part of her wasn't thinking about the hunky man before her taking off his clothes and stepping into a shower.

When Sam went upstairs, Katie wandered into the living room. This space, too, looked like the aftermath of a tornado, complete with a second carpet of tiny little bricks. Now that it was just her and the two kids, she wasn't quite sure what to do or how to engage them. She glanced at the television. Some cartoon sponge-shaped guy was running around in his underwear and letting out an annoying nasal laugh. "Hey, guys, what are you watching?"

"SpongeBob," Libby said. "He lives in the water. With Mr. Krabs. And Patrick."

"Sounds, uh…educational." Whatever happened to *Sesame Street*? *The Electric Company*? Shows she remembered and understood.

A commercial came on and Libby turned toward Katie. "Do you have a boyfriend?"

"Uh…no." She'd *had* a boyfriend. Who had dumped her the second he found out she was pregnant. She'd never in a million years thought nerdy Leonard Backstrom, another accountant at the firm, would be the one to break up first. He'd talked a lot about wanting to settle down, buying a house in an up-and-coming neighborhood, then starting joint retirement and 529 accounts. One stupid night when they both had too much to drink, and his tune had changed. He was, apparently, all talk and no real action. Last she heard, Leonard was dating Meredith the receptionist. He'd never even called Katie after she told him she was pregnant, as if he figured it was all her problem now.

After Katie had accepted that she was pregnant, she'd begun to think of a future with a child. A future of just the two of them. Those thoughts had grown into dreams, a plan—

Until she'd started cramping ten weeks later and lost everything.

So yeah, that was the complicated answer to *do you have a boyfriend?* Probably best to keep it to *uh...no.*

"My father says I can't have a boyfriend until I'm thirty," Libby said, and once again, Katie was struck by how mature she sounded. She sat down and Libby leaned closer. "Are you thirty?"

Katie laughed. "Almost. I'm twenty-nine."

"My father is thirty-four." Libby held up all her fingers, then flashed the digits three times. "That's old."

"You won't think so when you're thirty-four." Interacting with these kids wasn't so hard. She could do this. And she and Libby seemed to get along okay. The tutor thing should work out perfectly. In and out, an hour at a time. No biggie.

Libby considered that, then glanced over at Henry. "That's my brother. He's three."

Henry sat there, a blanket curled in one hand, just watching the exchange. He was a quiet kid. Probably easy to handle, Katie was sure. "He seems very nice."

Libby's nose wrinkled. "He smells funny and he takes my toys and he makes a mess with his food."

Katie laughed. "My brother was like that. But you know, he grew up to be really cool. Henry probably will, too."

Libby's nose wrinkled more. "My father makes me eat vegetables."

"Vegetables are good for you," Katie said.

"Are you gonna make me eat vegetables?"

"I don't think that's in my job description."

"Good. Because I don't wanna eat them," Libby said.

"Libby Bear, be nice to Katie. She's only here to help you with your schoolwork. No broccoli involved." Sam's voice came from behind Katie. She turned in her seat and her pulse did a little skip.

If she'd thought he looked handsome in a T-shirt and jeans, he was positively devastating in a suit and tie, with his hair still wet from the shower, smelling of fresh aftershave and soap. He was adjusting the cuffs on his white shirt, and for some reason, she thought that was one of the sexiest things she'd ever seen. Everything from the dark blue windowpane-pattern suit to the crimson tie at his neck and the black wingtip shoes gave him an air of power and manly confidence. Like a lion stepping onto the prairie and claiming his turf.

"I don't want to do schoolwork!" Libby sat back on the couch, crossed her arms over her chest and let out a huff. "You're mean."

"Yup. I am." He gave Katie a grin. "Still want the job?"

A job that came with perks like seeing Sam in a suit? Sign her up. "Yes, yes. I… I do."

Good Lord, she was stammering. The confident partner at the accounting firm had been replaced by a hormone-crazed teenage girl. She got to her feet, smoothed her skirt and cleared her throat. "Perhaps it's best if we went over any additional rules or expectations now."

He didn't say anything for a second, then he seemed to refocus, and nodded. "Yes. Yes, you're right."

She followed him out to the kitchen and they took the same seats as before. "So, do you have a list of things that Libby needs to work on?"

"Her teacher said she needed help with times tables and three-digit addition and subtraction problems. The whole carrying the one thing, you know? Then there are word problems, which I swear were created to stump parents." He laughed.

"Lucy has seven cantaloupes and Dave has three apples, so what time will the train arrive at the station?" Katie asked.

"Exactly." He crossed to a pile of papers on the back kitchen counter and riffled through it. "Her teacher sent home a list that I've got here somewhere. My late wife was the planner and organizer. Since she's been gone, I've just kind of…held on for dear life. I'm not very good at this whole juggling act."

"My childhood was like that. I guess it's why I'm the opposite. I like everything to add up, and for all the columns to balance."

He pulled a sheet out of the pile, then handed it to Katie as he sat down again. "Well, one thing I've learned about having kids, no matter how organized and planned you make your days, you're never going to get everything to add up perfectly. Kids…" His voice trailed off and his gaze drifted to the sofa, where Libby and Henry were laughing at the antics of the sponge and his starfish friend. "Kids change everything."

"Yes," she said softly, and her hand strayed to her empty belly, "yes, they do."

He turned back and his gaze met hers, and held, for one long second. "Thank you."

The praise made her shift in her seat. "I haven't even done my job yet. Why are you thanking me?"

"Because…" Sam's face clouded and his eyes filled, and his voice grew rough. "Because you got Henry to talk. I haven't heard his voice in a long, long time." Then, as if the emotion was too much, Sam got to his feet and grabbed a piece of paper and a pen from the middle of the table. He cleared his throat and dropped his gaze to the paper. "I'm going to write down my cell number. Call or text me if you have any problems. I'll be back after the interview, and Charity will be here any second, so you should be fine. Libby has a folder of practice sheets in her backpack that her teacher needs her to work on. If you and Libby get along, and this works for you, we'll talk about a schedule for the next week when I get home. Sound good?"

She rose, too, and closed the gap between them to take the paper, adding it to the one from Libby's teacher. "Sounds good."

His gaze dropped to her lips, then to her eyes. "And…thank you."

She was close. Too close to him. But she couldn't seem to make her feet move in reverse. "You…you said that already."

"I'm sorry. I'm just…distracted."

She wanted to ask him if that was because of her or the job interview or something else, but the doorbell rang just then. The dog started barking, the kids started shouting, and a second later, a sullen twenty-year-old was in the kitchen, and the moment was gone. Charity looked about as happy to be there as a grandparent at a death metal concert.

Sam made the introductions and filled Charity in on Katie's role. "Call me or text me if either of you have any problems at all. I'll be back before you know it."

A few minutes later, Sam was gone. Charity leaned

against the counter, her arms crossed over her slim frame. "Good luck," she said.

"Thanks, but I'm sure I'll be fine. It's just third grade math and reading."

Charity scoffed. "Yup. And with Libby, that's about as much fun as negotiating a nuclear war. So I say again, good luck."

Charity stalked out of the room, scooped up Henry and took him into the backyard to play on the swing set. Katie turned and saw Libby standing in the doorway, arms crossed, defiance in her eyes.

Good luck.

Chapter Four

"Welcome to the team, Sam." Hank Osborn got to his feet and put his hand out. "We look forward to working with you."

Relief filled Sam. He had a job again. Thank God. If there was one worry that had consumed his every thought, it was how he was going to provide for his family. There was no wife to fall back on for an additional income, no partner to help pick up the slack. It was all on Sam's shoulders, a weight that damned near seemed to kill him some days. The house, the kids, the bills, the…the loneliness. That was a place in his mind he didn't dare dwell upon. That hole in his world, that empty spot in his bedroom, his bathroom. The way he missed Wendy's chirpy *good mornings* and her sweet, whispered *good nights*.

Sam pushed those thoughts away. One thing at a time—right now, he had the job. That alone made him want to shout from the rooftops. Instead he settled for a professional smile and a nod of gratitude.

"When I looked back over some of your deals, I was really impressed," Hank went on. "You did a great job negotiating that multi-property deal in Raleigh. One of my guys was trying to win that battle, but you had that creative idea to find tenants before the negotiations started, and we were out of the running before the race even started. That was one hell of a deal, son."

"Thank you."

"And I expect the same kind of ingenious thinking while you're working for me. I like a man who thinks outside the box. Sound good?"

"Definitely, sir." Sam was glad to find Hank was a lot like him when it came to getting the deal done. It was part of the reason he had liked the gregarious older man immediately. Hank had owned Osborn Properties for thirty years, and brought it from a small one-man operation up to a three-office company with two dozen brokers, serving all of North Carolina and parts of the rest of the South. It was a big step for Sam, going from the small company he'd been at before to this one. The opportunities and support structure would be better, but the performance expectations were also going to be higher.

"I'll put you on the Midway Mall project right away," Hank said, handing Sam a file folder. "We have five open spaces in there, and want to get them filled before the mall opens in two months. One hundred percent capacity by opening day. Nothing less. Think you can do that?"

A huge task. It would mean working a lot of hours, and he still had a shaky child care solution. But the last thing he wanted to say to his new boss was no. "Yes, sir."

"One more thing," Hank said as he came around the desk. He put a hand on Sam's shoulder and walked with him to the door. "Don't call me sir. That's for my dad or my grandpa. Around here, I'm just Hank."

"Sounds good… Hank." Sam shook hands with the other man one more time, then said goodbye and headed out the door. It wasn't until he got in his car that he allowed himself a giant exhalation of relief.

The loss of his job had weighed on him like a ten-ton Mack truck. But now, with Hank's offer—even if it came wrapped up in some pretty high expectations—that weight had been lifted. He had a job, Libby had a tutor—a beautiful and capable tutor at that—and life was finally improving, a little at a time.

He wound his way through the bucolic, hilly roads of Stone Gap, mentally running through a list of potential clients to call for the mall project. If he could talk to Charity and convince her to sign on long-term for babysitting, then achieving Hank's goal was doable. Plus, if things had gone well with Katie today, then all the better—it would get Libby back on track in math and reading, and reduce the number of arguments he had with his daughter.

Not to mention how Katie had transformed his little family in the space of a morning. Sam could still hear the echoes of Henry's voice in his head. His son had turned a corner today, thanks to Katie Williams, and it was one that Sam hoped spelled good changes ahead.

Such a small thing, one that too many people took for granted, but oh, how he never would again. He owed Katie something huge—something impossible to grasp—for bringing his little boy back from the world of silence. Even if it was only a tiny step forward, and lasted only a moment, Sam would be eternally grateful.

For the first time in a long time, Sam allowed himself an emotion he thought had died in that car accident with Wendy—

Hope.

He pulled into the driveway, parked the car, then got out and paused a moment in the driveway. The sound of children laughing, of Bandit barking, filled the air.

Life was good. In this moment, in this space. It was something he'd been trying to work on—learning to appreciate the small moments. After the dark days he and the kids had gone through, every small moment seemed like a miracle.

Sam allowed himself another smile, then circled around through the side gate to the backyard. "Sounds like you guys are having a great—"

His step faltered. For several long seconds, he was sure he was seeing things. But no, there was Katie, mud-spattered, her hair a wild jumble around her head, trying to clean up a spilled pot of red finger paint on the patio, while Henry and Libby ran barefoot through the grass, taking turns aiming the hose at each other and the dog.

"You're home!" Katie got to her feet, and brushed at her hair with the back of her hand, but all that did was smear a long streak of red paint across her temple. "That's so…great."

He tried not to laugh at the paint on her face, the clear relief in her features. He glanced around the yard again, and when he noticed one less person than he'd left here this morning, alarm bells went off in his head. "Where's Charity?"

"She's inside. She said she had to make a call."

He'd had a feeling Charity wasn't going to last long when he hired her, but he'd hoped she would at least make it until he found a suitable replacement. He'd have to talk to her about taking personal calls when he was paying her to watch his kids. "Did the kids dip her in paint and mud, too?"

"No. That was all my doing." Katie laughed. "After Libby and I finished working on her math, I got them the paints because they were complaining that they were bored, and I didn't want to just park them in front of the television. I asked Charity, and she said she thought it was a good idea to do a craft. Except I'm not exactly the crafty type." Katie gave him a sheepish grin. "Libby got paint on her hands and wanted to clean it off, but I didn't think you'd want her to do that in the bathroom sink, so I turned on the hose and…" She waved at the yard and grimaced.

Sam could read that look of being overwhelmed from a mile away. How many times had he felt totally over his head when it came to the kids? He'd been so used to putting it all into Wendy's hands, into letting her take the lead while he worked too many hours. When his wife was gone and the family who had hovered over him for the first two weeks after she died had left, Sam was left floundering, beleaguered and clueless.

A lot like Katie looked right now. Actually, she looked kind of cute with the mud and paint peppered all over her shirt and skirt. She'd kicked off the heels, and there was something about her bare feet on the grass that just seemed…sweet. A part of him wanted to just draw her against his chest and kiss that spot of paint right above her brow.

"Come on," he said to Katie, waving toward the door. "Why don't you go inside and clean up? I'll corral the wild beasts and then we'll all get some lunch."

"Are you sure? I can clean up this mess out here first."

"I can handle it. Don't worry."

Katie gave him a grateful smile, then headed inside. Sam watched her go for a moment, then dragged his gaze away from the intriguing woman crossing his yard.

The guilt washed over him again. He shouldn't be concentrating on anything other than his kids and his job right now. The kids needed him—needed a parent who kept his crap together, not one who got distracted by a pretty woman with mud on her face.

He headed for the kids, reached out and took the hose from Libby just before she turned it on her brother again. Both kids were dripping wet, sodden messes from head to toe. He was about to chastise them, when he looked down and realized something else.

Both kids were happy. Goofy grins filled their eyes and brightened their cheeks. "We had fun!" Libby said. "Can we do that again?"

Beside her, Henry nodded. His face was a blur of paint, half of it smeared by the water and now running crimson into his orange T-shirt. There was no trace of the somber, withdrawn boy who had appeared the day Sam had sat on the sofa and hugged his kids to him and told them Mommy was never coming home again.

He glanced over his shoulder at the house. It was amazing what a few hours of Katie in their lives could do. And that was a very good thing.

When the pain hit her, it hit her hard and fast.

For three days, Katie had been coming to Sam's

house for an hour or two at a time after school, to work with Libby. They had slowly winnowed down the pile of papers her teacher had sent home and she had nearly mastered her times tables. Then, when they were done with schoolwork, Katie would draw with both kids, a break Charity seemed to welcome, because the nanny immersed herself in her phone the second Katie appeared. Maybe because Charity was there a longer portion of the day, picking up Henry from storytime at the community center and watching him until Libby got home from school.

The kids had kept clamoring for more finger painting, so Katie had finally caved today. This time without the need to hose off in the yard.

Everything had been going fine until Charity announced she was quitting. She said she'd gotten a call back from a job at the mall, and was done being a nanny. She was gone two minutes later, leaving a stunned Katie alone with the kids for a half hour until Sam came home.

It was in that thirty minutes that things had changed. Maybe it was because it was just the three of them, or maybe the kids were starting to bond with Katie, but just as she was helping Libby mix up some purple paint, Henry had leaned in and put his head on Katie's arm.

A simple movement, really. She'd looked down and seen this little boy curving into her like he'd known her all his life. Then Libby turned to Katie and said, "Our mommy used to draw with us. I'm glad you do, too." A pause, then Libby's eyes met hers, wide and serious. "Are you gonna stay, Katie?"

Katie glanced up and saw Sam standing there, his face filled with a mixture of surprise and something unreadable.

Katie had scrambled out of the seat, made up an excuse about needing to clean up, then barreled toward the bathroom. One second she was soaping up her hands, and the next, a sharp fissure pierced her chest. Her breathing tightened, her heart crumpled into a fist and tears rushed into her eyes. She braced her still dirty hands on either side of the sink, heedless of the soapy, purplish drops puddling on the tile below.

She glimpsed her face in the mirror, looking harried and messy and so out of her normal buttoned-up world. *This is what a mom looks like*, her mind whispered, *and these are the kinds of things a mom does.*

Wham, the pain had hit her.

She wasn't a mom. She might never be a mom. The one chance she'd had to be a mother, her body had failed…no, *she* had failed. She'd lost the baby and all those hopes and dreams she'd had. What had made her think she could be here, around these kids, and not be reminded of that fact? Maybe she should tell Sam she couldn't tutor Libby. Or maybe she should just keep working here, because maybe it would force her to confront all those things she had run from.

Yeah, and considering how often in her life she'd confronted any of the things that bothered her, those chances were pretty slim.

A light rap sounded on the door. "You okay in there?" Sam's voice, warm and concerned. Just four words, but they seemed to ease the tightness in her chest.

Katie released her grip on the porcelain, drew in a breath, then nodded at her reflection. Another breath, then she could speak. "Yeah, just cleaning up."

"Okay. Just checking. I was afraid you might have

climbed out the window and run off, especially since Charity quit."

That made her laugh. "Nope, I haven't left. Not yet."

"That's good."

She paused, sensing Sam lingering outside the door. A moment later, she heard the fading sound of footsteps as he headed back down the hall. She finished rinsing and drying her hands, then emerged from the bathroom. In the kitchen, Sam was bent down, Libby standing before him, with one of the pictures she had painted that day in her hands. Libby's face held a hushed hesitancy.

Katie's chest squeezed. In a split second, she was eight years old again, standing in front of her mother with a test she'd brought home from school. Her first A in math class, decorated with a giant smiley face sticker. She'd wanted her mother to be as proud as Mrs. Walker had been, wanted to hear those same words *you did it, kiddo.*

"This is awesome, Libby Bear," Sam said to his daughter, taking the picture and pointing at the center. "I love the rainbow. And the flower."

Libby frowned. "I thought the flower was kinda messy."

Sam cupped his daughter's cheek. "It's not messy. It's perfect."

Katie waited for that echoing grin of pride to appear on Libby's face, for her to acknowledge she'd heard the words she wanted to. The *you did it, kiddo.*

Instead, Libby shook her head and stepped back. "It's not! It's messy!"

She yanked the picture out of her father's hand and dashed out of the kitchen. The screen door closed behind her with a hard slap. Sam watched her go, then let out a long sigh and slowly straightened.

He turned and saw Katie. "Sorry about that. Sometimes Libby is…" He shrugged. "I don't know. I honestly don't know."

"She's a great kid," Katie said. Because she didn't know what else to say. How to explain Libby's reaction to what seemed like a regular conversation between a father and daughter. A part of Katie wanted to run after Libby and tell her that parents who made a big deal out of every painted rainbow and hand-drawn flower weren't as common as she thought. That perfection wasn't all it was cracked up to be.

"Yeah, she is." Sam pivoted back to the bay window, watching his daughter through the glass. She toed back and forth on the swing, one foot dragging listlessly against the worn oval in the grass. The picture lay in a crumpled ball beneath her. "But she's been going through a lot and there are days…"

Katie's heart went out to him. He was so clearly worried about his children and desperate to reestablish a connection with them. It was as if there was this invisible wall between Sam and his children, one none of them knew how to scale. Katie was no expert in these matters, but she knew what it felt like to be on one side of that wall.

Before she could think about it, she put a hand on his shoulder. He was solid and warm beneath her palm. "She'll come around. You're a great dad."

"I'm *trying* to be a great dad," he said. "That's not the same thing."

Katie's hand dropped as she thought of her own mother. A woman too self-involved to be any kind of parent. Colton had shouldered most of that responsibility, an older brother thrust into a role he'd never asked for. Maybe it was because Katie had been the second surprise baby, an unwelcome intrusion into a life already strained by the birth of Colton a few years earlier. Her mother had never married, never made more than just enough to keep a roof over her head. "When it comes to kids, trying is important. And noticed."

He studied her for a moment. "Sounds like you have some experience with that."

Katie shrugged. "I had a mother who was…busy a lot."

"Back in Atlanta?" He crossed to the sink, filled two glasses with water and returned to hand one to her. "Did you grow up there?"

The past three days, their conversations had centered entirely around the kids. How Libby had done with her homework, whether they'd finished the book she had to read for reading class, things like that. The personal question threw Katie for a bit of a loop. "I've never really lived anywhere else, or had a chance to travel anywhere. Until now."

He chuckled. "I don't know if I'd call Stone Gap a destination city."

"It is for some people," she said quietly. Her brother, after all, had found happiness here. A life.

"I always vowed I was going to leave town when I grew up. But then I met Wendy and…" His gaze strayed to Libby. "Anyway, it's a great place to raise kids."

"I can see that," Katie said. "It has that Mayberry feel to it."

He laughed. "You say that like it's a bad thing."

She arched a brow.

He leaned against the wall and faced her. "Okay, yes, living in a small town does mean that everyone knows everything you do on any given day. But it also means that people are there when you need them, people like Della, who has been a huge help in the last year and a half."

Katie thought of the cold, sometimes scary neighborhoods where she'd grown up. There were years when they had moved so often she didn't know a single neighbor. "I bet that was nice."

"When I was a kid, there was this little old lady who lived next door to me. Mrs. Hanratty. She'd sit on her porch and watch the neighborhood kids walk to school, and on hot days, she'd be out there after school, giving us all ice-cold Popsicles. On really cold winter mornings, she'd have little cups of hot chocolate for us. She never had any kids of her own, and I think she kinda felt like all the kids around her were hers."

"I had a neighbor like that once," Katie said. "For a few months. Then we moved again."

"That had to be tough on you when you were growing up."

She shook her head, as if it hadn't been. "I had Colton. And I turned out okay."

"Maybe kids are more resilient than we think."

His gaze had gone to his daughter again, still drifting back and forth in the swing. Katie wanted to stay, wanted to help, but she was starting to feel those panicky feelings again. The ones that told her she had no business trying to be anything other than the tutor. "I should probably get going."

"Wait." Sam turned toward her. "I...uh, wanted to thank you."

She picked up her purse from the counter and hung it over her shoulder. "Thank me? For what?"

"For...everything." He waved a hand in a circle. "The house looks amazing, and I know Charity didn't do it, not unless I was paying her extra. I don't think I've ever seen the kitchen this clean. The whole house looks...cheery."

She shrugged and placed her hand on his arm. "It wasn't a big deal. I finished up with Libby, then decided to stay and clean up a little before we did the painting, which turned out to be a good thing, since Charity ended up quitting. Chalk it up to my CPA brain. I like things organized."

"It was a big deal. Everything you've done over these last few days has been." He shifted toward her, and Katie's hand dropped away. He was wearing a pale yellow button-down shirt and a dark green tie. A part of her wondered what it would be like to run that silky material between her fingers.

"You're really great with both kids," Sam went on. "You've got them learning, and doing art projects, and as soon as you leave, you're all they talk about. Libby told me she likes you, and she's never said that about any of the nannies I've hired. I know I hired you to be Libby's tutor, but would you consider—" he put up a hand, warding off her objections before she could voice them "—being the nanny? Just until I have time to find someone permanent, because I know you aren't staying here for very long. My schedule is flexible, Libby has school, Henry has storytime and sometimes other activities at the community center, so it will really only be for a few hours a day. Heck, you've been here that long almost every day, and done more than Charity did in a month."

She flashed back to that moment in the bathroom. Of how being around these kids, seeing how attached they were getting to her, had hurt, deep in her chest. Could she deal with this all day? Every day?

Then she looked out the window at Libby, a sad little girl drifting back and forth in the swing, and she saw…

Herself.

What if someone had stepped in when Katie was little, in all those hours she'd sat at home on the sofa, waiting for Colton to get home from softball practice or her mother to come home from work? What if someone had been there to bake cookies and spill finger paints and fix broken teddy bears? What if someone had been there to say that A on the math test was amazing? Would it have made a difference?

"I don't have much experience," Katie said.

"You've been here every day for three days, and even Charity told me you've been great. I know the kids can be…overwhelming sometimes. Especially when they're armed with finger paints and a hose." He grinned.

Sam's smile was a little lopsided, with a slight dimple in his left cheek. She liked his smile. Liked it a lot. Wouldn't mind seeing it more often. And if he was going to be popping in throughout the day to help with the kids…

Was she seriously considering this job?

She didn't have anything to rush back to, no fire in her belly to get back to Atlanta. "I could maybe extend my time here," she said. "So the kids don't have a lot of change in a short period of time."

"So you'll take the job?" Sam asked. "And be the nanny?"

Her gaze traveled again to Libby, then to Henry, dwarfed by an oversize chair in the living room. He had a stuffed dog clutched to his chest, and his knees drawn up against him, while he watched TV. There was a smudge of finger paint on his cheek, like a royal blue fingerprint.

That smudge tugged at something deep inside Katie, something she hadn't even been sure existed until she walked into this house and met these children. This man.

"Okay," she said. "I'll do it."

Chapter Five

Sam noticed the flowers first. The window boxes, neglected for a long, long time, now bloomed with pink and white geraniums. A slight breeze moved the petals back and forth, almost as if they were waving. The terra-cotta planters that flanked the front porch had also been refilled, with more of the same kind of flowers cascading over the edges.

Sam fingered one of the flowers, thinking it had been ages since he'd seen anything growing in his yard. The flowers looked happy, bright. Hopeful.

He'd spent six frenzied hours at work today, zipping from client to client, answering calls and sending emails in the snippets of time he had between meetings. He'd had three showings to potential renters for the mall property, but none of them had made an offer. Since it was Katie's first day as nanny, Sam cut out early and grabbed some take-out Chinese food on his way home.

He'd never expected to see flowers. He hadn't realized how much he'd missed that kind of thing until he saw the geraniums. They were a change. A good change.

Then the guilt hit him, coming from left field like a rogue wave. Should he be enjoying the flowers another woman had planted on Wendy's porch? When his late wife would undoubtedly rather he worry about the kids, his job, everything else?

Or was it just that he was finding himself more and more drawn to Katie, and the guilt over having feelings for another woman was eating away at him? He had loved Wendy, Lord knew he had loved her, and he didn't want to tarnish the memory of a good wife and good mother by moving on too soon.

Best just to focus on the kids. That was what Wendy would want, too, he was sure.

He opened the front door and heard Libby's voice. He quieted his steps as he headed down the hall, trying to catch the gist of what she was saying.

"And then Kayla says that she wants to wear her pink shoes tomorrow, so I think I'm gonna wear my pink shoes, because Kayla is my best friend, and we both love pink," Libby said, her voice rising with excitement.

"That'll be awesome," Katie said. "Does Kayla like playing soccer, too?"

Sam lingered against the wall, watching his daughter, her head bent over a drawing she was working on as she talked. This normal moment, missed for so long in his house, was like seeing the flowers. Bright, happy. Hopeful.

"Kayla doesn't like soccer as much as me," Libby said. "But she said maybe she'll join the soccer team, if I do it, too."

"I used to play soccer in high school." Katie handed Libby a red crayon, then turned to Henry and slid a straw into his juice box. He climbed onto the chair beside them and started scribbling on a second coloring book. "My brother was a really great soccer player and he taught me all kinds of awesome moves."

"He did? Can you…" Libby hesitated, then looked up at Katie. "Can you teach me them, too?"

Katie laughed. "I don't know if I remember them, but I bet my brother does. Maybe I can have him come over tomorrow afternoon and show you. He's a firefighter."

That piqued Henry's interest. "A firefighter?"

"Yup. And if it's okay with your dad, I can take you guys down to the station and let you see the fire trucks."

The whole exchange was so normal, so uncolored by the sadness that had hung over this house like a heavy drape. Coloring books and soccer and visits to the firehouse. Regular family stuff, the kind of thing so many people took for granted.

Until it was gone.

Sam didn't know whether to cheer or cry. He'd wanted this…normalcy for his kids for so long. But it came attached to another woman, one he thought about way too often.

Sam pushed off from the wall and went into the kitchen. "Hey, a trip to the fire station sounds great to me. I want to go, too. As long as I get to toot the horn on the big truck."

Katie turned toward him and smiled, the kind of smile that said she was happy to see him. "I think you are a little too old for that."

Sam grinned. "A boy is never too old to do that, isn't that right, Henry?"

Henry nodded, clambered down from the chair, then

plowed into Sam's legs. He held on tight, while Sam ran a hand through his son's scraggly brown locks.

Libby stayed at the table, coloring and mostly ignoring Sam. The wall between himself and his daughter sometimes seemed impossible to scale. The moment of hopefulness began to fade.

Sam lifted the Chinese food up and away from Henry's now reaching arms. "Hold on a second, buddy. Let me put this—"

Katie was there, taking the bag from him. She had this uncanny ability to read his mind. "Here, let me help."

He smiled at her, then hefted his son into his arms. Henry settled against Sam's chest like he was made for that space. "Thank you," Sam whispered.

She smiled. "It was nothing."

But Sam looked at his daughter, coloring a picture of a farm, and his son, who was grinning from ear to ear, and disagreed. Things weren't perfect, but they were a sight better than they had been before. The house was clean, the kids were happy and engaged. There was an air of…hope around everything that he hadn't felt in a long time.

Sam lowered Henry to the floor. "Hey, buddy, go finish your picture for me, okay?"

Henry nodded and went back to the table. Katie was laying out the Chinese food on the counter. She added a pile of plates and silverware, then stepped back and brushed her hands together. "Well, I should go," she said. "Same time tomorrow?"

She'd done the same thing every day this week, leaving right after he got home. He felt like he barely knew her, and wanted to get to know her. Not just as a tutor for his daughter, but as a woman. He wanted to know what it was about her that was changing his life and breathing life into the dark spaces.

It was the flowers. Those damned flowers.

Sam caught Katie's hand as she started to pass by him. Like the first time they'd touched, an electric jolt ran through him. Her lips parted and her eyes widened, and he wondered if she'd felt the same thing. "Stay for dinner?"

She grinned. "I already eat lunch here every day after I pick Henry up from the community center. Feeding me wasn't part of the deal."

"Consider it a tip." He returned her smile.

"But the kids…" She glanced over at the table, where Libby and Henry were back to coloring again.

"Surely want you to stay as much as I do." Had he just said that out loud? To a woman other than his wife? It was for the kids, he told himself, only for the kids' benefit. He turned toward the table. "Hey, guys, do you want Katie to stay for dinner?"

"Yes!" Libby dropped her crayon onto the page and ran over to Katie. "Can you sit next to me? I wanna sit next to you."

Katie laughed. "Okay, okay. With an invitation like that, how can I say no?"

The four of them divvied up the Chinese food, then settled around the kitchen table. As they ate, Libby began to open up, nudged by strategic questions from Katie, about her day at school, about the decision to wear pink shoes with Kayla the next day, about the cool dog they saw at the park. Bandit sat beside the table, tail swishing against the floor, hoping for a dropped morsel.

When the take-out boxes were empty and the last crab Rangoon eaten by Henry, Sam gathered the plates and got to his feet. "You kids can either help with the dishes or—" he gave them a grin "—play in the yard."

A half second later, both Libby and Henry had escaped to the backyard, with Bandit hot on their heels. Katie started the hot water and loaded the few plates and pieces of silverware into the sink. "That was great Chinese food. Thank you for inviting me to stay."

"Thank you for staying."

She laughed. "You had me at Moo Shu Pork."

He slipped into place beside her and started drying as she washed. They fell into an easy rhythm, working together seamlessly. Wendy had always done the dishes alone, preferring the time to think, she'd said. It wasn't until he was on his own that he'd stayed in the kitchen longer than the time it took to finish a meal. But this was nice, working beside Katie on something as simple as washing a few plates. It felt odd, but also nice. He wasn't sure how to process that, so he didn't. He just kept on doing the dishes.

"I can't remember the last time we ate off of real plates," he said, slipping the blue-rimmed dinner plate into the cabinet. "I've pretty much stuck to whatever was disposable and quick."

"I'm sorry. I shouldn't have—"

He put a hand over hers, and that connection hit him again. "Stop apologizing. I'm glad you did it. It's about time all of us started…living again. Like a normal family."

She stiffened at that, and he wondered what he'd said that had caused the sudden coolness between them. Before he could ask, she had shut off the water and pulled the drain plug. "Well, that's it. I guess I'll see you tomorrow."

The kids were still playing outside, with the dog

chasing around them and barking. The sun was starting to ease behind the horizon, and soon it would be dark and the kids would be inside and this moment would be lost. Sam wasn't sure if he would be better off holding on to it or letting go.

Katie was gathering her purse and getting ready to leave. Sam stood there like a fool, so new to dating again that he wasn't quite sure how to go about it, or if he even should. She was the nanny, after all, and it wasn't a good idea. But she'd filled his chest with something that had been missing for a long, long time, and he wasn't prepared to let that go just yet.

"I saw the flowers," he said, just as she waved and started down the hall.

"The flowers? Oh, yeah." Katie turned back. "I hope you're not mad. I thought it would be a great project for the kids. And it's spring and, well, flowers just go with spring and…" She grimaced. "I presumed too much. Those are your planters and I shouldn't have just done that without asking first."

"They're…perfect."

"I'm glad you like them." She fiddled with her keys for a moment. "Well, I should go."

"Wait. Please." He came down the hall, where the light was dimmer and Katie's features seemed almost iridescent. He shifted closer to her, inhaling the light floral fragrance she wore. Her eyes widened, her lips parted and the desire that had been simmering inside him for hours began nudging him forward, until a fraction of space separated them.

"I'm glad you like the flowers," she said again, but her gaze lingered on his lips, and her body shifted ever so slightly in his direction.

"I do. Very much." He wasn't talking about the impatiens or geraniums or whatever the hell they were. He was talking about this woman who had come into his life and, in a handful of days, changed damned near everything. Things he wasn't sure should be changed, but he seemed powerless to stop any of it. Maybe because deep down inside, a part of him craved this change, craved...

Her.

Sam reached up and traced the side of her cheek, along the line of her jaw, holding her gaze with his own. Something so simple, yet so intense, with her brown eyes locked on his and their breaths mingling in the small space.

Then before he could think about what he was doing, Sam leaned in and kissed Katie. A short kiss, a momentary touch, but as he began to pull back, something pushed him forward again. He cradled the back of her head, she let out a soft, sweet sound and he opened his mouth against hers.

She curved into him, with her body, with her mouth, with everything. Desire roared through Sam, not just for a woman, but for this woman, this intriguing, captivating woman. He'd been alone for so, so long. In all that time, no one had tempted him like Katie did.

There was a sound outside, a shriek of laughter from Libby, a loud bark from Bandit. Sam jerked to his senses and pulled back. What was he doing? He'd taken his focus off the kids, off the most important thing in his life. Guilt rolled through him. What about Wendy? What about her memory? Was he doing his wife a disservice by kissing another woman?

Then he saw Katie, her cheeks still flushed, and all he could think about was kissing her again. How long was he going to wait to start his life over again?

"I'm out of practice, and I know I just did all this in the wrong order, with kissing you first and…" It was like he was fourteen again and asking Mary Sue Matlin out on a date. He was nervous and stammering and a jumbled mess. "Anyway, I'd really like to ask you out. For dinner, for drinks, for…whatever."

Hesitation flickered on her face. "I…I don't think I should."

"Because you're the nanny or because you're not interested?" He was pretty sure he'd read interest in that kiss. A whole lot of interest. Or maybe she was feeling just as conflicted as he was.

"Because…I'm complicated." She gave him a half smile, then reached up and touched his cheek. It was a flutter of a touch, just a second, but it warmed him. The smile faltered on her face and she stepped back. "I'll see you tomorrow, Sam."

Then she was gone, and Sam was left in his hall, wondering what she'd meant, and why the answer intrigued him so much.

"So, are you going to tell me?"

Katie looked up from her sandwich and grinned at her brother. They were sitting in the Good Eatin' Café, grabbing a late night snack, a few days after she'd started working full-time for Sam. She hadn't even been that hungry, but once she heard Colton order a grilled cheese sandwich, she couldn't resist getting one, too. Plus, it was always good to see her brother. Grounding, in a way. "Tell you what?"

"What are you doing? Taking on a nanny job for Sam, going around with that goofy grin on your face—"

"I do not have a goofy grin on my face."

"You do indeed. Every time I mention Sam's name that goofy grin pops up, like a balloon in a box."

She dropped her gaze to the plate. Was it that obvious that she was interested in Sam Millwright? Was that why he had kissed her? Why he had asked her out? Because she was as obvious as an infatuated teenager whenever he walked in the room? "I'm his children's nanny," Katie said, "nothing more."

Except she was 100 percent sure kissing Sam was not in her job description. Try as she might to pretend that kiss hadn't happened, it hung in the air every time she was at his house.

Colton had picked up on it several times during the last week when she'd seen him. He'd also latched onto the fact that she had extended her "vacation," although she hadn't told him the real reason why she wasn't going back to Atlanta yet.

"Remind me again, you're working as a nanny because…?" Colton prompted.

"Colton, this isn't a remake of the *Sound of Music*. I'm not there to marry the handsome bachelor dad." She shook her head. "Can we change the subject, please?"

"Okay, then let's talk about…weddings." He grinned.

She groaned. "I just told you. I'm not marrying anyone. For Pete's sake, all I did was take a job—"

"Not you. Me. Rachel and I are planning our wedding. If you ask me, the big day can't come soon enough. I love that woman like crazy." Now a goofy grin spread across Colton's face, the kind that said he was madly in love.

A flicker of envy ran through Katie. That was crazy. She didn't need or want a relationship right now. All relationships did was bring disappointment. Colton had gotten lucky—that one-in-a-million chance of finding someone who wasn't going to break your heart—but that didn't mean there was another one-in-a-million out there for Katie. Best to just not get involved at all.

Even with sexy widowers who had a tender touch and a deep voice. Who also happened to be amazing kissers. Her mind wandered back to that moment in the hall, to the way he had touched her face, made her melt, then—

"I'm so happy for you," Katie said. "Really."

"Since there's going to be a wedding in my near future, I wanted to ask… Are you going to be here for that?"

"Of course. You know I'd come back to Stone Gap for your wedding, even if I have to wear an ugly bridesmaid's dress."

Colton didn't laugh. His face was sober, serious. "I meant stay here. Don't go back to Atlanta. Live in Stone Gap. You already have a job, after all."

Katie was halfway to another bite and stopped. "Stay here? I only arrived a little over a week ago. I'm on vacation, not relocating."

"A vacation that now doesn't have any discernible end date, a vacation where you are working as a nanny? What kind of person takes on a job when they're on vacation?"

Someone who wants to keep too busy to think. Someone who doesn't actually know how to unwind. Someone who is a little lost and trying to buy some time before making a decision. "Sam was desperate," Katie said instead. "I told him I'd help him. It's only a few hours a day and it was a temporary thing."

"Uh-huh. You do know you've never been able to lie to me, right?"

"I'm not lying."

"Then answer me this, Abe Lincoln." He gestured toward her purse, closed and sitting on the bench seat beside her. "Your phone isn't out on the table. You're not checking it every half second. You're not pausing every five minutes to call someone back or shoot off an email or anything else. You're completely unplugged, and you are *never* completely unplugged. You, my sister, are a workaholic, who isn't working."

Katie fiddled with her silverware and finally pushed the remains of her sandwich away. "I sort of came to an agreement with my boss that I wasn't going to work there anymore."

"Wait. You got *fired*? *You?*"

"Not fired–fired. It was a mutual decision." Of sorts.

He arched a brow.

"It's a long story." One she'd managed to avoid telling, since Colton worked long hours and was often with Rachel.

"I've got all night." Colton leaned back and draped his arm over the vinyl edge of the bench. "And a running tab for decaf here."

"Have I told you lately that you are a total pain in the ass?"

Colton checked his watch. "Uh, not in the last thirty minutes."

That made her laugh and eased the wall in her mind. Maybe it *was* time to talk about everything. After all, not talking about what bothered her hadn't helped. Bottling it all up had, in fact, led to a volcanic explosion at work. Hence the not fired–fired events and the temporary nanny job and the muddle in her mind. Not to mention that kiss with Sam. Whatever that had been and whatever that had meant.

"I don't even know where to start," Katie said. "Or how to explain what happened."

Colton reached across the table and took her hand.

His was bigger, stronger, more solid. The same as he had been when she'd been three and scared of monsters in the closet, and when he walked with her into every new school, and when he'd been there with a hug when her heart had been broken in tenth grade. Colton had been there every single time, with his goofy smile and his big strong hands and his patient gaze. "Just start with why you came to Stone Gap."

"I was running away." Tears burned her eyes and she shrugged, trying to pass it off as nothing. But the pain surged to the surface all over again, like a wave she couldn't hold back. "I couldn't stay there one more day and be reminded of..."

"Of your job?" he finished, when her voice trailed off.

"Of..." She drew in a breath, held it, then let it out. She'd told no one about what had happened, and suddenly, the burden seemed too heavy, the ache too deep. "The baby."

Colton blinked. He sat back again and let out a low whistle. "Did you say *baby*?"

She nodded. And now that she had said that word, the rest came tumbling out, breaking past all those strongholds she'd put in place to keep her from having to feel anything. Really, all it had done was keep her stuck in place. She wanted to move forward, wanted to put it all far, far behind her. "Remember I was dating that guy Leonard? Well, one night we were drunk and in a rush, and I thought he had put protection on, but he hadn't, and... I got pregnant."

Her brother's gaze dropped to her belly. "Are you...? Did you...?"

The tears spilled over her eyelashes and trailed down her cheeks. She was back in the doctor's office all over again, knowing what he was going to say before he even spoke a word. She'd known it the minute her body began to betray her, that the dream she'd had was gone before she had a chance to hold on to it. "I lost the baby. Ten weeks in, and I lost it. I was just getting used to the idea, and as crazy as it sounds, looking forward to having my own family. I know I always said I never wanted to have kids, not after living with Mom, but you know, I really thought—" her voice caught, but she kept pushing the words out "—that I would be a good mother."

"Of course you would have been," Colton said. "Hell, you were half mother to me, Piglet."

"Me? I was the annoying tagalong. You were the one who was there for me all the time."

"Because you were the one who always worried about me. You still do."

"You're a big grown man." She waved off his words. "I don't worry about you."

He grinned. "Liar. I have some text messages that say the opposite."

It was true. She did text him from time to time to make sure he was okay. Even more in the year after he'd lost two friends at the scene of a fire. For a while there she'd been pretty worried that Colton wouldn't come out of the depression that had swept over him after the accident. But he had, and now he was back doing the job he loved, and moving forward with Rachel. "Those texts are just me ensuring you're still alive so I'll get a decent Christmas present this year."

"What, you didn't like the Scrooge and Marley action figures I sent you last year? Or the subscription to the NASCAR magazine the year before?"

"Not as much as I bet you enjoyed the *Dating for Dummies* book I sent you."

He mocked offense. "I'll have you know that book is

a godsend. After all, I'm getting married. Which means I'm going to have an excuse to see you in some lime-green bridesmaid dress with poufy sleeves."

"I've changed my mind. I'll only wear an ugly bridesmaid dress if it's to attend your funeral." She grinned. The moment of levity eased the sadness, dried up Katie's tears and gave her a moment to breathe. "How do you do that?" she asked Colton. "I can be telling you the saddest story ever and somehow, you make me laugh and make it all seem…not so bad."

"It's my secret power." He signaled for some more coffee, and waited to speak again until after the waitress had topped off their mugs. "I'm sorry about the baby, Katie."

"It's okay. It wasn't meant to be." The platitude didn't give her any comfort. It was simply a way to fill the hole in the conversation.

"You would have been a great mom and you will be someday," Colton said again. "A really great mom."

"Almost as great a mom as you were."

He grinned. "You weren't too much of a brat, so it was easy." He took a sip of coffee, then leaned closer. "So how did all that lead to you not exactly being fired from your job?"

She told him about the meltdown, about the clients they had lost, about the argument with her boss. "Around that same time, you texted me, asking me again to come to Stone Gap, so…here I am."

"I'm glad you are. I think you needed this town more than you knew. It's been good for me, Katie, and I'm sure it'll be good for you." He ate a french fry. "I still don't understand how that all led to you being Sam's nanny, though."

She circled the rim of her mug with her finger a few

times before answering. "I needed to keep busy, so I wouldn't keep thinking about everything. Della told me he needed a tutor, and I thought, great, I could work an hour or two a day and make a little money. Then his babysitter up and quit on him and he was desperate and…"

"And you took the opportunity to keep even busier."

She nodded. "You know me well."

"I share your DNA. That makes me an expert." He ate another couple fries, dunking them in ketchup before they disappeared in his mouth. Colton had the appetite of ten men, but worked out enough that he never seemed to gain an ounce. "So, are you planning on doing any actual vacationing while you are here?"

"If I vacation, I'll think, and I'm trying not to do that."

"Exactly why you should do it." He covered her hand again. "Take it from someone who spent a long time trying not to think about my biggest screwups. It's not until you finally look at the elephant in the room that you can figure out how to get it outside again."

She laughed. "I think that is the most convoluted piece of advice I've ever heard."

"Confucius say it's wise and profound. Because it's coming from your older brother. So you'd be smart to listen. And to have dessert with me."

"Why should I have dessert with you?"

"Because dessert, dear sister, makes everything better." Then he ordered pie, and told her a bunch of funny stories about the firehouse, and before Katie knew it, Colton had worked his magic again. Rescuing her one more time.

Chapter Six

Sam got up extra early, got Libby off to school, Henry off to a morning of crafts and stories at the community center, then rushed through his day like a man on fire. Every time he glanced at the clock, he was hoping it was noon, so that he could finagle some kind of excuse to stop by the house.

Because from the minute he'd woken up, his every other thought had revolved around Katie. Her smile. The way she touched him. How insanely amazing it had been to kiss her the other day. How she had turned down his dinner invitation.

Because I'm complicated.

Her response had left him confused. Okay, so he was a guy, and what women wanted and what they meant when they said things like that pretty much left him confused all the time. Still, he wanted to know what she meant. And why she had kissed him, yet turned him down.

Was it wrong to look forward to coming home to her? To think about kissing her? Holding her?

For several days, he'd tried to concentrate on work. He'd sold two commercial properties—a vacant warehouse outside of Stone Gap and a small office building in a neighboring town, which had put him in Hank's good graces. But all that work hadn't done much to keep him from thinking about Katie.

He turned his gaze to the blue, blue sky above. Wisps of clouds dotted the vast cornflower-colored canvas, seeming to promise anything was possible. That answers were there, if only he asked the right questions.

What would Wendy want?

It was a question Sam had asked himself every day since his wife had died. Would she want him to move on? Or would she want him to wait, to keep that space in his heart reserved a little longer?

"I wish I knew," he whispered to the sky. Because as wrong as it was to feel this happy coming home, there were many times when it felt so very right.

So there he was, in his own driveway a little after twelve, even though he had an appointment across town at one. Five minutes, tops, then he'd get back in the car and go back to work. Just a quick visit to say hi to Henry after his morning at the community center. The program had been a godsend—keeping Henry busy and playing with other kids, but not putting the pressure on him to talk like school would.

"I'm home," Sam called as he walked in the door. Something smelled good inside the house. There was music playing on the sound system in the dining room, and everything seemed to sparkle and shine. Sam hadn't realized how much he missed coming home to a house that was an actual home until these last couple days.

Katie was in the kitchen, mixing some kind of batter in a bowl. Henry was sitting at one of the kitchen bar stools, holding a big wooden spoon. Katie had her hair up in one of those clip things, which left a few long brown tendrils in tempting curls along the valleys of her neck. Today, she had on a pair of jeans that hugged her hips and outlined some very, very nice curves. Her bright green V-neck T-shirt sported a logo for the Green Bay Packers and a reminder of the four Super Bowl championships they'd won.

She glanced up as he entered the kitchen, and a bright smile burst on her face. "Hi."

"Hi. Sorry. I wasn't checking on you, just stopping by on my way to a meeting."

"You're just in time. Henry and I are busy making cookies to give to the firefighters later today. Isn't that right, buddy? Here, your turn to mix." She turned the bowl in front of Henry, and he dug in with this spoon for one quick flip of the batter.

"Cookies!" Henry said, and held up his spoon. "Daddy have some?"

Sam's throat closed, but he worked a smile to his face that hopefully didn't say every time he heard Henry speak it damned near turned him into a baby. "Maybe later. I have to go back to work in a few minutes."

Henry's bright features dimmed. He went back to stirring the batter, but his movements were listless, slow. "Okay."

Sam had been here for ten seconds and already disappointed his son. He shot a glance at Katie, who gave him a sympathetic smile.

"How about I meet you guys at the fire station later?" Sam did a mental rundown of his schedule and figured if nothing ran over its allotted time, he should be able to be there on time.

"That would be great," Katie said. "The kids would love it if you were there."

"I'm gonna play with the fire truck!" Henry spread his arms wide, sending a spray of batter onto the kitchen floor.

"Hey, let's keep the dough in the bowl, buster." Katie took the spoon out of Henry's hands, then grabbed a paper towel to wipe up the mess. Sam reached for one at the same time, his arm brushing against Katie's shoulder.

It was a small touch, a whisper, really, but it sent a shock wave through Sam. Katie's gaze darted to his, held for a moment, then Henry ran over and tried to climb onto Sam's back. That was enough to break the spell, to keep him from leaning in for another amazing kiss with Katie. Later, Sam promised himself, there would be time for that. He'd make sure of it.

"Let me clean this up," Sam said, swinging Henry off his back with one arm, and cradling him against his waist. "And let this monkey here help me."

Henry giggled. "I's a boy!"

"Monkey boy." Sam tweaked Henry's nose, then handed him half the paper towel. "Help Daddy clean up."

Henry did as he was told, taking great pride in swiping up the clumps of batter, then dumping the mess into the trash. While the boys did that, Katie finished mixing the dough and adding in the chips, then she turned to get a stack of cookie sheets out of the drawer beneath the stove.

Henry was already gone, running off to play with whatever toy had caught his eye, the dog hot on his heels, and Sam was left alone in the kitchen with Katie, with a very appealing view of her rear.

Damn. This nanny thing was adding complications he hadn't expected. Like every five seconds he was wondering how he could get her alone. "You, uh, need some help?" he said.

"I've got it." She straightened, and laid two cookie sheets on the counter.

"I didn't even know I had those."

"And here you struck me as the baker type." She gave him a grin.

"My baking skills extend to once, and only once, slicing up one of those logs of dough and then forgetting about it."

"You forgot about them? What happened?" She scooped up balls of dough with a spoon and began sliding them onto the cookie sheet.

"Let's just say I was airing the house out for three days and going through a couple cans of oven cleaner. I'm not exactly domesticated." He slipped into place beside her and picked up the second tablespoon beside the bowl. "Do I just put it on there? None of that spray stuff first?" He'd seen Wendy spray that nonstick stuff on pretty much everything before she cooked.

"Nope. They'll spread too much if you do that. Just try to make sure all the cookies are about the same size so they bake evenly."

He did as she said, working at a slower pace than Katie, who seemed to have some kind of magic scooping and dumping skills. They each filled one cookie sheet, three across, four down. "This is nice," he said as they worked. "I've never done this before."

"Your wife must have made cookies all the time."

He steeled himself. In the months after his wife died,

every mention of her had felt like ripping open an old wound. But this time…not so much. Talking about her felt like he was warming himself by a familiar fire.

"Wendy was one of those moms who colored the pictures and decorated the rooms and baked the cookies, but the kitchen was her domain, and she was pretty particular about it." A bittersweet smile crossed his lips. If there was one thing his late wife had excelled at, it was being a mother. It was as if she had been born for that singular purpose. She had loved the kids, and been so close to them it was almost as if they were three parts of one person. She would have loved Katie, the way she handled the kids, got Henry to talk, encouraged Libby with her schoolwork. "Wendy was great, she really was. I don't want to make it sound like she was anything but a great mother."

"No wonder the kids miss her so much."

And he was a poor substitute for the mother they had lost. He didn't bake cookies or do crafts or remember their favorite bedtime story. He did the only thing he knew how to do—he worked and kept the bills paid. But in the long, long months since their mother had died, he had realized how much more his kids needed. They needed the cookies and the finger paints and the silly jokes. For the thousandth time, he was grateful that Katie had shown up on his doorstep. "Do they talk about their mother with you?" he asked.

She turned and slid the cookie sheets into the oven, then set the timer. "Libby has. She tells me stories about your wife. About the books she read her, the way she liked her ice cream, the times she took her to the park."

Sam leaned against the counter and let out a sigh. Libby was the oldest and had taken the loss of her mother the hardest. His heart broke for the days ahead—

the proms, the first heartbreaks, the wedding day, when Libby would need her mother and her mother wouldn't be there. Would he be able to fill those gaps? "My kids miss her a lot. It's been tough."

"I'm no expert, but they seem to be doing okay," Katie said. "You're a great dad, Sam."

He scoffed. "I'm a fair to middling dad. I'm trying to do better than I did before. When Wendy was alive, I worked too many hours and left too much on her shoulders. Then she died, and I still worked too many hours. Mostly because I didn't want to think about losing her. I didn't want to come home to an empty house. So I left the kids with a nanny and I worked too much…"

"And became even more distant."

"Yeah. It's like my kids grew up when I wasn't looking. I used to know Libby's favorite song and what kind of cereal she liked. Now I'm just trying to keep my head above water." He grabbed a sponge and wiped up the dusting of flour on the counter. "After the last nanny quit and I lost my job, I was here all the time, doing everything. The problem was, I don't know how to do everything. I don't remember that Libby likes the edges cut off her sandwiches or that Henry needs a certain stuffed animal to sleep with. And I sure as hell don't do anything the way Wendy did."

"Who says you have to do things the same way? And for the record, I don't think anyone knows how to do everything when it comes to raising a family. Last I checked, they didn't hand out instruction manuals in the delivery room."

He chuckled. "I think they should."

"Heck, I think they should give everyone one at high school graduation." She turned back to the cabinet, giving him that appealing view of her behind again, then straightened and put two wire racks on the counter. Another thing he didn't know he owned. "Did you eat lunch? I'm no chef, but I did make a pretty spectacular turkey-and-cheese sandwich for Henry."

"If I can take it to go. I have a meeting at one."

She got the ingredients out of the fridge, then put the sandwich together, sliced it on the diagonal and handed it to him on top of a paper towel. "Here you go."

He chuckled lightly. "You divided it on the angle. My mom used to cut my sandwiches like that. Is that why you do?"

"My mom didn't do much sandwich making in my house." Katie's gaze dropped to the sink. "Colton pretty much did all that stuff."

"Colton? Really?" Sam couldn't imagine the firefighter cutting sandwiches for his little sister. He remembered Colton telling him that his childhood had been tough, but he'd never gone into detail.

"Our mother...wasn't around much, and I never knew my father," Katie said. "Colton did a lot of the things she should have done."

That made Sam admire Katie even more. She had fit in so easily in this house, better than any of the previous nannies. "So how is it that you knew just what to do to get my kids to relax and open up and laugh for the first time in forever?"

"Easy," Katie said. "I just did the opposite of what my mother did."

"Well, you're doing a fabulous job. Even if you are a Packer fan." He gestured toward the shirt.

"Let me guess. You're more of a Pats fan. Or the Colts."

"Bears all the way, baby." He grinned, then grinned some more when the "baby" made her blush.

"A Bears fan? I knew you were too good to be true." She grinned back at him.

He took a step closer, his sandwich forgotten. "You thought I was too good to be true?"

"For maybe a blip of a second."

"And yet you won't go out with me?"

"It's...complicated."

He stared down into her eyes and thought he could spend hours right here. "You keep saying that, but I don't see anything complicated about you, Katie. So what do you say? Dinner tonight after the fire station? I can ask Della to take the kids for a couple hours."

"I'm not dressed for dinner and—"

"Where we are going, you don't need anything but what you have on right now." He placed his palm on the counter, a millimeter from hers. He wanted to kiss her again, wanted to do a whole lot more than that, but Henry was twenty feet away, playing with his trucks, and the cookies were nearly done, and...

Sam didn't want to screw it up. He was new to dating again, not even sure he should be dating, but unable to resist this woman. The last thing he wanted to do was rush it. Maybe that was why she had said no yesterday. Because he had gone and kissed her first, asked her out second.

"So, it's a date?" he said. Was it? Even he wasn't sure.

She hesitated. "I'm not looking for anything permanent, you know."

"I'm not asking you to." Now he did reach up and brush one of those stray tendrils off her cheek. "It's just a date, Katie, not a lifetime commitment."

Just a date, not a lifetime commitment.

Uh-huh. If that was so, then why was Katie so nervous? It wasn't like she'd never dated before. And whatever happened with Sam would be temporary. Despite how wonderful it felt to be in his arms, and how the way he looked at her made everything inside her warm. Eventually, she was going back to Atlanta, and pursuing anything with Sam would be a mistake.

"Is this how I do it?" Libby asked, drawing Katie's attention back to the present, to her job. As the nanny, not the girlfriend.

"Almost," Katie said. She took the needle from Libby's hand and slid it near the edge of the bear's torn head. Katie had bought a sewing kit last night, and given the small basket of needles and thread to Libby, then taught her how to use it. Katie had done half the reattachment, and then showed Libby how to sew the two pieces together. "You want little stitches, so it won't show."

"Like this?" Libby slid the needle into the faux fur, then wriggled it out the other side.

"Exactly like that. Great job, Libby."

The little girl beamed. She was snuggled up against Katie on the couch, while Henry sat at their feet, building something out of blocks. While Katie was feeling like a fraud. These kids and Sam all looked at her like she was some kind of maternal wonder. All she could hear in her head was the doctor's voice telling her she had lost her baby.

The doctor had added all the normal platitudes— *these things happen, nothing you could do*—but deep down inside, Katie was sure if she had slept more or eaten better or worked less, none of it would have happened.

She was already growing attached to these kids, to this town, and that was a dangerous thing. She needed to get back to Atlanta, back to accounting, where all the credits and debits added up in neat little rows. Then maybe she could rid herself of this aching need for something she couldn't have.

"I'm glad we're fixing George, 'cuz he's my favorite bear," Libby said.

Katie cleared her throat and forced herself back to the present. "Why is he your favorite?"

"My mommy bought him when I was just a baby. She said it was my first toy." Libby stroked the bear's head. Tears glistened in her eyes. "I let Henry play with it sometimes, but it's my bear."

"George is a great bear. And it's really nice of you to let your brother play with it, too."

Libby slid another stitch in, a second, a third, before she spoke again. "Do you think my mommy is mad at me for breaking George?"

These were the moments when Katie wished she could call in a relief nanny, one who would know what to say to these heartbroken kids. "Oh, sweetie, no. Moms know that kids argue sometimes. She's not mad at all. And I bet she's really proud to see you fixing George. You're doing a great job." The stitches were even and tight. Libby had gotten the hang of sewing pretty quickly.

The praise seemed to warm Libby even more. She worked hard on the bear, her lips pursed in concentration, while Katie gave her little pointers. Katie glanced at the two kids, and for a second wondered if this was what it would have been like if she had gotten married and had kids of her own.

Would she have been the kind of mother who made pancakes and bought teddy bears and tied hair bows? Or would she have been distracted and busy and absent? Would she have had the best of intentions to be an involved, hands-on mom, or would she have let work take over her days?

Would her baby have had her brown hair and eyes, or ended up with Leonard's black hair?

Katie's hand strayed to her abdomen, to the empty cavern there that almost seemed to ache sometimes. She'd never have the chance to know those answers, never see the baby that almost was.

Her throat closed and her eyes burned. Everything would have been different if only...

"Is George all fixed now?"

Libby's voice drew Katie back again. She looked down at the reattached teddy bear head, now mostly back in place, lolling just a bit to the left. Katie choked back the lump in her throat. "He looks perfect, Libby. That's awesome. I'm so proud of what a good job you did."

"Thank you, Miss Katie." Libby beamed and leaned into Katie's side, nestling her tiny body under Katie's arm. "Thank you for helping me."

Katie hesitated a second, then wrapped her arm around Libby and drew her close. The sweet scent of strawberry shampoo wafted into the space. Libby didn't say anything, just clutched Katie's side, pressing the bear against her belly, and burrowed closer. "Thank you," she whispered again.

When she was a little girl, Katie had climbed into her mother's chair more than once and leaned into Vanessa's shoulder, seeking a hug the same as Libby was doing. Only in the cramped, musty apartments where she'd grown up, hugs had been as rare as hundred dollar bills. *You're too old for that*, her mother would say, pushing Katie down. *I'm tired and I can't deal with you kids.*

Katie might never know what kind of mother she would be with her own children, but right now, in this moment, she could be the mother she'd always wanted with these two motherless children. She could fill in those gaps as best she could, and never, ever make them feel unwanted or bothersome or unloved.

She could fix a bear and teach a girl to sew and make finger paintings and return hugs. And maybe, just maybe, doing so would begin to ease the ache in Katie's heart, too.

She drew Libby in a little closer, then pressed a gentle kiss to the girl's forehead. "You're welcome, Libby. You're very, very welcome."

Two hours later, Katie put Henry in the stroller, then took Libby's hand and set out for the fire station. Katie still had a bit of trepidation about her date with Sam afterward, and had spent way too much time fixing her hair and redoing her makeup before they'd left.

Libby carried George the entire way, holding the bear against her hip like it was a football made of gold. Henry was making small talk with an action figure he'd brought along, happy as a clam in the sun. He was a pretty happy kid overall, and talking more and more each time Katie saw him.

"Fire trucks," Henry said, reaching forward. "I see fire trucks!"

"You have to be good," Katie said. "And listen to the firemen. They're going to let you see all the trucks, and climb inside them, but only if you listen."

Libby scoffed. "He's three. He doesn't listen to anyone." Then she let out a long, dramatic sigh. The earlier moment of tenderness after the teddy bear got fixed had disappeared, and Libby was back to perfecting her annoyed eight-year-old face. "Why do we have to go see stupid fire trucks, anyway? I don't want to see any stupid trucks."

"Because Henry loves fire trucks and firemen, and my brother is going to show him the inside of the station. Besides, your dad is meeting us here."

Libby cast her gaze to the ground. "He always says that. Then he works and doesn't come."

"He'll be here," Katie said. "I'm sure of it."

Actually, she wasn't sure of any such thing. She hardly knew Sam. He could be the kind of guy who broke promises or showed up late, or never showed up at all. But he had seemed pretty adamant earlier today that he would be there, and after everything he'd said about not being involved when his kids were younger, surely he wouldn't miss this opportunity. Nor, she was sure, would he miss their date.

Katie's heart sang at the thought of seeing Sam again, and her steps seemed to lighten. She had run through her meager, hastily packed wardrobe in her mind, and realized the only dressy thing she had was a simple black dress and a pair of red pumps. Hopefully, Sam would like them. Ever since he'd stopped by this afternoon, she'd been nervously and excitedly anticipating their date.

Her gaze scanned the sidewalk, but she didn't see Sam anywhere. They reached the fire station, and Colton came out to greet them, dressed in dark blue pants and a dark blue T-shirt with the Stone Gap Fire Department logo above his heart. "I heard someone really likes fire trucks."

Henry raised his arms. "Me! Me!"

"Well, come on in, kids. I've got a lot of cool things to show you."

Katie bent down to unbuckle Henry, handing him the plastic container of cookies at the same time. "Go give those to Colton, okay?"

Henry toddled over to Colton and thrust the container up at him. "Here. I didn't eat any."

Colton laughed and took the cookies. "Maybe I'll share one later."

That made Henry smile, and he happily followed alongside Colton as the four of them went into the fire station. Libby brought up the rear, her gaze straying to the sidewalk again and again. Her face was sour, her eyes watery and her disappointment clear.

"Who wants to climb into the big engine?" Colton opened the door and helped Henry up and inside the cab. The little boy could hardly see above the dashboard, but he happily slipped into place and spun the steering wheel from side to side. Colton showed him how to honk the horn and play with the lights.

Libby hung back, her bear now in the stroller seat, while she stood listless and sad by the door. "I told you he wouldn't come," she said.

"He can still make it. We'll be here for a little while." Katie dug her phone out of her pocket and checked the text messages. Nothing from Sam. She debated contacting him, then thought maybe he'd forgotten what time they were meeting.

At the fire station with the kids. Libby is really missing you. Are you on your way?

She snapped a picture of Henry in the driver's seat of the fire engine, then sent the message off. She held the phone awhile longer, sure that there would be a quick response back. Nothing.

"See? I told you he isn't coming," Libby said. She gestured toward Katie's phone. "He probably didn't call or anything. He does that."

"I'm sure something important came up," Katie said. "Why don't you go on up in the truck with your brother? I'm sure Henry would love that."

Libby rolled her eyes, but did as Katie requested. A few other firefighters had joined Colton, and they took the kids over to the next engine parked in the bay.

Colton slipped into place beside Katie. "Thanks for the cookies."

"Thanks for doing this. I'm sure Henry's going to be over the moon for days now that he got to see inside a real fire truck."

"You know, that's how I ended up as a fireman myself. Uncle Tank took me to the fire station one day and I was hooked after that."

Uncle Tank, who both Katie and Colton had always thought was a family friend, had turned out to be Colton's natural uncle. He was the brother of Bobby Barlow, Colton's real father, and he had sort of kept tabs on Colton as he was growing up. He'd been an uncle to Katie, too, filling in for the father she'd never had.

Whoever her father had been. Vanessa had forgotten that detail in the long line of bad boyfriends she'd had. By the time Katie was old enough to ask, her mother couldn't remember which of her boyfriends had been the one to get her pregnant. Katie sometimes missed having a father, but between Colton and Uncle Tank, it had been enough. Yet at the same time, she had never given up hope that one day her father would come in, like a prince on a white horse, and whisk her into his arms and apologize for being gone so long.

Katie could understand how losing one parent could

leave a gaping hole for a child. How it had done that for Libby and Henry. Surely, Libby's mother would have known the right words to turn Libby's frown into a smile. Katie had just kept on echoing that Sam would be there, but as the minutes ticked by and the kids went from truck to truck, it became painfully clear he wasn't going to show up. Disappointment filled Katie as the excuses she'd made in her head became thinner and thinner.

"Sam's a good guy," Colton said, as if he'd read her mind. "A lot overwhelmed, but a good guy."

"His kids need him to be here," she whispered. "That's all they care about."

"He'll be there when it counts. That's the kind of man Sam Millwright is. Just give him some breathing room, let him get back on track."

Katie glanced up at Libby and Henry in the truck, Henry playing with the controls, Libby grudgingly sitting beside him. Even though it was clear Sam wasn't going to make it on time, Libby kept glancing at the door from time to time.

A little girl much like Katie had once been. A little girl who still had hope.

Chapter Seven

Sam trudged up the front steps a little after six, exhausted, his mind awhirl with the massive to-do list still waiting on him. He had calls to make, emails to send, a brochure to write up…the list was long and daunting. And it all needed to be done yesterday. He'd run behind all day, then had a last-minute showing that took five times longer than he expected. At least those extra hours—hours he had spent touring a vacant mall space instead of being with his kids—had resulted in an offer, which meant a hefty commission to come soon. That would go a long way toward easing the financial albatross around his neck.

Except it had meant missing the kids at the fire station, and the date he and Katie were supposed to have afterward. By the time he had a chance to text Katie, they were already walking home. Apparently, he was a star student in Failing at Being a Dad 101.

Sam sighed. Every time he turned around, he was screwing things up, with the kids, with Katie. Everything had seemed to be going so well between him and Katie, with an attraction that he could no longer deny, and didn't want to. But if he kept standing her up like this, she was going to be gone before he even had a chance to see where that attraction might lead.

At least he was home now. Just as he reached for the door, his phone rang. Work, interfering again. "Hello?"

"Sam, it's Hank Osborn." The owner of the firm had a deep, booming voice, made even more so by him being on speaker. "I want to know how that mall property is coming."

"I've had several showings. I've got one fabulous offer—"

"I need all five closed by the end of the month. The anchor tenant wants to open up a month earlier, so we need the other properties settled. Signed, sealed, money in the bank. Come on, Sam, you promised you could deliver. Show me that I didn't make a mistake hiring you."

"I'm on it, Mr. Osborn," Sam said, though he wasn't sure he could pull off the miracle Hank was asking of him, and on an even tighter deadline than before. With showings booked for the weekend and two nights this week, he was already working extra hours, but somehow he was going to need to work even more. And hopefully convince Katie to watch the kids a lot more than he'd originally hired her on for. He let out a long breath. It was almost one of those be-careful-what-you-wish-for things. He had the job he needed—and he was right back to working too many hours and being home too few.

He tucked his phone away and went inside. The scents of spaghetti sauce and garlic bread greeted him, followed by the sound of the music. Some pop song, sung by a singer he couldn't name, but with a catchy beat. He put his briefcase down by the door, then headed into the kitchen.

Katie had Henry on her hip, one of his hands in hers, sashaying around the kitchen island, while Libby followed along, dancing with her bear. The three of them were singing along with the song as they danced, their faces bright and animated and happy.

Just like a family should be.

Sam stood on the periphery, watching his family have fun without him. He should have been here, should have been the one making the spaghetti and dancing with the kids. Should have been at the fire station today. Should have been home earlier. Should have upheld his promise of a date tonight. He'd missed it all—because work had been his priority again. Guilt weighed on him like a too-heavy winter coat.

He was glad Katie had made dinner. She'd probably realized the restaurant plans would have to be changed and instead of getting mad, she'd taken care of dinner. He was beyond grateful for her thoughtfulness. Now, he could stay, spend time with the kids and Katie. Maybe the day could still be salvaged, after all.

He dropped his keys on the counter, then slipped in behind the three of them. "Looks like I'm just in time for the dance party."

Libby looked back at him, then made a face, and immediately Sam felt the coolness in the air between himself and his daughter. At the same time, the song came to an end, and she stopped dancing. "You're too late. We're done now."

"It's not too late, Libby Bear. We can put on another song—"

"You're too late!" she shouted. "You're always too late!" Then she spun on her heel and ran out of the room. A second later, Sam heard the slam of Libby's bedroom door.

Katie put Henry down. "Why don't you go play with your blocks while I finish up dinner?"

Henry nodded and took off for the living room. Katie leaned over and switched off the radio, then went back to the stove. She didn't talk to him, didn't so much as acknowledge his presence.

Great. He'd ticked everybody off.

"I'm sorry I'm home so late," he began. "And I hate to do this, but I need to work Wednesday and Thursday night and both weekend days. Just a few hours, I swear. I'm hoping you can take the kids for me."

She shook her head. "I thought you told me just yesterday how you regretted working too much and not being here with your kids."

"I did. I do. But I'm just starting at a new firm and they expect a lot out of me since I'm new and I thought I'd have the flexibility I had at my old job, but there's this big mall project and…" He ran a hand through his hair. "I'm sorry, Katie."

"I'm not the one you need to apologize to." She stirred the pasta, then the sauce, and paused to check the bread sitting under the oven broiler, toasting to a golden brown. Katie tugged off her apron and laid it on the counter. She didn't look at him, didn't grace him with one of those amazing smiles. Instead, she was as distant as she would have been with a stranger. "Dinner should be ready in five more minutes. All you have to do is drain the pasta and take the bread out of the oven in a couple minutes. Everything else is done."

He glanced at the table. Three place settings had

been laid out. The fourth empty chair seemed to mock him. "You're leaving?"

"My job is done today. Enjoy your dinner."

"Wait." He reached for her and stopped her. She turned and looked at him, but her face stayed impassive and cold. The warmth and light from yesterday had dimmed. "Stay. Eat dinner with us."

"I can't." She broke away from his grip, grabbed her purse and crossed the kitchen. "I'm sorry, Sam. I'll see you tomorrow."

"Katie…"

She turned back at the doorway. Her eyes filled; her face took on a shadow. Whatever warmth had been between them the last few days was gone now. "Libby and Henry weren't the only ones disappointed today, Sam. But they're the only ones you need to make it up to. Go spend time with your kids. I'll see you tomorrow."

Later that evening, Katie was sitting on the front porch, nursing a glass of wine. After leaving Sam's house, Katie had stopped in town to do a little shopping and grab a bite to eat. When she'd gotten back to the inn, she'd sent out several emails to contacts she had in the accounting industry in Atlanta, asking about job opportunities. *Moving forward*, she told herself. Or maybe just avoiding the present. Either way, she was going to sit here and drink her wine and unwind, and not dwell on how Sam had let the kids down today.

Let her down.

"I'm heading home to my man," Della said, joining her on the porch. "Do you need anything else? Mavis is inside, and she'll have breakfast ready first thing in the morning."

Katie liked Mavis, Della's partner in the B and B.

She was a buxom African-American woman, warm and friendly, with a ready smile and a fondness for peanut butter fudge. Mavis lived on-site while Della went home to her own house a few blocks away every night. "No, I'm good. Thanks, Della."

"What happened with Sam? I thought I was supposed to watch the kids tonight while you guys went out. But he texted a while ago and said plans had changed."

"Nothing happened. We just…changed our minds." Katie took a long sip of the wine. It didn't ease her disappointment. She should be glad. After all, not dating Sam allowed her to focus on her game plan going forward. She wasn't going to be Sam's nanny forever, which meant she needed to get back to her real job. Send out some more emails tonight, make use of the contacts she had in her database. Eventually she would have to leave Stone Gap and go back to reality in Atlanta. To her apartment, her life.

Della sank into the opposite wicker chair. "You okay, honey? You look…sad."

"I just thought Sam was…different." But in the end, he did what every other man she knew did—he said a lot of fancy words about wanting to settle down and be a family man, and instead made work his family.

It all told her one thing: when she needed him, Sam wouldn't be there and she'd be left to deal with things alone. Hadn't she learned that lesson with Leonard? Seen it firsthand tonight with Sam? All those extra hours he was going to work, the trips and dinners he was going to miss?

Losing the baby had been devastating. Katie could still picture the doctor, clutching his medical chart, with this uncomfortable look of sympathy on his face. "Do you have someone to drive you home?" he'd asked.

She'd had no one to hold her hand, no one to tell her it would all be okay. She wasn't going to be stupid enough to get involved with another man who wasn't there when things got rough.

Della put a hand on Katie's. "Some men are afraid to slow down. I think they're afraid they won't be up to the challenge of kids. They can tackle a ten-hour meeting with a roomful of lawyers, or negotiate for half a day on a piece of equipment, but when it comes to kids... they get scared."

"But it's Sam's own kids. If anything, it should be easy for him." Easier, certainly, than it had been for Katie. Every time Libby or Henry hugged her or took her hand, she could sense them seeking that connection with someone maternal. Those moments still caused a little hiccup of pain in Katie's heart, a reminder that she'd blown her one and only chance at being a mother.

"I think some men feel out of their element around kids," Della went on. "All that playtime and pretending and silly song singing. And then there are all those expectations. Kids are...precious and men know that. And so many of them are afraid that if they say the wrong thing or do the wrong thing, they'll screw them up and the whole family will end up on Dr. Phil." Della smiled. "My Bobby was like that when the boys were little. He held them like they were bombs that were ready to detonate at any second. It took him a long time to relax and have fun with them. But still there were years..."

Katie waited for Della to continue, sensing that whatever she was about to say was something she didn't share often. Della toyed with the wicker arm for a long moment.

"We had some hard years when we were married," she said finally. "Bobby worked a lot, spending more time under a Buick than he did at home. And when he was there, the boys didn't know how to engage with him. They gravitated toward me, even though they loved their dad and would do anything to spend more time with him."

"What changed? Because from what Colton says, all the Barlow boys are close to their dad." Since Colton had met his biological family, he'd kept Katie updated on everything Jack, Luke, Mac and Bobby were up to. She almost felt like she knew them all, just from the conversations she'd had with her brother. She was glad he'd found a family to love, a family who clearly loved him back. And maybe she was also a teeny bit jealous, too, that he had all that. Katie would never know her real father, and had no real relationship with her mother, but she could live vicariously through Colton and maybe that would be enough.

"What changed? The flu." Della laughed softly. "I know that sounds crazy, but that's what it was. Bobby got sick first, spent three days in bed, which was unheard of for a man who worked six days a week. Then the boys got it, and then me. I could barely lift my head, I was so sick, and Bobby had to stay home and tend to the boys. At first, it was all changing sheets and making chicken soup from a can, but then the boys got better, and Bobby took them with him, fishing and to the garage, to give me time to rest. By the time I was better, the boys and Bobby were thick as thieves."

Maybe that was what Sam needed. Some one-on-one time with his kids where they were all having fun. Katie had a feeling that all Sam did when he was home alone with the kids was clean and cook and try to keep the house running. He needed to be out there, finger painting and running the hose and dancing in the kitchen.

Maybe if her own mother had done more of that, Katie would have felt like she was living with an actual parent, and not a detached roommate. "And they stayed that way ever since?"

Della nodded. "Bobby would need a little nudging from time to time, to remember what was important, but yes, he did work hard at having a relationship with his sons. And in turn, that made our marriage stronger. We were a team, in every sense of the word. And I'll tell you, when the going gets tough, that's what you need to be—a team."

Katie scoffed. "I don't think I've ever felt like that with any man."

Della got to her feet. She gave Katie's shoulder a pat. "Those kind of men are out there. They're rare, but that's what makes them so special."

She twirled the wineglass, watching the liquid rise and fall against the curved edge. "I don't know where I'm going to find one."

A smile curved across Della's face. "There are an awful lot of men like that right here in Stone Gap. You might have already met one." Then she said good-night and headed down the stairs and out to her car.

Katie sipped the rest of her wine and watched the lights of Stone Gap turn on and off. People going home, having dinner, reading bedtime stories, saying goodnight. The night was warm, the air carrying the faint scent of ocean, and the streets were quiet, punctuated by the occasional call of a night bird. Katie started to get to her feet when she saw a set of headlights coming down the street, then stopping outside the Stone Gap Inn.

Sam stepped out of his car and stood in the pale white glow of the streetlight. Katie's heart stuttered.

"Can we talk?" he said.

"Where are the kids?"

"After they were asleep, I asked Colton to come by. I figured if Henry woke up, he'd be in heaven, with a real-life firefighter in his house." Sam gestured toward the porch. "Can I come up there?"

If he sat beside her, she'd be tempted to touch him, to lean into him, despite everything that had happened this afternoon. "Do you want anything to drink?"

"A beer would be fabulous."

"I'll go grab one." She welcomed the opportunity to go in the house, to take a few seconds to grab a beer for Sam and on the way back, primp in the mirror. Not that she cared what he thought, of course. But that didn't stop her from smoothing a few flyaway strands of hair or checking to make sure her eye makeup hadn't smudged. She went outside to the porch and handed Sam his drink. "Here you go."

"Thanks." He took the beer in both palms, but didn't drink. "I'm sorry about today. And tonight."

"It's okay. I told you."

"No, it's not okay. You're right. But I just can't seem to find a way to make it all work. My new job is more demanding than I had expected, and that means I need to put in the hours, make the connections, send out the emails. But I can't do that and be home and be present, too. There are only so many hours in the day."

"Then you have to prioritize." She sat back in the wicker chair, easing into the thick cushion. "Your kids need you, Sam. They want to have a relationship with you. I'm just the nanny and I won't be there forever. But you will be."

She'd taken steps tonight to make her return to Atlanta. She'd thought it would make her sleep easier, but instead, the thought of going back there made her…sad.

He sighed. "There's so much to worry about, so many things to remember, to do."

"You don't have to do everything, Sam. Just the things that are important."

"It's all important, Katie. Making sure the kids have a roof over their heads, food in their bellies, shoes to wear to school—those are my first priorities. Those have to come before watching Henry climb on a fire truck."

She thought of what Della had said, and about what she herself had seen in Sam over the last couple weeks. How he escaped instead of being plugged in. With his kids, with her. He'd missed more than just a fire truck adventure tonight, and she had to wonder if she was lumped in there in his mind with all the other things that he had to do. "Are you sure you aren't just using work as an excuse?"

"What kind of excuse could I be looking for?"

"Maybe…" She fiddled with the stem of the wine-glass. "Maybe you're afraid that you lost that connec-tion to the kids and you're working so you don't have to deal with that. Or find out that it's too late to restore it."

He got to his feet. "You don't have children, Katie. You don't know how tough this is. You know what I'm most afraid of? Letting my kids down. Losing the only things they have left—the house, the toys, the things that remind them of their mother. So I go to work every day and pay the bills and pray that I don't end up in a car accident, too, and leave my kids with no one."

The words hit her hard. She scrambled to her feet and took several steps away. "Just because I don't have kids doesn't mean I don't understand or that I can't sympathize with you."

"I… I don't mean to say that. It's just different when

you finally hold your child. There's this feeling that comes over you, and it's so powerful and so overwhelming. In that moment, when you look down at your baby's face, you know there is nothing in the world that could ever be more important than that child."

Her hand went to her belly, to the space that had once held her own baby. From the minute she'd realized she was pregnant, she'd felt that sense of protection. But in the end, her body had betrayed her, and the baby she'd sworn to keep safe had died, without ever seeing the world. Then she thought of her mother. Had there ever been a moment when Vanessa had looked at Katie and felt that kind of overpowering love and protection? Or had she seen only the work, the responsibilities involved?

"Maybe someday I'll know what that's like," Katie said softly.

He laid a hand on her shoulder. "When that day comes, I'm sure you'll be a great mom, Katie."

She shook her head and cursed the tears that burned the back of her eyes. "You don't know that."

"I've seen you with my kids. They love you, and are doing so well with you. And I know you're right. I should be there more." Sam sat still for a long time, not saying a word. His gaze dropped to the floor, and he dangled the beer between his fingers. "What if…"

"What?" she prompted, when he didn't finish.

"What if I suck at being with them? What if I can't do the crafts or remember Libby's favorite cereal or tuck Henry in with the right bedtime story? What if I'm not—" he lifted his gaze now, and she saw a shimmer in his eyes "—as good of a parent as my wife was?"

"You won't be the same parent your wife was, no matter what you do, Sam." She drew in a breath. "You're you, and that's awesome just the way you are. I see the way they light up when you are around."

"Henry, yes, but Libby…" He shook his head. "When I was a kid, my dad worked all the time. I vowed I would be a different father, that I would be there to build the tree houses and play the games and read the stories. Then we brought Libby home from the hospital and she cried for, I swear, six months straight. Wendy was the only one who could soothe her, get her to eat, sleep. I felt…left out. So I worked and worked, and by the time Henry came along, my career was in full swing and it just—" he let out a breath "—became easier to work instead of…"

"Failing again," she finished. She knew that avoidance technique. Heck, she could have written the book on it. "You're not the only one who uses work to avoid the hard stuff, Sam. When I was young, it was school. I was OCD student of the year. I kept thinking if I got better grades, my parents would show up in my life. They never did. Later, I replaced that with work. It was a…"

"Refuge," Sam finished for her.

She nodded. "Exactly."

He ticktocked the beer back and forth. "We're so much alike, Katie. It's no wonder I'm attracted to you."

Just like that, the tone between them shifted. She could feel the wine kicking in, making her a little warmer, a little braver. "You're attracted to me?"

He got to his feet, then reached out and crossed to her. "I think that's been pretty obvious from the beginning."

"Hot for teacher, huh?" She gave him a flirty smile.

"Hot for a teacher who makes a simple skirt look like a sin." He smiled back, then closed the gap between them and kissed her. Like their first kiss, it was sweet and tender, slow and easy.

Or at least it started that way. As soon as Katie leaned into him, Sam's body responded. He clutched her tighter and kissed her deeper. She curved her small frame into him, yet she fit exactly against his chest. His hands roamed over her back, her buttocks, her hips, then back up again, wanting more, yet at the same time painfully aware that they were standing on Della's front porch, and a kiss was as far as they could go.

With reluctance, he stepped back. But he didn't let go. His hands cupped her cheeks, his brown eyes locking on hers. Heat filled the space between them. "Tomorrow, I swear I will work a half day. Libby has a half day at school, Henry will be back early from the community center. As soon as the kids are home, let's take them to the beach."

"Both of us? But you don't need me there. You'll be fine with the kids."

"I don't *need* you there. I *want* you there. Will you go?"

Her eyes were wide and shiny in the dim light from the porch. She hesitated only a second, then nodded. "You had me at beach day."

He laughed. God, it felt good to laugh. To smile. To flirt. "Then I'm going to have to say that more often. Much, much more often."

Chapter Eight

Bandit darted in and out of the water, barking at the small waves that rolled onto the sandy shore. Libby waded in up to her ankles, while Henry, the more adventurous one, sat in the surf and let the water wash up to his waist while he tried to build a sand castle in between waves. The remains of the kids' sandwiches—a result of a quick pit stop at the Good Eatin' Café on the way over to the beach—lay atop paper plates on a checkered blanket.

It was a perfect way to spend the afternoon. Absolutely perfect.

That didn't mean that Sam wasn't thinking about work, though, or worrying that the appointment he had rescheduled, the emails he hadn't had a chance to send, and the calls that were going to his voice mail, were going to cost him down the road. The mall project wasn't going to rent itself.

But then Sam thought about the surprise on his kids'

faces when he'd walked into the house, and the whoop of joy Libby had let out when he'd said they were going to the beach. That alone was worth him working late tonight or getting up super-early tomorrow to finish up. For now, there was the beach, the sandwiches, the kids and Katie.

Sam leaned back on one elbow and stretched his legs. The sun warmed his skin, danced sparkles on the sand. "Thank you again for reminding me to take time off," he said to Katie. "This is…awesome. I feel like I don't spend hardly any time outside anymore."

"Me, too. I spent way too much time indoors at my job." She leaned back on both elbows beside him and tipped her face to the sun. Her dark hair hung like a curtain down her back, and there was a look of pure contentment on her face. He could just catch the faint scent of her perfume stirring in the air between them. Something dark, floral. Tempting. "This is nice."

"Very nice."

He'd stopped noticing the weather and the ocean because all he saw was Katie. She was beautiful, graceful. He took in the long curve of her neck and the gentle ridges of her shoulders, the delicate lines of her arms. She was wearing khaki shorts and a dark blue V-necked T-shirt. Specks of red paint from this afternoon's art project with Henry dotted her clothes, freckled her arms, and only enticed Sam more.

He wanted to ask her a thousand questions, wanted to know what made her smile, whether she was a chocolate or vanilla ice cream kind of girl, what movies made her laugh, which books made her cry.

Sam cleared his throat and returned his attention to the kids instead of staring at the woman he'd hired to be the nanny. That blanket of guilt still hung on his shoulders. He barely had enough time to be more than a token dad to his kids—what was he doing pursuing the woman working for him? If anything had cliché written all over it, it was the idea of falling for the nanny.

Libby came running up the beach, Bandit and Henry hot on her heels. Still wet from the surf, Henry's shorts dripped onto the sand, while Bandit panted beside him, tail wagging. "I'm bored," Libby said.

The most common words ever spoken by kids, Sam thought. How many times had he heard that from Libby? Heck, how often had he said it himself when he was a kid?

His father's solution—if his father had been there at all—would have been to send his two boys out back and tell them to find something to do. Their mother, often overwhelmed by raising two rambunctious boys, would opt to lie down for a nap or get lost in a soap opera, leaving Sam and Dylan to fend for themselves. He refused to let his kids grow up that way.

"Why don't we build a sand castle?" Sam said.

"I'm too old for that. That's what babies do and I'm not a baby anymore." She crossed her arms over her chest and pouted. "I wanna go home."

They'd been here only a half hour. If they went home, the kids would beeline for the TV, Sam would opt for his computer and this sweet moment in the sun would end. But when he tried to think of things that Libby might want to do, he drew a blank. When had it gotten this way? When had he lost track of his kids and what made them happy?

He knew that answer. When his wife had died and taken with her the gentle reminders to put down his work and engage with his kids, along with all that inside knowledge of a woman who had spent every spare second with her kids. Somehow, he needed to navigate these murky waters without Wendy.

"We could take a walk," Sam said.

Libby rolled her eyes. "I don't wanna do that with you. I wanna go home."

I don't wanna do that with you. The words pierced his heart. Sam could see Libby digging in her heels, and braced himself for the battle that was about to storm in. Henry lingered behind his sister, eyes downcast, face somber. Even Bandit had plopped down on the sand, his tail still, ears drooping.

There'd been a day when Libby would have rushed into his arms whenever he got home from work. When she had called out "Daddy!" like she'd just won the lottery. When she would have walked for hours with him, chattering on about her day or her toys or the little girl who lived next door. Now, Libby looked like she'd rather be anywhere but here with him.

He had only himself to blame. Those years of working too late, getting home after the kids were in bed, putting in extra hours on the weekend, or "spending time" with the kids while he was on his laptop and not really doing much more in common than breathing the same air, had taken their toll. There was no Wendy here to remind him to put down the keyboard or to take an hour off. There was just him, trying to balance everything without losing it all in the process. Judging by the look on Libby's face, he wasn't doing very well at either.

He might as well cave now to Libby's request and stave off the foot stomping and tears. If she didn't want to be here, the whole day would end up a bust, and that wasn't going to help anything. "Okay." He let out a breath. "Let me just get all this stuff packed up."

"Before you do that, I have an idea," Katie said, laying a hand on his for a second, saying *trust me* in that touch, before she turned her attention to Libby. "When I was a kid, and I got bored, my brother would take me on what he called adventure trips."

"What's an adventure trip?" Libby asked. She still wore that sullen look, but her eyes had brightened with interest. Sam shifted toward Katie, just as intrigued. Her idea already sounded a heck of a lot better than the two options he'd proposed.

"We didn't have a beach in Atlanta," Katie explained, "so we'd go down to a creek in our neighborhood or into the woods behind my school, and we'd look for animals and weird objects. Whoever found the coolest animal or the weirdest thing won a prize."

"A prize?" That had piqued her interest even more. "What kind of prize?"

"Well…" Katie glanced over at Sam, saying *fill in the blanks*.

He thought of what would make Libby the most excited, what kind of prize would entice her to play the game instead of insisting on going home. "How about first dibs on what movie we watch before bed tonight?"

"Even if it's *Frozen*?" Libby narrowed her gaze and propped a fist on her hip.

Sam bit back a groan. He had seen Libby's all-time favorite movie twelve trillion times already and usually vetoed it at bedtime because there was only so many times a grown man could listen to "Let It Go." But it was the one thing guaranteed to bring a smile to Libby's face, so that meant he'd listen to Elsa all night if he needed to. "Even if it's *Frozen*."

Libby turned back to Katie. She bounced on her heels. "Okay, I wanna do an adventure. What do we have to find?"

Katie got to her feet and brushed the sand off her palms. "It's the most fun when you have teams. So... how about me and Henry go against your dad and you, Libby?"

Libby sobered and looked up at Katie. "But I wanna be with you, Katie."

She caught Sam's gaze over Libby's head. He nodded, saying *let it go*. If he pushed Libby too hard and too fast, it would only make things worse.

"Okay, Libby," Katie said, "but I think we're going to have our work cut out for us." Sam hoisted Henry onto his hip and ruffled Libby's hair. Henry looked from his sister to his father, then rested his head on Sam's shoulder.

"Don't count on it," Sam said. "Us boys are serious competitors."

"Want to put a wager on it?" Katie asked him.

When she looked at him like that, with that little bit of a tease in her eyes, he'd agree to pretty much anything. "What kind of wager?"

"Winning team—" she thought for a second, a finger against her lip "—buys dessert on the way home."

"You're on." He put out a hand. When she slipped her palm into his, a little jolt ran up his arm. She had small, delicate fingers, but a firm grip. He didn't want to let go, but didn't think standing here and holding the nanny's hand was going to do anything other than confuse everyone. Especially him. Not that those kisses hadn't already muddled everything, anyway. He kept wavering between wanting to take her to bed and staying hands-off. Since he didn't have an answer to any of those dilemmas, he got back to the game. "Okay, where do we start?"

"With the little stuff, Sam." Her eyes met his, and

in them he could read understanding, compassion. She had seen his struggle with Libby and stepped in, with this simple game. That made him like Katie on a whole new level. "The big stuff will follow."

Katie didn't know what it was about Sam, but every time she looked at him, she wanted to melt. It wasn't just that he was handsome as heck, or that he had that sweet lopsided smile. It was the way he tried so hard to connect with his kids. She could see his heart breaking every time Libby gave him the cold shoulder or Henry refused to talk, and she wanted to do whatever she could to make that all better.

She'd lingered after lunch because she enjoyed spending time with Sam, with the kids. She'd have stayed even if she wasn't getting paid. She enjoyed the kids, and most of all, enjoyed seeing Sam smile.

Then she'd proposed the adventure game, the same one Colton had played with her. Only, when she was little, he hadn't taken her on adventures to stave off boredom or get her out of the house when their mother was in a bad mood. He'd done it to distract her from yet another disappointment. Another day in a house with a distant parent.

They had broken into two teams, with Sam and Henry running up ahead of Katie and Libby. Their goal: to find an intact clamshell. She'd given Henry and Libby each one of the plastic bags that had held their lunch, and told them there were extra points for finding the most interesting piece of trash.

"Look, Katie!" Libby held out her palm and revealed a sandy plastic army man, a little worse for wear. "I found this!"

"That's pretty cool," Katie said. "When I was a little

girl, my brother had army men like this. I took them and buried them in the backyard."

Libby gasped. "Did you get in big trouble with your mommy?"

Big trouble? Her mother had barely noticed Katie was home, never mind anything she did. "My mom worked a lot," Katie said. "So she didn't really know. But Colton, oh, he was mad at me for about a day. Longest day of my life." She laughed. "I love my brother, even if he sometimes drives me crazy."

"Kinda like how I feel about Henry. He's kinda cute but he cries a lot." Libby turned the army man over in her palm. "And he plays with my Barbies. I don't want him to 'cuz he eats their hair."

Katie laughed. "When he gets older, he won't do that anymore. And you never know, you two might even become friends."

Libby's nose wrinkled. "I don't think so."

"Give it time." Ahead of them, Sam was bent down, looking at something Henry had found, their two heads close together. Such a heartwarming image, with the sun glinting off their dark hair and twin smiles on their faces. For a second, Katie stopped walking and just stared.

There was something inherently sexy about a man who connected with children. Who could get down to their level. Sam was exclaiming over whatever Henry had in his hand, making as big a deal out of it as he would about finding a unicorn. Henry was smiling, clearly proud of himself.

She wondered for a second how things might have been different if she'd been dating Sam and gotten pregnant. Would Sam have left? Or would he have stayed by her side, every step of the way? Even in those dark days after she lost the baby?

"Katie, are we gonna find a clamshell? 'Cuz I really want to beat the boys."

"Uh, sure, sure." Katie turned her attention back to Libby and concentrated on scouring the beach.

A few minutes later, Sam ambled over, with Henry following right beside him. "Looks like somebody's buying me a slice of coconut cream pie," Sam said, then splayed his palm to reveal a complete clamshell, still hinged on one side.

"I don't know about that. I think someone's getting me a slice of chocolate cake." Katie held out the army man Libby had found. "Best trash piece."

"Hmm…looks like a tie." Sam grinned. "And what do we do in that case, oh adventure master?"

"We treat everyone to dessert," she said, thinking if he kept on smiling at her like that, she'd pay for dessert, dinner and breakfast the next morning. Damn, this man had so much power over her with something as simple as a smile.

"Ice cream?" Libby asked. "'Cuz I love ice cream!"

"I—scream," Henry echoed.

Sam glanced down at his son, his face lit with wonder, and his smile widened when he leaned closer to whisper in Katie's ear. "I'm never going to get tired of the sound of his voice. Thank you again."

She inhaled his cologne, and tried not to let her gaze linger on the dark stubble along his jaw. "I didn't do anything."

"You opened a door that had been shut," he said softly. "And for that, I should be buying *you* dessert. And much more."

She wanted to ask what he meant by much more, but

Libby was tugging at her arm and charging back up the beach toward the car. Probably just as well. She wasn't staying here and wasn't going to become mom to these kids. All of this was temporary.

A few minutes later, they were all settled in Sam's Range Rover and heading toward downtown Stone Gap. She could see why Colton enjoyed this town so much. It was quaint, with pastel homes flanking tree-lined streets, small wrought-iron benches peppered between old-fashioned streetlights. Every couple blocks there was a green space, either a park or a giant water fountain or just a trio of benches, encouraging people to sit and talk awhile. And everywhere she looked, there were people, walking between stores or sitting together and sipping coffee, or tossing a ball for their spaniel to fetch.

"Is it always like this here?" She glanced over at Sam.

"What, boring?"

She laughed. "I think Stone Gap is the opposite of boring. It's just so…quaint."

"It is a great town. I've lived here all my life and as much as I complain about how things stay the same year after year, I love it here. I couldn't imagine living anywhere else." His gaze flicked to the rearview mirror's reverse image of the kids, belted into the backseat. "Or raising my kids anywhere else."

Even if Sam had gotten a little disconnected over the years, Katie could see he was clearly a man who put his family first. Her mind wandered again to the questions she'd had earlier. Would things have been different if she'd been with Sam instead of Leonard? She shook her head. It didn't matter. Thinking of what could have been never led anywhere productive. "It does look like a great family town," she said.

"Pretty much everyone who was raised here stays here. Every day is like a high school reunion." He chuckled. "Which means everyone knows everything about everyone else. There truly are no secrets in a small town."

"But there's also connections, like you said," Katie added, as they passed a group of women greeting each other with hugs. "I think that's nice. Always knowing your neighbors, seeing friends you've known for years in the grocery store. Where I grew up, it wasn't like that."

"Because Atlanta's a big city?"

"Because my mom was always moving us. She didn't make much money, and every year or two we'd have to find a new apartment. Which meant a new school for me, a new neighborhood. Nothing ever stayed the same." She danced her fingers across the window as they passed two families standing on the sidewalk, chatting, twin strollers between them. "I always wondered what it would be like to live someplace like this. I can see why Colton loves it."

"He's a good guy," Sam said. "Really helped this town out after Ernie's hardware store burned down. Colton and his brothers were there the next day, rebuilding it all so quick, Ernie barely lost a dollar of business."

It made her proud to hear someone else say such good things about her brother. "He's always been like that. Best big brother a girl could ask for."

"I have a younger brother myself," Sam said. "He was the one who got in so much trouble that by the time my parents got to me, they were plumb worn out. I hardly ever got grounded. But Dylan, well, let's just say there was a reason I made a sign for the door to his room that said Detention Center."

Katie laughed. "That's terrible. What did he do when he saw the sign?"

"He loved it. When my mom was at the store one day, Dylan painted black stripes on his door. Really going for the whole in-jail feel, he said. That stunt got him another week of being grounded."

"Did your parents make him clean off the paint?"

"My mother, like yours, was pretty uninvolved and my dad was always working, so the paint stayed. My father said if Dylan wanted to pretend his room was a prison, he could. Dylan left home a few years later, in his late teens." Sam's face softened. "Haven't seen my brother in a long, long time. Or my parents. I see them maybe once or twice a year."

"I understand that." She was already having trouble imagining the years ahead, with Colton living several hours away. They'd always been close, even after Colton had moved out when he was nineteen. He'd always been there, just a text or phone call away. Even though she didn't need him now like she had when she was little and her mother forgot to pick her up at school, there was a certain comfort in knowing he always had her back.

"Are we there yet?" Libby's voice came in a long, drawn-out whine from the backseat. "Henry is kicking me and I want ice cream and I have to pee."

Sam chuckled. "Just got here, Libby Bear. Remember how we used to go here every Tuesday? We'd get ice cream for dinner, and then everyone's bellies would be sore." He turned right, then parked the car and shut it off. "Now, wait—"

But Libby had already unbuckled her seat belt and was making a beeline for the shop. Sam called out to her, but she didn't slow, heading straight inside the busy ice cream store. Sam grabbed her bear and sighed. "I swear, there are times I'm talking to myself."

Katie could see his frustration. Despite the moment of détente at the beach today, Libby was still distancing herself from her father. "I'll get her."

"Thank you. I'll be in right behind you." He leaned over to unbuckle Henry while Katie headed inside. She weaved her way through the crush of people waiting to order ice cream. No little brunette girl anywhere.

Panic raced through her. "Libby?"

The salesgirl at the counter glanced up at Katie. "Looking for a little one, about eight years old?"

Katie scanned the small shop again. "Did she come in here?"

The girl handed an elderly woman a vanilla cone, then nodded in the other direction. "Bathroom, down the hall, on the right."

"Thank you." Relief washed over Katie and she headed toward the restrooms. The bathroom was small, just two stalls, and painted a bright pink with white trim. The sink was shaped like a chocolate dipped waffle cone, and there was an ice cream cone stool in one corner. Even the soap dispenser was shaped like a sundae, and probably dispensed vanilla scented soap. One of the stall doors was closed, but Katie could see a familiar pair of pink flip-flops.

"Hey, Libby? You should have waited for us," Katie said. "We didn't know where you went."

From the other side of the closed stall door came a sniffle and a muffled, "I don't care."

Was Libby crying? Why? "Uh, are you almost done?" Katie asked. "I bet your dad and brother are waiting in line for us."

Another sniffle, another mumbled, "I don't care."

Katie stood in the bathroom, hesitating. Should she leave Libby alone? Did a girl that age need help washing her hands or anything? Was she sniffling because she was upset or mad or throwing a tantrum? And what was Katie supposed to do about any of those? Maybe she should get Sam. Except this was the ladies' room, and not the best place for a dad to talk to his daughter. "Uh, Libby, I'm just going to wait with your dad, unless you need something…"

No answer. Just more sniffling, and then the soft sound of crying. That was definitely not a tantrum. Katie's heart broke. Oh, how she understood those tears, that feeling of not being understood and just wanting to escape.

Katie went to the pink metal door and laid a hand on the cool surface. "Libby? You okay?"

"Just leave me alone."

Katie considered doing just that. She wasn't a mom, she didn't know anything about raising kids, and this crying thing seemed like something Sam should handle. The soft sounds of Libby's sobs and heaving breaths tugged at Katie.

She thought of that first summer she'd gone to camp—long before the summer she was a camp counselor. She'd been seven and terrified from the minute her mother's car pulled away, because it was also the first time she'd been somewhere without Colton in the next room.

Scared and lonely, Katie had run and hid in the bathroom. She'd huddled in the corner stall until after lights out. One of the counselors, a college student named Michelle, had found Katie in the bathroom. Michelle had sat on the floor outside the stall door and talked to her for a long, long time, until Katie's tears dried up and she'd unlatched the door. Michelle wasn't old enough to know how to be a mother, but she'd done the one thing Katie could do for Libby—she'd talked and listened and simply been there.

Katie slid down against the corner of the stall and sat on the tiles. She drew her knees up to her chest and pressed her back against the cold hard metal panel. "I'll just wait here for you, Libby. Okay?"

"You don't have to. I'm a big girl."

"I know that. But I'm gonna wait, anyway." Katie brushed at some dirt on her knees and tried to think of something to talk about that would distract Libby and calm her down. "Did you know that one cow makes enough milk to make two gallons of ice cream every day? That's a lot of milk."

Libby didn't say anything, just sniffled some more. Cried a little more.

Katie had already exhausted her list of interesting ice cream facts. "So what's your favorite flavor of ice cream, Libby? I bet it's…strawberry. Am I right?"

"That was… Mommy's favorite." Libby's voice had gone soft and sad, with a little sob on the end of "Mommy."

Oh, damn. Why had Katie brought that up? Now Libby really was crying, and it was all Katie's fault. Libby was miserable and locked inside the bathroom stall, instead of out in the shop with her father and brother. Clearly, Katie sucked at this mothering thing. Heck, she wasn't even very good at the being-a-friend-to-a-kid thing.

Katie's cell buzzed with a text from Sam. Where are you two?

Libby's a little upset. Talking to her in the bathroom.
Out in a few minutes.

She hoped. Katie spun on the tile floor and rapped
at the base of the stall door. She could see two little feet
in pink flip-flops, swinging back and forth against the
cream ceramic floor. "Libby? Why don't you come out?
Your dad and brother are waiting for us to get some
ice cream."

"No." It was a muffled word, still caught in a sob.
Heartbroken. Lonely. Scared.

"I bet it's hard being here without your mom," Katie
said softly. Silence on the other side of the door was un-
derwritten by the Muzak sound system. "Did she like
ice cream a lot?"

"Uh-huh."

"And you said her favorite was strawberry?" Katie
wasn't so sure asking Libby about her dead mother was
the best way to get her to come out from behind that
bathroom door, but when she was seven and scared at
camp and Michelle was on the other side of the stall
door, Katie had talked about the things that scared her
and the things that made her sad, and after a while,
that feeling of being overwhelmed began to abate, and
the room that had felt so stark and cold began to feel…
warm. Maybe the same would work with Libby.

She hoped.

"My mom's favorite was chocolate," Katie went on,
filling the space between them with words. "But I only
remember going out for ice cream once with her."

"Only one time? How come?"

"My mom…wasn't home a lot," Katie said, couch-
ing the truth. "So my big brother took me for ice cream.
Every Wednesday, we went after school. I always got

a two-scoop cone. Chocolate on the bottom, vanilla on top, but he was more of a purist and got just one scoop of chocolate. So, what's your favorite, Libby?"

There was a long pause. The Muzak switched to an instrumental version of the Bee Gees' "Staying Alive." Another text from Sam, with another reassurance sent back from Katie. In the texts, she sounded a lot more confident that she had this under control than she felt.

"I like vanilla," Libby said after a long while. "And sprinkles. Do you like sprinkles?"

"I do. They're the best part of an ice cream cone."

"My mommy liked sprinkles, too. But she called them...um, jim...jim something."

"Jimmies," Katie supplied.

"Yeah, jimmies." The pink flip-flops toed a circle on the floor. "She said that's what they were called where she grew up."

Katie could hear the sadness in the little girl's voice, the wistful melancholy at the memories of her late mother. It made Katie want to reach her arms through the door and hug Libby, and tell her it would be all right. But she couldn't do that, and especially couldn't promise that. "What do you say we both get an ice cream with sprinkles on it? I bet that would make your mom smile."

"But...my mom can't see me," Libby said, her voice low and sad again.

"I think maybe she can," Katie said. "When I was about your age, Libby, my grandma got sick. I loved my grandma, and was really upset that I was going to lose her. I remember she was sitting in her favorite chair by the window. It was a great big chair, with pink floral fabric, but it was just the right size for her and me to sit together. She had me climb up beside her, and when I did, she pointed out the window, at the bright blue sky, and said to me, 'Do you see that space, the one just past that little cloud? That's where I'm going to be, watching over you.'"

Libby sniffled again, then asked, "Can you see her there?"

"I wish I could, but the clouds are just so far away that I can't. But I know she's there, and sometimes, I just send a little wave toward the sky, to tell her I miss her." Katie had done that dozens of times when she was younger, missing the grandmother who had been more of a mother than her own mother. Grandma Martha had been the one to bake cookies, decorate for Christmas and hang the pictures Katie colored on the fridge. Then she had died and Colton had stepped in to be the parent they were both lacking. "I've always liked knowing that she was up there, watching over me."

A long, long pause, then finally, there was a shuffling on the other side of the door, followed by the click of the lock sliding out of its home. Libby poked her head around the corner of the door frame. "Do you think my mommy could see me if I wave toward her?"

Libby's eyes shimmered with unshed tears, and her lower lip trembled. Katie's heart broke a little. "Yes, honey, I'm sure she can."

"After..." Libby drew in a breath, steeled herself a little. "After we get an ice cream with jimmies, can we go outside, so my mommy can see my ice cream, and I can say hi?"

"I think that's a wonderful idea. We can do that, for sure."

A tentative smile wobbled on Libby's face, before she dropped her gaze to the floor and gave a little nod. "Okay."

There was a knock at the bathroom door, then Sam poked his head in. "You girls okay in here?"

"We are now," Katie said. She gave Libby another smile, and this time Libby's smile held. Katie got to her feet, waited while they both washed their hands, then Libby put her palm into Katie's. The two of them crossed the room and fell into place beside Sam. "I think we're ready for some ice cream right now."

"With jimmies," Libby added softly.

"With jimmies," Katie promised, and gave Libby's hand a tender squeeze.

Chapter Nine

Sam wanted to ask Katie what had happened back in the bathroom, but didn't want to upset the delicate balance that had been restored to Libby. She no longer seemed angry or upset, but more...peaceful. She stood beside Katie, holding her hand, and as they shuffled forward in line, Libby leaned against Sam's arm. Henry had fallen asleep, his thirty pounds of body weight a solid chunk against Sam's chest. It was as close to a perfect moment as Sam had felt in a long time.

He glanced over at Katie. She was reading the long list of ice cream flavors chalked on the slate board behind the counter. For the tenth time, he marveled at how this woman—a complete stranger—had brought a little calm into the chaos that had been his life for the last year and a half.

Libby said something about cows and milk, but Sam didn't hear the words, because whatever Libby said made Katie smile. The curve of her lips, the way her re-action lit her eyes, captivated Sam. It was a warm smile, the kind that spread through him like a warm fire.

In the year and a half since Wendy had died, Sam had barely noticed other women. He hadn't dated, hell, hadn't had time to do the laundry, never mind date, but also hadn't had the desire to ask another woman out. He'd loved Wendy, loved her from the first day he'd met her when they'd been paired up in chemistry class and she'd added too much baking soda to their faux volcano and created a Vesuvius-worthy reaction. After she died, he'd never imagined he'd meet another woman who would intrigue him as much as his late wife had. Until now.

Guilty feelings still clung to the edges of his thoughts, but they were a little quieter. Maybe it was time to move on, to open his heart again.

Katie turned, and caught him staring. A faint blush filled her cheeks. "What? Do I have sand on my face or something?"

"No, not at all." He wanted to say something more about how beautiful she was, but figured doing that while waiting in line for an ice cream with his kids wasn't the best timing. "Uh, what flavor are you get-ting?"

"I'm going with the tried-and-true," Katie said. "A two-scoop cone, chocolate on the bottom and—"

"Vanilla on the top," Libby added. "I wanna try that, too."

"Sounds like a great idea," Sam said. "How about we make it three?" Five minutes later, the three of them had identical cones, all topped with sprinkles, and a small dish of vanilla for Henry. Sam weaved his way through the crowd and led them to the outside picnic tables. Just before they sat down, Libby looked at Katie, then the two of them raised their cones to the sky. They held that position for a second, Libby's eyes glistening.

Henry woke up, and scrambled down to get his ice cream dish from Sam. The two kids opted to sit at a small table a few feet away, while Sam and Katie chose a nearby bench. "What was that about?" Sam asked.

"Libby was missing her mom, so I told her that her mom was watching her from up above, and she'd want to see that Libby was getting their favorite ice cream today."

The thoughtfulness and the heartfelt meaning in that moment made Sam choke up a little. He glanced over at his little girl, and saw her smiling, laughing, engaged with Henry. She had her bear propped up on the seat beside her as she ate her ice cream, and from time to time she would glance up at the sky. A wistful smile ghosted on Libby's face, then she turned back to her brother, her mood lighter, the tension in her tiny frame eased.

"That's...really sweet," Sam said. "Thank you."

Katie shrugged. "It was nothing."

"No, really, it was great. Libby's been struggling so much. Heck, both kids have. I wish I had the right words to help them, and it seems all I do is make it worse." He was too busy making sure everyone ate dinner and got to school and went to bed on time, and knew he was missing these small moments. The kind of moments that mattered in the long journey of healing broken hearts. "Maybe I should get them into counseling or something."

"I'm no expert," Katie said, "but I think all they need is more of what they had today."

His gaze lingered on his kids, his heart full, his throat thick. Henry struggled to scoop up the next bite, his little face scrunched with frustration. Libby leaned over, wriggled the spoon into the ice cream, then held it out to her little brother. Sam knew there would be squabbles in the days ahead—heck, maybe even in the next five minutes—but he let this moment linger.

"I'm trying, Katie, but it's been tough. Especially with Libby." He sighed. "Libby wanted to leave almost the second she got to the beach. *You* were the one who convinced her to stay and play that game. *You* were the one who talked to her in the bathroom. *You* were the one who thought of how she could share her ice cream with her mother. I think I lost whatever relationship I had with her."

"Maybe. Or maybe—" Katie paused "—you need to treat parenting like buildings."

He chuckled and took a bite of his ice cream. "You're comparing raising kids to real estate?"

"Well, when you look at a building, you get this gut instinct, I'm sure, of what it could be in the future. You know which clients to call, how to advertise the property, how to make the qualities stand out and how to minimize the flaws."

"And how does that compare to raising kids?"

"Well, you try to put a positive spin on the stuff the kids don't want to do, like eat broccoli, and try to anticipate their needs and wants." She took a few bites of her ice cream, before it melted over the edge of the cone. "It's how I worked with clients at the accounting firm. Stands to reason that if it worked with high-maintenance adults, it should work with kids."

He laughed. "Very true."

Henry and Libby squabbled a little over space on the curved bench seat at the table, the argument settled by Libby putting George on her lap. "Maybe I worry too much," Sam said. "These kids have been through so much. The last thing I want to do is make a single second of their lives more difficult."

"I think you're doing great." Katie finished her ice cream and tossed the napkin in the trash, then returned to sit beside Sam. The kids finished their treats and asked if they could play on the swing set in the small grassy area beside the ice cream shop.

"For ten minutes," Sam said. "Then it's time to go home."

Libby made a face, but didn't argue. She left her bear on the bench with Katie and Sam, then spun on her heel and chased after Henry, both of them dashing up the slide. Libby took Henry's hand at the top and let him go first. For all her complaining about her brother, Sam could see this protective side in Libby that told him she secretly did love Henry. It was nice, and told him maybe—just maybe—he was doing a few things right.

"So what about you?" he asked Katie as they walked the perimeter of the small park. Sam had the stuffed bear tucked under his arm. "How is it that an incredible woman like you is still single? I'd expect you to be married and raising a couple kids of your own."

She paused a long time. So long, he almost asked the question again. "I guess the right opportunity hasn't come along," she finally said.

"Opportunity? You make it sound like a job search." He chuckled. "Marriage is great, you know. I really did enjoy being married. And having kids, as tough as it can be some days, is wonderful. I'd love to get married again, maybe even have more kids. If the right opportunity comes along." He winked at her, expecting her to laugh.

Instead a shadow passed over her face, and the light

mood from earlier evaporated. Her body seemed to tense, and her steps slowed. "I think the ten minutes are up. We should probably get going so you can get the kids home."

But if he did that, the day with Katie would end, and suddenly, Sam didn't want to say goodbye. "Why don't I call Della and have her come over after the kids go to sleep, and just you and I go out?"

She was already shaking her head. "Sam, it's been a long day and—"

"Are you always this difficult to date?" He grinned. "Because last I checked, you kissed me back, twice, and that doesn't communicate 'not interested in dating you.'"

She let out a long sigh. "It's just...complicated."

"You said that already. A dozen times." Yet he read clear attraction between them. Unless maybe he'd been out of the game for so long that he was reading her wrong. "How is it complicated? Is there a boyfriend back in Atlanta?"

Please say no.

"No boyfriend. It's not that." She tore a leaf from a low-hanging branch, and watched it flutter to the ground. "I'm not staying here forever. You know that. I have to go back to Atlanta. Back to my real career."

Yeah, she did. And he didn't want to think about that day or when it would come. All he wanted to focus on was the fact that she was here now. He wanted to see more of Katie—and not with his children in the background.

And he knew the kids were getting attached to her, as much as he was. He didn't want her to leave, didn't want her to ever return to Atlanta. Maybe he'd come up with some brilliant idea that would keep Katie in Stone Gap.

"Either way, I see no reason for you and me not to have a little adult time. So before you can say no again, I'll call Della." He did just that, pulling out his cell phone and dialing Della Barlow. A few minutes of conversation and he had a babysitter lined up. "Della's going to meet us at the house in a few hours. That's just enough time to get the kids some dinner, bathed, in bed and asleep, especially after the busy day in the sun."

A smile curved across Katie's face. "You don't give up easily, do you?"

"Nope. Not in real estate and not—" he turned to her and tipped a finger under her chin "—when it comes to beautiful and stubborn women."

Katie had opted to go back to the bed-and-breakfast to get changed, so Sam could have some alone time with his kids, and to give herself a few moments to process how she'd gotten swept up into agreeing to dinner tonight. She should keep her distance, but there was something about his smile that drew her even when she knew he was the kind of man who wanted a future she didn't think she could give him. Sam wanted marriage, maybe more kids.

So she'd done the only thing she could think to do— she'd checked her email to see if anyone in Atlanta was looking for a CPA. And there in her in-box were two job offers, both at firms she knew and liked. Which meant she had a decision to make—to stay or go back.

Either way, it was crazy to even consider something long-term with a man she had just met. Sam was the kind of guy a woman settled down with, living in a tiny town like Stone Gap, in the house with a fenced-in yard and a playful golden retriever. For a moment, she'd thought she was that kind of woman.

She wasn't even sure if she had it in her to risk all that again. To dream about a forever kind of life with a husband and kids, and in the end, see both taken away in a blink.

"You look beautiful," Della said, when Katie came into the kitchen a little while later. "I'm so glad you and Sam found a way to go out. As disappointed as I am that I won't get to spoil those two little munchkins of his, I understand him wanting to spend time with his kids before they go to bed. Those little-kid years disappear in the blink of an eye. I love my granddaughter, Maddy, to pieces, and can't wait for my sons to bless me with more grandchildren to spoil."

Katie sat down at the kitchen table, a space that already felt like home, even after little over a week. She loved this bed-and-breakfast, with its warm tones and fresh-baked-bread scent. "Can I ask you something, if it's not too forward?"

"Honey, I was raised by a woman who believed in living out loud. My mama, bless her heart, never let the sun rest without telling folks how she felt, or giving them advice they may or may not have asked for." Della smiled. "There's nothing you can say or ask me that I'm going to think is too forward."

Katie toyed with the edge of the red plaid place mat, her finger running along the woven edge. "How do you know if you're ready to settle down with one person?"

"I don't know if anyone ever feels ready to settle down," Della said. "It's a scary thing to do, because it means you're giving your heart to just one person, and trusting that they aren't going to break it."

Della's gaze took on a faraway look, and Katie wondered if she was thinking about the brief affair her husband had had, the one that had produced Colton. As much as Katie adored Della Barlow, she was grateful for her brother's existence.

"I never thought I'd want to have that white-picket life," Katie said. "My childhood was…rough, and I had decided when I was young that instead of settling down, I was going to work on my career and never end up like my mother. Then I had a chance at the very life I had avoided and…even though I…I lost it, it made me wish for that one thing."

Della's features softened with understanding. It was as if there was some unspoken language among women, where they knew the pain the other had gone through. "And you're scared to take that risk again, in case the same thing happens."

Tears burned the back of Katie's eyes. It was all she could do to nod.

"Life is about risk, honey." Della's warm hand covered Katie's. "You risk your heart and sometimes it gets broken, but sometimes it finds the greatest love you will ever know. A love that can withstand the harshest storms. A love that is there for you, especially when you suffer a loss you think you can't ever get past." Della's words seemed to come from a place deep inside her, a place of shared hurt.

"Did you lose a baby, too?"

Della nodded, and her eyes misted. Even all these years later, the pain still flickered on her face. "It was my second pregnancy. Mac was only a few months old, and when I got pregnant again right away, a part of me—" she swallowed, paused a moment "—a part of me was resentful. I had my hands full with my first baby, and all I can remember is feeling so overwhelmed, and thinking how on earth will I do this with two babies? Then a little over a month later, I woke up in the worst pain I'd ever felt, and I thought…" She took in a deep breath, held it for a moment. "I thought God was punishing me for wishing I wasn't pregnant. My Bobby was there for me, thank God, and we got through it, together. For a long time, I felt like a failure because my body had betrayed me."

"That's how I feel, too." The knowledge that she wasn't the only one feeling that way eased the ache in Katie's heart. "This is the one thing all women can do, and I…couldn't."

"It wasn't you, honey. It was just part of nature's plan. It took me a long time to work up the courage to try again, but I am so grateful I did, because I have Jack and Luke. Those boys are the best part of my life, and the family I've formed with Bobby is the only legacy I really care about leaving." Della got to her feet, leaned over and drew Katie into a short, tight hug.

"Take the risk, Katie. In the end, even if it doesn't work out, you will be stronger and better for it. And your life will have a meaning you can't find punching a time clock."

Tears sprang to Katie's eyes. This woman she barely knew was more of a mother than her own had ever been. Katie's arms went around Della and she leaned into the hug. It was as warm and comforting as the sunny yellow kitchen and the fresh baked bread on the counter.

After a long time, Della drew back and gave Katie a watery smile. "You have a wonderful time with Sam tonight. He's a good man, one of the best. And if you take a chance on him, you may just find the very thing you've been seeking all your life."

"What's that?"

Della's hand cupped Katie's jaw, and her big green eyes held pools of understanding. "A home."

Chapter Ten

Sam stood on the front porch of the Stone Gap Inn, as nervous as he had been in ninth grade when he'd gone to Amy Jean Mollering's house to ask her to the freshman dance. Tonight, he'd nicked himself shaving, spent a solid ten minutes looking for a belt, and nearly walked out of the house without his shoes.

After watching "Frozen," taking baths and hearing three stories, the kids had finally fallen asleep. Henry had curled up in Sam's arms as he'd read a book about pirates, but Libby had stayed on the end of the bed, like an island of one. Still, she had stayed through both books Henry picked, then requested a favorite of hers from years before—a story about a princess living in a forgotten castle. Sam had taken that as a good sign. Maybe things were turning in a better direction with his kids. Maybe he could find a way to balance everything.

All that optimism faded the minute he reached the

front steps of the Stone Gap Inn. It was insane to be this nervous about taking a woman he had already spent an entire day with out on a date. But it was the first time he'd been entirely alone with a woman in a long time, and he wasn't quite sure he remembered how this whole dating thing worked. Surely in the ten years since he'd married Wendy, the rules had changed. Somebody really should hand out a manual, because Sam didn't have a clue. And the friend he would most likely ask for advice was Katie's brother. Probably not the best resource for how to woo this particular woman.

There was still a lingering feeling of guilt in his chest. It wasn't just about how he began to date again, but whether he *should*.

He rang the bell, and Mavis Beauchamp pulled open the door a moment later.

"Well, if it isn't Sam Millwright!" Mavis exclaimed. She opened her arms and drew him into a tight hug. "I haven't seen you in months, young man."

"Evenin', Mrs. Beauchamp."

She drew back and assessed him, an ample hip cocked to one side, her bright floral housedress looking like a garden exploded. "And what brings you by?"

"I'm here to call on Katie." There was just something about being around Mavis that made a man revert to the more formal language of the old South. Maybe it was the way she was so deeply rooted in the traditions of this area, or the way she looked at folks, as if expecting them to trot out their Sunday best on a Tuesday afternoon.

"Oh, yes. Della said something about that, just before she headed out the door. You come right on in and make yourself comfortable. I'll go get Katie." Mavis ushered him into the front parlor and waved him toward a rose-colored love seat. "Do you want some iced tea? Lemonade?"

"I'm fine, ma'am, thank you."

"All right. I'll be back faster than a squirrel can shake his tail." She gave him a wave, then headed down the hall. He heard Mavis in the kitchen, telling Katie her gentleman caller had arrived, and Sam had to bite back a laugh. He didn't think he'd ever been referred to as a gentleman caller in his life.

He rose as Katie entered the room. She'd changed since their day at the beach, and wore a light blue dress that flared at the waist and danced around her calves. Her long brown hair hung in loose waves around her shoulders, and she'd done something different with her eye makeup, because her eyes seemed even bigger and browner. "You look beautiful," he said.

She blushed. "Thank you."

"I know we already ate, so I thought maybe we could head to one of my favorite places in Stone Gap."

"Where's that?"

He grinned. "It's a surprise."

"Don't you dare take Katie to Makeout Hill," Mavis called from the kitchen. "No lady should be sitting in the backseat of your car, getting busy."

Sam laughed. "Don't worry, Mrs. Beauchamp. I'm not a getting-busy-in-the-backseat kind of guy."

"Uh-huh. I don't know about that. Most every man I know is a getting-busy kind of guy." Mavis poked her head into the front parlor. "You two get on out of here before I shoo you out. I have things to do, and I can't be standing around, visiting all night."

Sam laughed again, then put out his arm to Katie. "I think that's our cue."

She slipped her hand in the crook of his elbow. "Good night, Mavis. Don't wait up."

"You know I will." Mavis waved them off, then headed back to the kitchen.

Sam led Katie out to his car, opened the door for her, then waited for her to settle into the seat before going around to the driver's side. Once he was behind the wheel, the nerves returned, so he defaulted to the common ground of talking about the kids. "Even after that day at the beach, I ended up reading three stories to the kids before they finally fell asleep. Even Libby requested a book she used to love when she was little. It's the first time she's done that in a long, long time."

"That's wonderful," Katie said.

"I think Della was a little disappointed that the kids were asleep when she got there," he said.

Katie laughed. "She wanted to spoil them. She's one of the most motherly people I've ever met, especially with the guests at the inn. I have hot coffee and warm fresh bread waiting on a tray outside my room every morning. And there are always fresh cookies in the kitchen, and heck, even the linens smell like lilacs."

"She's the mom everyone wishes they had, even the people that had cool moms." He liked Della, liked all the Barlows, in fact. They were a great family and had made Stone Gap proud.

He started the car, then pulled away from the curb. Night was falling and the streetlights winked on, one by one, as he headed away from the bed-and-breakfast.

"I don't know about you but I'm crazy nervous," Katie said.

He laughed. "You read my mind. Maybe it's because it's been a while since I dated, or maybe it's because you work for me—"

"But this feels a little weird." They both nodded. "Then how about we don't call it a date? Just…getting together. Nothing more."

Not calling tonight a date kept him from feeling like this was wrong—too soon, too much, too something for a man widowed only a year and a half ago. Though a part of him wondered if he was using those feelings as a way to not deal with the fact that he did, indeed, want very much to date Katie. "Okay, it's not a date. Technically."

"Good." She sat back in her seat. "So…where are you taking me on our not-date?"

"If I told you, it wouldn't be a surprise, now would it?" He turned left, then right, winding his way out of the neighborhoods near Stone Gap's downtown area. The house-lined streets gave way to more trees, fewer residences, and then finally to a long stretch of woods that nearly swallowed the moonlight above. He took another turn, down a rutted road, and pulled to a stop beside a decaying house that had stood on this land for so long nobody in town could remember who had first owned it. He parked the car and turned off the engine. "This is my favorite place in all of Stone Gap."

"This…place? But it's…"

"A piece of crap," he finished. "Yup. But it's a piece of crap with serious potential. Come on, let me show you."

He grabbed a flashlight from the glove compartment, got out of the car, then came around to her side and took her hand as she exited. She'd worn flats with her dress, which was a good thing, because the terrain by the house was rough. "It still has good bones," he said as they walked up the slope of the bumpy driveway, their path illuminated by the flashlight's beam. "And one hell of a view."

Sam led Katie up the porch steps and around to the back of the house. At the base of the hill, Stone Gap Lake spread its deep, dark waters before them like a man offering his palm. The moon caught the slight ripples and bounced off them in tiny sparkles. A loon called from somewhere far across the lake, a lonely cry that echoed in the quiet.

"It's beautiful," Katie said, her voice so soft the word was almost a breath. "Absolutely beautiful."

"When I was a kid, I'd come here after school, and just sit on the porch and do my homework and watch the lake. The birds diving for their lunch, the fish splashing away, the fishermen whiling away an afternoon. It was peaceful and quiet. I used to imagine that when I grew up, I'd buy this house and live here with a dozen kids of my own."

"Why didn't you?"

He shrugged. "Wendy wanted the subdivision life. She wanted the neighbors and the block parties and the sidewalks. So we lived in a neighborhood. But this house…it was always the one I wanted my kids to live in, so they could run in the yard and fish in the lake and swing on a rope swing."

Katie spun in a slow circle, taking in the rest of the lake view, the woods to the left, the long empty field to the right. "Who owns it now?"

"An overwhelmed commercial Realtor with two mortgages and two kids."

She turned back to him, her jaw agape. "You bought it, after all?"

He still remembered the day he'd passed papers on this old home, thinking he'd finally have his dream.

He'd been so excited to hand his wife the keys, to start taking the first steps toward their new future together. "I thought I'd surprise Wendy on our fifth anniversary. Libby was four, and I thought it was a great time to move out of the subdivision and into a great old house like this one. We rarely fought, but boy, did we fight that day. I finally agreed to sell this house, but in the end, I just couldn't do it. The mortgage isn't much, because the house isn't worth much, so I kept on paying for it, and we kept on arguing about it."

"I think it's a fabulous place." Katie walked down the back porch stairs, ignoring the creak of the old, faded wood. She spun in a circle again, drinking in the expansive view, the carved columns, the wide plank floors, illuminated by Sam's flashlight. "I lived in the city all my life. Cramped little apartments in concrete prisons. I would have loved to have grown up somewhere like this. Heck, I'd love to *live* somewhere like this even now, as an adult."

That made a little part of Sam happy. He had hoped Katie would have that reaction, but wasn't sure she would love this run-down old house like he did. He'd been toying with the idea of hiring Colton's sister-in-law-to-be, Savannah, who was engaged to Mac Barlow, to look at restoring the house. He'd seen some of Savannah's restoration work—including the Stone Gap Inn—and been very impressed. "Do you want to see the rest of the place?"

"I'd love to."

He put out his hand as they walked into the house, and when she slid hers into his palm, the touch felt right. Perfect. With the flashlight illuminating the way, they walked hand in hand through the rooms, and Sam told her the plans he had for the place. All these years of thinking about how he would restore the old house had filled his mind with dozens of ideas, and he rattled them off like a locomotive racing down the tracks.

They moved from the parlor to the dining room. Floor-to-ceiling windows looked out over the fabulous view out back. The previous owner had started to renovate the house more than twenty years ago, and stopped after the demolition stage, which left gaping holes in several places, and more than a few walls stripped back to the frame. But Sam could still see his vision, could imagine the house with all the changes he wanted to make. "I want to put a coved ceiling in the dining room and a chandelier in the center. There's a space there for a built-in hutch, and I think it would look awesome if I had one with a glass front, and opened the back to the kitchen on the other side. The wainscoting is still in great shape, and I think it all can be salvaged. If not, I know Savannah has a whole garage filled with pieces she's scavenged over the years."

"These wide plank floors are incredible," Katie said, toeing the hardwood beneath her feet. "Are you going to save them?"

"As best I can. There's some water damage in the kitchen, and one of the upstairs bedrooms had a roof leak that pretty much destroyed all the flooring and walls. I did a temporary patch on the roof, but it really needs to be redone."

She let out a low whistle. "That all sounds pretty expensive."

"It is. But if I can wrap up this mall occupancy project that I'm working on, the commission from that should be enough to get the changes started here." He ran a hand through his hair and wrestled with the same internal debate he'd been having for a year and a half.

Was the smartest plan starting over here? He'd always imagined his kids playing in the big yard, running through the water, hanging pictures on the long wall in the kitchen. He'd imagined notching their heights in the wooden molding around the doors, setting a Christmas tree in the foyer by the bay window...

"I just don't know if I want to uproot the kids and move them someplace else," he said. "All their memories of their mother are in that other house."

"No, they're not, Sam. They're here." Katie placed a hand on his chest, right above his heart. Her palm spread warmth through the layer of his shirt. "They're in Tuesday night ice cream dinners and the same bedtime story every night and even George the bear. If you talk to the kids, I think you'll find that they remember a lot about their mother. A lot of things that they want to talk about, too."

Libby had barely talked about her mother since she died. Henry hadn't talked at all. The last thing Sam wanted to do was make any of this harder on them. "I guess I thought if I brought up old memories, it would make them upset. Losing her was so hard on them, and the last thing I wanted to do was bring that pain to life again."

Katie left her hand on his heart, a delicate, comforting touch. "They want to share those memories, and I think they need to. And I think as long as you do that, it won't matter what house you live in."

He covered her hand with his own and smiled down at her. This woman seemed to know exactly what to say, and exactly when to say it. With a few sentences, she'd eased his doubts and fears. "How did you get so wise?"

"I read a lot of romance novels." She grinned.

"And in those novels, is the hero always rescuing the heroine?"

"Sometimes it's the opposite." She smiled wider, and her gaze dropped to their joined hands. Neither of them spoke for a moment.

The tension in the air began to thicken, shifting from comfort to something different. Something warmer. He wanted to act on it, wanted to kiss her, wanted more. But still he hesitated. This date/not-date they were on was still in an undefined limbo.

Holding tight to her hand, he lowered their clasped palms to his side. "Come on, I want to show you the kitchen."

He led her down a short hall and into the kitchen. It was a big room, fourteen by eighteen, with a hearth at one end and a long island at the other. The upper cabinets were missing, but the sink was still there, and he'd brought over two bar stools to set on either side of the island.

In the center were two candles and a vase of fresh flowers. He had bought sandwiches and one of those ready-made dessert plates from the grocery store filled with little bites of brownies, chocolate-covered strawberries and a few cookies. And a bottle of wine, flanked by two glasses, was chilling in a bucket of ice. He leaned over, lit the candles, and stepped back.

"Oh, Sam, when did you do all this?" Her hand squeezed his a little tighter, and Sam's heart lifted.

"On my way over to pick up you. I didn't know what kind of wine you liked, so I went with a chardonnay. I hope that's okay. I bought ham-and-cheese and turkey-and-cheese sandwiches, so you could choose." God, he sounded nervous.

"It all looks amazing. Thank you."

He pulled out one of the bar stools and made a sweeping gesture. "Best seat in the house, mademoiselle."

She laughed and slid onto the bar stool, then laid a napkin across her lap. He took the seat across from her, then divvied up the sandwiches and poured them each a glass of wine. The sexual tension was still there between them, playing like background music to the food and conversation. "So what made you get into real estate?" she asked, then took a bite of her sandwich.

"I was always fascinated with buildings when I was a kid," he said. "I thought about becoming an architect or a contractor, but then I met Wendy, and her uncle was a Realtor. He let me go along with him a few times and see how it worked. I loved the challenge of marketing a property, finding the right buyer, or discovering that one forgotten piece of real estate that's just perfect for a client. I still do love that part." He took a bite of his sandwich, chewed and swallowed. "So why did you become an accountant?"

"Well, not because I loved it." She let out a little laugh. "I was good at math in school. I liked the order of it, how everything would align just right. My guidance counselor suggested I look at accounting schools, and the first one I applied to offered me a scholarship, so I took it. I just…wanted to get out of there. Colton was working at the fire station, and I didn't want to live at home anymore. So I took the scholarship, and ended up as a CPA."

"Order in chaos." He nodded. "I can understand that. You did the same with the kids, you know. Things were kind of a mess before you came along."

She ran a finger along the rim of her wineglass and watched the shimmer of the white wine in the dim candlelight. "I think it's because I could relate to them," she said. "Colton and I bonded together, because our mother was absent. And I think after they lost their mom, Henry and Libby bonded, too."

"They did. I was working, and grieving myself, and I wasn't there as much as I should have been." He sighed. "I wish I could do all those months over again."

"You're doing it right now, Sam. That's what's important."

"With your help." He covered her hand with his own. "You have made everything better, Katie. I can't thank you enough."

She shook her head and glanced downward. "Just doing my job."

"Is that all it is? A job?"

She lifted her gaze to his. A moment passed, another. The thread between them tightened again, shifting like the winds. "No. It's more than that."

The words made him happy. Made him forget all the reasons this wasn't supposed to be a date. Made him think again how beautiful she looked, how alone they were, and how very much he wanted to kiss her. Hell, he'd wanted to kiss her from the minute he met her, and now that he had, he knew how sweet and wonderful it would be.

He got to his feet and took the empty paper plates from their sandwiches to toss in the trash. "Which dessert would you like? There's cheesecake, brownies, chocolate-covered strawberries. I didn't know what you liked, so I bought them all."

She looked up at him and smiled, a wide, breathtaking smile that hit him hard. She held his gaze for a heartbeat, and the tension between them coiled even tighter. She shifted her weight in his direction and entwined her fingers with his. "I like pretty much all wine, and as for dessert, I love anything that has chocolate on it."

"Anything?"

The smile on her face eased into one that held flirtation. The desire that Sam had managed to keep on low all day flared up a few notches. "Anything," she whispered.

He leaned over and scooped a dollop of chocolate onto his index finger, then placed it against her lips. They parted, and her tongue darted out and tasted the sweet icing, then ate the bite. Her gaze never left his, and he had to resist the urge to groan. He moved his hand away and kissed her, this time hard and fast, tasting the chocolate on her tongue.

She pressed against him, fitting perfectly in his arms. His hands roamed down her back, over her buttocks, up her sides. She clutched at his shirt, drawing him closer, hungry for him, as hungry as he was for her. He wanted to hitch up her dress and have her right here, right now, on the kitchen counter, but instead he scooped her into his arms and headed out of the kitchen.

She let out a giggle and tightened her grip on him. "Where…where are we going?"

"Not all the bedrooms were damaged by the rain." His gaze met hers, half question, half invitation. Did she want this to go further as much as he did? Had she been feeling that same fire between them?

A sexy smile curved across her face. "I'm very glad to hear that."

He kicked open one of the bedroom doors. Years ago, he'd put a bed in here, intending to have a place to rest when he was working on the house, or to spend the weekend if he took the family fishing at the lake, but he'd never really used it. Tonight, he was damned grateful to have that bed there.

He laid Katie on the queen mattress and stepped back to look at her. She was beautiful in the moonlight streaming through the windows, casting her features with a soft pale wash. He lay down beside her and traced a line from her neck to her belly, over the hills of her breasts, down the valley of her abdomen. "You are incredible," he whispered.

"And you are biased." But she smiled all the same.

She reached for his shirt, but he took her hand and stopped her. "I mean it. From the minute you arrived on my doorstep in those heels and that skirt, I have known you were different. Unique. Special."

"I thought the same about you. The handsome widower trying so hard to get it right."

He grinned. "You think I'm handsome?"

"Let me show you the answer to that question." She untucked the tail of his button-down shirt and slid a hand against the smooth skin of his chest, then reached over with her other hand to unfasten the buttons.

Damn. He'd thought he wanted her before, but when she took the lead like that it sent his pulse into overdrive. Sam wrangled his arms out of his shirt and tossed it to the side, then reached for the hem of her dress. She arched up on the bed, and he slid the dress up and over her, then threw it to wherever his shirt had landed.

His gaze traveled over her, drinking her in. She had on white lace panties and a white lace bra that cupped her perfect breasts. Her belly was flat, toned, and he ran his palm over the taut expanse of skin, sliding one finger under the edge of her bra, toying with the edge of her breasts. Desire darkened her gaze and danced along her smile.

Sam traced the outline of her face. "From the minute you showed up on my doorstep, overdressed and over-qualified, I started falling for you."

She hesitated, stilling beneath him. "Falling for me? Sam, we're not—"

He placed a finger over her lips. "Not talking about any of that right now. Let's just be here, with each other."

Her hand slipped between them and slid over his erection. "That sounds like a good plan."

"Just remember I'm a little rusty." He slid his palm beneath the lace cup of her bra and caressed her breast, letting his thumb trace a circle over her nipple.

She moaned and rose up into the touch. "I wouldn't, uh, call you...rusty at all."

He slid his hand into her panties and touched her sensitive center. That made her moan even more, and buck up against him, her body begging for more. She reached for the button on his shorts, but fumbled un-doing the fastener. Her cheeks flushed, which he found adorable and sexy all at the same time. "Maybe I'm the rusty one," she said.

"Then we can be rusty together." He flicked open the button and slid down his zipper. Before he kicked his shorts to the side, he tugged a condom out of his wallet. Then he removed his boxers, slid the condom on and returned to Katie's side.

He hesitated, braced over her, his eyes connecting with hers. "What is it?" Katie asked.

"It's just..." He shook his head. "I haven't been with anyone but my wife in a very long time."

"Do you want to wait?"

There was concern in her eyes, and caring. It touched him, and reminded Sam that Katie wasn't the kind of woman who would look at tonight as a fling. That it would mean something to her, just as it did to him. He didn't know what tomorrow would bring, but he was tired of letting today slip by in a blur. "I think I've waited long enough." He slid his hand beneath her panties again, and when she rose against him with a gasp, he nearly came undone. He slid off the lacy underwear, giving him full access to the hypersensitive nub. He stroked her there, slowly at first, then faster, until she was gasping and panting, and then, a moment later, an orgasm rippled through her body.

"Oh, God, Sam," she said. "If that's rusty, I can't wait to see what more practice brings."

He chuckled softly. "Me, too." With his other hand, he slid the straps of her bra down, then peeled back the lacy cups. He lowered his mouth to her neck, then kissed down the valley of her throat, across to one breast, teasing the nipple with his tongue, before giving the other the same attention.

She put a hand on his chest, her eyes wide in the dark. "Sam…"

"I know." He cupped her chin and kissed her, gently, slowly. "If we do this, it changes—"

"Everything."

He nodded. "Is that okay?"

She ran a hand over his hair, then down along the side of his jaw. A light touch, but it seemed to whisper a dozen messages. Her gaze never wavered from his, and he knew, in that look in her eyes, in the touch of her hand, that she was feeling the same powerful wave as him. "Yes," she said, the word caught on a breath.

He shifted until he was above her, then lowered himself, his elbows on either side of her head. He kissed her again, deep and slow, kissed her until she was writhing beneath him, her hands roving over his back, his legs, his buttocks. Kissed her until she was whispering his name with urgency.

He slid into her then, and she rose up to meet him, bringing her hips to his with every stroke. They fell into a perfect rhythm, matching each other move for move, building in intensity and pace, until she was gasping and calling his name and clutching at him. He sank into her, deeper this time, and his orgasm rushed over him like a tsunami.

His heart was still thudding when he rolled to the side and pulled Katie against him. She nestled in his arms, and for a moment, it seemed like everything was perfect in the world. "That was..." His brain short-circuited and his voice trailed off.

"Incredible."

"I think we're going to need a thesaurus, because *incredible* doesn't even begin to describe how amazing that was." He laughed with her, then drew her closer still and pressed a kiss to her temple. "How amazing you are."

As she curved into him and laid her head above his heart, Sam realized Katie was right. Making love had changed everything and had him desiring things he wasn't sure he had any right to desire. With a woman who had made it clear she had no intention of staying.

Chapter Eleven

Katie lay in Sam's arms, content and warm, while the clouds played with the moon and the night birds called to each other across the lake. She wanted to stay here forever, in this old, drafty house that seemed worlds away from everything she'd ever known.

But as the minutes ticked by, reality began to settle in and remind her that she wasn't staying in this town, with this man. She was going to have to move forward. She had savings, of course, and Sam was paying her, but that didn't mean she could afford to put off the future indefinitely.

As if on cue, she heard her phone ping. Email. She rolled to the side, fished out her phone and scrolled through the messages.

Hey, Katie, got your message. We'd love to have you start right away. Can you be here Monday? We have a new client...

The job she'd been offered at one of the firms she liked and respected wanted her to start immediately. With a little bit of a pay bump. She should have been excited, but the idea of going back to working with numbers all day depressed her. She'd had more fun than she'd expected tutoring Libby, coloring pictures with Henry, teaching Libby how to sew. And then there was Sam...

Already she cared more about him than she wanted to. *From the minute you showed up on my doorstep, overdressed and overqualified, I started falling for you.*

She'd tossed back a joke to his words, because it was easier than saying the same thing had happened to her. The minute she'd seen him with his children, the way he was so tender, so sweet, she'd begun falling for him. Wanting to be more than just the tutor to his kids, the fill-in nanny. Wanting the life she had only dared to dream of once before.

And that meant she was getting way too comfortable here in Stone Gap. From the way Sam had asked her about staying, she knew he was thinking about a future between them. A future she couldn't give him.

Sam wanted to get married again. To have more kids. Katie couldn't trust her body—what if she miscarried again? What if she wasn't meant to be pregnant? What if she settled into this life, and a year from now realized she wasn't a good mother at all? She'd already be indelibly inked in the kids' lives, and pulling away after that would be so much harder, more destructive. To them, to him and to her.

Sam rose up on one elbow and trailed a finger along her nose. "Hey, what's so important that you have to be on the phone?"

She wanted to joke back, or kiss him and delay this

conversation, but that wasn't going to do either of them any good. She had to be up front and honest. Maybe then this…whatever this was between them would end, and she could move on. And so could Sam.

The mere thought of him moving on without her caused an ache deep inside Katie. That alone verified that she was in way too deep. Better to be honest now than to hurt ten times more later.

She thought of the email. The job she'd be crazy to turn down. She had everything she needed—except the motivation to leave. Maybe if she said the words aloud, it would be easier to accept them. "I'm thinking about heading back to Atlanta."

His eyes clouded. "Already? But you've only been here a few weeks."

"I can't afford to be on vacation forever. I was offered a new job, with a great firm. I think it's time I… get back to my life." *Life? More like an empty apartment in a concrete high-rise in a cold gray world I never liked. My friends, who were really just work colleagues. My mother, who barely sets aside five seconds to ask how I am.*

Yeah, that life. It wasn't until Katie had arrived here, in Stone Gap, and seen the happiness in Colton's face that she realized how much she hated her life in Atlanta. She craved what Colton had found here, with the department, with Rachel, with his other family.

As for Sam…

Sam was everything she'd ever dreamed of and never believed she could have. The family man with the big heart, who tried his hardest to be the kind of person his children and spouse needed him to be. The kind of guy a girl could lean on, depend upon. Grow attached to, as well as to his kids…

And to his dream of having more of that.

The moon shone through the dusty windowpanes with a pale white haze. The light danced off the worn wainscoting and battered wood floors. This was a house with character, memories. It was no surprise that Sam wanted to build more of that here.

That wasn't who she was, wasn't the kind of life she saw in her future. She needed to accept that, and go back to her predictable days of numbers that added up just so. Instead of taking a risk on something that could very easily go wrong. Hadn't she learned that painful lesson already?

"A new job?" Sam asked. "I thought you were already a CPA, or at least you were."

"Well, I am a CPA. Just not an employed one." She drew in a deep breath. "I was sort of fired from my job when I screwed up a couple of accounts. That's not like me, but I was going through a lot of things at the time and I… I lost my focus."

It was more than losing her focus, but she didn't know how to tell Sam the rest.

He brushed a tendril of hair off her forehead. His eyes were kind, caring. "What kind of things?"

Damn it. When she looked in his eyes, she saw that he truly wanted to know, because he cared. That look nearly undid her.

She started to speak, then took in the moonlit walls and floors again. The old sleigh bed they were lying in. The home that Sam dreamed of having. If she told him about the miscarriage, about how she had fallen apart, then maybe he would stop looking at her like that, and they would end this now and she wouldn't be foolish enough to believe she could have the same dream as he did. She had no experience being a mother—heck, she had grown up without one. Sure, she could do this for a few weeks, but long term? Better to leave now, before either of them got any more wrapped up.

Yes, that was best. Or at least, that's what she told herself, even though every cell in her body was protesting and telling her to just shut up and lie here against him and soak up the moment.

Instead, she came down firmly in the middle, not telling him the truth, but not caving to her own desires. "I'll stay and help you with the kids until you find somebody else to be their nanny," Katie said. "But I think it's best that I go back to Atlanta."

"Find another nanny? You're really leaving?"

"We always knew this was temporary. You need someone else, and I don't want to leave you shorthanded." She averted her gaze from his because she couldn't stand to see the hurt and confusion in his eyes.

"What about us?"

The three words hung in the air, and for a second, Katie wanted to undo everything she had just said, turn back the clock.

"You and I want different things, Sam," she said finally, "and it's better if we don't get any closer than we already have."

His fingers dropped from her face and he drew back. "Did something happen in the last half hour that I missed? Because last I checked, we were making love and everything was great. Incredible, we both said."

It was. It had been. She wanted more, wanted this moment to last forever. But that was foolish and impractical, and if there was one thing Katie wasn't, it was that. "I shouldn't have done that, shouldn't have led you on."

"Led me on?"

"I wanted it as much as you did." Oh, Lord, how she

wanted that, wanted him, and still did, even now when she knew they were all wrong for each other. "But I don't want the same future you do and it's best that I tell you now and let you move on."

With someone else. The thought threatened to break her.

He didn't say anything for a moment, just stared at her as if she was a total stranger. "What are you talking about?"

"You want to get married again and have more kids." She toyed with the edge of the sheet, and wished she had waited to have this conversation when it wasn't so easy to lean into him again. They were so close she could feel the heat from his body, and oh, how she wanted to press herself to him, to make love again, to just *be* with Sam. "I'm…not the kind of woman who should do that. Who should be a mother."

"Not the kind of woman who should do that?" Sam said. "You are *fabulous* with Libby and Henry. You've created a home out of the chaos I was living in. And you've made my kids laugh and engage for the first time in forever. That says you are exactly the kind of woman who settles down and has kids."

"This is temporary, Sam," she said, even though the words scraped her throat and burned in her eyes. "And I think we should just accept that and move on in different directions."

Then before she could change her mind or undo all of what she had said, Katie sat up, swung her legs over the side of the bed and started getting dressed again. Her clothes settled into place and provided a little bit of distance, a little more of a wall.

Sam did the same, pulling on his shorts and shirt, then tugging the sheets back into place on the bed.

There was a cold divide between them now, erasing the blissful moment earlier. Oh, how she wished she could erase the last few minutes, but that would just make leaving that much harder.

"I guess I'll drive you home, then," Sam said.

"Thank you."

It was all very distant and icy, and Katie told herself that was exactly what she wanted. But as they passed by the kitchen and she saw the simple tableau of flowers, wine and dessert, her heart broke. She started to reach for his hand, but at the last second grabbed her purse instead and clutched it to her chest. The cold leather was no substitute for what she really wanted.

It wasn't until she was back in her bedroom at the bed-and-breakfast that Katie allowed herself to cry. She cried until her pillow was damp and the ache in her heart became a dull pain.

Sam couldn't concentrate. It took him five tries to dial the number of a longtime client, six attempts at sending an email before he finally typed it without mistakes. His mind kept reaching back to last night, to Katie's sudden 180.

Everything had been going so well, and then wham, out of nowhere she was talking about leaving. It wasn't as if he had expected her to stay here forever...

Okay, so maybe a part of him was thinking she'd love Stone Gap and the kids and working for him so much that she would stay. And he could date her, and maybe, just maybe find the future he never thought he could have again.

Realistically, he'd known deep down inside that she'd have to go back to Atlanta someday. She'd mentioned it a couple times before, but he hadn't really listened—or hadn't wanted to listen.

Only an idiot thought a CPA would be happy as a nanny, along with the drastic pay cut the job entailed. Of course she'd want to go back to her career, and it only made sense to return to the place where all her contacts lived, making it easier to find a new job. But still...

Lunchtime rolled around, and Sam debated going home and seeing Katie and Henry. Then a text from Colton asked if he wanted to meet the Barlow boys for lunch downtown, and Sam said yes. Maybe a few minutes with Colton would pull Sam out of this distracted mood. Or maybe a part of him was hoping her brother would give him a little insight into Katie's mind.

Colton was already sitting at a table for five when Sam arrived. He dropped into the chair beside Colton and put his phone in the space beside his plate. Hopefully, five minutes would go by without a call or text. "Hey, Colton, how are you?" Sam asked.

"Doing great. Making wedding plans with Rachel. I know more about calla lilies and tulle than any man should." He grinned that goofy grin that only a man in love would wear.

"That's great." Sam clapped him on the shoulder. "I'm happy for you."

"Thanks. She's amazing." Colton took a sip of his coffee. "Speaking of amazing women, is it true you're dating my sister?"

Direct and to the point. Sam couldn't avoid the question any more than he could avoid Colton's probing gaze. Protective older brother to the rescue.

"We...spent time together," Sam said, since he wasn't quite sure if last night qualified as a date. And considering she'd already essentially ended things between them, it wouldn't be fair to call it dating.

Except a part of him had been dating her and still wanted to. The same part that ached right now like he'd lost a limb.

Colton arched a brow. "Della says you two have spent lots of time together."

Sam scowled. That was the problem with small towns. Everyone knew everything. "Okay, yes, we went out last night. Then she told me she has to go back to Atlanta soon."

"Yup. Not surprising my little sister panicked when you got close." Colton sipped his coffee and took a few minutes to speak again. "One thing you should know about Katie—she's strong on the outside, but soft as a marshmallow inside. She had a tough life growing up, and I think that makes her scared to settle down. Hell, I was scared, too, until I met Rachel."

Sam nodded. "She told me a little about her childhood."

"It was rough." Colton waved off the waitress's offer of a refill. "Our mother wasn't the motherly type at all. She would often forget to pick Katie up from school or leave her behind at the store, or just plain ignore her. I did my best to pick up the slack, but you know, I was the older brother and a kid myself. I had my own things going on. I wish I'd done more, been there more." He sighed.

"Katie thinks you're awesome," Sam said. The close relationship between brother and sister was obvious. It made Sam miss Dylan. Maybe it wasn't too late to patch things up with his wayward brother. "Katie has had nothing but the best things to say about you."

Colton ducked his head, a small smile on his face. "Thanks. That means a lot."

"No problem." Praise from guy to guy was always an awkward thing, so Sam studied the menu for a moment while Colton drank some coffee and the moment ebbed.

Sam half expected Colton to say something like "How about those Pacers?" but instead he returned to the subject of his sister. "Deep in her heart, my sister really wants the white-picket-fence life. She even came close to having it once. But then she got her heart broken, and things sort of…fell apart for her. If you ask me, that's made her twice as gun-shy," Colton said. "She'd kill me for talking about her, but I think you're good for her, and I'd hate to see anything mess that up."

Things sort of…fell apart. Whatever those things were, Sam was pretty sure it was part of Katie's reluctance to get involved, her breaking it off. "It's too late. She broke up with me and is definitely going back to Atlanta."

Colton let out a long sigh. "Between you and me, I think she hates living in Atlanta, and I think living here would be great for her."

"But…?" Sam prompted, when Colton paused.

"But if she's scared, she's going to run and hide in her work or something else. All I'm saying is don't give up on her, okay? She's been through a lot, and some of that was fairly recent."

Before Sam had a chance to respond or ask what Colton meant by that, Colton's brothers ambled in and dropped into the other three chairs. Mac, Luke and Jack all had the same dark hair and blue eyes as Colton, and except for the few differences that age brought to their features, they could have passed as quadruplets. "Now we know your standards have dropped, Sam, if you're hanging around with this character." Jack gave Sam a gentle slug on the shoulder.

"Hey, hey," Colton said. "Who says it's not my standards that have dropped since I got you three as brothers?"

Luke grinned. "Because we're the cool ones."

Sam scoffed. "That was in high school." Luke had been the quarterback, Jack the popular one and Mac the high achiever. Sam had been the geeky one in band and architecture classes. The Barlow boys had always been good guys, though, even in high school.

Luke laughed. "True. Glory days are behind us and all that. How are you doing, Sam?"

"Good, good." Sam didn't get into the emotional roller coaster he'd ridden in the months after his wife died. They were guys. They talked *around* things instead of *about* them.

The men exchanged small talk for a little while, talking about their jobs, football and the Yankees chances of making it to the World Series this year. Mac talked about his plans for the solar company he was running with his fiancée, Savannah, and Luke bragged about the painting his daughter, Maddy, had exhibited in the school art show. Jack got the most ribbing, for his life as a newly married man and the little house by the lake that he was fixing up for him and Meri to live in. She was just getting her photography company off the ground, working some with Rachel, who was back to doing wedding planning while she worked part-time at her father's hardware store and planned her own wedding to Colton.

Sam marveled at how well all the brothers got along, how the entire Barlow family seemed to bond with each other, as did their wives. He missed his brother, and made a mental vow to track Dylan down and find a way to get together soon. Dylan rarely lingered in one spot, and his contact with his family was sporadic at best.

"Thanks for sending your sister to the Stone Gap Inn," Mac said to Colton. The mention of Katie drew Sam's mind back to the conversation. "Our mother's really got her heart set on making that place work."

"The house looks amazing," Sam replied. "Savannah did a great job on the restoration, and you all made quick work of getting the carpentry work done."

"We did when they listened to me," Jack said, giving his brothers the leadership look he'd perfected in the military. "Somebody had to be in charge of the clown show."

"Hey! As the family prankster, I resent that remark." Luke grinned to show he was joking, then got to his feet and tossed a couple dollars on the table for his drink. "Anyway, I'd love to stay and eat, guys, but I have to get back to the garage. I promised Peyton I'd get home early tonight. Maddy is at a sleepover and that means…" Luke's grin widened.

"That means he's ditching us in favor of his woman," Mac said.

"Duh. She's cuter than all of you put together." Luke waved goodbye, then headed out the door.

Sam's phone started buzzing, with a request for a showing from a potential client. He paid for his lunch, promised the Barlows he'd catch up another time, then headed out to the mall space. He tried not to care that Katie had texted only once, to let him know she'd picked Libby up at school.

He shouldn't let his mind dwell on a woman who was leaving, even if the thought of her doing that caused a fissure in his heart. Maybe if he focused on his job, on making those deals happen for the new mall, it would dull that ache.

A little part of him whispered that pouring his energy into work was exactly what had gotten him here in the first place. Maybe it was time for a new approach.

Or maybe he was just dreaming of things that were already too far to reach.

Chapter Twelve

The honeymoon period had come to an end.

Libby stood in the kitchen, her arms crossed over her chest. "You aren't my mommy. You can't make me do my homework."

Katie sighed. They'd been having this argument for twenty minutes now, ever since Libby got home from school. She'd stormed out of the car, stomped into the house and slammed the door. And had started arguing as soon as Katie mentioned the word *school*. "My job, Libby, is to help you with your homework."

"No, your job is to watch Henry and me. My father said so. Because you're the nanny."

"Well, yes, that's my job, too. I have two jobs." She gestured toward the math papers on the kitchen table. "Now, come on, let's get these worksheets done and then you can go play. Or maybe after your homework is done, we could walk downtown and see the new dance studio that opened up. I heard they have ballet lessons."

"I don't care."

Katie sighed again. "Libby, listen. You have to do your homework no matter what. If I help you, then we can do the hard parts together. And then—"

"No! I said no!" Then she spun on her heel and ran out the door.

Katie glanced over at Henry, who was standing on the living room carpet, George the bear clutched to his chest, his eyes wide. Katie debated going after Libby and decided maybe it would be best to give the girl a few minutes to cool down. She thought of texting Sam, but she was on a strict no-Sam diet, to try to ease the pain in her chest every time she thought of him.

So far, that wasn't working. Being in his house, around his kids, was a constant reminder that soon she would leave all this behind. Probably for good. It would be for the best, she told herself, because she wasn't cut out for this white-picket-fence life. She may have been a decent nanny for a few days, but everything in Katie said that long-term, she didn't have the first clue how to be a good parent. She had virtually no parenting role models, and the one chance she'd had at being a mother—

Was over before it began.

Outside, Libby sat on the swing, toeing back and forth, her head down, her gaze on the ground. Katie fixed Henry a snack, then turned on his favorite television show and went outside to Libby, leaving the patio door open so she could hear Henry.

"Go away," Libby said, when Katie approached.

Katie sat in the second swing. It creaked under her weight but held. "So, what happened today at school?"

"Nothing."

"Something happened. I could tell the second you got in the car. You were madder than a hornet in a jar."

Libby didn't say anything, just kept pushing the swing back and forth, back and forth. In the distance, one of the neighbors started mowing his lawn. There was the sound of another school bus stopping a few houses away.

Katie kept waiting and Libby kept silent. Katie could understand. When she'd been little, she'd been slow to trust other people. Colton had been her one rock, the only go-to person she trusted. "Do you want me to get your dad?"

"He's never gonna come. He's working." Libby made a face.

"He came to the beach that day. He doesn't always work."

Libby shook her head. "He won't come."

Katie debated. Should she call Sam? Or try to handle this on her own? She glanced over at the sullen girl on the swing and decided things weren't going so well. It wouldn't hurt to call in reinforcements. She tugged her phone out of her pocket and texted Sam.

Libby had a bad day at school but won't talk to me about it. Can you swing by for a minute and maybe cheer her up?

There was no instant reply, but for all Katie knew, Sam could be driving or on the phone or meeting with a client. The best bet was to keep Libby focused on something else, until Sam could get here. "Libby, if we just get a start on your homework—"

"No! I don't want to! I want my mother to help me! Not you!" Libby pushed off from the swing and ran across the yard, then around the side of the house. Just as Katie started after her, Henry let out a wail.

Katie dashed into the house and found Henry on the floor, holding his foot. A pile of building blocks were scattered beside him. "Hey, did you step on one of those?"

Henry nodded. Tears streamed down his face. He held out his foot to Katie. She looked it over and saw an angry red mark, but no cuts or bruises. She drew him to her and gave him a little hug. "It looks okay," she said. "We just have to pick these up, so no one gets hurt, okay?"

She had stepped on those tiny little buggers more than once and knew the pain Henry was feeling. She reached over and scooped most of the blocks into the bin. Henry picked up a few and proudly dumped them on top of Katie's pile. "Henry help."

"You did indeed. Thank you. Now, let's go get Libby." Hopefully, a few minutes alone had calmed Libby down. Katie got to her feet, hoisted Henry onto her hip, then at the last second grabbed the bear, too, and pressed him into Henry's arms. She headed out the back door and around the side of the house.

Libby wasn't there. Katie skirted to the front of the house. "Libby?"

No response. She passed the flowerpots, then checked the other side of the house and the backyard once more. She'd done a complete tour of the perimeter and hadn't seen Libby anywhere. Alarm raised the hairs on the back of Katie's neck. "Libby? Libby!"

No response. Panic climbed Katie's throat. She ran inside—maybe Libby had come in while she was helping Henry and she just didn't hear her. Katie checked every room, every closet, under every bed. She called Libby's name over and over again—

Nothing.

"Where Libby?" Henry asked. His little face was scrunched in worry.

"She's fine," Katie said. "Just playing a game of hide-and-seek."

"Henry play, too?"

"No, not now." That was the last thing Katie needed—both Sam's kids missing. Surely Libby couldn't have gone far.

Katie made another loop of the yard, then checked inside the garage. It wasn't until she turned to check inside again that she noticed Libby's bike was missing from its customary place by the side door.

Katie's heart clenched. Oh, God. She had lost Sam's daughter. She'd handled the entire thing all wrong and now Libby was gone, and Katie didn't have the first clue where to look.

She pulled out her cell phone and dialed Sam's number. It rang three times, then went to voice mail. Katie dialed again, reached voice mail again. She left a message, telling Sam to call her back immediately, then followed that with a text that said the same thing.

"Come on, come on," she muttered to the silent phone. It didn't ring, didn't ping with a message. Nothing. Katie gave Henry a smile that she hoped didn't betray the panic in her chest. Where was Libby? Nearby? Katie hoped so. When she'd been Libby's age and run away, she hadn't gotten far...

But that was because Colton had come after her. Colton, who knew her almost as well as she knew herself, and had anticipated where his little sister might go. Katie barely knew Libby, and hadn't a clue where the girl might run to. Guilt knotted in Katie's chest. If she had handled this better, if she'd paid more attention…

"Henry, how about we take a little walk?"

"Libby, too?"

"We'll see Libby soon," Katie said, and as she strapped Henry into his stroller, she prayed that was true.

Sam tried to hide a smile as Ginny Wilkins, soon to be Beauregard, grabbed her fiancé's hand and let out a squeal. "This is going to be perfect, baby. Can't you just see it?"

Bernard shuffled from foot to foot. He was a slight man with a lisp, and glasses that had trouble staying on his nose. Ginny was the opposite—loud and bright in a pink dress that bloomed from her waist, and pink heels that clacked on the tile floor. She dangled a daisy-shaped purse from her forearm, and called everything either "darling" or "perfect" or "divine."

"My Bernard is opening his own boutique men's clothing store and we were so glad to hear his uncle had this mall space available right away," Ginny said. "My Bernard has such a fashion sense that I'm sure it's going to be a wild success. Don't you agree, Mr. Millwright?"

Sam didn't quite see how Bernard's striped, button-down shirt and khaki pants qualified for a fashion sense. He was wearing red-and-green-striped socks, so maybe his fashion started at the bottom and worked its way up gradually. All Sam wanted was a deal inked on the small storefront, hopefully before day's end. Bernard was Hank's nephew, after all, and keeping both his boss and his boss's family members happy would bode well for Sam's future at the firm. Even if Ginny and Bernard had been walking around the same two-thousand-square-foot space for over an hour now, debating where to put clothing racks. "I think Bernard's store will be a great addition to the mall," Sam said.

"We are just so excited about the future. We're getting married soon—in a pink wedding that people will be talking about for centuries, I'm sure—and we're building the cutest little house off of Oak Street, and opening Bernard's business venture, with his daddy's money, because, well, honey, it is the South, and the best money is old money…"

Ginny went on and on as she paced the perimeter of the store again. Bernard followed along like a lonely puppy, agreeing with everything Ginny said. Sam tried hard not to look impatient. His phone buzzed a few times, but every time he went to check it, Ginny asked another question.

"So," Sam said, after they made their seventh round of the space, "would you like to make an offer? Demand is high for this area, and there's bound to be some competition for this location, since it's right next door to an anchor tenant. I know your uncle is anxious to get all the spaces rented soon so the mall grand opening can bring a lot of business in."

Inside his pocket, he felt his phone buzz again. Probably just a reminder for his next appointment in a half hour.

"I don't know…" Ginny put a finger to her lips. She glanced at Bernard, then back at Sam. "Can we decorate however we choose?"

"Of course you can."

Sam's phone buzzed one more time, the sound feeling even more insistent. He glanced at his watch. A little after four. He was supposed to call Hank at four with a status update, but the meeting with Ginny and Bernard had run way over the time he had allotted. Maybe Hank just wanted to know how his nephew had responded to the space. Sam pulled his phone out of his pocket.

"And what did you say the rent was again?" Ginny asked.

Sam rattled off the numbers, then answered Ginny's next three questions about the lease. By the time she took a breath, another five minutes had gone by and Sam's phone had buzzed twice more. "Just one second, Miss Wilkins. I really need to check this."

Ginny sighed. "Bernard and I are on a schedule, Mr. Millwright. We have two more locations we want to look at today. His uncle assured us you would give us your undivided attention."

"Just one second. I promise." As soon as he flipped the phone over, the on-screen messages made his throat close. The room swam before his eyes and the air whooshed out of his lungs.

He needed to read only three words before he turned on his heel and ran out the door.

Libby is missing.

Chapter Thirteen

It took all Katie had not to crumple into a sobbing puddle. She'd lost Sam's child. The one task he had given her—watch his kids and keep them safe—and she had failed. Henry sat in his stroller, playing with the stuffed bear, unaware that Katie was on the verge of a nervous breakdown.

She'd been texting Sam and calling for ten solid minutes that felt like ten hours. She was just about to call the police when her phone buzzed.

On my way. There in five.

Sam. He'd know what to do. How to find Libby. Katie texted him the address where she was—a street corner about four blocks from the house—part of an ever-widening circle she'd been walking with Henry, while she looked for Libby.

She'd figured Libby couldn't have gone too far. Maybe just to a neighbor's house? She had tried to think if Libby had mentioned any friends who lived in the neighborhood, or maybe where Charity, her old nanny, lived, but had drawn a blank. So Katie kept walking and calling Libby's name, her guilt and worry increasing with every passing second.

Sam's SUV came to a screeching stop beside them and he jumped out. "Where is she?"

"I… I don't know." The tears Katie had held back for so long began to stream down her cheeks. "We had an argument, and then I went inside and she was outside—"

"You left her *alone*?"

"She was just in the yard. She was upset about school and wouldn't talk to me," Katie said, the words jerking out of her between tears. "I tried to get her to do her homework, but she got mad and ran off, and then Henry stepped on a block and he was crying, and when I turned around, she was gone. I checked the yard, the house, but her bike is gone, and I've looked all over and I don't know what to do."

"I *trusted* you with my kids, Katie. How could you do this?"

There was fury in his eyes, recrimination in his words. He was right. She'd failed him, and now Libby could be anywhere. "I'm sorry, Sam. I'm really sorry. I didn't think she'd do this. I am so sorry." Katie felt like she couldn't say it enough. God, she'd really screwed up.

Sam gave her a harsh, stony look. He glanced down at Henry, who put out his arms. "Daddy!"

Sam unbuckled his son and held him tight to his chest for a long second. Over Henry's head, Sam's gaze met hers. Pain shimmered in his eyes.

She tried to put a hand on his arm, but he shrugged off her touch. "All right, buddy, you gotta sit back in your seat and go home with Katie."

Henry shook his head. "I wanna stay wif you, Daddy."

"You can't. I have to go get Libby. But when I get home, we'll get pizza, okay?"

That was enough to make Henry agree. He climbed back into the stroller and settled George on his lap. His gaze darted between both adults, as if he knew something was wrong, but wasn't sure what it was.

"You know where she is?" Katie said quietly, so Henry wouldn't overhear. "I tried to think like her, to try to figure out where she might go. But I just don't know Libby well enough yet."

"No, you don't." His words were curt, short, accusatory.

"I'm sorry, Sam. I—"

"Wendy knew her best. She wouldn't have—" he cut off the sentence.

The unspoken words—*Wendy wouldn't have lost their daughter.* Guilt rolled through Katie. This was exactly why she wasn't fit for this life that Sam wanted. Once Libby was home safe, Katie was going to head back to Atlanta. Let Sam find someone better suited than she was. Someone he could rely on, not a woman who had lost his child.

The only thing she could do now was help him look for Libby. "Do you want us to split up? I can search this direction and you can search—"

"You've done enough, don't you think?" He let out a gust. "I'm sorry. I'm just worried. Please, take Henry home. I'll go look for Libby. If I don't find her, I'll call the Stone Gap Police Department. Just keep an eye on my son. Okay?"

She nodded, and tried to apologize again, but Sam was already in his car and peeling away from the curb.

Sam had been unnecessarily harsh with Katie. He knew that, but he didn't have time to smooth those waters right now. He'd lashed out at Katie, not just because he was worried and scared, but because he was mad at himself.

He hadn't been here. He'd been working—again—instead of being a part of his family. He'd lost that bond he had with Libby long ago, and now he had no idea where she might have gone. He drove at warp speed through town, past the school, the ice cream parlor, the library. On any other day, Libby would have gone to one of those places. But today, something had upset her, and Sam prayed he knew his daughter well enough to guess where she might have gone.

Knew her well enough. Wasn't that what Katie had said? That she had tried to think like Libby, and couldn't, because she didn't know her well enough? Sam pulled the car to the side of the road and let out a deep breath. He could feel time ticking away, time where something terrible could happen, but he closed his eyes and centered himself, and tried to think.

What would Libby do? Where would she go? Where did she feel most safe and happy…

An idea sparked in Sam's brain. He took a left on Maple, then a right on Birch, and finally, came to a stop at the end of the road.

An old park, hardly used since Stone Gap had built a prettier, newer one closer to downtown, sat at the end of Birch Street. Once upon a time, there'd been an elementary school behind the park, but as Stone Gap's population grew, the one-story school hadn't been enough and the town had built a new one on land donated by a farmer who had died. The park fell into disuse, leaving only a couple swings standing and one play structure, built thirty years ago by men who believed in building things to last.

The castle-shaped building was probably going to be here long after Sam was gone. He'd played on it when he was a kid, and Wendy had taken Libby here when she was little. Once Henry was born, Wendy hadn't wanted to make the drive, preferring the newer playground with its baby swings and oversize tic-tac-toe board. Sam couldn't remember the last time Libby had been to this park, although she mentioned it with longing from time to time. Some of her best memories with her mom were here, and for a little girl who felt lost and alone, Sam was pretty sure this was where she'd go.

Sam got out of the car, and whispered a quick prayer before he crossed the grassy park and headed for the castle. Why hadn't he paid closer attention? Been there for his daughter all these months? He'd been so locked in his own grief that he'd missed the signs that Libby was still hurting.

His heart filled his chest, and he prayed he wasn't too late, that he'd come to the right place. Then he saw a familiar pink bicycle leaning against a tree, and hope leaped within him. He ducked his head to get inside, then climbed a small ladder up to the top of the turret.

And there, in the center of the circular space, he found his daughter, her knees hugged to her chest, her shoes scuffed with dirt, tears puddling on her arms. Relief flooded Sam, and his knees buckled for a second. *Libby.* Thank God.

He climbed the rest of the way up, then folded himself into the small space beside Libby. She flicked a

quick glance at him, then went back to staring at the
picture in her hands. It was worn and creased, but Sam
knew it well.

Wendy holding five-year-old Libby, their faces
smushed together in the little round window of the turret. It was one of the last times they'd come to this park,
before Henry was born and Wendy's time with Libby
became limited. Libby had carried that picture with her
ever since the funeral. Sam's heart broke a little as he
saw the wrinkled edges, the faded images. "Hey, Libby
Bear, you had us all worried."

She sniffled. "Sorry."

"You want to talk about it?"

She shook her head.

Sam sat there for a while, feeling helpless. This was
where Wendy would have stepped in, with a soothing
word or a fresh-baked cookie. His late wife had a way
of getting the kids to open up, of easing their fears and
worries. He lacked that ability, and worried every day
that he was going to lose touch with his kids before
those difficult teen years.

He could feel Libby's pain radiating off her tiny
frame. He didn't know what to do with pain like that,
the kind of pain that went bone-deep. Didn't know how
to ease the sorrow in her heart. He'd been trying to find
that answer ever since Wendy died.

But there was no Wendy here now, and there wasn't
going to be. Either Sam figured this out or he was going
to lose what relationship he had with his daughter.

"When I was a kid, I had a tree house," Sam said,
starting with just talking. He didn't know where he
was going with the story or if it would help, but it was
filling the silence. He thought of his childhood, of the
days when he had wanted to escape. Maybe that was

part of what had driven Libby to this space, a need to escape the empty spot in the house, in her life. "Did I ever tell you that?"

Libby nodded. Sniffled some more.

"I used to play up there all the time because my little brother, your uncle Dylan, couldn't get up there. Then he got older and could climb the ladder. I didn't want to share so I told him I was too old for the tree house and stopped going up there." Sam thought of that old rickety house his father had built a long time ago. It hadn't been much, just a box with a couple holes for windows and a rope with a bucket for bringing snacks up to the fort. "But then my parents got divorced and my dad moved out. It was really hard on me, because I was the oldest. Dylan was only four, but I was nine, just a little older than you."

Libby sniffled some more, but she had shifted her head in his direction to listen. Sam took that as a good sign and kept talking.

"I had a really hard time when my dad moved out, and that tree house, well, that became the place where I would go. I'd sneak up there when Dylan wasn't around and pretend nothing was changing. I'd convince myself that when I climbed down, my dad would still be there and everything would be better than it was before." That his dad would be home, involved. During those hours in the tree house, Sam used to think his life was perfect. Then he'd go in for dinner and see the empty place at the table, or see the empty hook on the wall that used to hold his dad's keys.

The commonality wasn't lost on Sam. The very thing he had hated about his childhood—his father's absence—was part of what was hurting his own kids.

Their mother was gone, forever, and their father was buried in work. Again.

Was that why Libby was here? Was she trying to pretend her life was the way it had been before? Exactly what he had done when he was her age...

"Like when Mommy used to bring me here," Libby said, her voice nearly a whisper. "That was the best. I miss that. I miss...her."

"Me, too, kiddo." He could still see Wendy pushing Libby on the swings, or darting from tree to tree, laughing, playing tag. Libby's hair a riot of curls, spreading behind her like wings as she ran. He fingered the picture in Libby's hands. "Your mom used to love bringing you here. You know why?"

Libby shook her head.

"Because she said she loved to pretend you were both princesses. She always called you that when you were little, remember? Her princess."

Libby's eyes misted. "I remember."

He brushed a tendril of hair off Libby's forehead. "I know she misses you as much as you miss her, Libby, and if Mommy could be here, she would be."

Libby shifted closer to Sam, until her thigh brushed his. "Katie said Mommy is up in the clouds. I thought maybe if I came here, I could see her better, 'cuz I'd be up high. I wanted to talk to her and..." Libby's voice caught on a sob, and tears started rolling down her cheeks. "But I can't see her and I can't talk to her. Forever."

"You can talk to me," Sam said, his voice gentle. "I'd love it if you would, Libby. Because sometimes I need someone to talk to about Mommy, too."

She turned to him then. Her eyes were wide and round, and her lower lip trembled. "You do?"

All this time, he'd thought he was making it easier on his kids by not talking about their late mother, by keeping his emotions in check, and concentrating on moving forward. But what if all they had really needed was to know they weren't alone? That he missed Wendy, too, and that there were days when he struggled to draw that next breath, take that next step. That he saw the echo of their mother in the places they'd been, the pictures they'd taken, the memories that filled every corner of their lives. "I miss her a lot, too. I miss the way she made pancakes that looked like Mickey Mouse and how she used to pile all those pillows on the couch—"

"And Henry and I would pretend to hide under them, and make a fort with the blankets."

He remembered coming home dozens of times to blanket forts. Why had he never thought to do that with the kids, too? How did he let the busyness of life replace all those things that mattered? The pancakes and the blankets and the memories? That was what his kids had needed, what Katie had been trying to tell him, all along. "And how she would make dinner into a picnic on the living room floor. Your mommy was really great, wasn't she?"

Libby nodded, and then her chin wobbled and the tears started again. She traced the outline of Wendy's face with her finger. A tear slid off her cheek and puddled on the image. "I wish Mommy was coming back."

He heard the acceptance and the loss tied up in Libby's words. It damn near broke his heart. "I know, sweetie, I know."

"Today, at school, my teacher said...to d-draw your f-family..." Libby's words came in fits and starts, mixed with tears. "And I didn't know if I should d-draw my mommy or not 'cuz…'cuz I…I don't have one anymore."

Sam would have given anything to have Wendy climb into this castle right now and ease the loss in his daughter's heart, erase the hurt in her voice. He could feel Libby's pain as if it were his own. It wasn't fair that his precious daughter was going to grow up without her mother, that she was going to miss the proms and wedding day and graduations. He couldn't change that, couldn't turn back time, but he could open his heart, and hope that was enough.

"You should draw your mom in that picture," he said, "because she's always going to be part of our family, because she's part of you and Henry. You guys are the best part of her. The part that will forever remind everyone how amazing she was."

Libby cocked her head. "How do we do that?"

"By being exactly who you are. She was always so proud of you, Libby. And I am, too." He opened his arms. "Come here, Libby Bear."

A breeze rustled through the trees, sent leaves dancing against the walls of the fort. A soft rain began to fall, pattering on the ground below, and misting through the turret window.

Libby hesitated for a second, her eyes wide, her lower lip trembling. Then she climbed into Sam's lap and slid her arms around him. Her grip tightened, bit by bit, until she leaned her head into the valley beneath his chin. Her tears fell, dampening his shirt, blurring into the cotton stripes.

"I love you, Libby," Sam whispered. He stroked her hair and held her tight, and whispered the words over and over. "I love you."

They sat there for a long time, while the world went

on outside the castle. Birds called, rain fell and the sun marched toward the horizon.

"Can you promise me something?" Libby whispered against his chest.

If she wanted him to capture the sun right now, he'd find a way to give it to her. "Anything, baby girl."

Libby raised her gaze to his. Her eyes were puddles of shimmering tears and her breath caught on a hitch. "You're never…never gonna leave me, Daddy."

Daddy.

Sam's heart swelled. Libby may have her mother's smile, but right now, she had her father's eyes—wide, scared, yet still holding a sparkle of hope. That was what Sam held on to, what he would always hold on to.

Daddy.

How he had missed that word. He folded Libby into his embrace again, and kissed the top of her head, inhaling the soft strawberry scent of her shampoo and, he swore, traces of that innocent scent of a baby. "I'm not going anywhere, Libby. I promise." He kissed her again, and felt his own tears drop onto her curls. "I promise."

Chapter Fourteen

She damned near paced a hole in the carpet, waiting on Sam to call or text. Every car that went by made Katie jump, every buzz from an email or Facebook notification on her phone made her heart skip a beat. And then finally, just when she was about to call the police herself...

Found Libby. On our way home. Order pizza.

Katie let out a whoop, then scooped Henry up from where he was sitting on the couch. She'd imagined all the worst scenarios, and every minute had dragged by like a century. But Libby was safe, and everything was going to be okay. "Libby's on her way home, Henry. Your dad says we should order pizza. Do you like pizza?"

Henry nodded. "Pizza!"

"Pizza it is!" Katie found the pizza place menu tacked to the fridge, ordered a couple pepperoni pizzas, then sat down with Henry to make a house out of his toy bricks, to keep him occupied and keep herself from looking out the window every five seconds.

The guilt that she had been the whole reason Sam was out looking for Libby hadn't abated. Katie had been beating herself up for the past hour. She had no business being a nanny, or staying here and pretending she could ever be what Sam wanted.

She heard the front door open, then Sam's voice. Thank God.

"Go on up and wash your face, Libby," Sam said from the hall. "Pizza should be here any minute."

There was the sound of light footsteps heading up the stairs, then Sam's heavier footfalls coming down the hall and into the living room. Katie scrambled to her feet. "She's okay?"

Sam nodded. "She's fine. She was upset because her teacher had everyone in the class draw a picture of their family. That made her miss her mom a lot, so she went to this playground Wendy used to bring Libby to when she was little. She was sitting at the top of the castle they have there, and holding a picture of her mom, because she thought maybe she'd get closer to heaven that way." He let out a long sigh and dropped into a chair. Exhaustion lined his face. "God, I was so worried."

"I'm so sorry, Sam. I didn't mean to lose track of her. She was gone so fast—"

Sam put up a hand, cutting off her words. "I'm the one who should apologize for being so harsh with you earlier. I was worried, and I took it out on you. I'm sorry."

"I completely understand."

He gave her a soft smile. "If you don't have to go anywhere right away, would you stay for pizza? I think we've all had a busy day and I know the kids would love to have you here a little longer."

Katie hesitated. She was the whole reason they were here right now. If she hadn't argued with Libby, then maybe the little girl wouldn't have run away. Maybe it was better that she just left for Atlanta tomorrow. "Even Libby?"

"You're half the reason she went where she did." He shook his head and put up a hand. "Sorry. That came out wrong. What I meant is, she said you told her that her mom was watching from up above. So when she got upset, she went to the highest place she knew to try to talk to her mom."

Katie sank onto the arm of the sofa. Sam might not realize that she was at fault for tonight, but Katie knew it. She wasn't good for this family, or this man. "I'm glad Libby went somewhere safe. I was so worried."

"Me, too." Sam's phone began buzzing. He gave it a glance, then turned it off. "Tonight, all of that can wait." He crossed the living room and sank onto the carpet. "Instead, I'm going to sit on the floor and build with Henry. What are we making, buddy?"

"A house." Henry gave a little nod of decision.

"A house, huh? Who's going to live in it?"

"Me and George." Henry stacked a couple blocks, then waited while his father added some more. "And Libby and Daddy and Katie."

Whoa. Had Katie just heard Henry right? She glanced over at Sam, who was looking up at her with a bemused expression on his face.

"Seems you can't go back to a certain city in Georgia," Sam said, "because Henry here is building you a mighty nice place to live in, right here in Stone Gap."

"I, uh, think I hear the pizza guy outside." She didn't, but she left the room anyway, to wait by the front door. Easier to do that than to answer the questions hanging in the air.

She wasn't staying here. She wasn't going to live in a house with Sam and Libby and Henry. If she'd learned anything today, it was that she definitely wasn't cut out to be a mother or a stepmother or, heck, even a nanny. She'd had one job—one solitary job—and she'd failed at it. Sam might forgive her now in the rush of relief that Libby was okay, but down the road, he'd realize that Katie was better off being in charge of tax returns instead of children.

There was a sound on the stairs behind her, and Katie pivoted, to see Libby standing on the third step from the bottom. "Hi, Katie."

"Libby. Honey, I'm so glad you're home and okay."

Libby's eyes were red from crying, but she was wearing a clean T-shirt and a smile, and that was good to see. She dropped onto the bottom step. "I'm sorry for running away."

Katie sat down beside Libby, and gave her a little shoulder-to-shoulder nudge. The whole day had felt like looking into a mirror. Katie had seen herself— that scared, lonely little girl who had gathered up her toys and headed for the street—in Libby's eyes. She understood this girl, maybe more than Libby even realized. "It's okay. I did it, too, when I was your age."

"You did?"

"Yup. I was eight years old, just like you. My mom wasn't a nice mommy like yours was, and sometimes she yelled at me and scared me," Katie said, trying to find the right words to describe a childhood that was the complete opposite of Libby's. "So I packed up my favorite stuffed animals and I ran away."

"What happened? Did your daddy find you?"

"My brother did. You met him—Colton, the firefighter. Even back then he was rescuing people." Katie smiled. She didn't want to think about what her childhood would have been like if she hadn't had Colton. "He carried me home and made me supper, and told me everything would get better. He was right. It did."

"Did you run away again?"

Technically, she had, when she'd come here. She'd run away from her fears and her problems and all the things she didn't want to think about. Running straight to a man with two kids who needed a mother. Either she was a masochist or this was some kind of message from up above about facing her fears.

"Running away doesn't fix anything," Katie said. Except Katie wasn't taking her own advice. Wasn't going back to Atlanta another form of running away? "You have to talk about what scares you, because that's the only way to make it less scary."

Yeah, she hadn't done that with Sam, had she? She hadn't told him about the miscarriage or her doubts about being a good fit for the future he dreamed of, or the real reasons she was going back to Georgia.

Libby picked at a hangnail and thought about that for a second. Her long brown hair swung forward, covering her face. "Sometimes I have a hard time talking. 'Cuz it makes me cry, and I don't like to cry."

Katie smiled. Oh, how she understood that. Her whole life had been spent trying to bring order from chaos, creating straight lines instead of emotional curves. "Honey, nobody likes to cry. But sometimes it's good for you."

Again, advice Katie should be taking herself. If she had talked and let her emotions out months ago, she probably wouldn't have screwed up at work and lost her job. She probably wouldn't have had to run away to Stone Gap. Even in the couple weeks or so that she had been here, the conversations she'd had with Colton and Della had helped.

The time with Sam, with the kids, had helped ease the loss in her heart. Katie's hand strayed to her abdomen. The loss was still there, but the pain had begun to ebb. Maybe that would make it easier to go back to Atlanta, back to work and back to her life.

Except Libby leaned in just then and gave Katie a one-armed hug and whispered, "Thank you," and Katie didn't want to go anywhere. She couldn't think of a single place on earth that was better than the bottom step of Sam's staircase, sitting beside a little girl who was a kindred spirit.

Katie reached out and hugged Libby back, and whispered the same words, except hers came with a little catch in her throat. "Thank you, Libby."

By the time the pizza arrived, life was back to normal. Henry and Libby were squabbling over a toy, the TV was playing *SpongeBob* and the dog was barking at his own shadow. Sam looked around at the mess, the noise, the kids, and thought he was one damned lucky guy.

Katie was quiet at dinner, but Sam attributed that to the kids making so much noise. After they were done with the pizza, he told them they could watch the last half of *Frozen* before they went to bed. He got to his feet at the same time Katie did. They nearly collided on their way to the sink.

He caught the scent of her perfume, watched the tick of her pulse in her throat. He'd gone from knowing she was there to being insanely aware of her presence. "Sorry," he said.

"Sorry." She laid the dirty plates in the sink and turned to box up the rest of the pizza. If she felt what he had, she gave no sign of it. The quietness from dinner lingered, and there was a distance between them now. "I should get going. Thanks for the pizza."

He had hoped maybe after tonight she would change her mind about breaking up with him, but there was nothing in Katie's demeanor or words that said she was thinking about kissing him half as much as he was thinking about kissing her.

He wanted to kick himself for yelling at her, for letting his fear and his doubts fill his words. All it had done was build a wall between them.

She started to turn away, but he laid a hand on her arm. "Stay. Please. Just give it a half hour, then it's time for the kids to go to bed and you and I can talk."

He could see the hesitation in her features, the reluctance. "I know I lashed out at you this afternoon. What happened with Libby wasn't your fault. I was worried and lost my temper. I'm sorry again." He kept his hand on her arm, thinking how nice it felt just to touch her. How much he wanted to hug her, kiss her. But the kids were only a room away, and Katie wasn't looking at him the same way anymore. Maybe if they talked, he could straighten this out and they could go back to where they were before. "Please stay."

She turned to the sink, her gaze on the dishes. "Okay.

But only for a few minutes after the kids go to bed. I have some things I have to do tonight."

Things that would bring her closer to returning to Atlanta? He didn't want to ask.

Either way, she was staying for now, and that was good enough for him.

"Sounds good." He couldn't stop a grin from swinging across his face. Whatever was bothering Katie they could clear up with a conversation, he was sure. Because he liked this woman—more than liked her—and didn't want her to slip away.

He started the water in the sink, but Katie stopped him. "I'll do the dishes. I'm sure you have some work to get caught up on," she said.

"Work can wait. I'll take you up on doing the dishes, because it's one of my least favorite chores, but I will take the opportunity to go watch Elsa for the thousandth time with my kids." Sam pressed a kiss to Katie's cheek, then headed for the living room.

He sank onto the sofa, and felt the world set itself to rights again when Henry and Libby curled under his arms. How long had it been since he had done this? Far too long, that was for sure. By the time the movie ended, Henry had fallen asleep and Libby was yawning. Sam hoisted Henry into his arms, then took Libby's hand. "Come on, Libby Bear, bedtime."

Libby nodded, too tired to mount her usual protest.

Sam paused in the kitchen, where Katie had stayed. She'd cleaned up from dinner and was doing something on her phone, probably answering emails. Accepting that job offer she'd mentioned? He hoped not, at least not until she heard him out tonight. "I'll be back down in ten minutes, tops."

"That's fine," she said.

He took the kids to bed, tucking Henry in first, then heading to Libby's room. She was already in her pajamas and under her covers. Sam sank onto her bed and smoothed the hair across her forehead. "Are you okay, Libby?"

She nodded. "I'm sorry I ran away, Daddy."

He'd never get tired of hearing that word again. Just hearing her say "Daddy" told him they'd come a long way in the last few days. "I'm just glad you're home. Next time you get upset, come talk to me, okay?"

Libby fiddled with the edge of her blanket. "Is it okay if I talk to Katie sometimes? Because she's a girl and sometimes…"

"It's girl stuff." He chuckled. "I understand."

Then he thought about how Katie was leaving soon. He debated telling Libby, then decided she had enough to deal with. Later, hopefully much later, he'd deal with that. "Good night, Libby Bear."

"Wait, Daddy. Can you read me a story?"

As long as she kept saying Daddy, he'd read every book on her shelf. He'd missed so much in the last year and a half and vowed not to miss a moment more.

Sam pulled out Libby's favorite book—the same one about the princess he had read a few nights ago—and sat back against Libby's headboard. This time, she curled onto his chest, and fell asleep before he got past page ten. He leaned down, tucked her under the covers, then pressed a kiss to her temple. "I love you, Libby Bear," he whispered. She smiled in her sleep, and Sam tiptoed out of the room, counting his blessings.

Katie had moved to the back deck while he was upstairs. He opened a bottle of wine, then came outside with two glasses, handing one to her.

"Thanks," she said.

He took a seat in the other Adirondack chair. Above them, the sky had turned purple as night began to take over the land. It was still warm out, with a light breeze that tickled the tops of the trees. "I should be thanking you," he said.

"For what? I lost your daughter today." She put up a hand when he started to speak. "And please don't apologize for getting mad at me. You were totally justified in that. I screwed up."

He took her hand in his. Her fingers were cold, and he rubbed the backs with his own. "You were human. There's nothing wrong with that. Heck, I lost Libby once in a supermarket. Wendy had just had Henry, so I told her I'd take the kids to the grocery store so she could get some rest. Henry was a handful, colicky, and I was trying to soothe him. Next thing I knew, I turned around and Libby was gone."

"Where did she go?"

"The toy aisle." Sam chuckled. "I should have known. I ran up and down all the other aisles, got the manager to call her name on the loudspeaker, and when we found her, she was sitting on the floor, playing with a Barbie doll. I felt like the worst parent in the world. I think maybe—" he paused "—maybe that's when I started to pull back, to be involved less. To work more. Wendy was such a fabulous mom, you know? I felt like all I was going to do was screw it up."

"Your kids love you, Sam. They don't expect perfection. They just want you to be there."

"You've been telling me that all along, but I haven't listened. I guess I was afraid..." He drew in a deep breath. "Afraid that I'd never be as good as their mother was. She really was a great mom. But I realized something today, when I was up in that castle at the playground with Libby. She didn't need me to do anything other than be there and listen and hold her when she cried." He drew in another breath and let it out again. He vowed that from this moment forward, things would be different. Never again would he forget what was important.

He thought of Libby curling into him, of her saying "Daddy" for the first time in months. Whatever it took, he wasn't going to lose that again. "I have to do a better job at balancing my career and being a good dad."

Katie took a sip of her wine and looked out over the lawn. "Trust me, you could be doing a lot worse. Your kids are happy and healthy. You are doing your best, and that's a lot better than the crappy job of parenting some people do."

"People like your mom." He thought of what Colton had said. Was that part of why Katie wanted to run? Because she was afraid of getting close to anyone again?

She hung her head and stared at the wine in her glass. From somewhere down the street, there was the sound of kids playing basketball. A horn beeping. A bird making one last call.

"Yeah, my mom," Katie said finally. "And when it mattered most, what happened? I was just as bad as she was."

"Are you talking about today? Like I said, Katie, that wasn't a mistake. You had no idea Libby was going to run off."

"I'm not talking about today." Katie pulled her hand out of his, then pushed off from the chair and got to her feet. She wrapped her arms around her waist and stood slightly to the right, her face averted from his. The crescent moon shone above her, like a halfhearted smile. "Listen, I know where a relationship with a guy like you ends. You told me yourself you want to get married and have more kids. I'm not the girl for that, so please, just stop trying to make this work."

He rose, leaving his wineglass on the arm of the chair. He came around in front of her, but still she wouldn't look at him. "And what makes you think you're not the right girl?" He leaned in closer, until only a breath separated them. Her eyes widened and her lips parted. He refused to let this woman go back to Georgia without a fight. "Because I think you're the right girl. I think you're very, very much the right girl, Katie."

Before she could pull away, he leaned in and kissed her. A sweet kiss at first, slow and easy, then her arms went around his neck, and his hands went to her waist and he pulled her close. Their kiss deepened, the heat building as quickly as it had before, and—

Katie jerked back and shook her head. "We can't do this, Sam. You're wrong about me. I'm not the right girl for you. Just let that whole idea go. Let *me* go."

"I can't." He took a step closer, then brushed a tendril of hair off her face. "I'm falling in love with you."

He hadn't realized that until this morning, until he'd finally stopped hiding behind the wall of work. The thing that kept him from being afraid of losing someone close to him again.

Katie's eyes widened. "You...you can't. Don't do this, Sam."

"I don't understand you. You kiss me, you make love to me, you fit in with my kids like adding cheese to chili." He grinned at the joke, but she didn't echo his smile. He took her hands in his, but they were cold again. "Why don't you think we're good together? Why don't you want the same thing as I do? Because I sure as hell thought you did."

"I do want it." She yanked her hands out of his and let out a gusty sigh. "I can't have it. I can't explain... I have to go."

She spun on her heel, but he stepped in front of her before she could escape. There was something Katie was leaving out, some missing piece to the equation. He hadn't been blind when he'd seen her light up around the kids or plan that beach adventure game or make love to him. That had all been real, and true, but now Katie was acting as if it had never happened. "Why are you not right for me? Tell me."

"Because...you want different things than I do." She glanced away from him, and he knew, deep in his gut, that for some reason Katie was lying. To him, to herself.

"You don't want to get married and have a family?"

"Once upon a time, I thought I did, but..."

"But what?" He put a hand to her cheek, searching her gaze. "Tell me, Katie."

"Why can't you let this go? I lost your daughter today. If anything proves I shouldn't be with you, it's that."

"Katie, you had an argument with Libby and she ran off. Kids do that. It's okay. Everyone's okay."

She shook her head. Tears filled her eyes. "Just let me go, Sam. Stop trying to make me into something I'm not."

"You're everything I want, Katie. Why can't you—"

"Because I lost the baby!" She tore away from him and stalked across the yard, coming to a stop in front of the large oak tree. A tire swing hung from its widest branch, drifting lazily in the breeze.

Lost the baby? He let those words roll around in his mind for a moment. They'd had sex only a few days ago and they'd used protection, so he knew she couldn't mean his child. He thought about what Colton had said, about how there had been events in Katie's recent past that had spurred her coming to Stone Gap. Was that part of it? "What do you mean, you lost the baby?"

The yard was quiet, with just the soft sound of crickets chirping and the whisper of a breeze in the trees. The rain had stopped and everything sparkled in the moonlight.

"Maybe if I tell you, you'll see why I'm so wrong for you, for this family." Her voice was hoarse, and tears welled in her eyes. "I got pregnant a few months ago. At the time, I was sure I didn't want to settle down, or have a family, because my mom was so terrible, you know? And I had always vowed I would never turn out like her, so I thought if I didn't have a family, I never could. But as I got used to the idea of being pregnant, I started to get excited about it. I started making plans, clearing out space for a nursery. Creating a future."

"What about the baby's father?"

She scoffed. "Turns out he wasn't interested in anything more permanent than a weekend. As soon as I told him I was pregnant, he was gone."

Bastard. Sam couldn't understand men who did that. Man enough to have sex, but not man enough to raise a child.

"But I was okay with that," Katie went on. "I wanted the baby and I was excited about it, but still scared, you know, that I wasn't ready. So…" She bit her lip and looked away for a minute, her gaze lingering on the darkness in the back of the yard. "So I worked. A lot. Extra hours, weekends, whatever I could do, to try to fatten up my savings so I'd be ready when the baby came."

He could understand pouring yourself into work to

avoid the memories, the things that hurt. He'd done it himself for so long. Too long.

"And then…" Her voice trailed off.

She didn't need to finish the sentence. He could see how much the memory hurt her. But as the tears welled again in her eyes, he put the pieces together. "You don't think working overtime caused that, do you? That you were at fault?"

"Maybe if I'd rested more and taken care of my body more…" She cursed and shook her head. The tears brimmed and spilled over her lashes, running in little rivers down her cheeks. "I woke up one morning and it was over. I knew it, the second I felt the pain. And it was *my* fault. I don't care what the doctor said, I was the reason the baby…" She swiped at her tears. "The reason I couldn't do the one thing that millions of women do every year."

His heart broke for her, for this woman who loved so much, and yet couldn't forgive herself. "Katie, miscarriages happen all the time. It doesn't mean it was your fault."

"Don't you understand? I can't be a mother. I can't keep track of your kid, and I can't even hold on to my own." She spun away from him, standing tall and cold in the dark. "So just let me go, Sam."

"I can't. Because I already love you." The minute he said the words, he knew they were true. He loved the way she smiled, the way she talked to his kids, the way she made every burden he had seem easier with her beside him.

She stood there, her back to him, for a long moment. "Please don't say that. You're not listening to me. I… I should go."

He came up in front of her and waited until she raised

her gaze to his. "You're running away because you're scared. I know, because I did it myself for years with my job. I ran away from my family because I was scared I was not going to be half the parent my wife was. I ran away because it was easier than facing that fear and being here. It almost cost me my relationship with my kids." He looped a finger under the stubborn lock of hair that had fallen across Katie's forehead again, and tucked it behind her ear. "You're scared, too. I get that. But don't let that fear ruin your life."

"I'm not," she said, and her voice caught on a sob. "I'm trying not to let it ruin yours."

Then she spun on her heel and left. Sam stood in his backyard while the moon moved across the sky and the world went to sleep. He stood there, thinking if he stayed long enough, his heart would stop aching.

He was wrong.

Chapter Fifteen

"If I tell you that you are an idiot, are you going to listen to me?" Colton said.

Katie looked up to see Colton grinning at her.

"And I say that with love," he added, "just in case you were wondering."

She was sitting across from her brother in a corner booth and picking at a breakfast she didn't really want. She'd asked to meet him this morning so she could have a chance to say goodbye before she hit the road. "I'm not an idiot. I'm just making the smartest choice for me and Sam."

Her brother took a bite of toast, chewed and swallowed. "Uh-huh. Sounds to me like you're running away."

"Sam said the same thing." She shook her head and pushed the coffee in front of her to the side. What was with the men in her life? Didn't they understand she wasn't running away? She was just making a smart decision. For her career, for her apartment. For all the things she could depend on, that didn't come with emotional attachments. Getting back to those ordered lines. "I have to go back to Atlanta. I need to find a job, pay my bills, feed the alley cat."

"You don't have an alley cat."

"I'll find one." Adopt one, rescue one, borrow one. Something to take her mind off how much it had hurt to pack her bags this morning. Her car was just outside the Good Eatin' Café, and before she knew it, she'd be behind the wheel and driving home.

Except Atlanta didn't seem like home. It never really had. This quirky little town with a restaurant owner who remembered her name and an inn owner who'd teared up when she said she was checking out this morning—this was what felt like home. Heck, it had felt like home from the minute she'd arrived.

For a second, she considered staying in Stone Gap. After all, there were accounting jobs here, too. She could surely find one or even open her own office. Staying here would mean seeing Henry, Libby, and most of all, Sam.

She couldn't do that. Not without dissolving into a puddle of tears every time.

Hence the need for an alley cat.

"So why don't you stay?" Colton asked, as if reading her mind. "Because the one thing you've never really done, Piglet, is stay."

"I do, too. I have an apartment in Atlanta."

"And have you done anything permanent at your place?" Colton arched a brow and leaned forward. "Like plant a garden or buy a desk?"

"I live in an apartment, Colton. I can't plant a garden. And the firm provided me with a desk. I didn't need to buy one."

"Which means when you were not fired–fired, you could pack everything you owned into a cardboard box and walk out the door." Colton took another bite of toast.

"Well, yeah, but I don't see—"

"And if your apartment was to burn down tomorrow, would you be upset about losing anything inside there?"

"Well, I have a photo album from when we were kids, but really, it's all replaceable—"

"And leavable."

She laughed. "I don't think that's a word."

"My point is that you don't even have things that tie you down, never mind people or places. You can leave at any time—or rather, you can run away at any time. In the two weeks you were here, you made connections. You made friends. You made memories. And if you ask me—" he leaned back in his seat and picked up a second piece of toast "—you're having a hell of a hard time running away from those, because you can't pack any of that in a cardboard box." Colton popped the toast in his mouth and gave her a told-you-so nod.

"That's not it. That's crazy. I'm…" Her voice trailed off as she thought about what her brother had said. There was no one in Atlanta she was rushing to get back to see. She had friends, yes, but most of them were people she joined for dinner after work. There was no one in her contacts list that she would call for a pizza and movie night. No one she wanted to explore an old house with. No one she wanted to go fishing with or search for treasures in the sand with.

No one except for Sam.

"You can tell me I'm right anytime you want." Colton gave her a cheesy grin.

"I'm not saying you're right…" She realigned her fork and knife beside the plate. "Just that you might… *might* have a point."

"Then why are you still sitting here with me?"

"We're having breakfast."

Colton reached over, grabbed her plate, forked up the last of her eggs, then drained her coffee. "There. Now we're done."

Katie laughed. "Has anyone ever told you that you're a pain in the ass?"

"You. Every day of my life." He got to his feet and pressed a kiss to her forehead. "I love you, sis. Now get the hell out of here."

"And go where?"

"The mall on Route 104. Sam has an appointment to meet an interested client there at 10:00 a.m."

"Oh, I shouldn't interrupt him if he's…" She glanced at her brother's face. She recognized that meddling look. She couldn't be mad, because she knew Colton always had the best of intentions, like when he'd gone up to the playground bully when she was in third grade and told him to stop stealing his sister's lunch money. Colton was always going to look after Katie's best interests, even when she didn't need him to. "You?"

"Me? I'm not interested in the real estate Sam's offering. But I bet you are." He shooed her toward the door and tossed a twenty dollar bill on the table. "Now hurry up, because after you're done falling in love with Sam—"

"Who said I was falling in love with Sam?"

"Your goofy grin and googly eyes whenever I talk about him. As I was saying, after you are done falling in love with Sam, I'd love to invite you to dinner at my fiancée's house. Because if you're going to be moving here, you should get to know your sister-in-law." Then he leaned in just as Katie was heading out the door. "And bonus, Rachel's a wedding planner. I have a feeling that might come in handy one day soon."

Sam paced the two-thousand-square-foot space that he'd stood in just days earlier with Ginny and Bernard. They were still debating between this space and the one next door, but had put earnest money on both, just in case. With that deal, it put the mall occupancy at 90 percent—making Hank very, very happy with his new Realtor. Only one more space to fill and Sam would have accomplished his goal. If this next client worked out, that was.

His ten o'clock was running late. He'd called the office and asked for more information, but the receptionist said she didn't have any details about who was meeting him, or have a call-back number. Weird, but he'd met eccentric investors who did that kind of thing from time to time. He just hoped the meeting wouldn't be a complete waste of his time.

He had called Katie and texted her several times after she'd left his house last night, but she hadn't responded. For all he knew, she was already on the road back to Atlanta.

It was Tuesday, and Della had agreed to watch his kids this week until he found a new nanny. If he could tie everything up with the properties he was showing by Friday morning, then he could pick the kids up after Libby got out of school and take a road trip to Georgia. The woman he had made love to, the woman he had laughed with on the beach, that woman was the one he loved—and the same one that he was sure was scared to settle down.

She'd been wounded by the loss of her baby, and he could understand why she would see that as somehow her fault. But she was wrong, and he intended to spend as much time as it took to show her that.

The door to the shop opened and Sam pivoted around. His heart leaped into his throat and he had to blink to be sure he wasn't seeing things. "Katie."

"Hi." She gave him a shy smile, then stepped inside. The door shut again with a soft whoosh. "Can we talk?"

"Sure. But I have an appointment—" He stopped talking when he noticed her smile widen. "*You're* the appointment?"

She put out her arms and shrugged. "Blame Colton, the closet matchmaker."

Sam laughed. "Your brother's become a big romantic since he met Rachel."

"Tell me about it. He's practically a walking Nicholas Sparks novel now, except with a happy ending." She walked around the room, looking up at the tall ceilings with their exposed pipes and oversize pendant lights. She was wearing jeans today, with little heeled boots and a short-sleeved blue sweater. She looked incredible and beautiful, and it took everything he had not to sweep her into his arms. "So, if someone were interested in renting this place, what would it have to offer?"

"You mean, someone who is interested in staying in Stone Gap and maybe opening up an office?" He grinned, then shifted into business mode when she didn't reply. Okay, so that joke went flat. Best to focus on business. "It's a standard triple-net lease, utilities included. The anchor store is opening in three weeks, which should drive a lot of traffic to this end of the mall. The entire space is customizable to your needs and there's a loading dock right out back."

"Sounds...promising." She'd stopped walking and now stood in the center of the room.

Sam crossed to her and tried to read Katie's mind. She was an enigma right now. He couldn't decide if she was seriously interested in the space, making small talk or speaking in some kind of code about them. He opted for the third possibility and hoped he wasn't going to look like a fool in the end. "It is a promising deal," he said. "It has a lot to offer, but you have to move quickly. There's more than one interested party."

"There is?"

He nodded. "They've already made an offer. They want it to be a long-term deal, even though it's really risky, because it's a brand-new venture for them."

The room was wide and empty, almost symbolic in its blankness. It could be a new beginning—for a business owner, for a shop operator or for him and Katie. He held his breath, waiting, not yet ready to bank on anything.

"What made them lock into a long-term deal?" Katie asked.

"They're either fools or optimists," he said. "I prefer to go with the optimists' option."

She laughed softly. "And I'm thinking they're fools. If it's a new venture and you don't have the data to back up your decision, better to not take the risk. Especially not a long-term risk."

Were they talking about the commercial space or about them? "Sometimes the best option is just to take the leap."

She cocked her head and studied him. "But what if you don't know what's on the other side?"

"None of us know what's on the other side, Katie." He took her hand in his. She didn't pull away. Hope bloomed in his chest. He'd spent too many months stuck in thick mud, not moving forward or backward.

He thought of the picture of Wendy that Libby had been holding in the castle. His wife had always been one to live every day with gusto, because she'd said she was never sure what tomorrow would bring. She wouldn't want him to stay in the mud—she would want him to move forward, to grab today, because tomorrow could bring something unexpected. The last bits of his guilt ebbed, and he took a step closer to Katie. To a new future. "Life is short, Katie. That's one thing I have learned in spades in the last year and a half. You need to take the risk."

"But what if I screw up?" Her grip tightened on his, and her face creased with worry. "In accounting, all the numbers add up, even out. That's not how it is with love, with kids. With a family."

He remembered feeling that way before his kids were born, and then letting that fear get in his way after the day Libby got away from him in the grocery store. He thought of how many things had changed in the last few days, and how the children he loved had come back around. Things were different now, and for the first time in a long time, he could see brightness on the horizon. Katie had been the one to foster those changes, to open his heart again. He wished she could see that. "Nothing is ever gonna line up perfectly with kids, with the people you love. But that's what makes it so great. Life is messy and complicated, but all you have to do is love each other, and it'll all be okay."

It was the lesson he had finally understood sitting in the turret of the playground castle. Libby just needed him to love her, to be there, to set her world to rights again.

Katie turned away and started walking the perimeter of the room again. Putting distance between them, every time they got close. "This space has good bones," she said. "And with a little renovation, it could be perfect. It's worth it, though, isn't it? To do the work?"

"Yes, it is. Then you can get what you really want." He sighed. She really was just talking about the rental space. He tried to mask his disappointment, but it sat like a stone in his gut. "We can work with whatever renovation timeline you have. Though you might want to look at one of the other two properties I still have available. Like I said, this one has an offer on it already."

She pivoted back toward him. "I don't want any other properties. I want this one."

"I can't…" He took two steps closer and saw the mischief lurking in her eyes. Again, his heart leaped, held, cautious. "You want this one?"

She put a hand on his chest and smiled up at him. "This one right here. And no other."

"But what about Atlanta and your job?"

"They need accountants here. In fact, I called the firm in downtown Stone Gap on my way over and I have an interview later this afternoon." She looked scared and excited all at once. "I don't have a job offer or a plan, so there are no guarantees, but it's a step. And if a job with another firm doesn't work out, I can always go out on my own."

"That's great." He tried to work up some enthusiasm. She hadn't mentioned him or if they had any kind of future together. "So…you're thinking about staying in Stone Gap?"

"I'd like to make it a permanent move. My very wise and bossy brother lives here, and my soon-to-be sister-in-law. I want to be the terrible auntie who spoils their kids rotten."

Again, no mention of him. It was almost more painful to stand here. For a second there, Sam had thought she was talking about wanting him, wanting them. But now... "That sounds great. I bet Colton will be happy."

"And what about you?"

"What about me?"

"Would you be happy if I stayed in Stone Gap and spoiled Colton's kids?" she said.

"First of all, I am totally on board with spoiling Colton's kids as long as it involves a drum set to make up for the bongos he bought my kids for Christmas." Sam closed the gap between them and settled his hands on her waist. She didn't back away, and the hope in his chest grew. "Secondly, nothing would make me happier than for you to live permanently in Stone Gap. If... if we were together."

Her gaze softened, and a smile curved across her face. "I'm tired of running away, Sam. I want...a life I can depend on. A life I build and take the time to enjoy."

He drew her to him, and murmured against the soft locks of her hair, "Then stop running, Katie."

"I'm still scared."

He pressed his forehead to hers. Their eyes met, held. "Me, too. But I don't want to put my life on hold anymore because of what might happen. I want to live in the present."

"Me, too." Katie's smile widened, and Sam thought he would love nothing more than to see that smile every day of his life. "I love you, Sam Millwright."

She loved him? The words lifted his heart, filled him with joy. "I love you, too, Katie, even if you are completely overqualified to be with me."

"Completely overqualified?"

"I don't think you're right for the nanny job," he said, and paused a beat when confusion filled her gaze. "I think you should be my wife."

Katie's eyes widened. "But what if I can't have any more children? What if—"

He placed a finger on her lips. "That's not a requirement for being my wife, Katie. I want you, and the magic you've brought back to my life, to my kids' lives. I want to laugh with you and eat pizza with you and find treasures on the beach with you. For the rest of my life."

"I already found the best treasure," she said. "Right here." Katie leaned into his chest, listened to his heart beat. Sam held her tight, in an empty space that would someday hold someone else's future, and for the first time in her life, Katie stayed exactly where she was, and began to put down roots.

Epilogue

Eighteen months later

Bright balloons waved in the slight breeze, while the sound of children's laughter rang like bells across the lawn. Stone Gap Lake sparkled in the spring sunlight, the water beckoning, even if it was still too cold to swim.

The house Sam had bought years ago was finally restored, after months of hard work by Savannah Barlow and her crew. Today was the official housewarming, now that Sam, Katie, Libby and Henry were all settled in. There were still some pictures to hang, some pillows to fluff, but overall, the house was a home. The kids loved the lake in their backyard, the room for the new swing set Sam had installed, and the tree house he'd begun constructing last weekend. All of the Barlow boys had been here to help with that one, though it seemed the men had spent more time ribbing each other than actually building. It didn't matter. Katie had loved looking out the kitchen window and seeing the big family that she'd always wanted, expanding by the minute.

Now, Katie lowered herself into a chair and let out a long breath. Her back ached, no matter how often Sam rubbed the sore spot at the base of her spine. She watched Della Barlow hand out cookies to Libby, Henry and Maddy, her face filled with joy at the sight of her grandchildren. She'd officially declared herself Libby and Henry's grandmother, even if the familial link was several times removed. Katie didn't mind. It was nice to be wrapped in the warm embrace of the Barlow family, sort of like cocooning under blankets on a cold winter's night.

"Here you go," Sam said as he handed her a plate and took a seat in the Adirondack chair beside her. "Though I have no idea how you're eating that."

She laughed. "Don't blame me for the menu. Blame the baby." The final stages of her pregnancy had left her with a lot of weird cravings, including hot dogs topped with potato chips and mustard. Not to mention the pickle and apple slices on the side.

Sam's hand slid across her belly with a soft, slow, proud swirl. The sun glinted off the gold in his ring. "I can't wait till we finally get to meet him."

"Her," Katie gently corrected as the baby let out a gentle kick. "I think it's a girl."

"And I'm betting on boy." He grinned. "Either way, we'll know in a week."

For months after she saw the positive result on the pregnancy test, Katie had held her breath, too afraid to hope. Then as the first trimester stretched into the second, and then the third, she'd begun to plan, to paint the nursery with Sam, to fill a crib with stuffed animals (and even a bear that Libby and Henry had picked out for their new sibling). Now, with only a few days to go, Katie was filled with nervous anticipation. Sam was ecstatic, as were the kids. It was a bright new beginning for all of them, a perfect start that had begun the day she'd said "I do" to Sam on this very lawn last year.

Her hand covered his and their fingers interlaced. "It's a first baby. It might be late."

Sam leaned in and kissed her. He pressed his forehead to hers and met her gaze. "It'll be worth the wait."

"Quit kissing my sister." Colton grinned at the two of them. His wife, Rachel, was holding his hand, looking up at Colton like the sun rose in his face. They still had that just-married look, fourteen months after their own wedding. There were days when Katie could hardly believe she'd first come to Stone Gap a year and a half ago. So much had changed in that time.

"You do know where that kissing business leads, don't you?" Colton added.

Katie laughed and gave her belly a pat. "I do indeed. And if I'm not mistaken, so do you."

Rachel blushed and a hand strayed to her abdomen, the kind of unconscious gesture of a woman with a new life inside her. "How did you know? We just found out ourselves a few days ago."

"This family is having a baby boom," Sam said. "It only seemed right that you guys would be next."

Meri Barlow came over to them, with Jack right beside her. Jack had a sleepy six-month-old on his shoulder, a little blonde girl who looked as beautiful as her mother. "As much as I'd love to let Sam take credit for some kind of familial ESP, I might have let the news slip," Meri said, then turned to her sister-in-law. "You kinda told me yourself, Rachel, when you asked if I still had Liz's newborn clothes."

Rachel's face reddened even more. "I said I was asking for a friend."

The Barlows and the Millwrights laughed. "Yeah,

we all know that's code for asking for yourself," Jack said. "Either way, I'm glad to see you and Colton joining the party."

Luke and Peyton came strolling over, hand in hand. Luke clapped a hand on his brother's back. "What are the girls roping you into now, Colton?"

"The one thing you and Mac haven't been roped into yet," Colton said. "Kids."

"I already have one of those, you know. If I want more, I can borrow from a wide selection of Barlow youngsters." Luke drew Peyton into his arms and pressed a kiss to her temple. His arm looped around her waist and his voice lowered when he spoke again. "Though I don't think I'd mind adding one or two to our mix."

Peyton's eyes widened and a smile took over her face. "Is that you saying you want to have a baby?"

"It is." Luke's love for his wife showed in his eyes, his voice. They were rarely apart, even when Luke was working at the family garage. Most days, Peyton and Maddy stopped by there to eat lunch or share an early dinner with Luke. He tore his gaze away from her, then shouted over his head at Mac, who was helping Savannah slice a watermelon. "What do you say, Mac? Want to see who can have a son first?"

Mac arched a brow. "Are you seriously challenging me to an offspring challenge?"

"Somebody's got to make you finish settling down." Luke grinned. Mac had been the last of them to get married. He and Savannah had had a simple affair in Della and Bobby's backyard just three months ago.

"If you all would quit keeping my wife so busy with renovation projects, maybe we could find time to have kids."

Savannah swatted at him. "Shush. I love doing this work."

"And you do it well, sweetheart," Mac said softly, then kissed her. As much as the other men teased Mac, Katie could see every one of the Barlow family members were glad to see so much happiness among the brothers.

Della came up the little hill with the nearly empty tray of cookies still in her hand. "Did I just hear something about more grandchildren?" When she saw Rachel and Colton's twin smiles and shy nods of yes, Della let out a whoop, handed off the cookies to Luke, then grabbed the two of them in an excited hug.

Life was good, Katie thought, as she watched her children running along the edge of the lake with Bandit, and treasured the warmth of her husband's hand in hers. How things had changed in the space of time since she first arrived in Stone Gap, a town she couldn't imagine ever leaving. Especially not since she'd put down roots, and watched them grow into a family tree.

Even though she'd had an offer from the Stone Gap accounting firm, Katie had opened a little accounting practice out of the house, using what would have been the parlor as a home office. She worked part-time, which left her enough time to be with the kids when they got home from school, and spend lots of time with Sam, going on family scavenger hunts along the lakeshore. The new mall project that Sam had worked on filling had gone so well that the developers had asked him to help them fill another mall being built thirty miles outside of Stone Gap. He worked hard, but he'd stuck to his promise to spend more time with his family and not let work bleed over into that precious personal time. He'd already planned for a two-week vacation for after the baby came. It'd be nice to have him around more often. Very nice.

"I hear Savannah designed one hell of a garage for

you, Sam," Jack said. "Want to take us guys on a tour so we can drool over it?"

"Yeah, and we'll take the cookies for sustenance since we might be in there awhile, making up our own wish lists for Christmas." Luke swiped the rest of them into his palm, then handed the tray back to his mother.

Sam chuckled, then got to his feet. He bent down toward Katie again. "Are you going to be okay if I leave you for a bit?"

She laughed and gave him a nod. "Yes, worrywart, I will be. We've got a week, remember? And besides, I'm not going anywhere."

Love warmed Sam's brown eyes. "I'm never going to get tired of hearing you say that," he whispered, then gave her a kiss before heading off with the Barlow brothers. The men joked and laughed as they walked away, teasing Sam about the "man cave" Savannah had built in one of the garage bays.

Della took a seat beside Katie and gave her a quick hug. "I'm so glad you came to town and joined our crazy clan," she said.

"Even if I'm barely related?"

Della took Katie's hand in hers and gave it a squeeze. "You've been family since the day you arrived at the Stone Gap Inn, Katie."

The words warmed Katie, and filled her heart. The family she had found—Sam, Libby, Henry, the Barlows—had welcomed her and Colton with open arms. She could feel her life becoming full and complete, becoming the world she had never dared to dream existed when she was little and staring at those cracks in the ceiling.

A low, heavy pain rippled across her abdomen, and Katie let out a little gasp. She'd had several of those throughout the day, and kept thinking they were just more Braxton Hicks contractions. But this one was different, stronger somehow, and Katie's instincts told her this first baby wasn't going to be late, after all.

Katie looked over at Della. "I think you need to go get Sam."

Della's gaze dropped to Katie's belly, then back up to her face. "It's time?"

Katie nodded, and felt tears of joy spring to her eyes. She may have taken almost three decades to get here, to this town, to this man, to the family she'd dreamed of, but the wait, as Sam had said, had been worth it. "It's time."

* * * * *

PRINCE DADDY
& THE NANNY

BRENDA HARLEN

To Kate Weichelt –
who has helped brainstorm solutions to many
story problems over the years, including a few
in this one. Thanks for being a friend, an
inspiration, and especially for being you!

Chapter One

So this is how the other half lives.

Hannah Castillo's eyes widened as she drove through the gates into the upscale neighborhood of Verde Colinas.

Actually, she knew it was more likely how half of one percent of the population lived, and she couldn't help wondering what it would be like to grow up in a place like this. Having spent the first eight years of her life moving from village to village with her missionary parents, she hadn't realized there was anything different until her uncle Phillip had brought her to his home in Tesoro del Mar.

And even then, she wouldn't have imagined that there was anything like *this.* She hadn't known that real people lived in such luxury. Not regular people, of course, but billionaires and business tycoons, musicians and movie stars, philanthropists and princes. Well, at least one prince.

Prince Michael Leandres was the thirty-eight-year-old president of a multimedia advertising company, cousin of the prince regent, widowed father of Tesoro del Mar's youngest princess, and the first man who had ever made her heart go pitter-patter.

As she slowed to wait for another set of gates to open so that she could enter the drive that led to the prince's home, she couldn't help but smile at the memory. She'd been twelve at the time, and as flustered as she was flattered when Uncle Phillip asked her to accompany him to the by-invitation-only Gala Opening of the Port Augustine Art Gallery.

She'd been so preoccupied thinking about what she would wear (she would have to get a new dress, because a gala event surely required a gown) and whether she might be allowed to wear makeup (at least a little bit of eyeliner and a touch of lip gloss) that she hadn't given a thought to the other guests who might be in attendance at the event. And then she'd walked through the doors on her uncle's arm and spotted Prince Michael.

To a preteen girl who was just starting to take note of the male species, he was a full six feet of masculine perfection. He was also a dozen years older than she, and already there were rumors swirling about his plans to marry his longtime sweetheart, Samantha Chandelle. But Hannah's enamored heart hadn't cared. She'd been content to admire him from afar, her blood racing through her veins just because he was in the same room with her.

Since then, she'd met a lot of other men, dated some of them and even had intimate relationships with a few. But not one of them had ever made her feel the same kind of pulse-pounding, spine-tingling excitement that she'd felt simply by being in the presence of Prince Michael—not even Harrison Parker, the earl who had been her fiancé for a short time.

Now, fourteen years after her first meeting with the prince, she was going to come face-to-face with him again. She might even have a conversation with him—if she could manage to untie her tongue long enough to form any coherent words—and hopefully persuade him that she was the perfect woman to take care of his adorable daughter. Of course, it might be easier to convince him if she believed it herself, but truthfully, she wasn't sure how she'd let Uncle Phillip convince *her* that the idea of working as a nanny for the summer wasn't a completely ridiculous one.

Or maybe she did know. Maybe it was as simple as the fact that she was in desperate need of an income and a place to stay for the summer, and working as a nanny at Cielo del Norte—a royal estate on the northern coast—would provide her with both. But on top of that, her uncle claimed that he "would be most grateful" if she would at least meet with the prince—as if it would be doing him some kind of favor, which made the request impossible for Hannah to deny. That the salary the prince was offering was more than enough to finally pay off the last of her student loans was a bonus.

As for responsibilities, she would be providing primary care for the widowed prince's almost-four-year-old daughter. She didn't figure that should be too difficult for someone with a master's degree, but still her stomach was twisted in knots of both excitement and apprehension as she turned her ancient secondhand compact into the winding drive that led toward the prince's home.

Having grown up in tents and mud huts and, on very rare occasions, bedding down on an actual mattress in a cheap hotel room, she was unprepared for life in Tesoro del Mar. When she moved into her uncle's home, she had not just a bed but a whole room to herself. She had clothes in an actual closet, books on a shelf and a hot meal on the table every night. It took her a long time to get used to living in such luxurious surroundings, but pulling up in front of the prince's home now, she knew she was about to discover the real definition of luxury.

The hand-carved double front doors were opened by a uniformed butler who welcomed her into a spacious marble-tiled foyer above which an enormous crystal chandelier was suspended. As she followed him down a long hallway, their footsteps muted by the antique Aubusson carpet, she noted the paintings on the walls. She had enough knowledge of and appreciation for art to recognize that the works that hung in gilded frames were not reproductions but original pieces by various European masters.

The butler led her through an open doorway and into what was apparently the prince's office. Prince Michael himself was seated behind a wide desk. Bookcases filled with leather-bound volumes lined the wall behind him. The adjoining wall boasted floor-to-ceiling windows set off by textured velvet curtains. It even smelled rich, she thought, noting the scents of lemon polish, aged leather and fresh flowers.

"Miss Castillo, Your Highness." The butler announced her presence in a formal tone, then bowed as he retreated from the room.

The nerves continued to twist and knot in her stomach. Was she supposed to bow? Curtsy? She should have asked her uncle about the appropriate etiquette, but she'd had so many other questions and concerns about his proposition that the intricacies of royal protocol had never crossed her mind.

She debated for about ten seconds, then realized the prince hadn't looked away from his computer screen long enough to even glance in her direction. She could have bowed *and* curtsied *and* done a tap dance and he wouldn't even have noticed. Instead, she focused on her breathing and tried to relax, reminding herself that Michael Leandres might be a prince, but he was still just a man.

Then he pushed away from his desk and rose to his feet, and she realized that she was wrong.

This man wasn't "just" anything. He was taller than she'd remembered, broader across the shoulders and so much more handsome in person than he appeared in newspaper photos and on magazine covers. And her heart, already racing, leaped again.

He gestured to the chairs in front of his desk. "Please, have a seat."

His voice was deep and cultured, and with each word, little tingles danced over her skin. She couldn't be sure if her reaction to him was that of a girl so long enamored of a prince or of a woman instinctively responding to an undeniably attractive man, but she did know that it was wholly inappropriate under the circumstances. She was here to interview for a job, not ogle the man, she sternly reminded herself as she lowered herself into the Queen Anne–style chair and murmured, "Thank you."

"I understand that you're interested in working as my daughter's nanny for the summer," the prince said without further preamble.

"I am," she agreed, then felt compelled to add, "although I have to confess that I've never actually worked as a nanny before."

He nodded, seemingly unconcerned by this fact. "Your uncle told me that you're a teacher."

"That's correct."

"How long have you been teaching?"

"Six years," she told him.

"Do you enjoy it?"

"Of course," she agreed.

He frowned, and she wondered if her response was somehow the wrong one. But then she realized that his gaze had dropped to the BlackBerry on his desk. He punched a few buttons before he looked up at her again.

"And I understand that you've met Riley," he prompted.

"Only once, a few months ago. I was with a friend at the art gallery—" coincidentally, the same art gallery where she'd first seen him so many years earlier, though it was unlikely that he had any recollection of that earlier meeting "—and Princess Riley was there with her nanny."

Phillip had explained to her that the nanny—Brigitte Francoeur—had been caring for the princess since she was a baby, and that Prince Michael had been having more difficulty than he'd anticipated in his efforts to find a replacement for the woman who was leaving his employ to get married.

"The way Brigitte told it to me was that my daughter ran away from her, out of the café—and straight into you, dumping her ice cream cone into your lap."

Hannah waited, wondering about the relevance of his recounting of the event.

"I kept expecting to read about it in the paper," he explained. *"Princess Riley Accosts Museum Guest with Scoop of Strawberry."*

She couldn't help but smile. "I'm sure, even if there had been reporters in the vicinity, they would not have found the moment newsworthy, Your Highness."

"I've learned, over the years, that a public figure doesn't only need to worry about the legitimate media but anyone who feels they have a story to tell. A lot of ordinary citizens would have happily sold that little tale to *El Informador* for a tidy sum. Not only did you not run to the press to sell the story of the out-of-control princess, but you bought her a new ice cream cone to replace the one she'd lost."

"It wasn't her fault that the strawberry went splat," she said lightly.

"A gracious interpretation of the event," he noted. "And one that gives me hope you might finally be someone who could fill the hole that Brigitte's absence will leave in Riley's life."

"For the summer, you mean," Hannah sought to clarify.

"For the summer," he agreed. "Although I was originally hoping to find a permanent replacement, the situation has changed. The current nanny is leaving at the end of this week to finalize preparations for her wedding, and my daughter and I are scheduled to be at Cielo del Norte by the beginning of next. None of the applicants I've interviewed have been suitable, and your uncle has managed to convince me to settle for an interim solution to the problem."

She wasn't sure if she should be amused or insulted. "Is that why I'm here? Am I—"

"Excuse me," he interrupted, picking up the BlackBerry again. He frowned as he read the message, then typed a quick response. "You were saying?" he prompted when he was done.

"I was wondering if I'm supposed to be your 'interim solution.'"

His lips curved, just a little, in response to her dry tone. "I hope so. Although my royal duties are minimal, my responsibilities to my business are not," he explained. "I spend the summers at Cielo del Norte because it is a tradition that began when Samantha—"

His hesitation was brief, but the shadows that momentarily clouded his dark eyes confirmed her uncle's suspicion that the prince was still grieving for the wife he'd lost only hours after the birth of their daughter, and Hannah's heart couldn't help but ache for a man who would have faced such an indescribable loss so quickly on the heels of intense joy.

"—when Samantha and I first got married. A tradition that she wanted to carry on with our children." He cleared his throat, dropping his gaze to reshuffle some papers on his desk. "But the truth is that I still have a company to run. Thankfully I can do that from the beach almost as easily as I can do it from my office downtown. I just need to know that Riley is in good hands so that I can focus on what I need to do."

Be a good girl and stay out of the way so that Daddy can do his work.

The words, long forgotten, echoed in the back of Hannah's mind and sliced through her heart.

Maybe they had been born into completely different worlds, but Hannah suddenly wondered if she and Princess Riley might have a lot more in common than she ever would have suspected.

Her own father had rarely had any time for her, and then, when she was eight years old, her mother had died. She still felt the void in her heart. She still missed her. And she wanted to believe that in some small way, she might be able to fill that void for the prince's daughter. If he would give her the chance.

"Are you offering me the job, Your Highness?" she asked him now.

"Yes, I am," he affirmed with a nod.

"Then I accept."

Michael knew he should be relieved. He'd needed to hire a nanny for the summer, and now he'd done so. But there was something about Hannah Castillo that made him uneasy. Or maybe he was simply regretting the fact that his daughter would have to say goodbye to her long-term caregiver. Brigitte had been a constant in Riley's life almost from the very beginning, and he knew it would take his daughter some time to adjust to her absence.

He wished he could believe that being at Cielo del Norte with him would give Riley comfort, but the truth was, his daughter was much closer to her nanny than she was to her father. It was a truth that filled him with grief and regret, but a truth nonetheless.

He and Sam had long ago agreed that they would both play an active role in raising their child. Of course, that agreement had been made before Sam died, so soon after giving birth to their baby girl. How was one man supposed to care for an infant daughter, grieve for the wife he'd lost and continue to run the company they'd built together?

It hadn't taken him long to realize that there was no way that he could do it on his own, so he'd hired Brigitte. She'd been a child studies student at the local university who Sam had interviewed as a potential mother's helper when the expectation was that his wife would be around to raise their daughter.

For the first couple years, Brigitte had tended to Riley during the day and continued her studies at night, with Michael's sister, Marissa, taking over the baby's care after-hours. Then when Brigitte finished university and Michael's sister took on additional responsibilities elsewhere, the young woman had become Riley's full-time nanny.

I don't want our child raised by a series of nannies.

Sam's voice echoed in the back of his mind, so clearly that he almost expected to turn around and see her standing there.

He understood why she'd felt that way and he'd shared her concerns, but he convinced himself that a wonderful and energetic caregiver like Brigitte was the exception to the rule. She certainly wasn't like any of the harsh disciplinarians who had been hired to ensure that he and his siblings grew up to become proper royals.

Still, he knew his failure wasn't in hiring Brigitte—or even in hiring Hannah Castillo. His failure was in abdicating his own responsibilities as a father.

He'd wanted to do more, to be more involved in Riley's life. But the first few months after Sam's death had been a blur. He'd barely been able to focus on getting up every morning, never mind putting a diaper on a baby, so those tasks had fallen to Brigitte or Marissa.

At six months of age, Riley had broken through the veil of grief that had surrounded him. He'd been drinking his morning coffee and scanning the headlines of the newspaper when Marissa had carried her into the kitchen. He'd glanced up, and when he did, the little girl's big brown eyes widened. "Da!" she said, and clapped her hands.

He didn't know enough about a baby's developmental milestones to know that she was speaking her first word several months ahead of schedule. All he knew was that the single word and the smile on her face completely melted his heart.

Sam had given him the precious gift of this baby girl, and somehow he had missed most of the first six months of her life. He vowed then and there to make more of an effort, to spend more time with her, to make sure she knew how much she was loved. But he was still awkward with her—she was so tiny and delicate, and he felt so big and clumsy whenever he held her. Thankfully, she was tolerant of his ineptitude, and her smiles and giggles gave him confidence and comfort.

And then, shortly after Riley's second birthday, Brigitte made a discovery. Riley had been an early talker—not just speaking a few words or occasional phrases but in complete sentences—and she often repeated the words when the nanny read her a story. But on this particular day, Brigitte opened a book that they'd never read before, and Riley began to read the words without any help or prompting.

A few months after that, Brigitte had been playing in the music room with the little girl, showing her how she could make sounds by pressing down on the piano's ivory keys, and Riley had quickly started to put the sounds together to make music.

Before she turned three, Riley had been examined by more doctors and teachers than Michael could count, and the results had been unequivocal—his daughter was intellectually gifted.

He was proud, of course, and more than a little baffled. As if he hadn't struggled enough trying to relate to the tiny little person when he'd believed that she was a normal child, learning that she was of superior intelligence made him worry all the more. Thankfully, Brigitte had known what to do. She'd met with specialists and interviewed teachers and made all of the arrangements to ensure that Riley's talents were being nurtured. And when the advertising company he and Sam had established ran into difficulties because an associate stole several key clients, Michael refocused his attention on the business, confident his daughter was in much more capable hands than his own.

It had taken a while, but the business was finally back on solid ground, Riley was happy and healthy, Brigitte was getting married and moving to Iceland, and he had a new nanny for the summer.

So why was he suddenly worried that hiring Hannah Castillo had set him upon a path that would change his life?

He didn't want anything to change. He was content with the status quo. Maybe it wasn't what he'd envisioned for his life half a dozen years earlier, and maybe there was an empty place in his heart since Samantha had died, but he knew that he could never fill that void. Because there would never be anyone he would love as he'd loved Sam. There was no way anyone else could ever take her place.

Each day that had passed in the years since Sam's death had cemented that conviction. He had no difficulty turning away from the flirtatious glances that were sent in his direction, and even the more blatant invitations did nothing to stir his interest.

Then Hannah Castillo had walked into his office and he'd felt a definite stir of…something.

The morning weather reports had warned of a storm on the horizon, and he'd tried to convince himself that the change in the weather was responsible for the crackle in the air. But he knew that there was no meteorological explanation for the jolt that went through his system when he'd taken the hand she offered, no logical reason for the rush of blood through his veins when she smiled at him.

And he'd felt an uneasiness in the pit of his belly, a tiny suspicion that maybe hiring a young, attractive woman as his daughter's temporary nanny wasn't the best idea he'd ever had.

Because as much as he'd kept the tone of the interview strictly professional, he hadn't failed to notice that the doctor's niece was quite beautiful. She wasn't very tall—probably not more than five feet four inches without the two-inch heels on her feet. And while the tailored pants and matching jacket she wore weren't provocative by any stretch of the imagination, they failed to disguise her distinctly feminine curves. Her honey-blond hair had been scraped away from her face and secured in a tight knot at the back of her head in a way that might have made her look prim, but the effect was softened by warm blue eyes and sweetly shaped lips that were quick to smile.

Even as he'd offered her the job, he'd wondered if he was making a mistake. But he'd reassured himself that it was only for two months.

Now that she was gone and he was thinking a little more clearly, he suspected that it was going to be a very long summer.

Chapter Two

Hannah went through her closet, tossing items into one of two separate piles on her bed. The first was for anything she might need at Cielo del Norte, and the other was for everything else, which would go into storage. Thankfully, she didn't have a lot of stuff, but she still had to sort and pack everything before she handed over her keys, and the task was much more time-consuming than she would have imagined.

Subletting her apartment had seemed like a good idea when she'd planned to spend the summer in China as an ESL teacher. Unfortunately the job offer had fallen through when she'd declined to share a tiny one-bedroom apartment with the coworker who'd made it clear that he wanted her in his bed. She felt like such a fool. She should have realized that Ian had ulterior motives when he first offered to take her to China, but she honestly hadn't had a clue.

Yes, they'd been dating for a few months, but only casually and certainly not exclusively. When she'd sidestepped his advances, he'd seemed to accept that she didn't want to take their relationship to the next level. So when he'd presented her with the opportunity to teach in China during the summer break, she'd trusted that he was making the offer as a colleague and a professional. Finding out that he expected them to share an apartment put a different spin on things.

Ian's ultimatum was further evidence that she had poor judgment with respect to romantic entanglements, a truth first revealed by her broken engagement three years earlier. Now she had additionial confirmation in the fact that she was fighting an attraction to a man who wasn't just a prince but grieving the death of his wife. With a sigh, Hannah taped up yet another box and pushed it aside.

When she finished in the bedroom, she packed up the contents of the bathroom. By the time she got to the kitchen, her legs were protesting all the bending and her shoulders were aching from all the lifting. But she still had to empty the pantry of boxed food and canned goods, which she was in the process of doing when the downstairs buzzer sounded.

She stopped packing only long enough to press the button that released the exterior door locks. It was six o'clock on a Friday night, so she knew it was her uncle Phillip at the door. Weekly dinners had become their way of keeping in touch when Hannah moved out of his house, and she sincerely regretted that she would have to skip the ritual for the next couple of months.

"It's unlocked," she said in response to his knock.

"A woman living alone in the city should lock her doors," her uncle chided, passing through the portal with a large flat box in his hand and the sweet and spicy aroma of sausage pizza enveloping him. "Didn't I ever teach you that?"

"You tried to teach me so many things," she teased, standing up and wiping her hands on her jeans. "I thought I'd seen more than enough boxes today, but that one just changed my mind."

"Packing is hard work." He set the pizza on the counter

and gave her a quick hug. He smelled of clean soap with subtle hints of sandalwood—a scent that was as warm and dependable as everything else about him.

"I'm almost done." She moved out of his embrace to retrieve plates from the cupboard. "Finally."

"How long have you been at it?" He opened the refrigerator, pulled a couple of cans of soda from the nearly empty shelves.

"It seems like forever. Probably about seven hours. But I've already moved a lot of stuff into a storage locker downstairs, so it shouldn't take me too much longer."

Hannah took a seat on the opposite side of the table from him and helped herself to a slice of pizza. She hadn't realized how hungry she was until she took the first bite. Of course, she'd been too nervous about her interview with Prince Michael to eat lunch earlier, which reminded her that she hadn't yet told her uncle about the new job.

But he spoke before she could, saying, "I heard you're heading up to Cielo del Norte on Monday."

Phillip was a highly regarded doctor in the community and his network of contacts was legendary, but she still didn't see how he could have learned the outcome of her interview with the prince already. "How did you hear that?"

He smiled, recognizing the pique in her tone. "The prince called to thank me for the recommendation."

"Oh." She should have considered that possibility. "Well, his appreciation might be a little premature."

"I have every confidence that you're just what his daughter needs," Phillip said.

She wasn't so sure. She was a teacher, and she loved being a teacher, but that didn't mean she was qualified to work as a nanny.

And yet that wasn't her greatest worry. A far bigger concern, and one she was reluctant to admit even to herself, was that she now knew she'd never completely let go of her childhood infatuation with Prince Michael Leandres.

She should have outgrown that silly crush years ago. And she'd thought she had—until she stood in front of him with her heart beating so loudly inside of her chest she was amazed that he couldn't hear it.

So now she was trying *not* to think about the fact that she would be spending the next two months at Cielo del Norte with the sexy prince who was still grieving the loss of his wife, and attempting to focus instead on the challenges of spending her days with an almost-four-year-old princess.

"I wish I shared your faith," Hannah said to her uncle now.

"Why would you have doubts?"

"I'm just not sure that hiring a temporary replacement is the best thing for a young child who has just lost her primary caregiver." It was the only concern she felt comfortable offering her uncle, because she knew that confiding in him about her childhood crush would only worry him.

"Your compassion is only one of the reasons I know you'll be perfect for the job," Phillip said. "As for Riley, I think she'll surprise you. She is remarkably mature for her age and very well-adjusted."

"Then why does the prince even need a nanny? Why can't he just enjoy a summer at the beach with his daughter without pawning off the responsibility of her care on someone else?"

"Prince Michael is doing the best that he can," her uncle said. "He's had to make a lot of adjustments in his life, too, since losing his wife."

Hannah used to wonder why people referred to a death as a loss—as if the person was only missing. She'd been there when her mother died, so she knew that she wasn't "lost" but gone. Forever.

And after her death her husband had handed their daughter over to his brother-in-law, happy to relinquish to someone else the responsibility of raising his only child. Just as the prince was doing.

Was she judging him too harshly? Possibly. Certainly she was judging him prematurely. There were a lot of professionals who hired caregivers for their children, and although Prince Michael kept a fairly low profile in comparison to other members of his family, she knew that he had occasional royal duties to perform in addition to being president and CEO of his own company. And he was a widower trying to raise a young daughter on his own after the unexpected death of his wife from severe hypoglycemia only hours after childbirth.

Maybe her uncle was right and he was doing the best that he could. In any event, she would be at Cielo del Norte in a few days with the prince and his daughter. No doubt her questions would be answered then.

"So what are you going to do with your Friday nights while I'm gone this summer?" she asked her uncle, hoping a change in the topic of conversation would also succeed in changing the direction of her thoughts.

"I'm sure there will be occasional medical emergencies to keep me occupied," Phillip told her.

She smiled, because she knew it was true. "Will you come to visit me?"

"If I can get away. But you really shouldn't worry about me—there's enough going on with the Juno project at the hospital to keep me busy over the next several months."

"Okay, I won't worry," she promised. "But I will miss you."

"You'll be too busy rubbing elbows with royalty to think about anyone else," he teased.

She got up to clear their empty plates away, not wanting him to see the flush in her cheeks. Because the idea of rubbing anything of hers against anything of Prince

Michael's—even something as innocuous as elbows—made her feel hot and tingly inside.

Heading up to Cielo del Norte on Saturday afternoon had seemed like a good idea to Michael while he was packing up the car. And Riley had been excited to start their summer vacation. Certainly she'd given him no reason to anticipate any problems, but if there was one thing he should have learned by now about parenting, it was to always expect the unexpected.

The trip itself had been uneventful enough. Estavan Fuentes, the groundskeeper and general maintenance man, had been waiting when they arrived to unload the vehicle; and Caridad, Estavan's wife and the longtime housekeeper of the estate, had the beds all made up and dinner ready in the oven.

As Michael had enjoyed a glass of his favorite cabernet along with the hot meal, he'd felt the tensions of the city melt away. It was several hours later before he recognized that peaceful interlude as the calm before the storm.

Now it was after midnight, and as he slipped out onto the back terrace and into the blissful quiet of the night, he exhaled a long, weary sigh. It was the only sound aside from the rhythmic lap of the waves against the shore in the distance, and he took a moment to absorb—and appreciate—the silence.

With another sigh, he sank onto the end of a lounge chair and let the peacefulness of the night settle like a blanket across his shoulders. Tipping his head back, he marveled at the array of stars that sparkled like an exquisite selection of diamonds spread out on a black jeweler's cloth.

He jolted when he heard the French door slide open again.

"Relax—she's sleeping like a baby." His sister's voice was little more than a whisper, as if she was also reluctant to disturb the quiet.

He settled into his chair again. "I thought you'd be asleep, too. You said you wanted to get an early start back in the morning."

"I do," Marissa agreed. "But the stars were calling to me."

He smiled, remembering that those were the same words their father used to say whenever they found him out on this same terrace late at night. They'd spent a lot of time at Cielo del Norte when they were kids, and Michael had a lot of fond memories of their family vacations, particularly in the earlier years, before their father passed away. Their mother had continued the tradition for a while, but it was never the same afterward and they all knew it.

Gaetan Leandres had been raised with a deep appreciation for not just the earth but the seas and the skies, too. He'd been a farmer by trade and a stargazer by choice. He'd spent hours sitting out here, searching for various constellations and pointing them out to his children. He'd once told Michael that whenever he felt overwhelmed by earthly burdens, he just had to look up at the sky and remember how much bigger the world was in comparison to his problems.

Marissa sat down on the end of a lounger, her gaze on something far off in the distance. "I know they're the same stars I can see from my windows in the city, but they look so different out here. So much brighter."

"Why don't you stay for a few days?" he offered, feeling more than a little guilty that she'd driven all the way from Port Augustine in response to his distress call.

"I wish I could, but I've got three full days of meetings scheduled this week."

"Which you should have told me when I got you on the phone."

She lifted a shoulder. "I couldn't not come, not when I heard Riley sobbing in the background."

And that was why he'd called. His daughter, tired from

the journey, had fallen asleep earlier than usual. A few hours later, she'd awakened screaming like a banshee and nothing he said or did seemed to console her. She'd been in an unfamiliar bed in an unfamiliar room and Brigitte—her primary caregiver—was on a plane halfway to Iceland. Michael had tried to console Riley, he'd cuddled her, rocked her, put on music for her to listen to, tried to read stories to her, but nothing had worked.

It hadn't occurred to him to call his mother—the princess royal wouldn't know what to do any more than he did. It wasn't in her nature to offer comfort or support. In fact, the only things he'd ever been able to count on his mother to do were interfere and manipulate. So he'd picked up the phone and dialed his sister's number. During the first year and a half after Sam's death, before he'd hired Brigitte full-time, Marissa had been there, taking care of both him and his daughter. And, once again, she'd come through when he needed her.

"Do you think I should have stayed in Port Augustine with her?" he asked his sister now.

"That would have meant a much shorter trip for me," she teased, "but no. I'm glad you're maintaining the family tradition."

Except that he didn't have a family anymore—for the past four summers, it had been just him and Riley. And Brigitte, of course.

"When does the new nanny arrive?"

Marissa's question drew him back to the present—and to more immediate concerns.

"Tomorrow."

She tilted her head. "Why do you sound wary?"

"Do I?" he countered.

"Are you having second thoughts about her qualifications?"

"No," he said, then reconsidered his response. "Yes."

Her brows rose.

No, because it wasn't anything on Hannah's résumé that gave him cause for concern. Yes, because he wasn't completely convinced that a teacher would be a suitable caregiver for his daughter—even on a temporary basis.

"No," he decided. "Dr. Marotta would never have recommended her if he didn't believe she was capable of caring for Riley."

"Of course not," his sister agreed. "So what are you worried about?"

He didn't say anything. He didn't even deny that he was worried, because his sister knew him too well to believe it. Worse, she would probably see right through the lie to the true origin of his concern. And he was concerned, mostly about the fact that he'd been thinking of Hannah Castillo far too frequently since their first meeting.

He'd had no preconceptions when he'd agreed to interview her. His only concern had been to find someone suitable to oversee the care of his daughter during the summer— because after conducting more than a dozen interviews, he'd been shocked to realize how *un*suitable so many of the applicants had been.

Almost half of them he'd automatically rejected because of their advanced age. Logically, he knew that was unfair, but he had too many unhappy memories of strict, gray-haired disciplinarians from his own childhood. Another few he'd disregarded when it became apparent that they were more interested in flirting with him than caring for his daughter. Two more had been shown the door when they'd been caught snapping photos of his home with the cameras on their cell phones.

At the conclusion of those interviews, he'd almost given up hope of finding a replacement for Brigitte. Then, during a casual conversation with Riley's doctor, he'd mentioned his dilemma and Phillip had suggested that his niece might be interested in the job—but only for the summer.

So Michael had agreed to interview her and crossed his fingers that she would be suitable. Then Hannah had walked into his office, and *suitable* was the last thought on his mind.

"Oh," Marissa said, and sat back, a smile playing at the corners of her lips.

He scowled. "What is that supposed to mean?"

"She's very attractive, isn't she?"

His scowl deepened.

"I should have guessed. Nothing ever flusters you—okay, nothing except anything to do with Riley," she clarified. "But this woman has you completely flustered."

"I am not flustered," he denied.

"This is good," Marissa continued as if he hadn't spoken. "And it's time."

"Mar—"

She put her hands up in a gesture of surrender. "Okay, okay. I won't push for any details."

"There are no details," he insisted.

"Not yet," she said, and smiled.

His sister always liked to get in the last word, and this time he let her. It would serve no purpose to tell her that he wasn't interested in any kind of relationship with Riley's temporary nanny—it only mattered that it was true.

And he would repeat it to himself as many times as necessary until he actually believed it.

With every mile that Hannah got closer to Cielo del Norte, her excitement and apprehension increased. If she'd been nervous before her previous meeting with the prince—simply at the thought of meeting him—that was nothing compared to the tension that filled her now. Because now she was actually going to live with him—and his daughter, of course.

She could tell herself that it was a temporary position, that she was only committing two months of her time. But two months was a heck of a long time to maintain her objectivity with respect to a man she'd fallen head over heels for when she was only twelve years old, and a little girl who had taken hold of her heart the very first time she'd met her.

Hannah cranked up the radio in the hope that the pulsing music would push the thoughts out of her head. It didn't.

She wrapped her fingers around the steering wheel, her palms sliding over the smooth leather, and was reminded of the feel of his hand against hers. Warm. Strong. Solid.

She really was pathetic.

She really should have said no when her uncle first suggested that she could be anyone's nanny. But as she drove through the gates toward the prince's summer home, after showing her identification to the guard on duty, she knew that she'd passed the point of no return.

Cielo del Norte was even more impressive than the prince's home in Verde Colinas. Of course, it had once been the royal family's official summer residence, bequeathed to the princess royal by her father upon the occasion of her marriage to Gaetan Leandres.

Hannah had been advised that there were two full-time employees who lived in a guest cottage on the property, the groundskeeper and his wife. Hannah had been thrilled to hear that Caridad, the housekeeper, also cooked and served the meals, because she knew that if she'd been put in charge of food preparation as well as child care, they might all starve before the end of the summer.

She parked her aging little car beside a gleaming black Mercedes SUV and made her way to the door. An older woman in a neatly pressed uniform responded to the bell.

"Mrs. Fuentes?"

"Sí. Caridad Fuentes." She bowed formally. "You are Miss Castillo?"

"Hannah," she said, stepping into the foyer.

"The prince has been expecting you." There was the slightest hint of disapproval beneath the words.

"I was a little late getting away this morning," she explained. "And then traffic was heavier than I expected. Of course, taking a wrong turn at Highway Six didn't help, either, but at least I didn't travel too far out of my way."

The housekeeper didn't comment in any way except to ask, "Are your bags in the car?"

"Yes, I'll get them later."

"Estavan—my husband—will bring them in for you," Mrs. Fuentes told her.

"Okay. That would be great. Thanks." She paused, just taking a minute to absorb the scene.

She'd thought passing through the gates at Verde Colinas had been a culture shock, but now she felt even more like a country mouse set loose in the big city. The house, probably three times the size of the prince's primary residence in Port Augustine, almost seemed as big as a city—a very prosperous and exquisite one.

"There's a powder room down the hall, if you would like to freshen up before meeting with Prince Michael," the housekeeper told her.

Hannah nodded. "I would."

"First door on the right."

"And the prince's office?"

"The third door on the left down the west corridor."

Michael sensed her presence even before he saw her standing in the open doorway. When he looked up, he noticed that she'd dressed less formally today than at their first meeting, and that the jeans and T-shirt she wore made her look even younger than he'd originally guessed. He'd told her that casual attire was acceptable, and there was nothing inappropriate about what she was wearing. But he couldn't help noticing how the denim hugged her thighs and molded to her slim hips. The V-neck of her T-shirt wasn't low enough to give even a glimpse of cleavage, but the soft cotton clung to undeniably feminine curves. She wore silver hoops in her ears, and her hair was in a loose ponytail rather than a tight knot, making her look more approachable and even more beautiful, and he felt the distinct hum of sexual attraction through his veins.

Uncomfortable with the stirring of feelings so long dormant, his voice was a little harsher than he'd intended when he said, "You're late."

Still, his tone didn't seem to faze her. "I told you that I would come as soon as possible, and I did."

"I had a conference call at 8:00 a.m. this morning that I had to reschedule because you weren't here."

He expected that she would apologize or show some sign of remorse. Instead she surprised him by asking, "Why on earth would you schedule a conference call so early on the first morning of your vacation?"

"I told you that I would be conducting business from here," he reminded her. "And your job is to take care of my daughter so that I can focus on doing so."

"A job I'm looking forward to," she assured him.

"I appreciate your enthusiasm," he said. "I would expect that someone who spends ten months out of the year with kids would want a break."

"Spending the summer with a four-year-old is a welcome break from senior advanced English and history," she told him.

Senior English and history? The implications of her statement left him momentarily speechless. "You're a *high school* teacher?" he finally said.

Now it was her turn to frown. "I thought you knew that."

He shook his head. "Phillip said you would be perfect for

the job because you were a teacher—I assumed he meant elementary school."

"Well, you assumed wrong." She shrugged, the casual gesture drawing his attention to the rise and fall of her breasts beneath her T-shirt and very nearly making him forget the reason for his concern.

"So what kind of experience do you have with preschool children, Miss Castillo?" he asked, forcing his gaze back to her face.

"Other than the fact that I was one?" she asked lightly.

"Other than that," he agreed.

"None," she admitted.

"None?" Dios! How could this have happened? He was the consummate planner. He scheduled appointment reminders in his BlackBerry; he took detailed notes at every meeting; he checked and double-checked all correspondence before he signed anything. And yet he'd somehow managed to hire a nanny who knew absolutely nothing about being a nanny.

"Well, my friend Karen has a couple of kids, and I've spent a lot of time with them," Hannah continued.

He shook his head, trying to find solace in the fact that their agreement was for only two months, but he was beginning to question why he'd been in such a hurry to replace Brigitte. Had he been thinking of Riley—or had he been more concerned about maintaining the status quo in his own life? Or maybe he'd been spellbound by Miss Castillo's sparkling eyes and warm smile. Regardless of his reasons, he knew it wasn't her fault that he'd hired her on the basis of some mistaken assumptions. But if she was going to spend the summer with Riley, she had a lot to learn—and fast.

"You'll need this," he said, passing a sheaf of papers across the desk.

In the transfer of the pages, her fingers brushed against his. It was a brief and incidental contact, but he felt the jolt sizzle in his veins. Her gaze shot to meet his, and the widening of her eyes confirmed that she'd felt it, too. That undeniable tug of a distinctly sexual attraction.

As he looked into her eyes, he realized he'd made another mistake in thinking that they were blue—they were actually more gray than blue, the color of the sky before a storm, and just as mesmerizing.

Then she glanced away, down at the papers he'd given to her, and he wondered if maybe he'd imagined both her reaction and his own.

"What is this?" she asked him.

"It's Riley's schedule."

She looked back at him, then at the papers again. "You're kidding."

"A child needs consistency," he said firmly, because it was something Brigitte had always insisted upon, and he usually deferred to the nanny with respect to decisions about his daughter's care.

"If you're referring to a prescribed bedtime, I would absolutely agree," Hannah said. "But a child also needs a chance to be spontaneous and creative, and this—" she glanced at the chart again, obviously appalled "—this even schedules her bathroom breaks."

Maybe the charts Brigitte had prepared for the new nanny did provide a little too much detail, but he understood that she'd only wanted to ease the transition for both Riley and her temporary caregiver. "Brigitte found that taking Riley to the bathroom at prescribed times greatly simplified the toilet-training process."

"But she's almost four years old now," Hannah noted. "I'm sure…" Her words trailed off, her cheeks flushed. "I'm sorry—I just didn't expect that there would be so much to occupy her time."

He'd had some concerns initially, too, but Brigitte had made him see the benefits for Riley. Maybe she was young, but she was so mature for her age, so focused, and she was learning so much. She had a natural musical talent, an artistic touch and a gift for languages, and there was no way he was going to let this temporary nanny upset the status quo with questions and criticisms on her first day on the job. Even if her doubts echoed his own.

"It is now almost eleven o'clock, Miss Castillo," he pointed out to her.

She glanced at the page in her hand. "I guess that means it's almost time for the princess's piano lesson."

"The music room is at the end of the hall."

She folded the schedule and dropped a curtsy.

He deliberately refocused his attention back on the papers on his desk so that he wouldn't watch her walk away.

But he couldn't deny that she tempted him in more ways than he was ready to acknowledge.

Chapter Three

Well, that hadn't gone quite as she'd expected, Hannah thought as she exited Prince Michael's office. And she couldn't help but feel a little disappointed, not just with their meeting but in the man himself. She'd thought he might want to talk to her about Riley's favorite activities at the beach, give her some suggestions on how to keep the little girl busy and happy, but she'd gotten the impression he only wanted her to keep the child occupied and out of his way.

As she made her way down the hall in search of the princess, she realized that she'd never actually seen him with his daughter. The first time she'd met Riley—the day of the ice cream mishap at the art gallery—the little girl had been in the care of her nanny. When Hannah had arrived at the prince's house to interview for the position, Riley had been out with Brigitte. She'd gone back for a second visit, to spend some time with the child so that she wouldn't be a complete stranger to her when she showed up at Cielo del Norte, but she hadn't seen the prince at all on that occasion.

Now he was in his office, and the princess was apparently somewhere else in this labyrinth of rooms preparing for a piano lesson. Did they always lead such separate lives? Did the prince really intend to spend most of his supposed holiday at his desk?

Once she'd gotten over her wariness about taking a job for which she had no experience, she'd actually found herself looking forward to spending the summer with the young princess. She'd imagined that they would play in the water and have picnics on the beach. She hadn't anticipated that the little girl wouldn't have time for fun and frivolity. Yes, she'd been born royal and would someday have duties and obligations as a result, but she wasn't even four years old yet.

Brigitte had made a point of telling Hannah—several times—that Riley was an exceptionally bright and gifted child who was already reading at a second-grade level—in French. She'd encouraged the young princess to demonstrate her talents at the piano, and Riley had done so willingly enough. Hannah couldn't help but be impressed, but in the back of her mind, she wondered why the child didn't seem happy.

Somehow that question had Hannah thinking about what she'd been doing as a four-year-old. Her own childhood had hardly been traditional, but it had been fun. In whatever village had been their current home, she'd always had lots of local children to play with. She'd raced over the hills and played hide-and-seek in the trees. She'd gone swimming in watering holes and rivers and streams. She'd created rudimentary sculptures out of riverbank clay and built houses and castles from mud and grass.

Her parents had never worried about the lack of formal education, insisting that the life skills she was learning were far more important than reading and writing. While the teacher in her cringed at that philosophy now, she did understand the importance of balance between life and learning.

At the princess's age, she'd picked up some words and phrases in Swahili and Hausa and Manyika, enough to communicate with the other kids on a basic level; Riley was studying French, Italian and German out of textbooks. And whereas Hannah had learned music by banging on tribal drums or shaking and rattling dried seed pods, Riley had lessons from professional instructors.

She could hear the piano now, and followed the sound of the sharp, crisp notes to the music room to find the prince's daughter practicing scales on a glossy white Steinway.

She was sitting in the middle of the piano bench, her feet—clad in ruffled ankle socks and white patent Mary Janes—dangling several inches above the polished marble floor. Her long, dark hair was neatly plaited and tied with a pink bow. Her dress was the same shade of cotton candy, with ruffles at the bottoms of the sleeves and skirt. The housekeeper was in the corner, dusting some knickknacks on a shelf and surreptitiously keeping an eye on the princess.

The soaring ceiling was set off with an enormous chandelier dripping with crystals, but the light was unnecessary as the late-morning sun spilled through the tall, arched windows that faced the ocean. The other walls were hung with gorgeous woven tapestries, and while Hannah guessed that their placement was more likely for acoustics than aesthetics, the effect was no less breathtaking.

Suddenly, the fingers moving so smoothly over the ivory keys stopped abruptly. Riley swiveled on the bench, a dark scowl on her pretty face. "What are you doing in here?"

"Hello, Riley," Hannah said pleasantly.

"What are you doing in here?" the princess asked again.

"I wanted to hear you practice."

"I like to be alone when I practice," she said, demonstrating that she'd inherited her father's mood as well as his dark eyes.

Hannah just shrugged, refusing to let the little girl's attitude affect her own. "I can wait in the hall until you're finished."

"I have my French lesson after piano."

Hannah referred to the schedule she'd been given, which confirmed Riley's statement. "I'll see you at lunch, then."

The princess's nod dismissed her as definitively as the prince had done only a few minutes earlier.

On her way out, Hannah passed the piano teacher coming in.

The older woman had a leather bag over her shoulder and determination in her step. Clearly *she* had a purpose for being here. Hannah had yet to figure out her own.

The conference call that Michael had rescheduled came through at precisely eleven o'clock and concluded twenty minutes later. A long time after that, he was still struggling to accept what he'd learned about Miss Castillo—high school teacher turned temporary nanny.

Phillip Marotta had said only that she was a teacher; Michael had assumed that meant she had experience with children. Because he trusted the royal physician implicitly, he had taken the doctor's recommendation without question. Apparently he should have asked some questions, but he acknowledged that the mistake had been his own.

Still, despite the new nanny's apparent lack of experience, he knew that the doctor had stronger reasons than nepotism for suggesting his niece for the job. And from what Brigitte had told him, Riley seemed to accept her easily enough. Of course, his daughter had had so many doctors and teachers and instructors in and out of her life that she accepted most newcomers without any difficulty.

So why was he uneasy about Miss Castillo's presence at

Cielo del Norte? Was he really concerned about Riley—or himself?

When Sam died, he'd thought he would never stop grieving the loss. He was certain he would never stop missing her. But over the years, the pain had gradually started to fade, and Riley's easy affection had begun to fill the emptiness in his heart. He'd been grateful for that, and confident that the love of his little girl was enough.

He didn't need romance or companionship—or so he'd believed until Hannah walked into his life. But he couldn't deny that the new nanny affected him in a way that no woman had done in a very long time.

A brisk knock at the door gave him a reprieve from these melancholy thoughts.

"Lunch will be served on the terrace as soon as you're ready," Caridad told him.

He nodded his thanks as he checked his watch, surprised that so much time had passed. Twenty minutes on the phone followed by an hour and a half of futile introspection. Maybe he did need a vacation.

The housekeeper dropped a quick curtsy before she turned back toward the door.

"Caridad—"

"Yes, Your Highness?"

"What is your impression of Miss Castillo?"

Her eyes widened. "I'm not sure I understand why you'd be asking that, sir."

"Because I value your opinion," he told her honestly. "During the summers that I spent here as a kid, you were always a lot more of a mother to me than my own mother was—which makes you Riley's honorary grandmother and, as such, I'd expect you to have an opinion of her new nanny."

"We've only spoken briefly, sir, I'm certainly not in any position—"

"Quick first impressions," he suggested.

"Well, she's not quite what I expected," Caridad finally admitted.

"In what way?"

"She's very young and…quite attractive."

He didn't think Hannah was as young as Brigitte's twenty-four years, though he could see why the housekeeper might have thought so. Brigitte had dressed more conservatively and she hadn't been nearly as outspoken as the doctor's niece.

"Not that Brigitte wasn't attractive," she clarified. "But she was more…subtle."

She was right. There was absolutely nothing subtle about Hannah Castillo. While she certainly didn't play up her natural attributes, there was something about her—an energy or an aura—that made it impossible for her to fade into the background.

"But I'm sure that neither her age nor her appearance has any relevance to her ability to do her job," she hastened to add.

No—the most relevant factor was her employment history, which he decided not to mention to the housekeeper. No doubt Caridad would wonder how he'd ended up hiring someone with a complete lack of experience, and he was still trying to figure that one out himself.

"If I may speak freely…" Caridad ventured.

"Of course," he assured her.

"You should spend more time around young and beautiful women and less behind your desk."

"Like the young and beautiful woman you 'hired' to help in the kitchen when you sprained your wrist last summer?" he guessed.

"I wasn't sure you'd even noticed," she admitted.

"How could I not when every time I turned around she was in my way?" he grumbled good-naturedly.

"Maybe she was a little obvious, but I thought if I had to

hire someone, it wouldn't hurt to hire someone who might catch your eye."

"Caridad," he said warningly.

"Your daughter needs more than a nanny—she needs a mother."

The quick stab that went through his heart whenever anyone made reference to Samantha's passing—even a reference as veiled as Caridad's—was no longer a surprise, and no longer quite so painful.

"And in a perfect world, she would still have her mother and I would still have my wife," he stated matter-of-factly. "Unfortunately, this is not a perfect world."

"Four years is a long time to grieve," she said in a gentler tone.

"When Sam and I got married, I promised to love her forever. Is that time frame supposed to change just because she's gone?"

"Unless your vows were different than mine, they didn't require you to remain faithful forever but only 'till death do us part.'"

"Could you ever imagine loving anyone other than Estavan?" he countered.

"No," she admitted softly. "But we have been together forty-one years and I am an old woman now. You are still young—you have many years to live and much love to give."

He glanced at the calendar on his desk. "I also have another quick call to make before lunch."

"Of course, Your Highness." She curtsied again, but paused at the door. "I just have one more thing to say."

He knew it was his own fault. Once he'd opened the door, he had no right to stop her from walking through. "What is it?"

"No one questions how much you loved your wife," she told him. "Just as no one would raise an eyebrow now if you decided it was time to stop grieving and start living again."

He hadn't been with anyone since Sam had died, almost four years ago. And he hadn't been with anyone but Sam for the fourteen years before that. He'd loved his wife for most of his life. After meeting her, he'd never wanted anyone else—he'd never even looked twice at any other woman.

But Caridad was right—Hannah Castillo was beautiful, and he'd found himself looking at her and seeing not just his daughter's new nanny but a desirable woman.

Thankfully the buzz of his BlackBerry prevented him from having to respond to the housekeeper. Acknowledging the signal with a nod, she slipped out of the room, closing the door behind her.

Michael picked up the phone, forcing all thoughts of Hannah from his mind.

Lunch for the adults was pan-seared red snapper served with couscous and steamed vegetables. For Riley, it was chicken nuggets and fries with a few vegetables on the side. She eagerly ate the nuggets, alternately played with or nibbled on the fries and carefully rearranged the vegetables on her plate.

Throughout the meal, Hannah was conscious—almost painfully so—of the prince seated across the table. She'd pretty much decided that she didn't really like him, at least not what she'd seen of him so far, but for some inexplicable reason, that didn't stop her pulse from racing whenever he was near. Remnants of her childhood crush? Or the shallow desires of a long-celibate woman? Whatever the explanation, the man sure did interfere with her equilibrium.

Thankfully, he paid little attention to her, seeming content to make conversation with his daughter. Hannah found it interesting to observe their interaction, noting how alive and animated the princess was with her father. Certainly there was no evidence of the moody child who had banished her from the music room earlier.

"Is there something wrong with your fish?"

Hannah was so caught up in her introspection that it took her a moment to realize that the prince had actually deigned to speak to her. She looked down at her plate now, startled to notice that her meal had barely been touched.

"Oh. No." She picked up her fork, speared a chunk of red snapper. "It's wonderful."

"Are you not hungry?"

She *was* hungry. The muffin and coffee that had been her breakfast en route were little more than a distant memory, and the meal the housekeeper had prepared was scrumptious. But not nearly as scrumptious as the man seated across from her—

She felt her cheeks flush in response to the errant thought. "I'm a little nervous," she finally admitted.

"About seafood?"

The teasing note in his voice surprised her, and the corners of her mouth automatically tilted in response to his question. "No. About being here…with you."

"With me," he echoed, his brows drawing together. "Why?"

"Because you're a prince," she admitted. "And I'm not accustomed to dining with royalty."

"I'm a princess," Riley interjected, lest anyone forget her presence at the table.

"It's only a title," her father told both of them.

"That's easy to say when you're the one with the title," Hannah noted.

"Maybe," he agreed. "But the matter of anyone's birthright seems a strange reason to miss out on a delicious meal."

She scooped up a forkful of vegetables, dutifully slid it between her lips. "You're right—and it is delicious."

She managed to eat a few more bites before she noticed the princess was yawning. "Someone looks like she's ready for a nap," she noted.

"I don't nap," Riley informed her primly. "I have quiet time."

"Right, I saw that on the schedule," Hannah recalled, noting that Brigitte had indicated "nap" in parentheses.

And then, as if on schedule, the little girl yawned again.

"I think you're ready for that quiet time," the prince said, glancing at his watch.

His daughter shook her head. "I want ice cream."

He hesitated.

"Please, Daddy." She looked up at him with her big brown eyes.

"Actually, Caridad said something about crème caramel for dessert tonight," he said, attempting to put off her request.

"I want ice cream now," Riley insisted.

"One scoop or two?" Caridad asked, clearing the luncheon plates from the table.

"Two," the princess said enthusiastically. "With chocolate sauce and cherries."

The housekeeper brought out the little girl's dessert, but as eagerly as the child dug in to her sundae, Hannah didn't believe she would finish it. Sure enough, Riley's enthusiasm began to wane about halfway through, but she surprised Hannah by continuing to move her spoon from the bowl to her mouth until it was all gone.

"Could I please have some more?" Riley asked when Caridad came back out to the terrace, looking up at the housekeeper with the same big eyes and sweet smile that she'd used so effectively on her father.

"You can have more after dinner," the housekeeper promised.

The upward curve of Riley's lips immediately turned down. "But I'm still hungry."

"If you were really still hungry, you should have asked

for some more chicken, not more ice cream," the prince told his daughter.

"I didn't want more chicken," she said with infallible logic.

Hannah pushed away from the table. "Come on, Riley. Let's go get you washed up."

"I'm not a baby—I don't need help washing up."

It seemed to Hannah that the young princess didn't need help with much of anything—certainly not with manipulating the adults in her life, a talent which she had definitely mastered.

But she kept that thought to herself, at least for now.

She didn't want to lose her job on the first day.

"Riley," Michael chastised, embarrassed by his daughter's belligerent response. "Hannah is only trying to help."

"Actually," Hannah interjected, speaking to Riley, "maybe you could help me."

The little girl's eyes narrowed suspiciously. "With what?"

"Finding my way around this place," the new nanny said. "I've only been here a few hours and I've gotten lost three times already. Maybe you could show me where you spend your quiet time."

Riley pushed away from the table, dramatically rolling her eyes as she did so. If Hannah noticed his daughter's theatrics, she chose to ignore them.

"If you'll excuse us, Your Highness," she said.

"Of course." He rose with her, and watched as she followed Riley into the house.

He wasn't pleased by his daughter's behavior, but he didn't know what to do about it. As much as he loved Riley, he wasn't blind to her faults. But the adolescent attitude in the preschooler's body was just one more of the challenges of parenting a gifted child, or so he'd been told. Was Riley's behavior atypical—or did he just not know what was typical for a child of her age?

Surely any four-year-old going through a period of adjustment would need some time, and losing her longtime nanny was definitely an adjustment. He hoped that within a few days, after Riley had a chance to get to know Hannah and settle into new routines with her, her usual sunny disposition would return.

After all, it was a new situation for all of them, and it was only day one.

But as he made his way back to his office, he found himself thinking that he probably missed Brigitte even more than his daughter did. Everything had run smoothly when Brigitte was around.

More importantly, he'd never felt any tugs of attraction for the former nanny like the ones he was feeling now for Hannah.

Chapter Four

According to Brigitte's schedule, Riley's quiet time was from two o'clock until three-thirty. When that time came and went, Hannah didn't worry. She figured the little girl wouldn't still be sleeping if she wasn't tired, and since there wasn't anything else on her schedule until an art class at four-thirty, she opted not to disturb her before then.

Hannah was staring at her laptop screen when she heard, through the open door across the hallway, what sounded like drawers being pulled open and shut. She immediately closed the lid on her computer, wishing she could as easily shut down the shock and betrayal evoked by her father's email announcement.

He'd gotten married, without ever telling her of his plans, without even letting her meet the woman who was now his wife. But she forced herself to push those emotions aside and crossed the hall to the princess's room, a ready smile on her lips, determined to start the afternoon with Riley on a better foot.

Riley didn't smile back. Instead, she scowled again and her lower lip trembled.

"I want Brigitte," she demanded.

"You know Brigitte isn't here," Hannah said, attempting to keep her tone gentle and soothing.

"I want Brigitte," Riley said again.

"Maybe I can help with whatever you need," she suggested.

The young princess shook her head mutinously, big tears welling in her eyes. "It's your fault."

"What's my fault?"

"You made me wet the bed."

Only then did Hannah notice that the little girl wasn't wearing the same dress she'd had on when she'd settled on her bed for quiet time. She was wearing a short-sleeved white blouse with a blue chiffon skirt now, and the lovely pink dress was in a heap on the floor beside her dresser. A quick glance at the unmade bed revealed a damp circle.

"Accidents happen," Hannah said lightly, pulling back the covers to strip away the wet sheet. "It will only—"

"It wasn't an accident," Riley insisted. "It was your fault."

Hannah knew the child was probably upset and embarrassed and looking to blame anyone else, but she couldn't help asking, "How, exactly, is it my fault?"

"You're supposed to get me up at three-thirty—when the big hand is on the six and the little hand is halfway between the three and the four," Riley explained. "But now it's after four o'clock."

She probably shouldn't have been surprised that the child knew how to tell time—that basic skill was hardly on par with speaking foreign languages—and she began to suspect that the next two months with Riley would be more of a challenge than she'd imagined.

"Brigitte would have woke me up," Riley said, swiping at the tears that spilled onto her cheeks.

"*Woken*," Hannah corrected automatically as she dropped the sheet into the hamper beside Riley's closet. "And I know you miss Brigitte a lot, but hopefully we can be friends while I'm here."

"You're not my friend, you're the new nanny, and I hate you."

"I promise that you and I will have lots of fun together this summer. We can go—"

"I don't want to go anywhere with you. I just want *you* to go *away!*" Riley demanded with such fierce insistence that Hannah felt her own eyes fill with tears.

She knew that she shouldn't take the little girl's rejection personally. Despite her extensive vocabulary and adolescent attitude, Riley was only a child, reacting to her feelings of loss and abandonment. But Hannah understood those feelings well—maybe too well, with the news of her father's recent marriage still fresh in her mind—and she hated that she couldn't take away her pain.

"What's going on in here?" a familiar, masculine voice asked from the doorway.

Riley flew across the room and into her father's arms, sobbing as if the whole world had fallen down around her.

The prince lifted her easily. "What's with the tears?"

"I want Brigitte to come back." She wrapped her arms around his neck and buried her face against his throat, crying softly.

He frowned at Hannah over her daughter's head, as if the new nanny was somehow responsible for the child's tears.

"She's feeling abandoned," she told him.

His brows lifted. "Is she?"

She couldn't help but bristle at the obvious amusement in his tone. Maybe she didn't know his daughter very well yet, but she understood at least some of what the little girl was feeling, and she wasn't going to let him disregard the depth of those feelings.

"Yes, she is," she insisted. "She was upset when she woke up and the only person who was anywhere around was me—a virtual stranger."

The prince rubbed his daughter's back in an easy way that suggested he'd done so countless times before. "She'll get used to being here and to being with you," he insisted.

Hannah wished she could believe it was true, but she sensed that the princess would resist at every turn. "Maybe, eventually," she allowed. "But in the meantime, you're the only constant in her life and you weren't around."

"I was only downstairs," he pointed out.

"Behind closed doors."

"If I didn't have other things to deal with, Miss Castillo, I wouldn't have hired you to help take care of Riley for the summer." Now that the little girl had quieted, he set her back on her feet.

Hannah wanted to ask if his business was more important than his daughter, but she knew that it wasn't a fair question. She had to remember that the prince wasn't her own father, and she couldn't assume that his preoccupation with other matters meant he didn't care about the princess.

"You're right," she agreed, watching as Riley went over to her desk to retrieve a portfolio case. "I'm sorry. I just wish this wasn't so difficult for her."

"I get the impression she's making it difficult for you, too."

She hadn't expected he would see that, much less acknowledge it, and she conceded that she may have been a little too quick to judgment.

"I teach *Beowulf* to football players—I don't mind a challenge," she said lightly. "Although right now, the challenge seems to be finding a spare set of sheets for Riley's bed."

"I'll send Caridad up to take care of it," he told her.

"I don't mind," she said, thinking that it would at least

be something useful for her to do. "I just need you to point me in the direction of the linen closet."

Before he could respond, Riley interjected, "I need flowers for my art project."

"Why don't you go outside with Hannah to get some from the gardens?" the prince suggested. "I'm sure she would love to see the flowers."

"Can't you come with me, Daddy?" she asked imploringly.

"I'm sorry, honey, but I have a big project to finish up before dinner."

With a sigh, Riley finally glanced over at Hannah, acknowledging her for the first time since the prince had come into the room.

"I need freesias," she said. "Do you know what they are?"

Hannah smiled. "As a matter of fact, freesias happen to be some of my favorite flowers."

Michael was going to his office to pick up a file when the phone on the desk rang. He'd just tucked Riley into bed and didn't want her to wake up, so he answered quickly, without first bothering to check the display. The moment he heard his mother's voice, he realized his mistake.

"I have wonderful news for you, Michael."

"What news is that?" he asked warily, having learned long ago that her idea of wonderful didn't always jibe with his own.

"Your daughter has been accepted for admission at Charlemagne Académie."

"I didn't even know she'd applied," he said dryly.

Elena huffed out an impatient breath. "I pulled a lot of strings to make this happen, Michael. A little appreciation would not be unwarranted."

"I didn't ask you to pull any strings," he pointed out. "In fact, I'm certain I never mentioned Charlemagne at all."

"Your sister went there—it's a wonderful educational institution."

"Even so, I'm not sending Riley to boarding school."

"Of course you are," Elena insisted. "And while they don't usually accept children as young as five—"

"Riley's not yet four," he interrupted.

His mother paused, as if taken aback by this revelation, but she recovered quickly. "Well, if they could take a five-year-old, they can take a four-year-old."

"They're not taking her at all," he said firmly.

"Be reasonable, Michael. This is the perfect solution to your child-care dilemma."

"There's no dilemma, no reason for you to worry."

"I thought your nanny was leaving."

"Brigitte did leave, and I hired someone new for the summer."

"And what will you do at the end of the summer?" she challenged.

"I'm not worrying about that right now."

"The fall term starts in September."

"I'm not sending my four-year-old daughter away to boarding school in Switzerland."

"The child will benefit from the structure and discipline."

"The child has a name," he pointed out.

"A wholly inappropriate one for a princess," his mother sniffed.

"You've made your opinion on that perfectly clear," he assured her. "But it doesn't change the fact that Riley is her name."

"Getting back to my point—*Riley* will benefit from the structure and discipline at Charlemagne, and you will no longer be burdened—"

"Don't." Though softly spoken, the single word silenced her as effectively as a shout. "Don't you dare even suggest that my daughter is a burden."

"I didn't mean that the chi—that *Riley* was a burden," she hastened to explain. "But that the responsibilities of caring for a young daughter must seem overwhelming at times."

He couldn't deny that was true any more than he could expect his mother to understand that Riley was also the greatest joy in his life, so he only said, "I'll let you know if I change my mind about Charlemagne."

"I really do believe it would be best for Riley and for you," she said.

"I appreciate your concern," he lied.

Elena sighed. "I'll look forward to hearing from you."

Michael began to respond, but she'd already disconnected the call.

He dropped the receiver back in the cradle and went around his desk. Only then did he notice the figure curled up in the oversized wing chair facing the fireplace.

"I beg your pardon, Your Highness." Hannah immediately rose to her feet. "I should have made my presence known, but I didn't have a chance to say anything before the phone rang. Then I wanted to leave and to give you some privacy for your call, but you were blocking the door."

He waved off her apology. "It's okay."

"I really didn't intend to eavesdrop," she assured him. "But for what it's worth, I'm glad you're not planning to send Riley to boarding school."

He shook his head. "I can't believe she would expect me to even consider such a thing."

"She?" Hannah prompted curiously.

"My mother."

Her eyes widened. "That was your mother on the phone?"

He could only imagine how his half of the conversation had sounded to her, and shrugged. "We don't have a traditional parent-child relationship," he said.

Truthfully, there was more apathy than affection between them, especially since his wife had died. Elena had never respected boundaries and had never trusted her children to make their own decisions, and he had yet to forgive her for interfering in his marriage and convincing Sam that it was her wifely duty to provide him with an heir—a decision that had ultimately cost her life.

"Riley's grandmother wanted to send her to Switzerland?" Hannah pressed, apparently unable to get past that point.

"She even pulled strings to ensure she would be accommodated," he said.

"But she's just a child."

"My mother isn't an advocate of hands-on parenting," Michael told her.

Hannah seemed to think about this for a minute, then asked, "Did you go to boarding school?"

He nodded. "My brother and sister and I all did, but not until high school. Before that, we attended Wyldewood Collegiate."

"It would be easy to send her away," she said. "To let someone else assume the day-to-day responsibilities of her care."

"No, it wouldn't," he denied. "It would be the hardest thing in the world."

Hannah's conversation with the prince gave her some unexpected insight into his character and a lot to think about, but she was mostly preoccupied with trying to figure out his daughter. She tried to be patient and understanding, but as one day turned into two and then three, it seemed that nothing she said or did could change the princess's attitude toward her. And if there was one thing Hannah was certain of, it was that the princess's attitude very definitely needed changing.

On Saturday, after Riley had finished her lessons for the day, Hannah decided to take the little girl down to the beach. She'd made a trip into town the day before to get buckets and shovels and various other sand toys, and she was excited to watch Riley play. She should have guessed that the child would be less than enthusiastic about her plans.

"I don't like sand," the princess informed her. "And I get hot in the sun."

"That's why we wear our bathing suits—so we can cool off in the ocean after we play in the sand."

Riley folded her arms over her chest. "You can't make me go."

"Go where?" the prince asked, stepping out of his office in time to catch the tail end of their conversation.

"Hannah's trying to make me go to the beach." She made it sound as if her nanny was proposing a new kind of water torture.

"That sounds like a lot of fun."

The little girl wrinkled her nose, clearly unconvinced. "Will you come with us?"

He hesitated, and Hannah knew he was going to refuse, so she spoke quickly, responding before he did in the hope that it might lessen the sting of his refusal for Riley.

"I'm sure your daddy would love to come if he didn't have important business that needed his attention right now."

"But it's Saturday," Riley said, looking up at him pleadingly.

"Well, in that case," he said, "I could probably play hooky for a couple of hours."

His daughter's eyes lit up. "Really?"

"Sure, just give me a few minutes to change."

While the prince disappeared to don more appropriate beach attire, Hannah made sure that the princess was covered in sunscreen. Although the little girl obviously didn't like having the cream rubbed on her skin, she didn't protest. Apparently she was willing to put up with the process—and even Hannah—so long as she got to go to the beach with her daddy.

Hannah glanced up when she heard his footsteps, and exhaled a quiet sigh of purely female admiration. Over the past week, she'd come to appreciate how good the prince looked in his customary Armani trousers and Turnbull & Asser shirts, but the more formal attire had given her no indication of how muscular and toned he was beneath the clothes. Now he was wearing only board shorts slung low on his hips with a striped beach towel draped across very strong, broad shoulders, and just looking at him made Hannah's knees go weak.

She'd admired him from afar for so many years. As a teen, she'd snipped every photo of him out of newspapers and magazines and created her own personal scrapbook. Back then, she'd never expected that their paths would ever cross again. And now he was only a few feet away from her—almost close enough to touch. In fact, if she took only two steps forward, she could lay her hands on his smooth, tanned chest to feel the warmth of his skin and the beating of his heart beneath her palms. She could—

"Are we ready?" he asked.

"I'm ready, Daddy!"

It was the excitement in the little girl's response that snapped Hannah out of her fantasy and back to the present. She reached down for the bucket of toys, conscious of the warm flush in her cheeks. She should have outgrown her adolescent crush on the prince long ago, but as embarrassing as it was to accept that some of those feelings remained, it was somehow worse to realize that the man she was ogling was her boss. Obviously she had to work on maintaining appropriate boundaries.

"Let's go," she said brightly.

She'd barely taken a dozen steps out the door when she heard a familiar chime. Startled, she turned back to see the prince reaching into the pocket of his shorts.

"You weren't really planning to take your BlackBerry down to the beach, were you?" she asked incredulously.

"I've been waiting to hear back from a new client," he said without apology. And without another word, he turned away and connected the call.

Riley watched him, her big brown eyes filled with disappointment.

Hannah shook her head, acknowledging that while the prince might have a fabulous body and a face worthy of magazine covers, his priorities were completely screwed up.

Then she remembered the telephone conversation she'd overheard and the prince's adamant refusal to send his daughter away to school. Obviously he loved his little girl and wanted to keep her close—so why did he keep himself so distant from her? And why was she so determined to uncover the reason for this contradictory behavior?

Pushing the question from her mind, at least for now, she continued toward the water and the expensive private beach that had been calling to Hannah since her arrival at Cielo del Norte. "Do you want to know one of my favorite things about the beach?" she asked the princess.

The little girl shrugged but trudged along beside her.

"When the waves break against the shore, you can give them your troubles and they'll take them back out to the sea."

"No, they won't," the princess protested.

But instead of her usual confrontational tone, this time the denial was spoken softly, and the quiet resignation in her voice nearly broke Hannah's heart.

"Well, not really," she agreed. "But I'll show you what I mean."

She found a long stick and with it, she wrote in the sand, right at the water's edge: M-A-R-K-I-N-G-T-E-S-T-S.

"I'm a teacher," she explained. "And I love teaching, but I don't like marking tests."

The little girl looked neither interested nor impressed, but she did watch and within a few moments, the movement of the water over the sand had completely erased the letters.

Hannah offered the stick to Riley, to give her a turn. The princess seemed to consider for a moment, then shook her head.

So Hannah wrote again: T-O-F-U. She smiled when the letters washed away.

"What's tofu?" Riley asked.

"Bean curd," Hannah said. "It comes from China and is used in a lot of vegetarian dishes."

Thinking of China made her think of Ian, so she wrote his name in the sand.

"Who's Ian?"

"Someone I thought was a friend, but who turned out not to be. He's in China now."

"Eating tofu?"

She chuckled at Riley's question. "I don't know—maybe he is."

The little princess reached for the stick. She paused with the point of it above the sand, her teeth nibbling on her bottom lip. Finally she began to make letters, carefully focusing on the formation of each one until she spelled out: R-A-M.

"You don't like sheep?"

Riley smiled, just a little. "It's 'Riley Advertising Media.'"

"Your dad's company?"

The little girl nodded.

Hannah frowned as a strange thought suddenly occurred to her. "Did he actually name you after his business?"

Now the princess shook her head. "Riley was my mommy's middle name—because it was her mommy's name before she married my granddad."

"Oh. Well, it makes more sense that you'd be named after your mom than a corporation," Hannah said lightly.

But the little girl was writing in the sand again, this time spelling out: H-A-N-A...

She tried not to take it personally. After all, this game had been her idea, and she should feel grateful that Riley was finally communicating with her, even if she didn't like what she was communicating.

"Actually, my name is spelled like this," she said, and wrote H-A-N-N-A-H in the sand.

Riley studied the word for a moment, and when it washed away, she wrote it again, a little further from the waves this time. "Your name is the same backwards as forwards."

Hannah nodded. "It's called a palindrome."

"Are there other palindromes?"

"There are lots, not just words—" she wrote R-A-C-E-C-A-R in the sand "—but phrases and even complete sentences."

"Do you know any sentences or phrases?" Riley challenged.

N-E-V-E-R-O-D-D-O-R-E-V-E-N.

"That's pretty cool," the princess admitted. Her gaze flickered back toward the house. The prince was pacing on the terrace, his phone still attached to his ear.

She took the stick from Hannah again and wrote D-A-D.

"Good job," Hannah said, then winced when the little girl crossed the word out with so much force the stick snapped.

"Do you want to go back inside?" she asked gently.

Riley shook her head again. "I need to wash off this sand."

Michael had just ended his call when he spotted Hannah and Riley coming out of the water. Obviously he'd missed the opportunity to join them for a swim, and he was as sincerely disappointed as he knew his daughter would be. But as she made her way up the beach with Hannah toward the lounge chairs where they'd left their towels, his attention and his thoughts shifted from his little girl to the woman with her.

He hadn't expected that she would swim in the shorts and T-shirt she'd worn down to the beach. Truthfully, he hadn't even let himself think about what kind of bathing suit she had on beneath those clothes. But it wasn't the bathing suit that snared his attention so much as the delectable curves showcased by the simple one-piece suit of cerulean Lycra.

He didn't feel the phone slip from his fingers until it hit the top of his foot. With a muttered curse, he bent to retrieve the discarded instrument—and smacked his head on the rail coming up again. This time his curse wasn't at all muted.

Rather than risk further bodily injury, he remained where he was, watching through the slats of the railing as the nanny helped Riley dry off. After his daughter's cover-up had been slipped back on, Hannah picked up a second towel and began rubbing it over her own body. From the curve of her shoulders, down slender, shapely arms. From narrow hips, down endlessly long and sleekly muscled legs. Across her collarbone, dipping into the hollow between her breasts.

There was nothing improper about her actions—certainly she wasn't trying to be deliberately seductive. But like a voyeur, he couldn't tear his gaze away.

She tugged her shirt over her head, then shimmied into her shorts, and Michael blew out a long, slow breath, urging the hormones rioting in his system to settle down. But he now knew that, regardless of what she might be wearing, he would forever see the image of her rising out of the water like a goddess.

It was a good thing he would be going out of town for a few days.

Chapter Five

By the time Michael joined his daughter and her new nanny, Riley was packing sand into a long rectangular mold. She glanced up when he lowered himself onto the sand beside her, but didn't say a word. She didn't need to say anything—he could tell by the reproachful look in her big brown eyes that she was displeased with him.

He could handle her quick mood changes and even her temper tantrums, but her evident disappointment cut him to the quick. He was trying his best to be a good father, though it seemed increasingly apparent to him that he didn't know how. Every time he thought he was getting the hang of things, the rules changed.

"Sorry I missed swimming," he said, tugging gently on a lock of her wet hair. "But that was a really important client."

"They're all really important." She turned the mold over and smacked the bottom of it, perhaps a little too hard, with the back of a plastic shovel.

She was right. And she certainly wouldn't be the first person to suggest that he might be too focused on his company. But his work was at least something he understood. In his office, he was competent and capable and completely in charge. With Riley, he often felt helpless and overwhelmed and absolutely terrified that he was going to screw up—as if he hadn't done so enough already.

He glanced over at the nanny, to gauge her interpretation of the stilted exchange with his daughter, but Hannah's eyes were hidden behind dark glasses so that he couldn't tell what she was thinking. He decided he would wait to tell both of them of the meeting that would take him back to the city on Monday.

"What are you making?" he asked Riley instead.

"What does it look like?"

He wasn't pleased by her sarcastic tone, but he knew that she wasn't pleased with him at the moment, either, so he only said, "It looks like a sand castle."

She didn't respond.

"Is it Cinderella's castle or Sleeping Beauty's?" he prompted.

"Uncle Rowan's."

He should have realized that a child who had run through the halls of an authentic castle would be less fascinated by the fairy-tale versions. He should also have realized that she would be as methodical and determined in this task as with any other. Riley didn't like to do anything unless she could do it well. As a result, she quickly grew frustrated with any task she couldn't master.

Though Hannah didn't say anything, she pushed a cylindrical mold toward him with her foot. He let his gaze drift from the tips of her crimson-painted toenails to the slim ankle, along the curve of her slender calf—

She nudged the cylinder again, with a little less patience

this time. He tore his attention away from her shapely legs and picked up the vessel.

"Building a castle is a pretty big project for one person," he said to Riley. "Do you think maybe I could help?"

She just shrugged, so he picked up the small shovel and began filling the receptacle.

"You can't use that sand," she said impatiently, grabbing the mold from him and tipping it upside down to empty it out. "You need the wet stuff, so it sticks together."

She looked to Hannah for verification, confirming that this castle-building knowledge had been recently imparted by the new nanny, and was rewarded by a nod. Then she demonstrated for him—showing him how to pack the container with sand, then turn it over and tap it out again.

There were a few moments of frustration: first when one of the walls collapsed, and again when she realized the windows she'd outlined weren't even. But Michael patiently helped her rebuild the wall and assured her that sand-castle windows wouldn't fall out if they weren't perfectly level. That comment finally elicited a small smile from her, and he basked in the glow of it.

While he remained outwardly focused on the castle-building project, he was conscious of the nanny watching their interactions. He was conscious of the nicely rounded breasts beneath her T-shirt, and of the long, lean legs stretched out on the sand. He noticed that her hair had dried quickly in the sun and that the ends of her ponytail now fluttered in the breeze.

She could have passed for a teenager who'd skipped school to hang out at the beach with her friends, the way she was leaning back on her elbows, her bare feet crossed at the ankles and her face tipped up to the sun. And his immediate physical response to the sexy image was shockingly adolescent.

Dios, it was going to be a long two months. Especially if, as he suspected, he was going to spend an inordinate amount of that time fighting this unexpected attraction to her. On the other hand, the time might pass much more quickly and pleasantly if he *stopped* fighting the attraction. If he reached over right now to unfasten the band that held her hair back in order to slide his hands through the silky mass and tip her head back to taste her—

"Is it okay to dig a moat?" Riley asked, and the fantasy building in his mind dissipated.

He forced his gaze and his attention back to her construction.

"Every castle should have a moat," he assured her.

"Uncle Rowan's doesn't."

"But it should, to protect the princes and princesses inside from ogres and dragons."

She giggled. "Ogres and dragons aren't real, Daddy."

"Maybe not," he allowed. "But a moat is a good idea, just in case."

Riley tipped her head, as if considering, then nodded and began digging.

"What do you think?" he asked Hannah. "Is it worthy of the Sand Castle Hall of Fame?"

"An impressive first effort, Your Highness," she replied, and he knew she wasn't just talking about the construction.

"But I shouldn't quit my day job?" he guessed lightly.

"I don't imagine you would ever consider doing so."

He winced at the direct hit.

"But if you did, you might have a future in castle-building," she relented. "Your spire looks pretty good."

His brows rose. "My spire?"

Her cheeks colored as she gestured to the cone shape on top of the tower he'd built. She was obviously flustered by his innuendo, and he couldn't help but smile at her.

"But your flagpole is crooked," she said, and smiled back at him.

His gaze dropped automatically to her mouth, to the seductive curve of her lips. He wondered if they would feel as soft as they looked, if they would taste as sweet as he imagined. And he thought again about leaning forward to press his mouth to hers, to discover the answers to those questions.

Instead, he straightened the twig that was the castle flag and mused that it had been a long time since he'd shared this kind of light, teasing banter with a woman. A long time since he'd felt the slightest hint of attraction for a woman who wasn't his wife, and what he was feeling for Hannah was more than a hint.

He pushed himself up from the sand and picked up an empty bucket.

"Let's get some water for your moat," he said to Riley.

When the moat was filled and the finished project adequately *ooh*ed and *aah*ed over, they returned to the house. Hannah ran a bath for the princess so that Riley could wash the salt off her body and out of her hair. When she was dried and dressed, the little girl had taken a book and curled up on her bed. Hannah suspected that she would be asleep before she'd finished a single page.

After she'd showered and changed, the nanny ventured back downstairs, looking for Caridad to inquire if the housekeeper needed any help with the preparations for dinner. Hannah was embarrassingly inept in the kitchen but with so much time on her hands, she thought she might start hanging around while Caridad cooked. Even if she didn't learn anything, she enjoyed spending time with the older woman.

Unfortunately, the kitchen was empty when she entered. But more distressing to Hannah than the missing housekeeper was the absence of any suggestion that dinner might be in the oven.

She opened the door and scanned inside, just to be sure. Then she opened the fridge and surveyed the shelves.

"Looking for something?"

She started at the unexpected sound of the prince's voice behind her. When they'd returned to the house, she'd assumed that he would retreat to his office and stay there for the rest of the evening. That was, after all, his pattern.

"Caridad," Hannah said. "I haven't seen her all day."

"Well, I can assure you that you won't find her in either the oven or the refrigerator."

He smiled, to show that he was teasing, and she felt her cheeks flush. She hadn't yet figured out the prince or her feelings for him—aside from the jolt of lust she felt whenever he was in the same room. But as attracted as she was to Prince Michael, she was equally frustrated with the father in him. There were times he was so oblivious to his daughter and her needs that Hannah wanted to throttle him. And then there were other times, such as when he'd reached for his little girl's hand on the beach or when he'd slip into his daughter's room late at night just to watch over her while she slept—as she noticed he did almost every night—that his obvious love and affection for the princess made her heart melt. How could one man be both so distant and so devoted?

And how, she wondered, could one man have her so completely tied up in knots? Because there was no doubt that he did, and Hannah had absolutely no idea how to cope with her feelings.

She tried to ignore them, all too aware that Michael was completely out of her league, not just because he was her boss but because he was a prince. Her short-lived engagement to a British earl had forced her to accept that royals and commoners didn't mix, at least for the long term. Unfortunately, ignoring her feelings for the prince hadn't diminished them in the least.

"She and Estavan have weekends off," Michael continued

his response to her question about Caridad. "Unless I have formal plans for entertaining."

"Oh," Hannah replied inanely, thinking that was another check in the 'good prince' column. She also thought it was great for the housekeeper and her husband—and not so great for a woman whose kitchen expertise was limited to reheating frozen dinners.

"You don't cook, do you?" the prince guessed.

"Not very well," she admitted.

"Then it's a good thing I'm in charge of dinner tonight."

She stared at him. "*You* cook?"

"Why do you sound so surprised?"

"I just can't picture you standing over the stove with a slotted spoon in one hand and your BlackBerry in the other. Your Highness."

Rather than taking offense, he smiled. "You do that a lot, you know."

"What's that?"

"Tack my title on to the end of a reply, as if that might take the sting out of the personal commentary."

"I don't mean to sound disrespectful, Your Highness."

"I'm sure you don't," he drawled. "But getting back to dinner, maybe you could try picturing the stove as a barbecue and the slotted spoon as a set of tongs."

"I should have realized that when you said you could cook what you really meant was that you could grill meat over fire."

"You forgot the 'Your Highness.'"

She smiled sweetly. "Your Highness."

"And at the risk of spoiling your illusions, I will confess that I also make an exquisite alfredo sauce, a delicious stuffed pork loin and a mouthwatering quiche Lorraine."

"But do you actually eat the quiche?" she teased.

"You can answer that question for yourself as it's on the menu for brunch tomorrow."

"And what's on the menu for dinner tonight?" she asked, as curious as she was hungry.

"Steak, baked potato and tossed green salad," he told her.

Her mouth was already watering. "Can I help with anything?"

"You just said that you don't cook."

"Can I help with anything that doesn't involve preparing food over a heat source?" she clarified.

He chuckled. "Do you know how to make a salad?"

"I think I can figure it out."

While Michael cooked potatoes and grilled steaks on the barbecue, Hannah found the necessary ingredients in the refrigerator for a salad. When Riley came downstairs, she gave her the napkins and cutlery and asked her to set them on the table.

The princess did so, though not happily. Obviously she wasn't accustomed to performing any kind of menial chores. And when her father came in with the steaks and potatoes, she looked at the food with obvious distaste.

"Can I have nuggets?"

"Not tonight." The prince had earlier uncorked a bottle of merlot and now poured the wine into two glasses.

"But I want nuggets," Riley said.

"You had nuggets for lunch," Hannah reminded her, and gave herself credit for not adding "almost every day this week."

The little girl folded her arms across her chest. "I want nuggets again."

"If she'd rather have nuggets, I can throw some in the oven," the prince relented.

"Yes, please, Daddy." Riley beamed at him.

Hannah opened her mouth, then closed it again without saying a word.

"Excuse us," he said to his daughter, then caught Hannah's arm and steered her into the kitchen.

"What's the problem with Riley having chicken nuggets?" he demanded.

"I didn't say anything, Your Highness."

"No, you stopped yourself from saying whatever was on your mind," he noted. "And since you didn't seem to have any qualms about speaking up earlier, why are you censoring your comments now?"

"Because I don't want to get fired after less than a week on the job."

"I won't fire you," he promised.

"Then I'll admit that I'm concerned about your willingness to give in to your daughter's demands," she told him. "She's not even four years old, and if you let her dictate what she's going to eat, she might never eat anything but chicken nuggets."

"It's just nuggets."

"No, it's not just nuggets. It's that you always give in to her demands."

"I don't always," he denied.

"And if you give in on all of the little things," she continued, "she'll expect you to give in on the not-so-little things and then, suddenly, you have no authority anymore."

She picked up the salad to carry it to the table, giving the prince a moment to think about what she'd said.

"Where are my nuggets?" Riley demanded when he followed Hannah into the dining room.

"It will take too long to make nuggets now," he said gently. "Why don't you just have what we're having tonight?"

Hannah cut a few pieces of meat from one of the steaks and slid them onto a plate along with half of a baked potato and a scoopful of salad. Although the prince didn't sound as firm as she hoped he would, she gave him credit for at least taking a stand.

The princess scowled at the food when it was set in front of her, then looked straight at Hannah as she picked the plate up and dropped it on the floor.

"Riley!" The prince was obviously shocked by his daughter's behavior.

The little girl, equally shocked by her father's harsh reprimand, burst into tears.

Hannah simply retrieved the broken plate from the floor and scooped up the discarded food to dump it into the garbage. Then she got another plate and prepared it the same way again.

"I want nuggets," Riley said, but her tone was more pleading than demanding now, and tears swam in her big brown eyes.

"Your daddy cooked steak and potatoes. You should at least try that before asking for something else."

Two fat tears tracked slowly down the child's cheeks. "You're mean."

"Because I won't let you have your own way?" Hannah asked.

"Because you told Daddy not to let me have nuggets."

She caught the prince's eye across the table. He looked helpless and confused, and though her heart instinctively went out to him, she felt confident that the situation was of his own making.

"You should sit down and eat your dinner," she suggested quietly.

He sat, but he continued to cast worried glances in his daughter's direction.

"If Riley's hungry, she'll eat," Hannah reassured him.

"I'm hungry for nuggets," the princess insisted.

"You're hungry for power." The retort slipped out before she could clamp her lips together.

Riley frowned at that.

"Don't you think that's a little unfair?" Michael asked.

"No, but I do think your daughter's demands are some-times unreasonable." Hannah finished making up Riley's second plate, but the mutinous look in the little girl's eyes as they zeroed in on the meal warned her that the food was likely destined for the floor again. So instead of setting it in front of her, she put it aside, out of Riley's reach.

Then Hannah deliberately cut into her own steak, slid a tender morsel into her mouth. Riley watched through nar-rowed eyes, her bottom lip quivering. Hannah ate a few more bites of her meal while the child watched, her gaze occasionally shifting to her own plate.

"I'm thirsty," Riley finally announced.

"There's milk in your cup," Hannah told her.

The princess folded her arms across her chest. "I don't want milk."

"Then you can't be very thirsty."

"I want juice," Riley said, and pushed the cup of milk away with such force that it hit Hannah's wineglass, knock-ing the crystal goblet against her plate so that it spilled all over her dinner and splashed down the front of Hannah's shirt.

She gasped and pushed away from the table, but the wine was already trickling down her chest, between her breasts. The prince grabbed his napkin and rounded the table, his gaze focused on the merlot spreading across her top. He squatted beside her chair and began dabbing at the stain.

Hannah went completely still. She couldn't move. She couldn't think. Heck, she couldn't even breathe, because when she tried, she inhaled his distinctly masculine scent and her hormones began to riot in her system. So she sat there, motionless and silent, as he stroked the napkin over the swell of her breasts.

Her blood was pulsing in her veins and her heart was pounding against her ribs, and he was all but oblivious to the effect he was having on her. Or so she thought, until his movements slowed, and his gaze lifted.

His eyes, dark and hot, held hers for a long minute. "I guess I should let you finish that," he said, tucking the linen into her hand.

She only nodded, unable to speak as his gaze dipped again, to where the aching peaks of her nipples pressed against the front of her shirt, as if begging for his attention.

"Or maybe you should change," he suggested, his eyes still riveted on her chest.

She nodded again.

"I want juice!"

Riley's demand broke through the tension that had woven around them. The prince moved away abruptly, and Hannah was finally able to draw a breath and rise to her feet.

"I'll be right back," she said, and retreated as quickly as her still-quivering legs would allow.

Michael sank back into his chair, then turned to face his daughter. He wasn't sure if he was angry or frustrated or grateful, and decided his feelings were probably a mixture of all those emotions—and several others he wasn't ready to acknowledge.

"Well, you've certainly made an impression today," he told Riley.

"I'm thirsty," she said again.

"Hannah gave you milk," he told her, trying to be patient. "And you spilled it all over the table and all over Hannah."

"I don't want milk, I want juice."

"You always have milk with dinner."

"I want juice," she insisted.

Though he had misgivings, he got up to get her drink. As he poured the juice into another cup, Hannah's words echoed in the back of his mind. *If you give in on all of the little things, she'll expect you to give in on the not-so-little things and then, suddenly, you have no authority anymore.*

He knew that she was right, and it irritated him that after less than a week with his daughter, Hannah had a better understanding of the child's needs than he did after almost four years. But the truth was, as much as he wanted to be a good father, he'd felt awkward and uncomfortable in the role from the very beginning. He'd constantly second-guessed everything he said and did around Riley, and whether it was a result of his ineptitude or not he knew Hannah was right: his daughter was turning into a pint-size dictator.

It was as if he was missing some kind of parenting gene— or maybe he'd deliberately suppressed it. When he and Sam got married, he knew that any pregnancy would be high-risk because of her diabetes and accepted that they might never have children. When she got pregnant, he'd been not only surprised but terrified. He knew what kind of risks she was facing, and he'd been so focused on her that he hadn't let himself think about the baby she carried.

Now that baby was almost four years old, the only care-givers she'd ever known were gone, and he'd hired a high school teacher to play nanny while he buried himself in his work, unwilling to even play at being a father. Was it any surprise that his daughter was acting out?

"Where's my juice?" she asked again when he returned to the table empty-handed.

"You can have juice with breakfast," he told her, trying to maintain a patient and reasonable tone.

"Now." She kicked her feet against the table.

"If you don't stop this right now, you'll have to go to bed without anything to eat or drink," Michael warned.

"You can't do that," Riley said, though there was a note of uncertainty in her voice now.

"I can and I will," he assured her.

His heart nearly broke when she started to cry again.

"It's Hannah's fault," she wailed. "She's making you be mean to me."

"Maybe, instead of always looking to blame someone else when you don't get your own way, you should start taking some responsibility for your own actions," he suggested.

She stared at him, completely baffled. He knew it wasn't because she didn't understand what he was saying but because the concept was completely foreign to her—because he had never before let there be consequences for her misbehavior. Instead, he'd made excuses—so many excuses, because she was a little girl without a mother.

While Riley considered what he'd said, Michael tried to tidy up the mess his daughter had made. He used another napkin to mop most of the spilled wine off of Hannah's plate, which made him recall the tantalizing image of the merlot spreading across her shirt, and the round fullness of the spectacular breasts beneath that shirt, and the blood in his head began to flow south.

He scowled as he righted her overturned goblet and refilled it. It had been a long time since he'd become aroused by nothing more than a mental image, and a lot longer since he'd been affected by a mental image of anyone other than Sam. He felt betrayed by his body's instinctive response to this woman, guilty that he could want a woman who wasn't his wife.

He knew that having sex with someone else wouldn't mean he was unfaithful. Sam was gone—he was no longer her husband but a widower. But he'd loved her for so long that even the thought of being with someone else felt like a betrayal of everything they'd shared and all the years they'd been together.

By the time Hannah returned to the table, the steaks and potatoes were cold. He offered to throw her plate in the microwave, but she insisted that it was fine. He didn't bother to heat his own dinner, either. He was too preoccupied wondering about the flavor of her lips to taste any of the food that he put in his mouth.

He'd been so tempted to kiss her. When he'd been crouched down beside her chair, his mouth only inches from hers, he'd very nearly leaned forward to breach the meager distance between them.

He didn't think she would have objected. It might have been a lot of years since he'd sent or received any kind of signals, but he was fairly certain that the attraction he felt wasn't one-sided. He was also fairly certain that he'd never experienced an attraction as sharp or intense as what he felt for Hannah Castillo.

He and Sam had been friends for a long time before they'd become lovers; their relationship had blossomed slowly and rooted deep. What he felt for Hannah was simple lust, basic yet undeniable.

It seemed disloyal to make any kind of comparison between the two women. Sam had been his partner in so many ways and the woman he loved with his whole heart; Hannah was a stranger on the periphery of his life, his daughter's temporary nanny—and the woman with whom he was going to be living in close quarters for the next two months. And he was definitely tempted to take advantage of that proximity.

"Are you hungry now?"

Though she wasn't speaking to him, Hannah's question interrupted his musings. Forcing his attention back to the table, he noticed that Riley was eyeing the plate Hannah had prepared for her, this time with more interest than irritation.

"If you dump it again, you won't have any dinner left," Hannah warned before she set the meal in front of the child.

His daughter immediately picked up a piece of potato and put it in her mouth.

"Use your fork, Riley," Michael said.

She didn't look at him, but she did pick up the fork and

speared a wedge of tomato. It was obvious that she was still angry with him, but at least she was eating. Though he'd tried to sound firm when he'd threatened to send her to bed without any dinner, he wasn't entirely sure he would have been able to follow through on his threat.

When the meal was finally over, Riley had eaten most of her potato and picked at the salad, but she'd adamantly refused to touch the steak.

"Dinner was excellent," Hannah said, pushing her chair away from the table. "Thank you."

"You're welcome," he replied, just as formally.

"I'll clean up the kitchen after I get Riley ready for bed," she told him. "And then, if you've got some time, I'd like to talk to you about a few things."

Michael nodded, though he wasn't certain he wanted to hear what Hannah was going to say. He was even less certain that he should be alone with the nanny without the buffer of his daughter between them.

Chapter Six

Riley had made it clear to her new nanny that she was neither needed nor wanted, and as Hannah finished tidying up
the kitchen after the princess was tucked in bed, she began
to question her true purpose for being at Cielo del Norte.
Maybe she was being paranoid, but when she finally cornered the prince in his office, the first question that sprang
to her mind was "Did my uncle ask you to fabricate a job
for me so that I wouldn't go to China?"

The prince steepled his fingers over the papers on his
desk. "I didn't know anything about your plans to go to
China," he assured her. "And this job is most definitely not
a fabrication."

She had no reason to distrust his response, but she still
felt as if he could have hired a local high school student to do
what she was doing—and for a lot less money. "But Riley's
instructors spend more time with her than I do," she pointed
out to him, "which makes me wonder why I'm even here."

"You're here to ensure that the status quo is maintained."

"Your daughter needs more than a supervisor, Your Highness. And if you can't see that, then I'm wasting my time."

He leaned back in his chair, his brows lifted in silent challenge. "After less than a week, you think you're an expert on what my daughter needs?"

"I don't need to be an expert to know that a child needs love more than she needs lessons," she assured him.

"Riley isn't a typical four-year-old," the prince pointed out.

"Maybe she's not typical, but she is only four."

"She is also both gifted and royal, and she has a lot to learn in order to fulfill the duties and responsibilities that will be required of her in the future."

"In the future," she acknowledged. "But right now, knowing how to make friends is more important than speaking French."

"I disagree."

"I'm not surprised," she said, and couldn't resist adding, "but then, you probably speak impeccable French."

His gaze narrowed. "Is there a point to this conversation, Miss Castillo?"

His tone—undeniably royal-to-servant—gave her pause. She hadn't been sure how far she intended to push, but in light of his apparent refusal to give any consideration to her opinions, she felt that she had no choice but to make him face some hard truths. Even if those truths cost her this job.

"I took Riley into town yesterday afternoon," she said, then hastened to reassure him—though with an undisguised note of sarcasm in her tone—"Don't worry. We weren't gone any longer than the allotted two hours of free time."

"Did Rafe go with you?" he demanded.

She nodded, confirming the presence of the security guard whose job it was to protect the princess whenever she went out in public. Although Riley was young enough to be of little interest to the paparazzi, there was always the possibility of encountering overzealous royal watchers or, worse, a kidnapper.

"Where did you go?"

"To the bookstore."

The furrow between his brows eased. "Riley enjoys visiting the bookstore."

"Right inside the door was a display case for a new book she wanted, but the case was empty. Then Riley spotted another child at the cash register with a copy in her hands. When I told Riley it was probably the last one, she tried to snatch it out of the other girl's hands."

"She is used to getting what she wants when she wants it," he admitted a little sheepishly.

"Because you give her what she wants when she wants it," she pointed out. "And it's turning her into a spoiled brat."

"Miss Castillo!"

She ignored the reprimand, because as angry as he was with her, she was still angrier about Riley's behavior the previous afternoon.

"And when the child counted out her money and realized she was two dollars short, Riley actually smirked at her—until I gave the extra two dollars to the clerk so the other girl could take it home, and then the princess threw a tantrum like I've never seen before."

Michael scrubbed his hands over his face as he considered his response. "Riley's status as a royal combined with her exceptional talents make it difficult for her to relate to children her own age," he finally said.

"Her behavior has nothing to do with her blue blood or superior IQ and everything to do with her sense of entitlement."

"If this arrangement isn't working out for you, maybe we should consider terminating our agreement," he suggested in an icy tone.

She shook her head. "I'm not quitting, and I don't think you really want to fire me."

"I wouldn't bet on that," he warned.

"If you were sincere about wanting someone to help with Riley, then you need me," she told him. "You might not want to admit it, but you do."

His brows rose imperiously. "Do you really think so?"

"I doubt you'd have much difficulty replacing me," she acknowledged. "I'm sure you could find someone who is willing to step in and manage Riley's schedule and defer to her every command, and at the end of the summer, you and your daughter would be exactly where you are now."

"I'm not seeing the downside."

Hannah had never doubted that the princess came by her attitude honestly enough. She forced herself to draw in a deep breath, then let it out slowly. She was a commoner and he was a royal and her bluntness bordered on rudeness, but someone needed to shake up his comfortable little world to make him see the bigger picture—for his sake, and certainly his daughter's.

"The downside is that, if you let this continue, the princess's behavior will be that much more difficult to correct later on," she told him.

"Don't you think you're overreacting to one little incident?"

"If it was only one little incident, I might agree, Your Highness. But you saw how she was at dinner. And I suspect that her behavior has been escalating for a long time."

"Do you really think she knocked your wineglass over on purpose?" His tone was filled with skepticism.

"I believe that she was acting out of frustration, because she's so accustomed to getting her own way that she doesn't know how to cope when she doesn't."

He was silent for a moment, as if he was actually considering her words. And when he spoke, his question gave her hope that he had finally heard what she was saying. "So what am I supposed to do?"

"You need to make some changes." She spoke gently but firmly.

"What kind of changes?" he asked warily.

Before Hannah could respond, his BlackBerry buzzed.

"That's the first one," she said, as he automatically unclipped the device from his belt to check the display.

"It's my secretary. I have to—"

"You have to stop putting your business before your daughter."

"That statement is neither fair nor accurate," he told her, as the phone buzzed again. "There is nothing more important to me than my daughter."

"And yet, when I'm trying to talk to you about her, it's killing you not to take that call, isn't it?"

Even as he shook his head in denial, his gaze dropped to the instrument again.

"Answer the phone, Your Highness." She turned toward the door. "I'll set up an appointment to continue this discussion when it's more convenient for you."

Hannah's words were still echoing in the back of his mind while Michael gathered the files and documents that he needed for his meetings in Port Augustine. He didn't expect her to understand how important his business was, why he felt the need to keep such a close eye on all of the details.

He did it for himself—the business was a way to be self-supporting rather than living off of his title and inheritance, and it was something to keep him busy while his daughter was occupied with her numerous lessons and activities. He also did it for Sam—to ensure that the business they'd built together continued not just to survive but to thrive. And while it did, his sense of satisfaction was bittersweet because his wife wasn't around to celebrate with him.

Ironically, the company's success was one of the reasons that Sam had been anxious to start a family. The business didn't need her anymore, she'd claimed, but a baby would. Michael had assured her that he still needed her, and she'd smiled and promised to always be there for him. But she'd lied. She'd given birth to their daughter, and then she'd abandoned both of them.

He knew that she would never have chosen to leave them, that she would never have wanted Riley to grow up without a mother. But that knowledge had done little to ease his grief, and so he'd buried himself in his work, as if keeping his mind and his hands occupied could make his heart ache for her less.

Except that he rarely did any hands-on work himself anymore, aside from occasional projects for a few of the firm's original clients, his pro bono work for the National Diabetes Association and a few other charitable causes. For the most part, he supervised his employees and worked his connections to bring in new clients. And although he'd claimed that he was too busy to take a two-month vacation, the truth was, he could easily do so and know that his business was in good hands. The knowledge should have filled him with pride and satisfaction, but he only felt…empty.

Truthfully, his greatest pride was his daughter. She was also his biggest concern. After almost four years, he felt as if he was still trying to find his way with her. Their relationship would be different, he was certain, if Sam had been around. Everything would be different if Sam was still around.

Your daughter needs more than a nanny—she needs a mother.

He knew it was probably true. But he had no intention

of marrying again just to give Riley a mother. He had no intention of marrying again, period.

You are still young—you have many years to live, much love to give.

While he appreciated Caridad's faith in him, he wasn't sure that was true. He'd given his whole heart to Sam—and when he'd lost her, he'd been certain that there wasn't anything left to share with anyone else.

Of course, Riley had changed that. He'd never understood the all-encompassing love of a parent for a child until he'd held his baby girl in his arms. And as Riley had grown, so had the depth and breadth of his feelings for her. But knowing what to do with a baby didn't come as instinctively as the loving, and for the first year of her life, he'd relied on Marissa and Brigitte to tend to most of Riley's needs.

And then, just when he'd thought he was getting the hang of fatherhood, he'd realized that Riley needed so much more than he could give her. So he made sure that there were people around to meet her needs—tutors and caregivers—and he turned his focus back to his business.

When he told Hannah about his intended trip back to Port Augustine after lunch on Sunday, she just nodded, as if she wasn't at all surprised that he was leaving. Of course, she probably wasn't. She'd made it more than clear the previous night that she thought he valued RAM above all else. While that wasn't anywhere close to being the truth, he wasn't prepared to walk away from the company, either.

"I'm the president and CEO," the prince reminded her. "Fulfilling those positions requires a lot of work and extended hours at the office."

"I didn't ask, Your Highness," she said evenly.

"No, you'd rather disapprove than understand."

"Maybe because I can't understand why you don't want to spend any time with your daughter," she admitted.

"It's not a question of want."

"Isn't it?" she challenged.

He frowned. "Of course not."

"Because it seems to me that a man who is the president and CEO of his own company—not to mention a member of the royal family—would be able to delegate some of his responsibilities."

"I do delegate," he insisted. "But ultimately, I'm the one who's responsible."

"But it's your wife's name on the door, isn't it?"

"What does that have to do with anything?"

She shrugged. "Maybe nothing. Maybe everything."

"Could you be a little more indecisive?" he asked dryly.

"I just can't help wondering if your obsession with the business isn't really about holding on to the last part of the woman you loved."

"That's ridiculous," he said, startled as much by the bluntness of the statement as the accusation.

"I agree," she said evenly. "Because the business isn't the only part you have left of your wife. It's not even the best part—your daughter is."

"And my daughter is the reason you're here," he reminded her. "So you should focus on taking care of her and not lecturing me."

She snapped her mouth shut. "You're right."

"Especially when you couldn't be more off base."

"I apologized for speaking candidly, but I was only speaking the truth as I see it, Your Highness."

"Then your vision is skewed," he insisted.

"Maybe it is," she allowed.

"The potential client is only going to be in town a few days," he said, wanting to make her understand. "If the meeting goes well, it could turn into a big contract for RAM."

"What would happen if you skipped the meeting?" she challenged. "Or let one of your associates handle it instead?"

"The client specifically asked to deal with me."

"And if you said you were unavailable?"

"We would lose the account," he told her.

"And then what?" she pressed.

He frowned. "What do you mean?"

"Would you miss a mortgage payment? Would the bank foreclose on your home?"

"Of course not, but—"

"But somehow this meeting is more important than the vacation you're supposed to be sharing with your daughter?"

She was wrong, of course. But he could see how it appeared that way, from her perspective.

"The timing of the meeting is unfortunate and unchangeable," he told her, "which is why you're here to take care of Riley in my absence."

"Don't you think it would be better if Riley had more than a week to get to know me before you left?"

"I agree the circumstances aren't ideal," he acknowledged. "But I trust that you can manage for a few days."

That was apparently her job—to manage. While her lack of experience had given her some concern about taking a job as a nanny, Hannah had sincerely looked forward to spending time with the young princess. But the truth was, she spent less time with Riley than did any of the little girl's instructors.

And while she rarely saw the prince outside of mealtimes, their weekend beach outing aside, just knowing he had gone back to Port Augustine somehow made the house seem emptier, lonelier. Or maybe it was the weather that was responsible for her melancholy mood. The day was gray and rainy, Riley was busy with one of her countless lessons, leaving Hannah on her own.

After wandering the halls for a while—she'd spent hours just exploring and admiring the numerous rooms of Cielo del Norte—she decided to spend some time with Caridad.

Although she'd only been at the house for a week, she'd gotten to know the housekeeper quite well and enjoyed talking with her. But Caridad was up to her elbows in dough with flour all over the counters, so she shooed Hannah out of her way.

Hannah felt as if she should be doing something, but when she finally accepted that there was nothing she *had* to do and considered what she *wanted* to do instead, she headed for the library.

It was, admittedly, her absolute favorite space in the whole house. She had always been a voracious reader, and on her first visit to the room she'd been thrilled to find that the floor-to-ceiling bookcases were stocked with an eclectic assortment of materials. There were essays and biographies; textbooks and travel guides; volumes of short stories, poetry and plays; there were leather-bound classics, hardback copies of current bestsellers and dog-eared paperbacks. She spent several minutes just perusing the offerings, until a recent title by one of her favorite thriller writers caught her eye.

She settled into the antique camelback sofa with her feet tucked up under her and cracked open the cover. As always, the author's storytelling technique drew her right in, and her heart was already pounding in anticipation as the killer approached his next victim when a knock sounded on the door.

The knock was immediately followed by the entrance of a visitor and, with a startled gasp, Hannah jumped to her feet and dropped a quick—and probably awkward—curtsy.

"I beg your pardon, Your Highness, you caught me—"

"In the middle of a good book," the princess finished with a smile, as she offered her hand. "I'm Marissa Leandres, Michael's sister."

Of course, Hannah had recognized her immediately. Although the princess kept a rather low profile and wasn't a usual target of the paparazzi, she made frequent public appearances for her favorite charities and causes.

"I recently read that one myself and couldn't put it down," Marissa admitted. "So if I'm interrupting a good part, please tell me so, and I'll take my tea in the kitchen with Caridad."

"Of course not," Hannah lied, because after being banished by the housekeeper, the prospect of actual human company was even more enticing than the book still in her hand.

"Good," the princess said, settling into a balloon-back chair near the sofa. "Because I would love for you to join me, if you have a few minutes to spare."

"I have a lot more minutes to spare than I would have anticipated when I took this job," Hannah admitted.

The other woman's smile was wry. "I guess that means that my brother, once again, chose to ignore my advice."

"What was your advice?"

"To give Riley a break from her lessons, at least for the summer."

"So I'm not the only one who thinks that her schedule is a little over the top for a not-quite-four-year-old?" Even as the words spilled out of her mouth, Hannah winced, recognizing the inappropriateness of criticizing a member of the royal family—and to his sister, no less.

"Please don't censor your thoughts on my account," Marissa said. "And I absolutely agree with you about Riley's schedule. Although, in his defence, Michael believes he is doing what's best for Riley."

"I'm sure he does," she agreed, even if she still disagreed with his decision to leave Cielo del Norte—and his daughter. Thinking of that now, she apologized to the princess. "And I'm sure the prince must not have known of your plans to visit today because he went back to Port Augustine this morning."

Marissa waved a hand. "I didn't come to see him, anyway. I came to meet you. And I would have come sooner, but I've been tied up in meetings at the hospital, trying to get final approval for the expansion of the neonatal department at PACH."

"The Juno Project."

Marissa smiled. "Of course you would know about it—your uncle has been one of my staunchest allies on the board."

"He believes very strongly in what you're doing."

"Don't encourage me," the princess warned. "Because if I start talking about what we want to do, I won't be able to stop, and that really isn't why I'm here."

Another knock on the door preceded Caridad's entrance. She pushed a fancy cart set with a silver tea service, elegant gold-rimmed cups and saucers, and a plate of freshly baked scones with little pots of jam and clotted cream.

"Thank you," Marissa said to the housekeeper. "Those scones look marvelous."

Though she didn't actually smile, Caridad looked pleased by the compliment. "Would you like me to serve, Your Highness?"

"No, I think we can handle it."

"Very well then." She bobbed a curtsy and exited the room, closing the door again behind her.

"She makes that curtsying thing look so easy," Hannah mused. "I always feel like I'm going to tip over."

Marissa smiled as she poured the tea.

"It does take some practice," she agreed. "But I wouldn't worry about it. We don't stand on ceremony too much in my family—well, none of us but my mother. And it's not likely you'll have occasion to cross paths with her while you're here."

The statement piqued Hannah's curiosity, but she didn't feel it was her place to ask and, thankfully, the princess didn't seem to expect a response.

"So how are you getting along with my brother?" Marissa asked, passing a cup of tea to her.

"I don't really see a lot of the prince," Hannah admitted.

"Is he hiding out in his office all the time?"

"He's working in his office all of the time," she clarified.

"He does have the National Diabetes Awareness Campaign coming up in the fall," the princess acknowledged. "He always gives that a lot of time and attention—and pro bono, too."

Her surprise must have shown on her face, because Marissa said, "I know Michael sometimes acts like it's all about making money, but he does a lot of work for charities—Literacy, Alzheimer's, the Cancer Society—and never bills for it."

Hannah knew that his wife had been diabetic, so she should have expected that awareness of the disease was a cause close to his heart, but she hadn't expected to learn that he had such a kind and generous heart.

"I didn't know he did any of that," she admitted.

"Michael doesn't think it's a big deal," the princess confided. "But giving back is important to him. After Sam died…I don't know how much you know about his history, but he went through a really tough time then."

"I can't even begin to imagine," Hannah murmured.

"Neither can I," Marissa confided, "and I was there. I saw how losing her completely tore him apart—nearly decimated him. I tried to be understanding, but I don't think anyone really can understand the magnitude of that kind of grief without having experienced the kind of love that he and Sam shared.

"It took him a long time to see through the fog of that grief—to see Riley. But when he finally did, he put all of his efforts into being a good father to his little girl. He prepared her bottles, he changed her diapers, he played peekaboo."

As hard as Hannah tried, she couldn't imagine the prince

she'd only started to get to know over the past week doing any of those things. While it was obvious that he loved his daughter, it seemed just as obvious to Hannah that he was more comfortable with her at a distance.

"He made mistakes, as all new parents do, but he figured things out as he went along. Then he found out that Riley was gifted, and everything changed."

"Why?"

"Because Michael was just starting to find his way as a father when one of the specialists suggested that Riley would benefit from more structured activities, as if what he was doing wasn't enough. So he asked Brigitte to set up some interviews with music teachers and language instructors and academic tutors, and suddenly Riley's day became one lesson after another. Honestly, her schedule for the past six months has been more intense than mine."

While Hannah doubted that was true, she did think the princess's insight might explain Riley's bed-wetting episode. It wasn't that the little girl was regressing to her toddler habits, just that the signal of her body's need hadn't been able to overcome the absolute exhaustion of her mind.

"I think that's when he started spending longer hours at the office, because he felt like Riley didn't need him."

"I've tried to talk to the prince about his daughter's schedule," Hannah admitted now. "But he seems...resistant."

The princess's brows lifted. "Are you always so diplomatic?"

She flushed, recalling too many times when she'd freely spoken her mind, as if forgetting not just that he was a prince but also her boss. "I'm sure His Highness would say not."

Marissa laughed. "Then I will say that I'm very glad you're here. My brother needs someone in his life who isn't afraid to speak her mind."

"I'm only here for the summer," Hannah reminded her.

"That just might be long enough," Marissa said with a secretive smile.

Hannah didn't dare speculate about what the princess's cryptic comment could mean.

Chapter Seven

It was ten o'clock by the time Michael left the restaurant Tuesday night, but he did so with the knowledge that the prospective clients were going to sign a contract at nine o'clock the following morning. He didn't need to be there for that part of things—he'd done his job, gotten the client's verbal commitment; the rest was just paperwork. The documents had already been prepared by his secretary and the signing would be witnessed by the company vice president, so there was no reason that Michael couldn't head back to Cielo del Norte right now. True, it would be after midnight before he arrived, but he wasn't tired. In fact, the drive would give him a chance to let him unwind.

But for some reason, he found himself following the familiar route toward his home in Verde Colinas.

He unlocked the door but didn't bother turning on any lights as he walked through the quiet of the now-empty house toward his bedroom. It was the bedroom he'd shared with his wife during their twelve-year marriage. Even the bed was the same, and there were still nights that he'd roll over and reach for her—and wake with an ache in the heart that was as empty as his arms.

For months after she'd gone, he could still smell her perfume every time he walked into their bedroom. It was as if her very essence had permeated every item in the room. Each time, the scent had been like a kick to the gut—a constant reminder that while her fragrance might linger, his wife was gone.

He wasn't sure when that sense of her had finally faded, but now he was desperate for it, for some tangible reminder of the woman he'd loved. He drew in a deep breath, but all he could smell was fresh linen and lemon polish.

He stripped away his clothes and draped them over the chair beside the bed, then pulled back the covers and crawled between the cool sheets.

He deliberately shifted closer to Sam's side of the bed, and he was thinking of her as he drifted to sleep.

But he dreamed of Hannah.

The prince had told Hannah that he would probably be away overnight, but he was gone for three days.

At first, despite the nightly phone calls to his daughter, it didn't seem as if Riley was even aware of her father's absence. But then Hannah noticed the subtle changes in the little girl's behavior. She went about her daily routines, but she was unusually quiet and compliant at mealtimes, and she wet her bed both nights. The first morning that Hannah saw the damp sheets in a heap on the floor, she waited for Riley's tirade. But the little girl only asked if she had time to take a bath before breakfast.

By Wednesday, Hannah was desperate for something—anything—to cheer up the little girl. It was the only day of the week that Riley's lessons were finished by lunchtime, so in the morning, she dialed the familiar number of her best friend.

"I'm calling at a bad time," she guessed, when she registered the sound of crying in the background.

"Gabriel's teething," Karen replied wearily. "It's always a bad time."

"Maybe I can help," Hannah suggested.

"Unless you want to take the kid off of my hands for a few hours so I can catch up on my sleep, I doubt it."

"I was actually hoping to take Grace off of your hands for a few hours, but I might be able to handle the baby, too."

She must have sounded as uncertain as she felt, because Karen managed a laugh. "The new nanny gig must be a piece of cake if you want to add more kids to the mix."

"I wouldn't say it's been a piece of cake," Hannah confided. "But I really would appreciate it if Grace could come over and hang out with Riley for a while."

The only response was, aside from the background crying, complete and utter silence.

"Karen?" she prompted.

"I'm sorry. I'm just a little—a lot—surprised. I mean, Grace is a great kid, but she goes to public school."

Hannah laughed. "She is a great kid, and I think it would be great for Riley to play with someone closer to her own age." Although her friend's daughter had just turned six and the princess wasn't quite four, Hannah didn't have any concerns about Riley being able to keep up with Grace. "So—will you come?"

"I'm packing Gabe's diaper bag as we speak," Karen assured her.

"Could you bring some of Grace's toys and games, too?"

"Sure. What does the princess like to play with?"

"That's what I'm trying to figure out," Hannah admitted.

For the first time since Hannah arrived at Cielo del Norte, she felt as if she and Riley had a really good day. Of course, it was really Grace's visit that made the difference for the princess. After Riley got past her initial hesitation about meeting someone new, the two girls had a wonderful time together. They played some board games, made sculptures with modeling clay, built towers of blocks—which Gabe happily knocked down for them—and sang and danced in the music room. The adults observed without interference until Grace suggested playing hide-and-seek, then Karen insisted on limiting their game to only four rooms, to ensure that her daughter didn't wander off too far and get lost.

Hannah was amazed by the transformation of the princess into a normal little girl. And while Karen still looked like she would benefit from a good night of uninterrupted sleep, she thanked Hannah for the invite, insisting that the change of venue and adult conversation were just what she needed to feel human again. For her part, Hannah was happy to have the time with her friend—and thrilled to cuddle with ten-month-old Gabe.

"Did you have fun playing with Grace today?" Hannah asked when she tucked Riley into bed later that night.

The princess nodded. "Her mommy is very pretty."

The wistful tone in her voice made Hannah's heart ache for the little girl who didn't have any memories of her own mother. "Yes, she is," she agreed. "Her mommy is also one of my best friends."

"I don't have a best friend," Riley admitted. "I don't have any friends at all."

"Only because you haven't had a chance to make friends. That will change when you go to school in September."

Riley looked away. "I don't want to go to school."

"Why not?"

The little girl shrugged. "Because I won't know anyone there."

"It can be scary," Hannah admitted. "Going new places,

meeting new people. But it's going to be new for all of the other kids, too."

"Really?"

"Really," Hannah assured her.

"When did you meet your best friend?" Riley wanted to know.

"The first year that I came to Tesoro del Mar to live with my uncle Phillip."

"He's my doctor," Riley said, then her little brow furrowed. "But why did you live with your uncle? Where was your daddy?"

Hannah thought it was telling—and more than a little sad—that Riley didn't ask about her mother. Because, in her experience, it was more usual for little girls to live with their daddies than with both of their parents.

"My daddy lived far away."

"Why didn't you live with him there?"

"I used to," Hannah told her. "Before my mother died."

The princess's eyes went wide. "Your mommy died, too?"

Hannah nodded. "When I was a few years older than you."

"Do you miss her?"

She nodded again. "Even though it was a very long time ago, I still miss her very much."

"I don't remember my mommy," Riley admitted, almost guiltily.

Hannah brushed a lock of hair off of the little girl's forehead. "You couldn't," she said gently, hoping to reassure her. "You were only a baby when she died."

"But I have a present from her."

"What's that?"

The princess pointed to the beautifully dressed silken-haired doll on the top of her tallest dresser. Hannah had noticed it the first time she'd ever ventured into the room, partly because it was so exquisite and partly because it was the only doll the little girl seemed to own.

"I call her Sara."

After the little princess in the story by Frances Hodgson Burnett, Hannah guessed, having seen a copy of the book on Riley's shelf of favorites.

"That's a very pretty name," she said. "For a very pretty doll."

The child smiled shyly. "Daddy said she looks just like my mommy, when she was a little girl. And he put her up there so that she could always watch over me." Then she sighed.

"Why does that make you sad?" Hannah asked her.

"I just think that she must be lonely, because she has no one to play with."

"Are you lonely?"

Riley shook her head, though the denial seemed more automatic than sincere, and her gaze shifted toward the doll again. "There's always a teacher or someone with me."

"You are very busy with your lessons." Hannah took Sara off of the dresser, smoothed a hand over her springy blond curls. The princess watched her every move, seemingly torn between shock and pleasure that her beloved Sara had been moved from her very special place. Hannah straightened the velvet skirt, then adjusted the bow on one of her black boots, and finally offered the doll to Riley.

The child's eyes went wide, and for a moment Hannah thought she might shake her head, refusing the offer. But then her hand reached out and she tentatively touched a finger to the lace that peeked out from beneath the doll's full skirt.

"But maybe you could spend some time with Sara when you're not too busy?"

She nodded, not just an affirmation but a promise, and hugged the doll against her chest.

"And maybe Grace could come back to play another time," Hannah continued.

The last of the shadows lifted from the little girl's eyes. "Do you think she would?"

"I think she'd be happy to." She pulled the covers up to Riley's chin. "Good night."

"'Night," Riley echoed, her eyes already drifting shut.

Hannah switched off the lamp on the bedside table and started to tiptoe out of the room.

"Hannah?"

She paused at the door. "Did you need something?"

There was a slight hesitation, and then Riley finally said, "Daddy sometimes sits with me until I fall asleep."

And as Michael hadn't been home for the past two nights, his daughter was obviously missing him. "I'm not sure when your daddy's going to be home," she admitted, because he never spoke to her when he called except to ask for his daughter and she hadn't felt entitled to inquire about his agenda.

"Could you stay for a while?" Riley asked. "Please?"

"I would be happy to stay," Hannah told her.

The princess's lips curved, just a little. "You don't have to stay long. I'm very tired."

"I'll stay as long as you want," she promised.

Hannah wasn't very tired herself, but the night was so dark and quiet that she found her eyes beginning to drift shut. She thought about going across the hall to her own bed, but she didn't want to tiptoe away until she was certain that Riley wouldn't awaken. So she listened to the soft, even sounds of the little girl's breathing...

Michael had stayed away longer than he'd intended, and he was feeling more than a little guilty about his extended absence. And angry at himself when he finally recognized the real reason behind his absence—he'd been hiding.

His sister would probably say that he'd been hiding from life the past four years, and maybe that was true to a certain extent. But for the past three days, he'd been hiding from something else—or rather some*one* else: Hannah Castillo.

Since she'd moved into Cielo del Norte, she'd turned his entire life upside down. She made him question so many things he'd been certain of, and she made him feel too many things he didn't want to feel.

After two long, sleepless nights alone in his bed in Verde Colinas, he'd accepted that he couldn't keep hiding forever.

Besides, he missed his daughter, and hearing her voice on the phone couldn't compare to feeling the warmth of her arms around his neck.

Whether Hannah believed it or not, Riley was the center of his world. Maybe he spent more hours in his office than he did with his child, but it was the time he spent with her that made every day worthwhile. It was her smile that filled the dark places in his heart with light, and her laughter that lifted his spirits when nothing else could.

Even now, as he tiptoed toward her room, his step was lighter because he was finally home with her.

Of course, being home also meant being in close proximity to Hannah again, but he was confident that he would figure out a way to deal with the unwelcome feelings she stirred inside of him. And anyway, that wasn't something he was going to worry about before morning.

Or so he thought until he stepped into Riley's room and saw her in the chair beside his daughter's bed.

He stopped abruptly, and her eyelids flickered, then slowly lifted.

"What are you doing here?" Though he'd spoken in a whisper, the words came out more harshly than he'd intended.

Hannah blinked, obviously startled by the sharp demand. "Riley asked me to sit with her until she fell asleep."

"I would hope she's been asleep for a while," he told her. "It's after midnight."

"I guess I fell asleep, too."

"You should be in your own bed," he told her.

She nodded and eased out of the chair.

He moved closer, to adjust Riley's covers. As he pulled up the duvet, he noticed that there was something tucked beneath her arm. He felt a funny tug in his belly as he recognized the doll that Sam had bought when she learned that she was having a baby girl.

It was the only thing Riley had that was chosen specifically for her by her mother. Now its dress was rumpled and its hair was in disarray and one of its boots was falling off. He tried to ease the doll from Riley's grasp, but as soon as he tried to wriggle it free, her arm tightened around it. With a sigh of both regret and resignation, he left the doll with his daughter and caught up with Hannah outside of the room.

He grabbed her arm to turn her around to face him. "What were you thinking?" he demanded, the words ground out between clenched teeth.

The nanny blinked, startled by his evident fury, and yanked her arm away from him. "I don't know what you're talking about, Your Highness, but if you're going to yell at me, you might not want to do so right outside of your daughter's bedroom."

He acknowledged her suggestion with a curt nod. "Downstairs."

Her eyes narrowed, and for just a second he thought she would balk at the command. Maybe he wanted her to balk. Her defiance would give him a reason to hold on to his fury, because touching Hannah—even just his hand on her arm—had turned his thoughts in a whole other direction. But then she moved past him and started down the stairs.

She paused at the bottom, as if uncertain of where to go from there.

"My office," he told her.

She went through the door, then turned to face him, her arms folded over her chest. "Now could you please explain what's got you all twisted up in knots?"

"The doll in Riley's bed."

He saw the change in her eyes, the shift from confusion to understanding. Then her chin lifted. "What about it?"

"It's not a toy."

"Dolls are meant to be played with," she told him firmly.

"Not that one."

She shook her head. "You don't even realize what you're doing, do you?"

"What *I'm* doing?" he demanded incredulously, wondering how she could possibly turn this around so that it was his fault.

"Yes, what *you're* doing. You told Riley this wonderful story about how her mother picked out the doll just for her, then you put it on a shelf where she couldn't reach it, so that the only tangible symbol she has of her mother stayed beautiful but untouchable."

He scowled at her. "That's not what I did at all."

"Maybe it's not what you intended, Your Highness," she said in a more gentle tone, "but it's what happened."

He'd only wanted to preserve the gift for Riley so that she would have it forever. But he realized now that Hannah was right, that in doing so he'd ensured that she didn't really have it at all.

He shook his head, the last of his anger draining away, leaving only weariness and frustration. "Am I ever going to get anything right?"

He felt her touch on his arm. "You're doing a lot of things right."

He looked down at her hand, at the long, slender fingers that were so pale against his darker skin, and marveled that she would try to comfort him after the way he'd attacked her. She truly was a remarkable woman. Strong enough to stand up to him, yet soft enough to offer comfort.

"That's not the tune you were singing the last time we discussed my daughter," he reminded her.

Her hand dropped away as one side of her mouth tipped up in a half smile. "I'm not saying that you're doing *everything* right," she teased. "But I do think you have a lot of potential."

"If I'm willing to make some changes," he said, remembering.

She nodded.

"Do you want to talk about those changes now or should we just go up to bed?"

He didn't realize how much the words sounded like an invitation until she stepped back. He didn't realize how tempted he was by the idea himself until he'd spoken the words aloud.

"I meant to say that if you're tired, you can go upstairs to your own bed," he clarified.

"Oh. Of course," she said, though he could tell by the color in her cheeks that she had been thinking of something else entirely. Unfortunately, he couldn't tell if she was intrigued or troubled by the something else.

"I apologize for my poor word choice," he said. "I didn't mean to make you uncomfortable."

"You didn't."

He took a step closer to her, knowing that he was close to stepping over a line that he shouldn't but too tempted by this woman to care. "You didn't think I was propositioning you?"

"Of course not," she denied, though her blush suggested otherwise.

"Why 'of course not'?" he asked curiously.

She dropped her gaze. "Because a man like you—a prince—would never be interested in someone like me."

There was a time when he'd thought he would never be interested in anyone who wasn't Sam, but the past ten days had proven otherwise. Even when he wasn't near Hannah, he was thinking about her, wanting her. He knew that he shouldn't, but that knowledge did nothing to diminish his desire.

"You're an attractive woman, Hannah. It would be a mistake to assume that any man would not be interested."

"You're confusing me," she admitted. "In one breath, you say that you're not propositioning me, and in the next, you say that you find me attractive."

"Actually, my comment was more objective than subjective," he told her. "But while I do think you're a very attractive woman, I didn't hire you in order to pursue a personal relationship with you."

"Okay," she said, still sounding wary.

Not that he could blame her. Because even as he was saying one thing, he was thinking something else entirely.

"In fact, I wouldn't have invited you to spend the summer here if I thought there was any danger of an attraction leading to anything else."

"Okay," she said again.

"I just want you to understand that I didn't intend for this to happen at all," he said, and slid his arms around her.

"What is happening?" she asked, a little breathlessly.

"This," he said.

And then he kissed her.

Chapter Eight

She hadn't anticipated the touch of his lips to hers.

Maybe it was because her head was already spinning, trying to follow the thread of their conversation. Or maybe it was because she would never, in a million years, have anticipated that Prince Michael might kiss her. But whatever the reason, Hannah was caught completely off guard when the prince's mouth pressed against hers.

Maybe she should have protested. Maybe she should have pushed him away. But the fact was, with the prince's deliciously firm and undeniably skillful lips moving over hers, she was incapable of coherent thought or rational response. And instead of protesting, she yielded; instead of pushing him away, she pressed closer.

It was instinct that caused her to lift her arms and link them behind his head, and desire—pure and simple—that had her lips parting beneath the coaxing pressure of his. Then his tongue brushed against hers, and everything inside of her quivered.

Had she ever been kissed like this? Wanted like this? She didn't know; she couldn't think. Nothing in her limited experience had prepared her for the masterful seduction of his lips. And when his hands skimmed over her, boldly sweeping down her back and over her buttocks, pulling her closer, she nearly melted into a puddle at his feet.

She couldn't have said how long the kiss lasted.

Minutes? Hours? Days?

It seemed like forever—and not nearly long enough.

When he finally eased his lips from hers, she nearly whimpered with regret.

Then she opened her eyes, and clearly saw the regret in his.

It was like a knife to the heart that only moments before had been bubbling over with joy. Being kissed by Prince Michael was, for Hannah, a dream come true. But for Prince Michael, kissing her had obviously been a mistake, a momentary error in judgment.

Her hand moved to her mouth, her fingertips trembling as they pressed against her still-tingling lips. Everything inside her was trembling, aching, yearning, even as he was visibly withdrawing.

"I'm sorry." He took another step back. "I shouldn't have done that."

He was right. Of course, he was right. What had happened—even if it was just a kiss—should never have happened. He was Riley's father and her employer. But, even more importantly, he was a prince and she was *not* a princess. She was nobody.

That was a lesson she should have learned years ago, when Harrison Parker had taken back his ring because she didn't have a pedigree deemed suitable by his family. But all it had taken was one touch from the prince, and she'd forgotten everything but how much she wanted him.

How had it happened? One minute they'd been arguing

and in the next he'd claimed that he was attracted to her. Then he'd kissed her as if he really wanted to. And when he'd held her close, his arms wrapped around her, his body pressed against hers, she'd had no doubt about his desire. But then he'd pulled away, making it clear that he didn't want to want her.

Proving, once again, that she simply wasn't good enough.

"Hannah?"

She had to blink away the tears that stung her eyes before she could look at him.

"Are you okay?"

The evident concern in his voice helped her to steel her spine. "I'm fine, Your Highness. It wasn't a big deal."

He frowned, and she wondered—for just a moment—if he might dispute her statement. If maybe he, too, felt that it *had* been a big deal.

But in the end, he only said, "I was way out of line. And I promise that you won't be subjected to any more unwanted advances."

"I'm not worried about that, Your Highness," she said confidently.

And she wasn't.

What worried her was that his kiss hadn't been unwanted at all.

He dreamed of her again.

Of course, this time the dream was much more vivid and real. And when Michael finally awakened in the morning with the sheets twisted around him, he knew that it was his own fault.

He never should have kissed her.

Not just because he'd stepped over the line, but because one simple kiss had left him wanting so much more.

It wasn't a big deal.

Maybe it wasn't to Hannah, but to Michael—who hadn't

kissed anyone but Sam since their first date so many years before—it was.

He didn't feel guilty, not really. His wife had been gone for almost four years, and he knew she would never have expected him to live the rest of his life as a monk. But he did feel awkward. If he was going to make a move on anyone, he should have chosen a woman he would not have to interact with on a daily basis from now until the end of the summer, and especially not an employee.

He winced as he imagined the headlines that a sexual harassment suit would generate, then realized he was probably being paranoid. After all, to Hannah the kiss "wasn't a big deal."

He would just have to make sure that he kept his promise, that absolutely nothing like that ever happened again. And count down the days until the end of the summer.

After Hannah ensured that Riley was wherever she needed to be for her first lesson of the day, she usually returned to the kitchen to enjoy another cup of Caridad's fabulous coffee and conversation with the longtime housekeeper of Cielo del Norte.

But when she approached the kitchen Thursday morning, she could hear that the other woman already had company—and from the tone of her voice, she wasn't too pleased with her visitor.

"This isn't open for discussion," Caridad said firmly.

"But it isn't fair—"

"Whoever said life was supposed to be fair?"

"You never made Jocelyn go to summer school," the male voice argued.

"Because Jocelyn didn't struggle with English Lit."

"She would have if she'd had Mr. Gaffe as her teacher."

"You complained about the teacher you had last year, now you complain about this teacher—maybe the problem isn't the teachers but the student. And maybe you should have paid a little more attention to the lessons and a little less to Serik Jouharian last term."

Based on the dialogue and the tones of their voices, Hannah guessed that Caridad was talking to her son. She knew that the housekeeper and her husband had five children—four girls and, finally, a boy. Kevin was the only one still living at home and, according to Caridad, he was responsible for every single one of her gray hairs.

"The only reason I even passed that course was because Serik was my study partner," the boy told her now.

"Then you'd better pick your study partner as carefully this time."

Hannah peeked around the corner in time to see Caridad kiss her son's cheek, then hand him his backpack. "Now go, so you're not late."

"Serik," Hannah said, as Kevin exited the room. "That's a beautiful name."

"Serik was a beautiful girl. An exchange student from Armenia, and I thanked God when school was done and she went back to her own country." Caridad sighed. "He was so smitten. And so heartbroken when she said goodbye."

"I guess he's at that age."

"The age when hormones lead to stupid?"

Hannah laughed. "He seems like a good kid."

"He is," Caridad admitted. "And smart. He's always got good marks in school, except for English. I thought if he took the next course at summer school, when he only has to focus on one subject, he might do better, but he's done nothing but complain since the course started."

"He's a teenager and it's the summer," Hannah said. "Of course he's going to complain about being stuck in school."

"He says he'd rather be working, and if I let him get a job, he could help pay for his education. But I worry that a job would take time away from his studies, jeopardizing his chances of getting a scholarship."

"I could tutor him," she offered.

"No offense, but I can't imagine that a nanny knows too much about senior English."

"You might have noticed that I don't know too much about being a nanny," she said. "That's because I'm a teacher in my real life."

"Your real life?"

"Well, nothing about this seems real to me." She looked around at the kitchen that was bigger than her whole apartment in the city. "It's as if I've fallen through the rabbit hole."

"Should we call you Alice?"

She smiled. "No. Riley's already confused enough without giving a new name to the new hire."

"So how did an English teacher end up taking a summer job as a royal nanny?"

"Desperation."

"Prince Michael's desperation or your own?"

"Both, I guess. He needed someone who could step in right away while he continues to look for a full-time caregiver, and I needed a job and a place to stay for the summer because I sublet my apartment with the intention of spending the break teaching in China." She shook her head in response to the lift of Caridad's brows. "Don't ask."

"We can't afford a tutor," Caridad admitted. "Prince Michael offered to hire one when he heard that Kevin was struggling, but I couldn't let him do that when he already does so much for us."

"I'm already getting a paycheck, and I really do love to teach."

"I wouldn't feel right—taking something for nothing."

"We could exchange services," Hannah suggested. "Maybe you could teach me to cook?"

"Not likely," the housekeeper said.

Hannah couldn't help but feel disappointed by her response. Cooking lessons would at least give her something to do while Riley was busy with her tutors, but unlike her, Caridad probably had more than enough to keep her busy.

"You don't think you'd have the time?" she guessed.

"I don't think you could learn," the older woman admitted bluntly. "You don't know the difference between browning and burning."

Hannah couldn't deny it was true—not when the housekeeper had asked her to keep an eye on the garlic bread while she put a load of laundry in the wash. All Hannah had to do was take the tray out of the oven when the cheese started to brown. But then Riley had come into the kitchen to get a drink and she'd spilled her juice, and while Hannah was busy mopping up the floor, the cheese was turning from brown to black.

"Don't you think that's a little unfair?" she asked, because she had explained the extenuating circumstances behind the mishap.

"Maybe," Caridad agreed. "But not untrue."

Hannah had to laugh. "No, not untrue," she admitted as she poured herself a fresh cup of coffee. "But is that any reason to let your son struggle?"

The housekeeper hesitated. "It's only the first week. I want to see him at least make an effort before you bail him out."

Hannah and Riley spent the following Saturday afternoon on the beach again, but the prince made no effort to join them. And although the three of them had dinner together, as usual, the prince immediately retreated to his office after the meal was done.

It was Monday before Hannah worked up the nerve to knock on his office door.

She could hear him talking, and she pictured him pacing

in front of his desk with his BlackBerry in hand. It seemed as if it was *always* in hand. His voice rose, as if to emphasize a point, and she took a step back. Maybe she should come back later. Maybe she should forget trying to talk to him at all—or at least choose a different venue for their conversation. The last time she'd been in his office with him was when the prince had kissed her.

Okay, it probably wasn't a good idea to think about that kiss right now. Except that since Wednesday night, she'd barely been able to think about anything else.

She realized that she couldn't hear him talking anymore, and knocked again, louder this time.

"Come in."

She pushed open the door and stepped inside.

He looked up, as if surprised to see her. He probably was. They'd both been tiptoeing around each other for the past several days.

"We never did finish the conversation we started to have about Riley," she reminded him.

"I assumed if there was cause for concern I would hear about it."

"Well, actually, I do have some concerns. Primarily about her eating habits."

"I have lunch and dinner with my daughter almost every day," he said. "Other than her preference for chicken nuggets, I haven't observed any problem."

"I wouldn't say it's a problem," she hedged. "At least not yet."

His brows lifted. "You came in here to talk about something that isn't yet a problem?"

She felt her cheeks flush. "Riley seems to eat a lot for such a young child, and she has dessert after lunch and dinner—every day."

"So?"

"If she continues to eat the way she does now, it won't be

long before she's battling weight and possibly even health issues."

"She's not even four."

She didn't disagree with what he was saying, and it wasn't Riley's weight that worried her. It was the pattern that she could see. She knew there was an easy fix for the problem, but only if the prince agreed to cooperate.

"She eats too much and exercises too little," she said bluntly.

"Should I hire a personal trainer for her?"

"No, Your Highness, you should stop hiring people and start spending time with her."

His brows lifted in silent challenge.

"I know I haven't been here very long," Hannah said. "But I've noticed that you don't interact with Riley very much outside of mealtimes."

"Then maybe you've also noticed that I have a lot of work to do and Riley is busy with her own lessons."

"Yes, I have noticed that, too," she admitted. "And I think that's why Riley is overeating."

"I'm not following."

She hesitated, torn between reluctance to disturb the status quo that obviously mattered to him and determination to open his eyes to some harsh truths. In the end, she decided his relationship with Riley was more important than anything else—her job included.

"The only time Riley sees you throughout the day is at lunch and dinner, so she does everything that she can to extend those mealtimes," she explained. "As soon as her plate is cleared away, you disappear, and I think that she's asking for second helpings so that you stay at the table with her. It's not because she's hungry, but because she's starving for your attention, Your Highness."

His gaze narrowed dangerously. "How dare you—"

"I dare," she interrupted, "because you entrusted Riley

into my care and I'm looking out for her best interests, Your Highness."

"Well, I don't believe it's in my daughter's best interests to put her on a diet."

She was horrified by the very thought. "That isn't what I'm suggesting at all."

"Then what are you suggesting?"

"That you rearrange your schedule to spend a few hours every day with Riley, somewhere other than the dining room."

"You can't be serious," he said, his tone dismissive. "And even if you are, she doesn't have that much time to spare any more than I do."

"Which is the other thing I wanted to talk to you about," she forged ahead before she lost her nerve.

"Go on," he urged, albeit with a decided lack of enthusiasm.

"A four-year-old needs time to play, Your Highness."

"Riley has plenty of time to play."

She shook her head. "She plays the piano, but she doesn't do anything else that a typical four-year-old does—anything just for fun. She paints with watercolors but doesn't know what to do with sidewalk chalk. She doesn't know how to jump rope or hit a shuttlecock, and she's never even kicked a soccer ball around."

"Because she isn't interested in any of those things."

"How do you know?" Hannah asked softly.

He frowned. "Because she's never asked to participate in those kinds of activities."

"Did she ask for piano lessons?"

"No," he admitted. "Not in so many words. But when she sat down and began to play, it was patently obvious that she had a talent that needed to be nurtured."

"And how do you know she's not a potential all-star soccer player if you don't give her the opportunity to try?"

"If she wants to kick a ball around, I have no objections," he said dismissively. "Now, if that's all—"

"No, it's not all," she interrupted. "There's the issue of her French lessons—"

"If there's any issue with her French lessons, you should discuss it with Monsieur Larouche."

"And I suppose I should direct all inquires about her Italian lessons to Signora Ricci and about her German lessons to Herr Weichelt?"

"You're starting to catch on."

She bristled at the sarcasm in his tone. "I thought we were past this already. Why are you acting like you don't care when I know that you do?"

"You're right," he agreed. "I do care—enough that I've hired qualified people to ensure she has everything she needs."

"When we talked the other night—" she felt her cheeks flush and prayed that he wouldn't notice "—you said that you were willing to make some changes. All I'm asking for is a couple of hours of your time every day."

He drummed his fingers on his desk, as if considering. Or maybe he was just impatient for her to finish.

"You said you wanted to get it right," she reminded him. "The only way to do that is to spend time with your daughter. To get to know her and let her get to know you, and that's not going to happen if you insist on keeping nannies and business obligations between you."

"It's the business that allows me to pay your salary," he pointed out to her.

"I'll gladly take a cut in my pay if you promise to give Riley at least two hours."

Once again, Hannah had surprised him. "I don't usually let my employees set the conditions of their employment."

"But this isn't a usual situation, is it?" she countered. "And I know you want what's best for Riley."

How could he possibly argue with that? And truthfully, he didn't want to. Although it was against his better judgment to give in to a woman whom he was beginning to suspect would try to take a mile for every inch he gave her, he wasn't opposed to her suggestion. After all, his time at Cielo del Norte was supposed to be something of a vacation from the daily demands of his company.

It's hardly a vacation if you're working all the time.

He heard Sam's words, her gently chiding tone, clearly in his mind.

It had been a familiar argument, and one that he'd always let her win—because it hadn't been a sacrifice to spend time with the wife that he'd loved more than anything in the world. But Sam was gone now, and without her a vacation held no real appeal. And yet he'd continued to spend his summers at the beach house because he knew that she would be disappointed if he abandoned the tradition. Just as he knew she'd be disappointed if he didn't accede to Hannah's request.

During Sam's pregnancy, they'd had long conversations about their respective childhoods and what they wanted for their own child. Sam had been adamant that their daughter would grow up in a home where she felt secure and loved. She didn't want Riley to be raised by a series of nannies, as he had been raised. Michael had agreed. He had few fond memories of his own childhood—and none after the death of his father—and he couldn't deny that he wanted something more, something better, for Riley. Except that without Sam to guide him, he didn't know what that something more and better could be.

Now Hannah was here, demanding that he spend time with his daughter, demanding that he be the father that Sam would want him to be. And he couldn't—didn't want to—turn away from that challenge. But he had to ask, "How do you know that spending more time with me is what Riley wants or needs?"

"Because you're her father and the only parent she has left," she said simply.

It was a fact of which he was well aware and the origin of all his doubts. He knew he was all Riley had—and he worried that he wasn't nearly enough. And he resented the nanny's determination to make him confront those fears. "Why is this so important to you?" he countered. "I mean, at the end of the summer, you'll walk away from both of us. Why do you care about my relationship with my daughter?"

He saw a flicker of something—sadness or maybe regret—in the depths of her stormy eyes before she glanced away. "Because I want something better for her than to get an email from you twenty years in the future telling her that she has a new stepmother," she finally responded.

Dios. He scrubbed his hands over his face. He'd forgotten that Hannah wasn't just Phillip Marotta's niece but that she'd lived with the doctor since coming to Tesoro del Mar as a child. Obviously there were some unresolved father-daughter issues in her background, and while those issues weren't any of his business, he knew that his relationship with his own daughter *was* his concern. And if Hannah was right about Riley's behavior, he had reason to be concerned.

"Okay," he agreed.

"Okay?" She seemed surprised by his acquiescence.

He nodded and was rewarded with a quick grin that lit up her whole face.

"I'd like to start this afternoon," she told him.

He glanced at his schedule, because it was a habit to do so before making any kind of commitment with respect to his time, and because he needed a reason to tear his gaze away from her mesmerizing smile. She truly was a beautiful woman, and he worried that spending more time with her along with his daughter would be as much torment as pleasure.

"If that works for you," Hannah said, as if she was expecting him to say that it didn't.

"That works just fine," he assured her.

She started for the door, paused with her hand on the knob. "Just one more thing."

"What's that?"

"When you're with Riley, the BlackBerry stays out of sight."

Chapter Nine

When Caridad told her that Monsieur Larouche had called to cancel his morning lesson with Riley, Hannah took it as a positive sign. Not for Monsieur Larouche, of course, and she sincerely hoped that the family emergency wasn't anything too serious, but she was grateful for the opportunity to get Riley outside and gauge her interest in something a little more physical than her usual activities.

Whether by accident or design, Karen had left a few of Grace's toys behind after their visit the previous week, including the little girl's soccer ball. And when Riley's piano lesson was finished, Hannah lured her outside with the promise of a surprise.

The princess looked from her nanny to the pink ball and back again. "What's the surprise?"

"I'm going to teach you how to play soccer."

"Soccer?" Riley wrinkled her nose.

"It's fun," she promised. "And very simple. Basically you

run around the field kicking a ball and trying to put it in the goal."

"I know what soccer is," the child informed her. "I've seen it on TV."

"It's not just on television—it's the most popular sport in the world."

"I don't play sports."

Hannah dropped the ball and when it bounced, she kicked it up to her thigh, then juggled it over to the other thigh, then back down to one foot and over to the other, before catching it again. "Why not?"

"Because I'm a princess," she said.

But Hannah noticed that she was looking at the ball with more curiosity than aversion now. "Oh—I didn't realize that you weren't allowed—"

"I'm allowed," Riley interrupted. "But I have more important things to do."

"Okay," Hannah agreed easily, slipping her foot under the ball and tossing it into the air.

"What does that mean?" the child demanded.

"I'm simply agreeing with you," she said, continuing to juggle the ball between her feet. "Playing soccer isn't important—it's just fun."

"And it's time for my French lesson anyway," the princess informed her, the slightest hint of wistfulness in her voice.

"You're not having a French lesson today."

"But it's Monday. I always have French after piano on Monday."

"Monsieur Larouche can't make it today."

Riley worried her bottom lip, uncomfortable with last-minute changes to her schedule.

"But if you'd rather study than learn to play soccer, you can go back inside and pull out your French books," Hannah assured her.

"Can you teach me how to do that?" Riley asked, mesmerized by the quick movements of the ball.

"I can try." She looked at the girl's pretty white dress and patent shoes. "But first we'd better change your clothes."

As Hannah scanned the contents of the child's closet, then rifled through the drawers of her dressers, she realized that dressing Riley appropriately for outdoor play was easier said than done.

"Who does your shopping?" she muttered.

"My aunt Marissa."

"It's as if she was expecting you to have tea with the queen every day." She looked at the shoes neatly shelved in three rows on the bottom of the closet. There were at least fifteen pairs in every shade from white to black but not a single pair without tassels or bows or flowers.

"Tesoro del Mar doesn't have a queen," the princess informed her primly. "It's a principality."

Hannah continued to survey the child's wardrobe. "Do you even own a T-shirt or shorts? Or sneakers?"

Riley shrugged.

"Well, I think before we get started, we need to find a mall."

"There's a bookstore at the mall," the little girl said, brightening.

"Shorts and shoes first," Hannah insisted. "Then we'll see."

"Maybe we could find a book about soccer," Riley suggested.

Hannah had to laugh. "You're pretty clever, aren't you?"

"That's what my teachers say."

"We'll go shopping after lunch," Hannah promised.

Though Michael didn't believe that Riley was starved for his attention as Hannah had claimed, he did make a point of paying close attention to her behavior at lunch. And he was dismayed to realize that the nanny was right. As soon as he had finished eating and she thought he might leave the table, she asked if she could have some more pasta salad. And after she finished her second helping of pasta salad, she asked for dessert.

"What did you want to do after lunch?" he asked her, while she was finishing up her pudding.

"I have quiet time until four o'clock and then..." The words faded away, and Riley frowned when she saw him shaking his head.

"I didn't ask what was on your schedule but what you wanted to do."

The furrow in her brow deepened, confirming that Hannah hadn't been so far off base after all. His daughter truly didn't know what to do if it wasn't penciled into her schedule.

"Because I was thinking maybe we could spend some time together."

Riley's eyes grew wide. "Really?"

He forced a smile, while guilt sliced like a knife through his heart. Had he really been so preoccupied and neglectful that his daughter was surprised by such a casual invitation?

"Really," he promised her.

"Well, Hannah said we could go shopping after lunch."

He looked at the nanny, his narrowed gaze clearly telegraphing his thoughts: *I agreed to your plan but I most definitely did* not *agree to shopping.*

"Your daughter has an impressive wardrobe that is completely devoid of shorts and T-shirts and running shoes," she explained.

"So make a list of what she needs and I'll send—"

One look at his daughter's dejected expression had him changing his mind.

With an inward sigh, he said, "Make a list so that we don't forget anything."

* * *

After two hours at the mall, with Rafe and two other guards forming a protective circle around the trio of shoppers, Michael noted that Hannah was almost as weary of shopping as he. But they had one more stop before they could head back to Cielo del Norte—the bookstore. He bought her a latte at the little café inside the store and they sat, surrounded by shopping bags, and discreetly flanked by guards, in the children's section while Riley—shadowed by Rafe—browsed through the shelves.

"We got a lot more than what was on the list."

"You said she didn't have anything," he reminded her.

"But she didn't need three pairs of running shoes."

Except that Riley had insisted that she did, showing how the different colors coordinated with the various outfits she'd chosen.

"She gets her fashion sense from my sister," he told her. "One day when we were visiting, Marissa spilled a drop of coffee on her shirt, so she went to find a clean one. But she didn't just change the shirt, she changed her shoes and her jewelry, too."

Hannah laughed. "I probably would have put on a sweater to cover up the stain."

"Sam was more like that," he admitted. "She didn't worry too much about anything. Except official royal appearances—then she would stress about every little detail like you wouldn't believe."

He frowned as he lifted his cup to his lips. He didn't often talk about Sam, not to other people. It was as if his memories were too precious too share—as if by revealing even one, he'd be giving up a little piece of her. And he wondered what it meant—if anything—that he found it so easy to talk to Hannah about Sam now. Was it just that he knew he could trust her to listen and not pass judgment, or was it a sign that he was finally starting to let go of the past and look to the future?

"Well, I should have realized that Riley's closet wouldn't be filled with all those frills and ruffles if it wasn't what she liked," Hannah commented now.

"You weren't into frills and ruffles as a child?"

"Never. And when I was Riley's age…" She paused, as if trying to remember. "My parents were missionaries, so we traveled a lot, and to a lot of places I probably don't even remember. But I think we were in Tanzania then, or maybe it was Ghana. In either case, I was more likely running naked with the native children than wearing anything with bows."

He tried to imagine her as a child, running as wild as she'd described. But his mind had stuck on the word *naked* and insisted on trying to picture her naked now. After having seen the delectable curves outlined by her bathing suit, it didn't take much prompting for his imagination to peel down the skinny straps of sleek fabric to reveal the fullness of creamy breasts tipped with rosy nipples that eagerly beaded in response to the brush of his fingertips. And when he dipped his head—

"Look, Daddy, I found a book about soccer."

Nothing like the presence of a man's almost-four-year-old daughter to effectively obliterate a sexual fantasy, Michael thought.

Then Riley climbed into his lap to show him the pictures, and he found that he didn't regret her interruption at all.

"That's an interesting book," he agreed.

"Can we buy it?"

He resisted the instinct to tell her yes, because he knew from experience that it wouldn't be the only book she wanted and he was trying to follow Hannah's advice to not give her everything she wanted.

"Let me think about it," he told her.

She considered that for a moment, and he braced himself

for the quivering lip and the shimmer of tears—or the hands on the hips and the angry scowl—but she just nodded. "Can you hold on to it while I keep looking?"

"I'll keep it right beside me," he promised.

Hannah watched the little girl skip back to the stacks. "She's so thrilled that you're here," she told him.

"I guess I didn't realize that it took so little to make her happy," he admitted.

"We've already been here longer than the two hours I asked for."

"I'm not counting the minutes," he assured her. "Besides, I'm enjoying this, too."

"Really?"

He chuckled at the obvious skepticism in her tone. "Let's just say, the shopping part wasn't as bad as I'd feared. And this part—" he lifted his cup. "—is a definite pleasure."

"You better be careful," she warned. "Or you just might live up to that potential I was talking about."

He took another sip of his coffee before asking the question that had been hovering at the back of his mind. "Was your father so neglectful?"

"How did my father come into this?" she countered.

But the casual tone of her reply was too deliberate, and he knew that beneath the lightly spoken words was buried a world of hurt.

"I think he's always been there, I just didn't realize it before."

"It's true that my father and I aren't close," she admitted.

"Because he never had enough time for you," he guessed.

"He never had *any* time for me." She cupped her hands around her mug and stared into it, as if fascinated by the ring of foam inside. "I'm not even sure that he ever wanted to be a father," she finally continued, "but my mom wanted a baby and there was no doubt that he loved my mom, and I thought it was enough to know that my mom loved me."

"Until she died," he guessed.

"But then I had my uncle Phillip. He pretty much raised me after she was gone."

"I have to say, he did a pretty good job."

She smiled at that. "He was a wonderful example of what a father should be—of the kind of father I know *you* can be."

He hoped—for Riley's sake even more than his own—that he wouldn't disappoint her.

Despite the new outfit and the proper shoes, it didn't take Hannah long to realize that Riley was never going to be an all-star soccer player. It wasn't just that the child seemed to lack any kind of foot-eye coordination, but that she quickly grew discouraged by her own ineptitude. The more patient and understanding Hannah tried to be, the more discouraged Riley seemed to get.

So after a few days on the lawn with little progress and a lot of frustration, she took Riley into town again so that the little girl could decide what she wanted to try next. The sporting goods store had an extensive selection of everything, and Hannah and Riley—and Rafe—wandered up and down several aisles before they found the racquet sports section.

"I want to play tennis," Riley announced.

Since there was a court on the property, Hannah hoped it might be a better choice for the princess, who immediately gravitated toward a racquet with a pink handle and flowers painted on the frame.

Now she had a half-full bucket of tennis balls beside her with the other half scattered around the court. She'd been tossing them to Riley so that she could hit them with her racquet, with very little success. The child had connected once, and she'd been so startled when the ball made contact with the webbing that the racquet had slipped right out of her hand. But she'd scooped it up again and refocused, her big brown eyes narrowed with determination. Unfortunately, it seemed that the harder she tried, the wider she missed.

The prince would happily have paid for a professional instructor, but Hannah wanted to keep the lessons fun for Riley by teaching the little girl herself. But after only half an hour, neither of them was having very much fun. The more balls that Riley missed the more frustrated she got, and the more frustrated she got the less she was able to focus on the balls coming toward her.

"She needs to shorten her grip."

Hannah looked up to see a handsome teenager standing at the fence, watching them with an easy smile on his face.

"She needs a better teacher," she admitted.

"Kevin!" Riley beamed at him. "I'm going to learn to play tennis just like you."

The boy's brows lifted. "Just like me, huh?"

She nodded. "Hannah's teaching me."

"Trying to, anyway." She offered her hand. "Hannah Castillo."

"Kevin Fuentes," he said.

"Caridad and Estavan's son," she suddenly realized. "I've seen you helping out your dad around the yard." And she'd heard him in the kitchen, arguing with his mother, though she didn't share that information. "So you play tennis?" she queried.

"Every chance I get."

"Caridad says that Kevin's going to get a scholarship," Riley informed her. "But only if he pays attention in class and forgets the pretty girls."

Hannah couldn't help but laugh as the boy's cheeks flushed.

"You have an awfully big mouth for such a little kid," Kevin said, but the reprimand was tempered with a wry smile as he ruffled Riley's hair.

The little kid in question beamed up at him in obvious adoration.

"Do you want me to show her how to adjust her grip?" Kevin asked.

"I'd be extremely grateful," Hannah assured him.

The teenager dropped to his knees on the court beside her.

"I'm going to play just like you," the little girl said again.

"It took me a lot of years of practice." Even as he spoke, he adjusted the position of Riley's grip on the handle of her racquet.

"I'm a fast learner," she assured him.

"You need to learn to be patient," he told her, guiding her arm in a slow-motion demonstration of a ground stroke. "And to let the ball come to you."

He nodded toward Hannah, signaling her to toss a ball.

As soon as the ball left her hand, Riley was trying to reach for it, but Kevin held her back, waiting then guiding her arm to meet the ball.

The fuzzy yellow ball hit the center of the webbing with a soft *thwop,* and Hannah had to duck to avoid being hit by its return. Riley turned to Kevin, her eyes almost as wide as her smile. "I did it."

"You did," he agreed. "Now let's see if you can do it again."

After a few more easy tosses and careful returns, Riley said, "I want to hit it harder."

"You should work on accuracy before power," Kevin told her.

Riley pouted but continued to practice the slow, steady stroke he'd shown her.

"You're a lot better at this than I am," Hannah said, tossing another ball.

He gave a half shrug. "This comes easily to me. Trying

to figure out what Hamlet's actually saying in his infamous 'to be or not to be' speech doesn't."

"It's really not that complicated, although the language of the time can make it seem so," she said, not wanting to delve into the details of the tragic hero's contemplations about suicide in front of a four-year-old.

"And my teacher talks like he was born in Shakespeare's time."

"It can't be that bad," Hannah protested, tossing the last ball.

"It's worse," he insisted. "I have an essay due tomorrow in which I have to decide—in a thousand words—whether or not Hamlet really did love Ophelia."

She couldn't help but smile, thinking that—like most teenage boys—he'd much rather talk about the character's thirst for revenge than any of his more tender emotions. But all she said was, "*Hamlet* has always been one of my favorite plays."

He turned to look at her now, his expression a combination of surprise and disbelief. "Really?"

She shrugged, almost apologetically. "I like Shakespeare."

"Can we do some more?" Riley interrupted to demand.

"First lessons should be short," Kevin told her. "And the lesson's not over until you put all of the balls back in the bucket."

If Hannah had been the one to ask Riley to retrieve the scattered balls, she had no doubt the princess would have refused. But when Kevin spoke, the little girl happily trotted off to do his bidding.

"You're really good with her," Hannah noted.

"She's a good kid."

"Would you be willing to work with her on some other tennis basics some time?"

"Sure," he agreed readily. "It's not like I'm doing much of anything else these days, aside from summer school."

"Speaking of which," she said. "Why don't you bring your essay up to the main house tonight?"

His eyes lit up. "Are you going to fix it for me?"

She laughed. "You're assuming it needs fixing."

"It does," he assured her.

"Then we'll fix it together."

Friday morning after breakfast, Hannah and Riley were working on a jigsaw puzzle in the library when Caridad came in to water the plants. She looked from the little girl to the clock then back again and frowned.

"Signora Ricci is late today," she noted.

"Signora Ricci isn't coming today," Hannah told her.

The housekeeper held a towel beneath the spout of the watering can to ensure it didn't drip as she moved from one planter to the next. "Is she ill?"

"No, she's on vacation."

"She would not have gone on vacation without first arranging a replacement and certainly not without discussing the matter with the prince." The implication being that the prince would then have told her, which of course he would have—if he'd known.

"The vacation was my idea," Hannah admitted. "And more for the benefit of the princess than her teacher."

"You have talked to Prince Michael about this?" the housekeeper prompted.

"I tried, but the prince assured me that any concerns about his daughter's language instruction were best discussed with her instructor."

"I had my doubts," the housekeeper admitted, "when the prince first hired you. But now I think that maybe he knew what he was doing."

"Even if he would disagree?"

Caridad smiled. "Especially if he would disagree."

She finished watering the rest of the plants before she

spoke again. "Kevin said you're helping him with his Shake-speare essay."

"In exchange for him helping Riley learn to play tennis," Hannah explained, remembering their earlier conversation in which the housekeeper had expressed reluctance to accept help for her son without some kind of payment in return.

The housekeeper waved the towel in her hand, obviously satisfied by the exchange of services. "I have no objections," she said. "If you are half as good a teacher as you are a nanny, he will write a good paper."

Only a few weeks earlier, Hannah hadn't been certain that she even wanted to be a nanny, but in all of her years of teaching, she'd never received a compliment that meant as much to her as Caridad's.

Chapter Ten

There were still occasions when Michael had to return to Port Augustine for meetings with clients, but he rarely stayed away overnight. Unfortunately, today's meeting had stretched out longer than he'd anticipated because the client refused to be satisfied with any of the advertisement proposals presented to her.

Michael believed strongly in customer satisfaction, so he suggested that they continue their discussions over dinner. He'd learned that a less formal atmosphere often facilitated a more open exchange of information, but as they shared tapas and wine, he quickly realized that the client had chosen RAM less for the needs of her company and more for her personal interest in him.

He knew that he should be flattered, but truthfully he was growing tired of deflecting unwanted advances. Especially when he'd given her no indication that he was interested in anything more than a business relationship. But as he drove back to Cielo del Norte, he found himself wondering what was wrong with him that he wasn't attracted to an obviously attractive woman. A few weeks ago, he could have argued that he just wasn't ready, that he couldn't imagine himself with anyone who wasn't Sam.

Since Hannah had moved into Cielo del Norte, he'd realized that was no longer true. So why couldn't he be attracted to someone other than Hannah? What was it about his daughter's temporary nanny that had got under his skin?

As a result of his unproductive dinner meeting, he returned to the beach house much later than he'd intended. Not only had he missed hanging out with his daughter during the day, but he was too late to tuck her into bed, as had become their nightly ritual. When he went upstairs to check on her, he found that she was sleeping peacefully with Sara tucked under her arm. He brushed a light kiss on her forehead and her lips curved, just a little, in response to the touch.

He went back downstairs, thinking that he would pour a glass of his favorite cabernet and sit out under the stars for a while. When he approached the kitchen, he heard the sounds of conversation. The soft, smoky tone was definitely Hannah's; the deeper, masculine voice wasn't as familiar.

It occurred to him then that she'd given up her whole life to spend the summer at Cielo del Norte, and in the first month that she'd been in residence, she hadn't asked for any time off to go out. He knew that her friend Karen had visited a few times with her children, because Riley would tell him all about her "best friend" Grace and describe in great detail everything that they'd done together. But it was Hannah's visitor who was on his mind now.

Was the man in the kitchen an old friend? Maybe even a boyfriend? He frowned at the thought. His frown deepened when it occurred to him that there had been no other vehicles in the drive when he'd pulled in.

He paused in the doorway, shamelessly eavesdropping.

"Pay close attention to the characters of both Marlow and

Kurtz," Hannah was saying now. "And which one seems, to you, to be the real hero of the book."

It didn't sound like date conversation to him. On the other hand, he hadn't been on a date in more than sixteen years, so what did he know?

"But can't there be—"

Her guest looked up as he walked into the room, and the boy—Caridad's son, Michael realized with a sense of relief—pushed his chair away from the table to execute an awkward bow. "Your Highness."

He waved Kevin back to his seat. "I didn't realize you were...entertaining," he said to Hannah.

"I didn't realize you were home," she countered.

He noted the books that were open on the table, surrounded by scraps of paper with notes scribbled on them.

"We're working on the outline for Kevin's next assignment," she explained.

Michael surveyed the assortment of bottles in the wine rack, automatically reached for a familiar label. Maybe she did believe she was helping the boy study, but it was obvious to him that Hannah's student was more interested in her than in anything she was trying to explain to him.

"I thought school was out for the summer," he commented.

"For most people," Kevin said. "But my mom decided to torture me with summer school—as if spending ten months in the classroom wasn't already torture enough."

Hannah smiled as she gathered together the loose papers and inserted them into a folder. "Look on the bright side— if you get your credit this summer, you won't have to take another English course until college."

"That's still too soon for me," the boy grumbled.

"I want to see your draft outline by Wednesday," Hannah told him.

"I'll have it ready," he promised. Then he bowed again. "Good evening, Your Highness."

"Good evening, Kevin." He uncorked the bottle of wine. "So how long have you been tutoring my housekeeper's son?"

"It isn't a formal arrangement," she said. "And it doesn't interfere in any way with my taking care of Riley."

"I'm not worried—just curious as to how this arrangement came about, and whether Caridad knows that her son has a major crush on you."

"It came about because Kevin's been helping Riley with her ground stroke, and Caridad knows that his infatuation will be over before he signs his name to his final exam."

"How can she be so sure?"

"Teenage boys are notoriously fickle."

"That's probably true enough," he acknowledged, even as he mentally berated himself for being no less fascinated by the sexy curves outlined by her T-shirt than the teenage boy who had just left.

And no doubt he would have shown more interest in English Lit when he was in school if he'd had a teacher like Hannah Castillo. But all of the teachers at the exclusive prep school he'd attended had been male and seemingly as old as the institution itself.

She finished packing away her notes, then pushed away from the table. "I'm going to go check on Riley."

"I just did." He took two glasses out of the cupboard. "She's sleeping."

"Oh. Okay."

"Come on," he said, heading toward the sliding French doors that led out to the terrace. He bypassed the chairs to sit at the top of the steps, where he could see the moon reflecting on the water.

Hannah had paused just outside the doors, as if reluctant to come any closer. "It's late."

"It's not that late," he chided, pouring the wine. "And it's a beautiful night."

She ventured closer and accepted the glass he offered before lowering herself onto the step beside him. "How was your meeting?"

"I don't want to talk about the meeting." He tipped his glass to his lips, sipped. He didn't even want to think about the time he'd wasted, time he would much have preferred to spend with his daughter—and her nanny. "How did things go with Riley today?"

"I think we're making some real progress."

"I know she's enjoying the tennis lessons," he admitted.

Hannah smiled. "That's more because of Kevin than the game, I think."

He frowned. "Are you telling me that my daughter has a crush on the boy who has a crush on her nanny?"

"It's a distinct possibility," she told him. "At least the part about Riley's feelings for Kevin."

"I should have my brother talk to the Minister of the Environment about testing the water out here," he muttered.

She smiled again. "She's a little girl and he's a good-looking boy who pays her a lot of attention."

"You think he's good-looking?"

"That was hardly the most relevant part of my statement," she said dryly.

"Maybe not," he acknowledged. "But he's also seventeen years old."

"Relax, I don't think she's planning the wedding just yet," she teased.

"I was making the point of his age to you," Michael admitted.

"I know—oh!" She grabbed his arm and pointed. "Look."

Her eyes were wide with wonder as she stared up at the sky, but it was the press of her breast against his arm that snagged his attention.

"I've never seen a shooting star before," she told him.

She was still holding on to his arm, though he wasn't sure if she was conscious of that fact. And while he couldn't deny the quick jolt of lust that went through him, he realized that there was something deeper beneath the surface. A sense of happiness and contentment that came from just sitting here with Hannah. A sense of happiness and contentment that he hadn't felt in a very long time.

"It was right here on this terrace with my dad that I saw my first-ever shooting star," he told her.

She seemed surprised by the revelation, and he realized that she probably was. Over the past couple of weeks, they'd spent a lot of time together and engaged in numerous conversations, but either Riley was with them or was the center of those discussions. He certainly wasn't in the habit of sharing personal details of his own life.

"Did you spend a lot of time here as a kid?" she asked him now.

"Yeah. Although not as much after my dad passed away."

"It was probably hard for your mom, to return to a place with so many memories."

While he appreciated the sympathy in her tone, he knew that her compassion—in this instance—was misplaced. "It wasn't the memories she had trouble with, it was the lack of exclusive boutiques and five-star restaurants."

Hannah seemed puzzled by that.

"Do you know much about my family?" he asked.

"I know that your mother is the princess royal."

"And my father was a farmer."

"I didn't know that," she admitted.

"She claimed that she loved who he was, and then she spent the next fifteen years trying to change him into someone else. Someone better suited to her station."

She didn't prompt him for more information or pry for details, and maybe that was why he found it easy to talk to her. Why he found himself telling her things that he'd never told anyone else before.

"After my dad died, she changed her focus to my brother and I. She had such big plans and ambitions for us."

"I would think she'd be very proud of both of you."

His smile was wry. "She refers to RAM as my 'little company' and despairs that I will ever do anything worthwhile. And even Cameron's position in the prince regent's cabinet isn't good enough, because she wanted him sitting on the throne."

"What were her plans for Marissa?" she asked curiously.

"Lucky for her, my baby sister pretty much flies under Elena's radar."

"How does she manage that?"

"She's female."

Hannah's brows lifted.

"I'm not saying it's right—just that it is what it is. Even though the Tesorian laws were recently changed to ensure equal titles and property would be inherited regardless of gender, she's always believed that it's the men who hold the power.

"I remember how thrilled she was to find out that Sam was expecting—and how disappointed she was when she learned that we were having a daughter. She didn't even pretend otherwise."

"But Riley is such a wonderful little girl," she protested.

"And my mother barely knows her," he admitted. "She's the only grandparent my daughter has, and she doesn't even make an effort to spend time with her."

Not only did Elena not spend time with Riley, the princess royal had suggested sending his little girl away to boarding school, the mere idea of which still made Michael's blood boil.

"She's lucky, then, to have a father who's making such an effort to be part of her life," Hannah told him.

"I missed her today," he admitted, pushing all thoughts of his mother aside. "And I hated not being here to tuck her in."

"She was disappointed, but thrilled when you called from the restaurant to say good-night."

"She said you had a picnic on the beach at lunch."

"I thought it might take her mind off of the fact that you weren't here."

"She sounded as if she really enjoyed it," he said.

Hannah smiled. "She got a bit of a surprise when she threw the crusts of her sandwich away and the gulls swooped in to take them."

"Was she scared?"

"She did shriek at first, but then she was okay. She's already decided that she's keeping the crusts of her toast from breakfast tomorrow so that she can feed them again."

"Then we'll have to make sure we have toast for breakfast," he agreed.

And that was how they ended up on the dock the next morning. Except Hannah noticed that while she and Riley were tossing bread to the birds, the prince had wandered farther back on the dock. After the little girl had tossed the last few pieces to the hungry gulls, Hannah took Riley's hand and guided her back to where her father was standing, with his back to the water and his BlackBerry to his ear.

She put her hands on her hips. "What do you think you're doing?"

Michael stopped in midsentence. "I'm just—"

Before he could finish speaking, she'd grabbed the phone from his hand.

"We had a deal," she reminded him.

And he'd stuck to the deal, which had been a pleasant surprise to Hannah. At least until now. In fact, he'd been so diligent about following the rules that she was prepared to cut him some slack—after she'd made him feel just a little bit guilty.

"I know, but—"

"No phones, Daddy." It was Riley who interrupted his explanation this time, and before he could say anything further, she took the phone from Hannah and flung it over her shoulder.

Hannah gasped as Michael's head whipped around, his gaze following the instrument as it sailed through the air, seeming to tumble end over end in slow motion before it splashed into the ocean.

She knew that Riley had acted on impulse, without any thought about what she was doing or the potential consequences, and that the prince was going to be furious. The only possible way to do damage control was to get Riley to apologize immediately and sincerely. But when Hannah opened her mouth to speak to the little girl, the only sound that came out was a muffled laugh.

"I was in the middle of a conversation with the vice president of a major telecommunications company," the prince informed her.

"You'll have to tell him that your call—" she tried to muffle her chuckle with a cough "—got dropped."

He glowered at her.

"I'm sorry. I know it's not funny…" But she couldn't finish, because she was laughing.

"If you know it's not funny, why are you laughing?" he demanded.

Riley looked from one to the other, measuring her father's stern visage against her nanny's amusement, as if trying to figure out how much trouble she was in.

"I don't know," Hannah admitted. "But I can't seem to stop."

"She threw my BlackBerry into the ocean."

She was turning red from holding her breath, trying to hold in the chuckles.

His eyes narrowed. "You really *do* think it's funny, don't you?"

She shook her head, wanting to deny it. But her efforts were futile.

"Well, then," Michael said. "Let's see if you think this is funny."

She fell silent when he scooped her into his arms, suddenly unable to remember why she'd been laughing. The sensation of being held close in his arms blocked everything else out. Everything but the heat and hardness of his body— the strong arms holding on to her, one at her back and one under her knees; the firm muscles of his chest beneath her cheek. She was tempted to rub her cheek against him and purr like a kitten, inhaling the encitingly spicy scent of the furiously sexy man. Oh, if only he would hold her like this forever—

The thought had barely formed in her mind when she realized that he was no longer holding on to her at all. Instead, she was flying through the air.

The shock of that had barely registered before she hit the water.

She came up dripping and sputtering, obviously as surprised as he had been when Riley had tossed his phone in the water, then she resolutely began to swim back to the dock. Any sense of satisfaction Michael had felt when he sent her on the same journey was gone. In fact, looking at her now as she pulled herself up onto the ladder, he was feeling distinctly unsatisfied. And very aroused.

He stared. He knew it was impolite, but he couldn't help himself. She usually dressed conservatively, keeping her feminine attributes well hidden. But now, with her pale pink T-shirt and white shorts soaked through and plastered to her body, there was no disguising the delicious curves she had tried to hide—or the sexy lace bra that covered her pert, round breasts but couldn't conceal the tight buds of her nipples.

He swallowed, hard.

She was at the top of the ladder now, and he offered his hand to help her up the last step.

She eyed him warily for a moment before she accepted.

Her hand was cool, but the touch heated his blood, and he realized that he was in serious trouble with this woman. Because even now, when he should be angry and amazed, he couldn't deny the attraction between them. An attraction that continued to grow stronger with each passing day.

"All in all, I'd say you fared better than my phone," he noted, trying to maintain some equilibrium.

She shoved a handful of sopping hair over her shoulder and, with obvious skepticism, asked, "How do you figure?"

"Your circuits aren't fried." As his were—or at least in serious danger of doing so.

"Are you going to throw me in the water, too, Daddy?" Riley looked at him with an expression that was half hopeful and half fearful.

"I might," he said, scooping her off of her feet and into his arms.

Riley shrieked and wrapped her arms tight around his neck. "No, Daddy, no."

"But you did a bad thing, throwing my phone into the water," he reminded her. "So there should be some kind of punishment."

She nodded her head, still clinging to him.

"What do you think that punishment should be?"

His daughter wrinkled her nose, as if seriously contemplating an answer to his question, then offered her suggestion. "Maybe no broccoli for me for a month?"

It was all he could do not to laugh himself—because he

knew how much she hated broccoli. "Nice try, Princess, but I think the punishment needs to be a little more immediate than that and more directly linked to the crime."

"An apology?" she suggested. "Because I am very sorry, Daddy."

"That's a good start, but not very convincing."

"Very, very sorry," she said, framing his face in her hands and kissing first one cheek and then the other.

"Much more convincing," he said.

She smiled at him, and it was the kind of smile he hadn't seen on her face in a very long time—a smile full of such pure joy that it actually made his heart ache.

He glanced over her head at Hannah, hoping to telegraph his appreciation to her because he knew that she was responsible for so many changes he'd seen in his daughter in the past few weeks. She was watching them and smiling, too, and he saw that there were tears in her eyes.

Since her first day at Cielo del Norte, Hannah had witnessed more and more examples of the strengthening bond between father and daughter. They'd come a long way in a short while, she realized. From virtual strangers who shared polite conversation across the dinner table to a father and daughter who genuinely enjoyed spending time together.

Watching them together filled her heart with happiness—and more than a little envy. Because as much as she wanted to believe that she'd played a part in bringing them together, her role had been peripheral. She was the outsider, as she'd been the outsider through most of her life.

Even when her uncle Phillip had brought her back to Tesoro del Mar, she'd been conscious of the fact that she didn't really belong. All she'd ever wanted was a home and a family of her own, a place where she was truly wanted and needed. But she'd be a fool to think she could find it here—even for a short while.

But there were moments—rare and precious moments that she knew she would hold in her heart forever—when she truly felt as if she was part of their world. Like when Riley reached for her hand as they walked on the beach. Or when the little girl spontaneously reached up to hug Hannah as she tucked her into bed at night.

She'd known from the beginning that her time with Riley and the prince wouldn't ever be anything more than temporary, but that knowledge hadn't stopped her from falling for the princess. There was simply no way she could have resisted a child who needed so much and somehow gave back so much more.

No, it didn't surprise her at all that the little girl had completely taken hold of her heart. The bigger surprise—and much bigger worry—was that she was very close to falling in love with the princess's father, too.

Chapter Eleven

It was the sound of Riley's screams that had Michael bolting out of his office a few days later. The screams were coming from the tennis courts, and he raced in that direction. Caridad, also summoned by the sound of the little girl's calls, was right behind him.

"Help! Daddy! Help!"

He would have been the first to admit that his daughter had a tendency to melodrama and that she did everything at full volume. But he'd learned to tell from the tone of her cries whether she was sad or frustrated or hurt, and he'd learned to distinguish between playful and fearful shouts. But he'd never heard her scream like this, and the sound chilled him to the bone.

"Someone! Please! Quick!"

As soon as she saw him, her screams turned to sobs. "Daddy, Daddy, you have to help."

He dropped to his knees beside her. "What happened? Where are you hurt?" He ran his hands over her as he spoke, his heart in his throat as he tried to determine the nature of her injury. The way she'd been screaming, he'd sincerely feared that she'd lost a limb or at least broken a bone. But aside from the red face streaked with tears, she appeared to be unharmed, and relief flooded through him like a wave.

"It's n-not m-me," she sobbed. "It's H-han-nah."

By this time, the housekeeper had caught up to them, and he saw that she had gone directly to where Hannah was kneeling on the court. Though the nanny had a hand to her head, she didn't seem to be in any dire straits.

With Riley clinging to his side, he ventured closer.

"I'm fine," he heard her saying, trying to shake Caridad off as she helped her to her feet.

But the older woman was resolute, and as she steered Hannah toward one of the benches along the sidelines of the court, he finally noticed the blood.

He halted abruptly, his stomach clenching.

"I d-didn't m-mean to d-do it," Riley managed between sobs. "It w-was an accid-dent."

He squeezed her gently, trying to reassure her but unable to tear his own gaze away from the crimson blood dripping down the side of Hannah's face.

"You are not fine," Caridad said to Hannah. "And you need to sit down while I get a towel and the antiseptic cream."

He'd yet to meet anyone who could ignore a direct order from the housekeeper when she spoke in that tone, and Hannah was no exception. She sat where Caridad directed.

"Come on, Riley," the housekeeper said. "You can help me find what we need."

Michael knew that Caridad didn't really need Riley's assistance but was trying to distract her from the situation. And Riley was eager to help, obediently falling into step behind the housekeeper. Michael moved over to the bench to check on Hannah.

"I guess that will teach me to walk up behind a little girl with a tennis racquet," she said ruefully.

"Is that what happened?" He kept his tone light, not wanting her to know how badly his insides were shaking. He guessed that she'd been cut right above the eye, because that's where she seemed to be applying pressure, but he couldn't tell for sure.

Hannah managed a smile. "Your daughter has a good set of lungs on her."

"That she does," he agreed.

"I'm sorry about the panic. I was trying to calm her down, but she saw the blood and then just started screaming."

Riley raced over with a neatly folded towel. "This one's for your head," she said, handing one to Hannah. "You're supposed to put pressure on the cut to stop the bleeding. Caridad's bringing the rest of the stuff."

The rest of the stuff turned out to be a washcloth and a basin of warm water, which she used to clean the blood off of the area around the cut, and a first-aid kit, from which she took an antiseptic wipe to dab gently against the wound. Then she instructed Hannah to keep the pressure on and went back inside to finish getting dinner ready.

"There's a lot of blood, Daddy." Riley spoke in an awed whisper.

"Head wounds always bleed a lot," Hannah said, trying to reassure her. "I'll put a Band-Aid on in a few minutes and—"

The prince laid his hand over hers, forcing her to lift the towel so that he could take another look at the gash. The blood immediately began to flow again. "I'm pretty sure it needs more than a Band-Aid."

"I'm sure it doesn't," she insisted.

"You're not a doctor," he reminded her.

"No, but I grew up with one, and he—"

"And he would want you to have this checked out," the prince said firmly.

As it turned out, her uncle Phillip had been at a day conference in San Pedro, so he arrived at Cielo del Norte within an hour of the housekeeper's call. By that time, the bleeding had mostly stopped and Hannah was lying down on a sofa in the library, reading.

Riley was sitting with her, keeping her company while she waited for the doctor to arrive. Despite her repeated assurances that she was okay, the child insisted on staying by her side.

"You only had to call and I would have come to visit," her uncle chided from the doorway. "You didn't need to create all this drama to get me out here."

"I'm having second thoughts about it now," she told him, easing herself back up to sitting position.

"Hi, Doctor Phil," Riley said.

He smiled at the nickname and offered the little girl a lollipop that he took out of his bag. "For after dinner."

She nodded and tucked it into the pocket of her shorts.

Phillip sat down beside his niece. "So how did this happen?"

"I hit Hannah with my racquet," Riley confessed.

"Forehand or backhand?" the doctor asked.

Riley had to think for a minute before answering that one. "Backhand."

"You must have a pretty powerful swing."

"I've been practicing lots," she admitted, sounding torn between pride and regret.

"Okay, let's see what kind of damage you did," he said, moving to examine the wound.

Hannah winced when he tipped her head back.

"Headache?" he asked, all teasing forgotten.

She nodded slowly.

"I'll give you something for that after I stitch this up."

He offered to let Riley stay to watch while he fixed up the wound. The little girl had seemed enthused about the prospect, but as soon as the needle pierced through the skin the first time, she disappeared quickly enough.

"Are you enjoying your job here?" Phillip asked Hannah when Riley had gone.

"Other than today, you mean?"

"Other than today," he agreed with a smile.

"I am," she said. "There was a period of adjustment— for all of us—but I think we've come a long way in a few weeks."

"The young princess seems very taken with you."

"I think she's feeling guilty."

"That could be part of it," he admitted.

Hannah sat patiently while he tied off the sutures, thinking about the little girl.

"I still miss my mom sometimes," she finally admitted.

If her uncle thought it was a strange statement, or one that came from out of nowhere, he gave no indication of it. Instead, he said, "I do, too."

"But I have a lot of memories of the time we spent together. Good memories."

"And Riley has none of her mother," he noted, following her train of thought.

"Do you think that makes it harder for her—because she doesn't have any memories to hold on to?"

"I'm sure there are times when she's conscious of a void in her life, but she seems pretty well-adjusted to me."

"How long do you think someone usually grieves?"

He taped a square of gauze over the sutures. "I'm not sure there's an answer to that question. Each relationship is different, therefore each grieving process is different."

She thought about her father's latest email again—and her

own surprise and anger when she read his note. "I thought my dad would love my mom forever."

"I'm sure he will," her uncle said gently. "But that doesn't mean he couldn't—or shouldn't—fall in love again."

She nodded, but her thoughts were no longer on her parents' relationship or her father's remarriage. "Do you think Prince Michael could fall in love again?"

"I'm sure he could," he said with a slight furrow in his brow. "But I wouldn't want to speculate on when that might happen, and I don't want you to forget that this is only a summer job."

"Don't worry—I have no desire to give up teaching to be a full-time nanny," she assured him.

"That's not what I meant."

"What did you mean?"

"I know you had a crush on the prince when you were younger, and I'm worried that being here may have rekindled those feelings."

"I did have a crush," she admitted. "But it was a childhood infatuation. I didn't know him then, and I didn't even like him when I first came here—he was so distant and reserved."

"And now you've fallen in love with him," he guessed.

She shook her head. "No. I have feelings for him—" deeper feelings than she was ready to admit even to herself "—but I'm smart enough to know that falling in love with a prince could never lead to anything but heartache."

"You're not nearly as smart as you think if you honestly believe that you can control what is in your heart," he warned her.

As Phillip finished packing up his bag, Caridad came in to invite him to stay for dinner. He declined the offer politely, insisting that he wanted to get on his way.

Hannah was sorry to see him go—she had missed him over the past several weeks, but she was also relieved by his departure. Apparently he had shrewder observation skills than she would have guessed, and she was very much afraid he was right. And if she was falling in love with the prince, she didn't want her uncle to be a witness to her folly.

Because she knew that it would be foolish to give her heart to a man who could never love her back because he was still in love with his wife. And she feared that her uncle was right—that loving the prince might not be a matter of choice, and that she already did.

After dinner, Hannah joined the prince and his daughter in the media room to watch a movie. Riley insisted on sitting between them with the bowl of popcorn in her lap, and while the action on the screen kept her riveted for nearly ninety minutes, she did sneak periodic glances at the bandage on Hannah's head to ensure that it wasn't bleeding again.

"Bedtime," the prince told his daughter when the credits began to roll.

"I can't go to bed," she protested. "I have to stay up in case Hannah has a concuss."

"It's *concussion*," Hannah said. "And I don't."

"But what if you do?"

"Doctor Phil checked me over very thoroughly."

"But the medical book says you should be 'specially vigi—" She wrinkled her nose, trying to remember the word.

"Vigilant?" her father suggested.

She nodded. "You should be 'specially vigilant when someone gets hit in the head."

So that was what she'd been doing while Phillip stitched up Hannah's wound—reading up on head injuries.

"I appreciate your concern," she told the little girl. "But I'm really okay—I promise."

"You're not going to die?" The little girl's eyes were wide, her tone worried.

"Not today."

"Does it hurt very much?" The child didn't sound worried so much as curious now.

"Not very much," she said, and it was true now that the acetaminophen her uncle had given her was finally starting to take the edge off of the pain.

"Do you want me to kiss it better?"

Hannah was as surprised as she was touched by the offer. "I think that would make it much better."

Riley leaned forward and very carefully touched her lips to the square of white gauze that had been taped over the wound.

"Okay?"

She nodded.

"You have to kiss it, too, Daddy."

Hannah's panicked gaze met with the prince's amused one.

"It's really much better now," she said to Riley.

"But if one kiss helps, then two should help twice as much," the little girl said logically.

"You can't argue with that," Michael told her.

"I guess not," she agreed.

"Kiss her, Daddy."

So he did. He leaned down and touched his lips gently to her forehead, just above the bandage. It was nothing more than a fleeting touch, barely more than a brush against her skin, but it made everything inside of her melt. Oh yeah, she was definitely falling.

He pulled back, looking into her eyes again. All traces of amusement were gone from his expression now, replaced by an intense awareness that rocked her to her very soul.

"Is that twice as much better?" Riley wanted to know.

Hannah forced a smile. "Twice as much."

"Now that Hannah's boo-boo has been kissed all better, it's bedtime for you," Michael reminded his daughter.

"Will you take me up, Daddy?"

"You bet," he said, and swept her off of her feet and into his arms.

Hannah let out an unsteady breath as they disappeared through the doorway. She felt the tiniest twinge of guilt knowing that she'd lied to the little girl. Because the truth was that the prince's kiss hadn't made anything better, it had only made her desire for him that much harder to ignore.

When Riley was all snug under her covers, Michael kissed her good-night and went back downstairs to find Hannah. He wasn't happy when he found her in the kitchen.

"You're supposed to be resting," he admonished.

"I'm not on my hands and knees scrubbing the floor—I'm just putting a couple of glasses in the dishwasher."

"Nevertheless—" He took her arm and steered her out of the room. "I don't want your uncle mad at me because you weren't following his orders."

"I can't imagine he would hold you responsible."

"And Riley is very concerned about you, too," he reminded her.

She smiled at that. "If I'd known a little cut above my eye would change her attitude toward me, I'd have let her take a swing at me weeks ago."

"I'm not sure that's a strategy I would actually recommend to her next nanny."

He was only responding to her teasing, but his words were a reminder to both of them that the summer was almost halfway over. And when it was done, Hannah would go back to her own life, and he and his daughter would go on with theirs.

Not so very long ago he'd been thinking about the two months he'd planned to spend at Cielo del Norte as an interminable amount of time. Now that the first month had nearly passed, it didn't seem long enough.

Hannah returned to the media room and resumed her

place at one end of the oversize leather sofa. He'd been sitting at the other end earlier, with Riley as a buffer between them, but he sat in the middle now.

She looked at him warily. "Don't you have phone calls to make or projects to complete?"

"It's almost ten o'clock."

"That hasn't seemed to matter on any other night."

She was right. He was in the habit of disappearing back into his office again as soon as he'd said good-night to his daughter. But what Hannah didn't know was that he often just sat behind his desk, doing nothing much of anything except ensuring that he kept a safe and careful distance between himself and the far-too-tempting nanny. And if he was smart, he would have done the same thing tonight, except that he'd made his daughter a promise.

"Riley asked me to keep an eye on you."

"I'm fine," she insisted.

"She made me pinky-swear," he told her.

Her lips curved. "It's sweet of her to worry, but I'm not concussed and I don't need anyone watching over me."

"I know it," he acknowledged. "But Riley seems really concerned."

"A lot of kids are preoccupied by death and dying," she said. "I would guess it's even more usual for a child who's lost someone close."

Somehow he knew that she wasn't just talking about Riley anymore. "How old were you when your mom died?" he asked.

"Eight."

"What happened?"

"There was a malaria epidemic in the village where we were living at the time. I got sick first, and my mom didn't trust that the Swazi doctors knew what they were doing, so she called Phillip. By the time he arrived, I was on my way to recovery, but—" Her gaze shifted away, but not before he caught a glimpse of the moisture in her eyes. "But while she'd been taking care of me, she'd ignored her own symptoms. By the time the doctors realized that she'd been infected, too, the disease had progressed too far."

She tucked her feet up beneath her on the sofa. "I thought my dad blamed me," she confided. "And that's why he sent me away after she died."

"He sent you away?"

"No one admitted that's what happened. Uncle Phillip said that I would be better off in Tesoro del Mar, that traveling from village to village was no kind of life for a child, and my father agreed. But no one had seemed too concerned about that while my mom was alive, and no one seemed to think about the fact that they were sending me away to live with a man I barely even knew."

"I'm sorry, Hannah."

And he was. He couldn't imagine how traumatic it had been for a child who'd just lost her mother to be taken away from her only other parent.

"I'm not. At the time, I was devastated," she admitted. "But now I realize it was the best thing that could have happened. My uncle gave me not just a home, but a sense of stability and security I'd never had before. He was—and is—a constant presence in my life, the one person I know I can depend on above all others."

"Where's your father now?"

"Botswana, I think. At least, that's where his last email came from."

"The one that told you he was getting married again," he guessed.

"How did you know about that?"

"You once told me that you wanted me to work on my relationship with Riley so that she didn't get an email from me telling her that she had a new stepmother."

She winced. "I was upset. The message wasn't that he

was getting married but that he'd already gotten married. He didn't even think to tell me beforehand. And probably the only reason he thought to share the news at all is that they're coming to Tesoro del Mar in the fall and he hopes I'll get a chance to meet her."

"I can see how that would have pulled the proverbial rug out from under you," he admitted.

"But it shouldn't have," she said now. "Because the truth is, I don't know him well enough to be surprised by anything he does. In the past eighteen years, since Uncle Phillip brought me here, I've only seen my father half a dozen times.

"His work has always been more important to him than anything else. And I guess, when you trust that you've been called to a higher mission, it needs to be a priority," she acknowledged. "And I know he believes in what he's doing. He goes to the darkest corners of the world, he sees families living in poverty and he sees children struggling to learn, but he never saw me."

She sighed. "It hurt. For a long time. But I finally realized that he was doing what he needed to do, because the people he helps out need him more than I ever did."

He didn't think it was as simple as that, and he was furious with her father for turning a blind eye to the needs of his child and angry with himself because he'd been doing the same thing to Riley. And he was so very grateful to Hannah for making him see it and helping him to be a better father to his daughter.

"So will you go to meet her—your father's new wife?"

"Probably." Her lips curved just a little.

He lifted a brow, silently inquiring.

"My friend Karen suggested I show up with a husband in tow," she explained.

"Getting married just to make a point seems a little extreme, don't you think?"

"More than a little, but I don't think she was suggesting an actual legal union."

"Have you ever been married?" he asked curiously.

"No."

"Engaged?"

"Haven't we covered enough of my family history for one night?"

He figured that was a *yes,* but decided to respect her wish not to talk about it. At least for now. "So what are we going to talk about for the rest of the night?"

"If you're really determined to hang out here babysitting me, that's your choice, Your Highness. But I'm going to watch some television."

"It's my choice," he agreed. "And it's my TV." And he snapped up the remote before she could.

She narrowed her gaze. "Don't make me wrestle you for it."

"Would you really?" He was certainly willing to let her tackle him. In fact, the more he thought about it, the more intrigued he was by the possibility.

"I would, but I'm supposed to be resting."

Another fantasy ruined, he handed her the remote.

Chapter Twelve

The rain was pouring down when Michael pulled into the drive at Cielo del Norte after a quick trip into town to meet with an old friend. It had been gray and drizzling for the better part of three days, but now the skies had completely opened up.

As he ran through the deluge to the front door, a flash of lightning split the sky, almost immediately followed by a crash of thunder. He winced, knowing how much Riley hated storms. If she was awakened by one in the night, he'd sometimes find her trying to crawl under the covers of his bed, her eyes squeezed tight and her hands pressed against her ears.

Inside, he shook the rain off of his coat and hung it in the closet. From the kitchen, he could smell the mouthwatering scents of roasted pork and sweet potatoes, but it was the music he heard in the distance that drew him down the hall.

Not surprisingly, it was coming from the music room. But

it certainly wasn't Riley practicing piano. In fact, it wasn't anything he had ever heard before. And when he pushed open the door, he saw something that he was certain he'd never seen before.

Riley was dancing—spinning and twirling, with her arms flying and her legs kicking. Hannah was right into the music with her, hips wriggling and body shimmying. And both of them were singing at the tops of their lungs about…he wasn't sure if he was unable to decipher the lyrics or if they just didn't make any sense, but both his daughter and her nanny seemed to know all the words.

He winced at the volume of the music, but he knew there was no way that Riley could hear the thunder over whatever it was that they were listening to—and no way they could have heard him enter the room. So he just leaned back against the wall and enjoyed the show for a few minutes.

One song led into the next, and they continued to sing and laugh and dance, and he continued to watch, marveling at the sheer happiness that radiated from his little girl. He couldn't remember ever seeing her like this—just being silly and having fun, and he realized that Hannah had been right about this, too. His daughter, despite all of her talents and gifts, needed a chance to simply be a child.

Impossible as it seemed, Riley's smile grew even wider when she finally spotted him.

"Look, Daddy! We're dancing!"

While Riley continued to move, Hannah's steps faltered when she realized that she and the child were no longer alone, and he would have bet that the flush in her cheeks was equal parts embarrassment and exertion.

"Don't let me interrupt," he said. "Please."

But she went to the boom box and lowered the volume, at least a little.

He picked up the CD case, looked at the cover, then lifted his brows.

"Grace let Riley borrow it," she told him, then grinned. "In exchange, Riley gave her a copy of Stravinsky's *Rite of Spring.*"

He was suprised to learn that his little girl, who had a profound appreciation for the classics, could find such pleasure in jumping up and down and wiggling her hips to something called *Yo Gabba Gabba,* but he wasn't at all disappointed by the recent changes in her behavior.

"So what precipitated this dance-a-thon?"

"The precipitation," Hannah said, and smiled. "The rain made us give up on the idea of going outside, but Riley had a lot of energy to burn off."

"She's changed so much in only a few weeks," he noted.

"You say that in a way that I'm not sure if you approve or disapprove of the changes," she said uncertainly.

"I approve," he assured her. "I guess I'm still just getting used to it. I would never have said that she was unhappy before—but I've also never seen her as obviously happy as she is now. And to hear her laugh—the sound is so pure and full of joy."

"She's a wonderful little girl," Hannah assured him.

He had to smile, remembering that it hadn't been so long ago that she'd warned him that his daughter was turning into a spoiled brat. But then she'd taken Riley out of the familiar, structured world that she knew and changed all of the rules.

And while there had been a few growing pains in the beginning—and he was sure there would be more to come—he couldn't deny that he was impressed by the results.

"With a real passion for dance," the nanny continued.

Watching his daughter move, he couldn't deny that it was true. She might not have a natural talent, but she certainly had enthusiasm.

"My sister has a friend who—"

"No," Hannah interrupted quickly, then softened her refusal with a smile.

He frowned. "How do you even know what I was going to say?"

"Because I know how your mind works. And Riley doesn't need any more lessons. At least, not yet. Just let her have some fun for a while. And then, if she does want more formal training, enroll her in a class where she can learn along with other kids."

When the current song came to an end, Hannah snapped the music off.

"It's not done," Riley protested. "There's still three more songs."

"How many times has she listened to this CD?" Michael wondered.

"I've lost count," Hannah admitted. Then to Riley she said, "It's almost time for dinner, so you need to go wash up."

The little girl collapsed into a heap on the floor. "I'm too tired."

Michael had to smile. "If you're not too tired to keep dancing, you can't be too tired to twist the taps on a faucet," he said, picking her up off of the floor to set her on her feet. "Go on."

With a weary sigh, the princess headed off.

Hannah took the CD out of the machine and returned it to its case.

"Did you have any formal dance training?" he asked curiously.

She nodded, a smile tugging at the corners of her mouth. "Ballet, because my uncle Phillip was a lot like you in that he wanted to give me every possible opportunity. But after two years, my teacher told him that she couldn't in good conscience continue to take his money when it was obvious that I had less than zero talent."

"She did not say that," Michael protested.

"She did," Hannah insisted. "And truthfully, I was relieved."

"You looked pretty good to me when you were spinning around with Riley."

"We were just having fun."

"Will you dance with me?" he asked her.

She looked up, surprise and wariness in her eyes. "Wh-what?"

He moved to the CD player, pressed the button for the satellite radio—and jumped back when heavy metal screamed out at him. Hannah laughed while he adjusted the volume and scrolled through the preset channels until he found a familiar song.

"This one was at the top of the charts in my first year of college," he told her, and offered his hand.

"I don't recognize it," she admitted.

"Then I won't have to worry about you trying to lead," he teased.

Though she still looked hesitant, she finally put her hand in his.

"You really don't know this song?" he asked, after they'd been dancing for about half a minute.

She shook her head.

"Okay, now I have to ask—how old are you, Hannah?"

"Twenty-six."

Which meant that she was a dozen years younger than he, and while he'd been in college, she'd still been in grade school. But that was a long time ago, and there was no doubt that she was now all grown up. And soft and feminine and undeniably sexy.

He drew in a breath and the scent of her invaded his senses and clouded his mind.

"Hannah—"

She tipped her head back to meet his gaze, and whatever

words he'd intended to say flew out of his mind when he looked into those blue-gray eyes and saw the desire he felt reflected back at him.

He'd been fighting his feelings for her from the beginning, and to what effect? He still wanted her, now more than ever. And if she wanted him, too—and the look in her eyes made him believe that she did—then what was the harm in letting the attraction between them follow through to its natural conclusion?

They were, after all, both adults…but the little girl peeking around the corner was definitely not.

"Caridad said to tell you that it's dinnertime," Riley announced.

Hannah wanted to scream with frustration.

For just a minute, she'd been sure that the prince was going to kiss her again. And his gaze, when it flickered back to her now, was filled with sincere regret.

Regret that they'd been interrupted?

Or regret that he'd almost repeated the "mistake" of a few weeks earlier?

"Thank you for the dance, Hannah," he said formally.

"It was my pleasure, Your Highness."

He lifted her hand to kiss it.

She wanted a real kiss—not some lame fairy-tale facsimile. But then his lips brushed the back of her hand, and she felt the tingles all the way down to her toes.

It wasn't the passionate lip-lock with full frontal contact that she craved, but it wasn't exactly lame, either. And that made her wonder: if a casual touch could wield such an impact, what would happen if the man ever really touched her?

She was almost afraid to find out—and more afraid that she never would.

* * *

The next day, the sun shone clear and bright in the sky. After being cooped up for the better part of three days, Riley was thrilled to get outside and run around. In the morning, Hannah took her for a long walk on the beach. Michael watched from his office as they fed the gulls and wrote messages in the sand, and he wished he was with them.

He tore his attention from the window and back to his work. He was putting the final touches on a project for the upcoming National Diabetes Awareness Campaign, and if he finished it up this morning, then he could spend the whole afternoon with Riley and Hannah.

He wasn't sure when he'd started thinking of Hannah as Hannah and not "Miss Castillo" or his daughter's nanny— or when he'd started looking forward to spending time with her, too. In the beginning, when every step in his relationship with Riley seemed both awkward and tentative, he'd been grateful for her guidance. But somewhere along the line, he'd begun to enjoy her company and thought they might actually be friends. Except that he was still fighting against his body's desire to get her naked.

He pushed that idea from his mind and forced himself to get back to work.

He did finish the project by lunch, and afterward Riley invited him down to the beach to build castles in the sand. It was an offer he couldn't refuse, and he wasn't just surprised but disappointed when Hannah begged off. She claimed to want to catch up on some emails, but he knew that she was really trying to give him some one-on-one time with his daughter.

He appreciated her efforts. After all, she was only going to be with them until the end of the summer, at which time he and Riley were going to have to muddle through on their own—or muddle through the adjustment period with another new nanny. The thought made him uneasy, but he refused to delve too deeply into the reasons why. It was easier to believe that he was concerned about his daughter than to acknowledge that he might actually miss Hannah when she was gone.

After castle-building, they went swimming to wash the sand off, then Riley talked him into whacking some balls around the court with her. Hannah had told him that Riley was learning a lot from Kevin, and he was pleased to see that it was true. By the time they were finished on the court, he noticed that Hannah had come outside and was sitting on one of the lounge chairs on the terrace.

Riley spotted her at almost the same moment, and she went racing ahead. By the time Michael had reached the bottom step, his daughter was already at the top. Then she climbed right up into her nanny's lap and rested her head against her shoulder.

"It looks like you wore her out on the tennis court," Hannah said to him.

"She's had a busy day," he noted, dropping down onto the edge of the other chair.

Riley nodded her head, her eyes already starting to drift shut. "I'm ready for quiet time now."

Hannah smiled at his daughter's code word for "nap." "Quiet time's okay," she agreed. "But you can't fall asleep because it's going to be time for dinner soon."

The little girl yawned. "I'm not hungry."

"Caridad was making lasagna," Michael reminded her. "And that's one of your favorites."

"Is Hannah going to burn the garlic bread again?"

The nanny sighed. "I'm never going to live that down, am I?"

His daughter giggled.

"Well, in answer to your question, I can promise you that I am *not* going to burn the garlic bread because Caridad won't let me in the kitchen while she's cooking anymore."

"I'm glad," Riley said. "Because if you were helping her cook, you couldn't be here with me."

Hannah's lips curved as the little girl snuggled against her, but the smile faltered as she caught Michael's gaze.

"Is something wrong?" she asked quietly.

"What?" He realized he was scowling, shook his head. "No."

But he could tell that she was unconvinced, and he couldn't blame her. Because the truth was, *everything* about this situation was wrong.

She shouldn't be there. She shouldn't be on *that* chair on *this* deck cuddling with his daughter. That was *Sam's* chair—he'd painted it that particularly garish shade of lime green because Sam had thought it was a fun color. And this was *their* special place—where they used to come to escape the craziness of the world together. And Riley was *their* little girl—the child that his wife had given her life to bring into the world.

He felt a pang in his chest. Caridad was right—Riley needed more than a nanny, she needed her mother. But that was something he couldn't give her. Sam was gone. Forever.

He thought he'd accepted that fact. After almost four years, he should have accepted it. During that entire time, while he'd gone through the motions of living, he'd been confident that Riley was in good hands with Brigitte, and he'd been comfortable with his daughter's relationship with her nanny.

So why did it seem so different when that nanny was someone else? Why did seeing his daughter with Hannah seem so wrong? Or was the problem maybe that it seemed so right?

How was it possible that after only one month, Hannah had become such an integral part of his daughter's life— and his, too? It was hard to believe that it had been four weeks already, that it was already the beginning of August, almost...

The third of August.

The pain was like a dagger through his heart. The stab of accompanying guilt equally swift and strong. He reached for the railing, his fingers gripping so tight that his knuckles were white.

Dios—he'd almost forgotten.

How had he let that happen? How had the events of the past few weeks so thoroughly occupied his mind and his heart that the date had very nearly escaped him?

He drew in a deep breath, exhaled it slowly.

"I just remembered that there are some files I need from the office," he announced abruptly. "I'll have to go back to Port Augustine."

"Tonight?" Hannah asked incredulously.

"Can we go, too, Daddy?" Riley asked.

Not *I* but *we,* he realized, and felt another pang. Already she was so attached to Hannah, maybe too attached. Because at the end of the summer, Riley would have to say goodbye to someone else she cared about.

"Not this time," he told her, stroking a finger over the soft curve of her cheek. "It would be too far past your bedtime before we got into town."

"When are you coming back?" Riley asked.

"Tomorrow," he promised.

Riley nodded, her head still pillowed on Hannah's shoulder. "Okay."

"Are you sure everything's all right?" Hannah asked.

Concern was evident in her blue-gray gaze, and as Michael looked into her eyes, he suddenly couldn't even remember what color Sam's had been.

"I'm sure," he lied.

He'd loved his wife—he *still* loved his wife—but the memories were starting to fade. She'd been the center of his world for so many years, and it had taken him a long time to put his life back together after she was gone. Losing her had absolutely devastated him, and that was something he wouldn't ever let himself forget. And that was why he wouldn't ever risk loving someone else.

Chapter Thirteen

Michael didn't remember many of the details of Sam's funeral. He didn't even remember picking out the plot where she was buried, and he wasn't entirely sure that he had. It was probably Marissa, who had stepped in to take care of all of the details—and his baby girl—who made the decision.

Thinking back to that time now, he knew that Sam would have been disappointed in him. She would have expected him to be there for their daughter, and he hadn't been. Not for a long time.

But he was trying to be there for her now, trying to be the father his little girl needed, and he thought he'd been making some progress. There was no awkwardness with Riley anymore. Not that everything was always smooth sailing, but they were learning to navigate the stormy seas together.

Hannah was a big part of that, of course. There was no denying the role she'd played in bringing him and Riley together. And sitting here now, on the little wrought-iron bench by his wife's grave as he'd done so many times before, he knew that Sam would be okay with that.

He caught a flicker of movement in the corner of his eye and, glancing up, saw his sister climbing the hill. She laid the bouquet of flowers she carried in front of Sam's stone.

"Are you doing okay?" she asked gently.

"You know, I really think I am."

She nodded at that, then took a seat beside him.

They sat in silence for a few more minutes, before he asked, "Why did you come?"

"Did you want to be alone?"

"No, I just wondered why you were here. Why you always seem to be there when I need you—and even when I don't realize that I do."

"Because you're my big brother and I love you."

He slipped his arm across her shoulders. "I'm the luckiest brother in the world."

She tipped her head back and smiled.

"It would have been our sixteenth anniversary today," he said.

"I know."

"I thought we would have sixty years together." He swallowed around the lump in his throat. "She was more than my wife, she was my best friend—and the best part of my life. And then she was gone."

"But now you have Riley," his sister reminded him.

He nodded. "The best part of both of us."

Marissa smiled again. "I heard she's learning to play tennis."

"Dr. Marotta told you, I'll bet."

She nodded. "How's Hannah?"

"The stitches should come out in a couple of days, and she's learned to keep a distance from Riley's backhand." He waited a beat, then said, "She canceled almost all of Riley's lessons for the summer."

"Good for her."

He hadn't expected such unequivocal support of the decision. "You were the one who encouraged me to find a piano instructor for Riley," he reminded her.

"Because she has an obvious talent that should be nurtured. But you went from music lessons twice a week to five days a week, then added language instruction and art classes. And I know the deportment classes were Mother's idea, but you could have said no. Instead, the poor child barely had time to catch her breath."

Which was almost exactly what Hannah had said. And while Riley never complained about her schedule, he should have seen that it was too much. He should have seen a lot of things he'd been oblivious to until recently.

"So other than tennis, what is Riley doing with her spare time?" his sister wanted to know.

"She's...having fun."

"You sound surprised."

"I'd almost forgotten what it sounded like to hear her laugh," he admitted. "It's...magic."

Marissa smiled again. "Maybe I was wrong."

"About what?"

"To worry about you. Maybe you are beginning to heal."

He knew that he was. And yet, he had to admit, "I still miss her."

"Of course," she agreed. "But you've got to move on. You're too young to be alone for the rest of your life."

"I can't imagine being with anyone other than Sam," Michael told her, but even as he spoke the words, he knew that they weren't entirely true. The truth was, he'd never loved anyone but Sam, and it seemed disloyal to even think that he ever could.

But that didn't stop him from wanting Hannah.

* * *

Hannah had sensed that something was wrong when the prince suddenly insisted that he needed to go to Port Augustine the night before. It seemed apparent to her that what he really needed was to get away from Cielo del Norte, though she couldn't figure out why.

Over the past few weeks, as Michael and Riley had spent more time together and grown closer, she'd thought that she and the prince were growing closer, too. But his abrupt withdrawal suggested otherwise.

She wasn't surprised that he was gone overnight. It didn't make sense to make the drive back when he had a house in town. She was surprised when he stayed away through all of the next day. But Caridad seemed unconcerned about his whereabouts. In fact, the housekeeper didn't comment on his absence at all, leading Hannah to suspect that she might know where the prince was.

It was only Riley, because she'd been spending more and more time with him every day, who asked for her daddy. Hannah tried to reassure the child without admitting that she had no idea where the prince had gone—or when he would be back.

It was late—hours after Riley had finally settled down to sleep—before she heard the door open. She told herself that she wasn't waiting up for him, but she'd taken the draft of Kevin's latest essay into the library to read because she knew if she was there that she would hear the prince come in.

"I didn't know if you'd still be up," he said.

"I had some things to do."

He opened a glass cabinet and pulled out a crystal decanter of brandy. She wasn't in the habit of drinking anything stronger than wine, and never more than a single glass. But when the prince poured a generous splash of the dark amber liquid into each of two snifters and offered one to her, it seemed rude to refuse.

"You haven't asked where I've been all day," he noted, swirling the brandy in his glass.

"I figured if you wanted me to know, you'd tell me."

He sat down on the opposite end of the sofa, but with his back to the arm, so that he was facing her. But he continued to stare into his glass as he said, "It was Sam's and my anniversary today."

"You went to the cemetery," she guessed.

"Just like I do every year." He swallowed a mouthful of brandy before he continued. "Except that this is the first time I almost forgot."

Hannah eyed him warily, uncertain how to respond—or even if she should. She sipped her drink cautiously while she waited for him to continue.

"We celebrated twelve anniversaries together. This is only the fourth year that she's been gone, and the date almost slipped by me."

"You're feeling guilty," she guessed.

"Maybe," he acknowledged. He tipped the glass to his lips again. "And maybe I'm feeling relieved, too. Because in the first year that she was gone, I couldn't seem to not think, every single day, about how empty my life was without her, so the important dates—like her birthday and our anniversary—were unbearable."

He looked into his glass, and frowned when he found that it was nearly empty. "And then there was Mother's Day. She wanted nothing so much as she wanted to have a baby, and she never got to celebrate a single Mother's Day."

Beneath the bitter tone, she knew that he was still hurting deeply, still grieving for the wife he'd loved.

"I wasn't happy when Sam told me she was pregnant," he admitted.

Coming from a man who obviously doted on his little

girl, the revelation startled her more than anything else he'd said.

"I knew it was a risk for her," he explained, and rose to pour another splash of brandy into his glass. "Though she'd successfully managed her diabetes for years, the doctors warned that pregnancy and childbirth would take a toll on her body.

"After a lot of discussion and numerous medical consults, we decided not to take the risk. It was enough, I thought, that we had each other."

Obviously, Hannah realized, at some point that decision had changed.

"She didn't tell me that she'd stopped taking her birth control pills," Michael confided. "We'd always been partners—not just in the business but in our marriage. Neither one of us made any major decisions without consulting the other, so I wasn't just surprised when she told me that we were going to have a baby, I was furious."

Hannah didn't say anything, because she knew the prince wasn't trying to make conversation so much as he was trying to vent the emotions that were tearing him up inside. So she just sat and listened and quietly sipped her drink.

"I was furious with Sam," he continued, "for unilaterally making the decision that would cost her life, even if neither of us knew that at the time. And I was furious with my mother, for convincing Sam that I needed an heir—because I found out later that was the motivation behind Sam's deception."

And that, she thought, explained so much of the tension in his relationship with his mother.

"But in the end, I realized that I was most furious with myself—because I should have taken steps to ensure that Sam couldn't get pregnant. If I had done that, then I wouldn't have lost my wife."

He sank into the chair beside hers, as if all of the energy

and emotion had drained out of him so that he was no longer able to stand.

She touched his hand. "You might not have lost your wife," she agreed softly. "But then you wouldn't have your little girl."

He sighed. "You're right. And now, when I think about it, I know that even if I could go back in time, I wouldn't want to. I couldn't ever give up Riley, even if it meant I could have Sam back."

"They say there's nothing as strong as a parent's love for a child," she said softly, her throat tight.

"The first time I held her in my arms, I knew there wasn't anything I wouldn't do for her," he admitted. "For a few glorious hours, I let myself imagine the future we would have together—Sam and Riley and myself. And then Sam was gone."

The grief in his voice was still raw—even after almost four years. And listening to him talk about the wife he'd obviously loved with his whole heart, Hannah experienced a pang of envy. Would she ever know how it felt to love like that—and to be loved like that in return?

She'd thought she was in love with Harrison, but when their relationship ended, she was more angry than hurt. She most definitely had *not* been heartbroken.

"I'm sorry," he said. "I didn't come in here with the intention of dumping on you."

"Please don't apologize, Your Highness. And don't worry—I can handle a little dumping."

"Strong shoulders and a soft heart?"

She managed a smile. "Something like that."

"Can you handle one more confession?"

She would sit here with him forever if it was what he wanted, but she had no intention of admitting that to him, so she only said, "Sure."

"I met Sam when I was fifteen years old and while I

didn't realize it at the time, I started to fall for her that very same day. I was lucky enough that she fell in love with me, too, because from that first moment, there was never anyone else. Even after she died…I never wanted anyone else." His dark eyes lifted to hers, held. "Until now."

She swallowed.

"I know it's wrong," he continued. "Not that it's a betrayal of my vows, because I've finally accepted that Sam is gone, but wrong because you're Riley's nanny and—"

She lifted a hand to touch her fingers to his lips, cutting off his explanation. She didn't want to hear him say why it was wrong—she refused to believe that it was. If he wanted her even half as much as she wanted him, that was all that mattered.

Somewhere in the back of her mind it occurred to her that the prince was still grieving and that if she made the next move, she might be taking advantage of him in a vulnerable moment.

Then his fingers encircled her wrist, and his thumb stroked slowly over the pulse point there as if to gauge her response. As if he couldn't hear how hard and fast her heart was pounding. Then he lowered her hand and laid it against his chest, so that she could feel that his heart was pounding just as hard and fast, and the last of her reservations dissipated.

She knew there was no future for them, but if she could have even one night, she would gladly take it and cherish the memories forever.

"I want you, Hannah," he said again. "But the first time I kissed you, I promised that I wouldn't do it again."

"You promised that you wouldn't make any unwanted advances," she corrected softly.

"Isn't that the same thing?"

"Not if I want you to kiss me," she said.

"Do you?" he asked, his mouth hovering above hers so

that she only needed to tilt her chin a fraction to make the kiss happen.

"Yes." She whispered her response against his mouth.

It was the barest brush of her lips against his, yet she felt the jolt all the way down to her toes. She caught only a hint of his flavor, but she knew that it was rich and dark and more potent than the brandy she'd sipped.

"I want you to kiss me," she repeated, in case there was any doubt.

He responded by skimming his tongue over the bow of her upper lip, making her sigh with pleasure. With need.

"I want you," she said.

His tongue delved beneath her parted lips, tasting, teasing. She met him halfway, in a slow dance of seduction.

It was only their second kiss, and yet she felt as if she'd kissed him a thousand times before. She felt as if she belonged in his arms. With him. Forever.

No—she wasn't going to let herself pretend that this was some kind of fairy tale. She knew better than to think that the prince wanted to sweep her off of her feet and take her away to live out some elusive happily-ever-after.

But he did sweep her off of her feet—to carry her up the stairs to her bedroom. And the sheer romanticism of the gesture made her heart sigh.

"Say my name, Hannah."

It seemed an odd request, until she realized that she'd never spoken his name aloud. Maybe because she hoped that using his title would help her keep him at a distance. But she didn't want any distance between them now.

"Michael," she whispered, savoring the sound of his name on her lips.

He smiled as he laid her gently on the bed, then made quick work of the buttons that ran down the front of her blouse. She shivered when he parted the material, exposing her heated flesh to the cool air. And again when he pushed the silk off of her shoulders and dipped his head to skim his lips over the ridge of her collarbone.

"Are you cold?"

She shook her head.

How could she be cold when there was so much heat pulsing through her veins? When her desire for him was a burning need deep in the pit of her belly?

His mouth moved lower. He released the clasp at the front of her bra and pushed the lacy cups aside, exposing her breasts to the ministrations of his lips and teeth and tongue.

She wasn't a virgin, but no one had ever touched her the way he was touching her. The stroke of his hands was somehow both lazy and purposeful, as if he wanted nothing more than to show her how much he wanted her. And with every brush of his lips and every touch of his fingertips, she felt both desire and desired.

Her hands raced over him, eagerly, desperately. She tore at his clothes, tossed them aside. She wanted to explore his hard muscles, to savor the warmth of his skin, to know the intimacy of his body joined with hers.

Obviously he wanted the same thing, because he pulled away from her only long enough to strip away the last of his clothes and take a small square packet from his pocket.

"I didn't plan for this to happen tonight," he told her. "But lately…well, I began to hope it would happen eventually and I wanted to be prepared."

"I'm glad one of us was," she assured him.

His fingers weren't quite steady as he attempted to open the package, and he dropped it twice. The second time, he swore so fervently she couldn't hold back a giggle. But he finally managed to sheath himself and rejoined her on the bed, nudging her thighs apart so that he could lower himself between them.

"Will you do me a favor?" he asked.

"What's that?"

"When you remember this night, will you edit out that part?"

She smiled. "Absolutely."

But it was a lie. She had no intention of editing out any of the parts. She wanted to remember every little detail of every minute that she had with Michael. Because she didn't have any illusions. She knew this couldn't last. Maybe not even beyond this one night. But she wasn't going to think about that now. She wasn't going to ask for more than he could give. She was just going to enjoy the moment and know that it was enough.

His tongue swirled around her nipple, then he drew the aching peak into his mouth and suckled, and she gasped with shock and pleasure. He shifted his attention to her other breast, making her gasp again.

Oh yes, this was enough.

Then his mouth found hers again in a kiss that tasted of hunger and passion. His tongue slid deep into her mouth, then slowly withdrew. Advance and retreat. It was a sensual tease designed to drive her wild, and it was succeeding.

She whimpered as she instinctively shifted her hips, aching for the hard length of him between her thighs. Deep inside her.

She rocked against him, wordlessly pleading.

He entered her in one hard thrust, and her release was just as hard and fast. Wave after wave of pleasure crashed over her with an unexpected intensity that left her baffled and breathless.

While her body was riding out the last aftershocks of pleasure, he began to move inside of her. Slow, steady strokes that started the anticipation building all over again.

Had she honestly thought that this might not be enough?

It was so much more than she'd expected, more than she'd even dared hope for, more than enough. And still, he somehow managed to give her more, to demand more, until it wasn't just enough—it was too much.

His thrusts were harder and faster now, and so deep she felt as if he was reaching into the very center of her soul. Harder and faster and deeper, until everything seemed to shatter in an explosion of heat and light and unfathomable pleasure.

Michael didn't know if he could move. He did know that he didn't want to. His heart was still pounding like a jack-hammer and every muscle in his body ached, and yet he couldn't remember ever feeling so good. So perfectly content to be right where he was.

But his own contentment aside, he knew that Hannah probably couldn't breathe with his weight sprawled on top of her. So he summoned enough energy to roll off of her. But he kept one arm draped across her waist, holding her close to his side. After another minute, he managed to prop himself up on an elbow so that he could look at her.

Her hair was spread out over the pillow, her eyes were closed, her lips were slightly curved. She looked as if she'd been well and truly ravished, and he felt a surge of pure satisfaction that he'd had the pleasure of ravishing her. And he wanted to do so again.

He stroked a finger down her cheek. Her eyelids slowly lifted, her lips parted on a sigh.

"*Dios,* you're beautiful."

She smiled at that. "Postcoital rose-colored glasses."

He shook his head. "Maybe I've never told you that before, but it's true. Your skin is so soft and smooth, your lips are like pink rose petals and your eyes are all the shades of the stormy summer sky."

"I didn't realize you had such a romantic streak, Your Highness," she teased.

"Neither did I." His hand skimmed up her torso, from her

waist to her breast, his thumb stroking over the tight bud of her nipple. "I always thought everything was black or white—and for the past few years, there's been a lot more black than white. And then you came along and gave me a whole new perspective on a lot of things."

She arched into his palm, as if she wanted his touch as much as he wanted to touch her. She had incredible breasts. They were so full and round, and so delightfully responsive to his touch.

Sam's curves had been much more modest, and she'd often lamented her tomboy figure. Even when she'd been pregnant, her breasts had never—

He froze.

Her gaze lifted to his, confusion swirling in the depths of her blue-gray eyes.

"Michael?"

The unmistakable smoky tone of Hannah's voice snapped him back to the present and helped him push aside any lingering thoughts of Sam. As much as he'd loved his wife and still grieved for the tragedy of a life cut so short, she was his past and Hannah—

He wasn't entirely sure yet what Hannah would be to him, but he knew that even if she wasn't his future, she was at least his present.

He lowered his head to kiss her, softly, sweetly. And felt the tension slowly seep out of her body.

Yes, she was definitely his present—an incredible gift. The only woman he wanted right now. And so he used his hands and his lips and his body and all of the hours until the sun began to rise to convince her.

Chapter Fourteen

Hannah didn't expect that Michael would still be there when she woke up in the morning. She'd known he wouldn't stay through the night. There was no way he would risk his daughter finding him there. But it would have been nice to wake up in his arms. To make love with him again as the sun was streaming through the windows.

Making love with Michael had been the most incredible experience. He'd been attentive and eager and very thorough. She stretched her arms above her head, and felt her muscles protest. Very very thorough. But while her body was feeling all smug and sated, her mind was spinning.

She'd been fighting against her feelings for the prince since the beginning, and she knew that making love with him was hardly going to help her win that battle. But as she showered and got ready for the day, she knew she didn't regret it.

After breakfast, while Riley was in the music room practicing piano—simply because she wanted to—Hannah was in the kitchen sipping on her second cup of coffee while Caridad was making a grocery list.

"How many people are you planning to feed?" Hannah asked, when the housekeeper turned the page over to continue her list on the other side.

"Only the three of you," she admitted. "But I want to make several ready-to-heat meals that you can just take out of the freezer and pop in the microwave."

"Are you going somewhere?"

"Just for a few days, and I'm not sure when, but I want to be ready to go as soon as Loretta calls."

Loretta, Hannah remembered now, was Caridad and Estavan's second-oldest daughter who was expecting her first child—and their fourth grandchild. "When is she due?"

"The eighteenth of August."

"On Riley's birthday," Hannah noted.

"She mentioned that to you, did she?"

"Only about a thousand times," she admitted with a smile.

"A child's birthday is a big deal—or it should be." Caridad tapped her pen on the counter, her brow furrowed.

Hannah knew that there was more she wanted to say. She also knew that prompting and prodding wouldn't get any more information out of the housekeeper until she was ready. So she sipped her coffee while she waited.

"The princess is going to be four years old," Caridad finally said. "And she's never had a party."

Hannah was startled by this revelation, and then realized that she shouldn't be. Samantha had died within hours of giving birth, which meant that Riley's birthday was the same day that Michael had lost his wife.

"I don't mean to be critical—I know it's a difficult time for the prince. And it's not like her birthday passes without any kind of recognition.

"There's always a cake," Caridad continued. "Because I bake that myself. And presents. But she's never had a party."

"Why are you telling me?" Hannah asked warily.

"Because I think this year he might be ready, but he probably won't think of it on his own."

"You want me to drop some hints," she guessed.

The housekeeper nodded. "Yes, I think just a few hints would be enough."

"Okay, I'll try."

"But not too subtle," Caridad said. "Men sometimes don't understand subtle—they need to be hit over the head."

Hannah had to laugh. "I'll do my best."

Michael had thought that making love with Hannah once would be enough, but the first joining of their bodies had barely taken the edge off of his desire. After four years of celibacy, it probably wasn't surprising that his reawakened libido was in no hurry to hibernate again, but he knew that it wasn't as simple as that. He didn't just crave physical release, he craved Hannah.

Every time his path crossed with hers the following day, his hormones jolted to attention. Now that he knew what it was like to be with her—the sensual way she responded to the touch of his lips and his hands, the glorious sensation of sinking into her warm and welcoming body, the exquisite rhythm of their lovemaking—he wanted only to be with her again.

But what did *she* want?

He didn't have the slightest clue.

She'd been sleeping when he'd left her room, so he'd managed to avoid the awkward "What does this mean?" or "Where do we go from here?" conversations that purportedly followed first-time sex. Since Hannah was the first woman he'd been with since he'd started dating Sam almost eighteen years earlier, he had little firsthand experience with those morning-after moments. And now he didn't know what was the next step.

They had lunch and dinner together with Riley, as was customary, and the conversation flowed as easily as it usually did. There were no uncomfortable references to the previous night and no awkward silences. There was absolutely no indication at all that anything had changed between them.

Until later that night, when he left Riley's room after he was sure she was asleep, and he found Hannah in the hall.

It wasn't all that late, but she was obviously ready to turn in for the night. Her hair had been brushed so that it fell loose over her shoulders, and she was wearing a long blue silky robe that was cinched at her narrow waist. A hint of lace in the same color peeked through where the sides of the robe overlapped, piquing his curiosity about what she had on beneath the silky cover.

He'd intended to seek her out, to have the discussion they'd missed having the night before. But now that he'd found her, conversation was the last thing on his mind.

"Wow" was all he managed.

But apparently it was the right thing to say, because she smiled and reached for his hand. Silently, she drew him across the hall and into her room.

The robe was elegant but discreet, covering her from shoulders to ankles. But when he tugged on the belt and the silky garment fell open, he saw that what she wore beneath was a pure lace fantasy. A very little lace fantasy that barely covered her sexy curves, held into place by the skinniest of straps over her shoulders.

And while he took a moment to appreciate the contrast of her pale skin with the dark lace, he much preferred reality to fantasy. With one quick tug, he lifted the garment over her head and tossed it aside.

* * *

Afterward, he let her put the lace-and-silk fantasy back on, and they sat on her balcony with a bottle of wine, just watching the stars.

"Are you ever going to tell me about that engagement?" he asked her.

"It was a long time ago," she said dismissively.

Considering that she was only twenty-six, he didn't imagine that it could have been all that long ago, and he was too curious to drop the subject. "What happened?"

"It didn't work out."

He rolled his eyes.

"We met at university," she finally told him. "He was a member of the British aristocracy, I was not. As much as he claimed to love me, when his family made it clear that they disapproved of his relationship with a commoner, he ended it." There was no emotion in her voice, but he sensed that she wasn't as unaffected by the broken engagement as she tried to appear.

"How long were you together?"

"Almost four years." She lifted her glass to her lips. "They didn't seem concerned about my lack of pedigree so long as we were just dating—apparently even aristocrats are entitled to meaningless flings—but to marry me would have been a blight on the family tree."

Again, her recital was without emotion, but he saw the hurt in her eyes and silently cursed any man who could be so cruel and heartless to this incredible woman.

"I didn't imagine there was anyone living in the modern world—aside from my mother—" he acknowledged with a grimace "—who had such outdated views about maintaining the purity of bloodlines."

"And yet your mother married a farmer," Hannah mused.

"Elena is nothing if not illogical. Or maybe she believed that her royal genes would trump his." He smiled as an old memory nudged at his mind. "The first time I scraped my knee when I was a kid, I didn't know what the red stuff was, because I honestly believed that my blood was supposed to be blue."

She smiled, too, but there were clouds in her eyes, as if she was thinking of the lack of blue in her own veins.

"So did you at least get to keep the ring?" he asked, in an attempt to lighten the mood.

She shook her head. "It was a family heirloom," she explained dryly.

"He didn't actually ask for it back?"

"Before we even left the ancestral estate," she admitted.

"And you gave it to him?" He couldn't imagine that she would have just slid it off of her finger and handed it over. No, if she'd cared enough about the man to want to marry him, she wouldn't have been that cool about the end of their engagement.

"I threw it out the window."

He chuckled.

"It took him three hours on his hands and knees in the immaculately groomed gardens to find it."

"He must have been pissed."

"Harrison didn't have that depth of emotion," she informed him. "But he was 'most displeased' with my 'childish behavior.'"

"Sounds like you made a lucky escape." And he was glad, because if she'd married that pompous British twit, she wouldn't be here with him now.

"I know I did. I guess I just thought I'd be at a different place by this point in my life."

"You're only twenty-six," he reminded her. "And I don't think there are many places in the world better than this one."

"You know I didn't mean this place specifically." She

smiled as she tipped her head back to look up at the sky. "This place is…heaven."

"Cielo," he agreed. "And you are…*mi ángel.*"

After almost a week had passed and Hannah's apparently too-subtle hints about Riley's approaching birthday continued to go unnoticed, she decided that Michael needed to be hit over the head. Not as literally as she had been, she thought, rubbing the pink scar that was the only visible reminder of her clash with Riley's racquet now that her stitches had been removed. But just as effectively.

So on Thursday morning, after the little girl had gone to the tennis court with Kevin, she cornered the prince in his office.

"It's Riley's birthday next week," she said.

"I know when her birthday is," he assured her.

"Well, I was thinking that it might be fun to have a party."

"A party?" he echoed, as if unfamiliar with the concept.

"You know—with a cake, party hats, noisemakers."

He continued to scribble notes on the ad layout on his desk. "Okay."

She blinked. "Really?"

He glanced up, a smile teasing the corners of his mouth. "Did you want me to say no?"

"Of course I didn't want you to say no," she told him. "But I thought there would be some discussion first."

He finally set down his pen and leaned back in his chair. "Discussion about what?"

"I don't know. Maybe the when and where, the guest list, a budget."

"When—sometime on the weekend. Where—here. As for the guest list, I figure if it's Riley's party, she should get to decide, and I don't care what it costs so long as I don't have to do anything but show up."

Happiness bubbled up inside of her. She couldn't wait to race into the kitchen and tell Caridad the good news.

"If you let Riley decide what she wants, it could turn into a very big party," she warned.

"I think we're overdue for a big party." He slipped his arms around her waist, drew her close. "And this year, I feel like celebrating."

Her heart bumped against her ribs, but she forced herself to respond lightly. "Okay, then. I'll talk to the birthday girl when she comes in and get started making plans."

"Where is Riley?"

"On the tennis court with Kevin."

"You'll have to give me an updated schedule," he said, not entirely teasing. "I never know where to find her these days."

"We don't have a schedule—we're improvising."

"I can improvise," he said, brushing his mouth against hers.

Hannah sighed. "Mmm. You're good at that."

"How long is she going to be busy with Kevin?"

"Probably about an hour. Why?"

"Because I want to show you some of the other things I'm good at."

Her cheeks flushed. "It's nine o'clock in the morning."

"But you don't have a schedule to worry about—you're improvising," he reminded her.

"Yes, but—"

"I really want to make love with you in the daylight."

He was a very lucky man, Michael thought with a grin as Hannah took his hand led him up to her room. And about to get luckier.

When he followed her through the door, his gaze automatically shifted toward the bed upon which they'd made love every night for the past nine days—and caught on the enormous bouquet of flowers in the vase on her bedside table.

He picked up the card. "With sincere thanks for helping me survive summer school, Kevin."

She paused in the process of removing the decorative throw cushions from the bed when she saw him holding the card. "Isn't that sweet?"

"Sure," he agreed stiffly. "He's finished his course, then?"

She nodded. "He got an A-plus on his final essay to finish with first-class honors."

"Caridad must be thrilled."

"She promised to make baklava, just for me," Hannah told him.

She said it as if that was her favorite, and maybe it was. He didn't know too much about what she liked or didn't like.

"I didn't know you liked flowers," he said, as if that was an excuse for the fact that he'd never thought to give her any.

"Who doesn't like flowers?" she countered lightly.

There was no accusation in her words, no judgment in her tone. Of course not—Hannah had made it clear from the beginning that she didn't have any expectations of him. Not even something as insignificant as a bouquet of flowers. And though he couldn't have said why, the realization annoyed him.

Or maybe he was annoyed to realize that he'd never really made an effort where Hannah was concerned. He'd never even taken her out to dinner, and they only went as far as the media room to watch a movie. They came together after dark like clandestine lovers, without ever having had anything that resembled a traditional date.

He knew that was his fault. He wasn't ready to subject Hannah to the media scrutiny of being seen in public together. Going shopping with Riley didn't really count, because the press accepted that the prince would require the assistance of a nanny when he was out with his daughter.

But he knew it would be very different if he and Hannah ventured out together without Riley as a buffer between them.

It was difficult to date when you were a member of the royal family, even one not in direct line to the throne. There was no such thing as privacy, and rarely even the pretense of it. Every appearance, every touch and kiss, became a matter of public speculation.

Not that Michael thought she couldn't handle it. He had yet to see Hannah balk at any kind of challenge. No, it was simply that he wasn't ready to go public with a relationship that felt too new, or maybe it was his feelings that were too uncertain. And that he was unwilling to look too deep inside himself to figure them out.

"I don't know if I like the idea of a much younger man bringing you flowers," he said, only half joking.

"He didn't just bring flowers," she teased. "He kissed me, too."

His brows drew together; Hannah laughed.

"It was a perfectly chaste peck on the cheek," she assured him.

"Lucky for him, or I might have to call him out for making a move on my woman."

Her brows rose. "*Your* woman?"

The words had probably surprised Michael even more than they'd surprised Hannah, and were followed by a quick spurt of panic. He immediately backtracked. "Well, you're mine until the end of summer, anyway."

Hannah turned away on the pretext of rearranging the colored bottles on her dresser, but not before he saw the light in her eyes fade. When she faced him again, her smile was overly bright.

"And that's less than three weeks away, so why are we wasting time talking?" She reached for the buttons on his shirt.

"Hannah—" He caught her hands, not sure what to say, or even if there were any words to explain how he felt about her.

He cared about her—he couldn't be with her if he didn't. And he didn't want her to think it was just sex, but he didn't want to give her false hope, either. He didn't want her to think that he could ever fall in love with her. Because he couldn't—he loved Sam.

"I never asked you for any promises," she told him.

And he couldn't have given them to her if she had. But he could give her pleasure, and he knew that doing so would give him pleasure, too.

He stripped her clothes away and lowered her onto the mattress. Then he knelt between her legs, stroking his fingertips slowly over the sensitive skin of her inner thighs. He brushed the soft curls at the apex of her thighs, and she gasped. He repeated the motion, parting the curls so that his thumb stroked over the nub at her center, and she bit down on her lip to keep from crying out.

"It's okay," he told her. "I want to hear you. I want to know how it feels when I touch you."

"It feels good. So good."

As his thumb circled her nub, he teased her slick, wet opening with the tip of a finger. She whimpered.

"Michael, please."

"Tell me what you want, Hannah."

"I want you."

He wanted her, too. He wanted to spread her legs wide and bury himself in her. To thrust into the hot wetness between her thighs, again and again, harder and faster, until he felt her convulse around him, dragging him into blissful oblivion.

But first, he wanted to taste her.

He slid his hands beneath her, lifting her hips off of the mattress so that he could take her with his mouth.

She gasped again, the sound reflecting both shock and pleasure. His tongue slid deep inside, reaching for the core of her feminine essence. Her breath was coming in quick, shallow pants, and he knew that she was getting close to her edge. It wouldn't have taken much to push her over the edge, but he wanted to draw out the pleasure for her—and for himself.

With his lips and his tongue, he probed and suckled and licked. He heard her breath quicken, then catch, and finally... release.

He stroked and kissed his way up her body until she was trembling again. Her belly, her breasts, her throat. She reached for him then, her fingers wrapping around and then sliding up the hard, throbbing length of him. He sucked in a breath. She stroked downward again, slowly, teasingly, until his eyes nearly crossed.

She arched her hips as she guided him to her center, welcoming him into her slick, wet heat. The last threads of his self-control slipped out of his grasp. He yanked her hips up and buried himself deep inside her.

She gasped and arched, pulling him even deeper, her muscles clamping around him as she climaxed again. The pulsing waves threatened to drag him under their wake. He reached for her hands, linking their fingers together over her head, making her his anchor as he rode out the tide of her release.

He waited until the pulses started to slow, then he began to move. She met him, stroke for stroke. Slow and deep. Then fast and hard. Faster. Harder. This time, when her release came, he let go and went with her.

Chapter Fifteen

Once the prince had given his nod of approval to the birthday party, Hannah was anxious to get started on the planning, so she turned to her best friend for advice. Karen
outlined the five essential ingredients of a successful children's party: decorations, such as colorful streamers and
balloons; games or crafts to keep the kids busy; cake to
give the kids an unnecessary sugar high; presents for the
guest of honor and loot bags for all of her friends—all of
which should somehow coordinate with the party theme.
And preferably, she added as an afterthought, outdoors so
that the sugar-high kids weren't tearing through the house
and destroying everything.

For Riley's first-ever birthday party, Hannah took her
friend's list and gave it the royal treatment. She decided to
go with a princess theme, since it was too obvious to resist.

The first glitch came when she asked Riley who she
wanted to invite. The little girl mentioned her new friend,
Grace, then added Kevin and Caridad and Estavan before

rattling off the extensive list of all her aunts, uncles and cousins. She didn't mention her grandmother, and when Hannah asked about adding her to the list, the princess wrinkled her nose.

"Do I have to?"

"She is your grandmother, and you invited everyone else in the family," Hannah felt compelled to point out, even as she wondered if she was making a mistake.

But she couldn't help remembering Michael's comment about his mother barely knowing his daughter, and though she didn't think an invitation to one birthday party was likely to change that, she couldn't help hoping that it might be a start. And maybe, if the princess royal got to know Riley, she would give up on the idea of sending her away to boarding school.

"Everyone else in my family is nice," Riley said simply.

Hannah didn't quite know how to respond to that. She'd never actually met the princess royal and she didn't want to prejudge, but the princess's response made her wary.

"Would it be nice to invite everyone except her?" she prodded gently.

"No." Riley sighed, and considered her dilemma for another minute before she finally said, "Okay, you can put her on the list. But she doesn't get a loot bag."

After the guest list was finalized, Hannah turned her attention to other details. Taking her friend's advice to heart and unwilling to trust in the capriciousness of the weather, she rented a party tent to ensure that the celebration remained outside. Of course, when she called about the tent, she realized that she needed tables and chairs for inside the tent, and cloths to cover the tables and dress up the chairs. By the time she got off the phone, she was grateful the prince wasn't worried about budget.

"I just ordered a bouncy castle," she admitted to Caridad.

The housekeeper's brows lifted. "One of those big inflatable things?"

"It fits the princess theme," she explained.

"Riley will love it."

"And a cotton-candy cart and popcorn machine."

Caridad's lips twitched. "Apparently you know how to throw a party."

"You don't think it's too much?"

"Of course it's too much, but after waiting four years for a party, it should be a party worth waiting for."

"It will be," Hannah said confidently.

And it was. The tent was decorated with thousands of tiny white fairy lights and hundreds of pink streamers and dozens of enormous bouquets of white and pink helium-filled balloons.

The younger female guests got to make their own tiaras—decorating foam crowns with glittery "jewels" and sparkling flowers. Thankfully Hannah had realized that the crowns wouldn't be a big hit with Riley's male cousins, so they got to decorate foam swords. After the craft, they played party games: pin the tail on the noble steed, musical thrones and a variation of Hot Potato with a glass slipper in place of the potato. And, of course, they spent hours just jumping around in the inflatable bouncy castle that had been set up behind the tennis court.

For a minute, Hannah had actually worried that Michael's mother was going to have a coronary when she spotted it. The princess royal had gone red in the face and demanded that the "grotesque monstrosity" be removed from the grounds immediately. But Michael had been unconcerned and simply ignored her demand, for which the kids were unbelievably grateful.

Riley loved all of it. And she was completely in her element as the center of attention. Hannah was happy to remain in the background, making sure everything was proceeding as it should, but Michael made a point of introducing "Riley's nanny and party planner" to everyone she hadn't yet met. There was nothing incorrect in that designation, and it wasn't like she expected or even wanted him to announce that they were lovers. But she wished he'd at least given a hint that she meant something more to him than the roles she filled in his daughter's life.

That tiny disappointment aside, she really enjoyed meeting his family. She already knew his sister, of course, and was pleased when Marissa jumped right in to help keep things running smoothly. She was introduced to Prince Cameron, his very pregnant wife, Gabriella, and their daughter, Sierra. The teenage princess was stunningly beautiful and surprisingly unaffected by her recently newfound status as a royal, happily jumping in to help the kids at the craft table.

She also met Rowan, the prince regent, his wife, Lara, and their sons Matthew and William; Prince Eric and Princess Molly and their kids, Maggie and Josh; Prince Christian—next in line to the throne—his sister, Alexandria, and their younger brother, Damon. Even Prince Marcus, who divided his time between Tesoro del Mar and West Virginia, happened to be in the country with his wife, Jewel, and their two daughters, Isabella and Rosalina, so they were able to attend.

They were all warm and welcoming, but it was their interactions with one another that Hannah observed just a little enviously. It had nothing to do with them being royal and everything to do with the obvious closeness they shared. As an only child, she'd never known anything to compare to that kind of absolute acceptance and unquestioning loyalty, but she was glad that Riley did.

As for Riley's "Grandmama"—well, Hannah didn't get any warm and fuzzy feelings from her, so she just kept a careful distance between them. And she succeeded, until she went into the house to tell Caridad that they were getting low on punch. On her way back out, the princess royal cornered her in the hall.

"I'll bet this party was your idea," she said.

And so was adding your name to the guest list, Hannah wanted to tell her. But she bit her tongue. Elena Leandres might be insufferably rude, but she was the princess royal and, as such, was entitled to deference if not respect.

"Riley doesn't need to play at being a princess," the birthday girl's grandmama continued. "She *is* one. And this whole display is tacky and inappropriate."

"I'm sorry you're not enjoying yourself."

The older woman's eyes narrowed on her. "But you are, aren't you?"

"I can't deny that I like a good party, Your Highness," she said unapologetically.

"Is it the party or the fairy tale?" she challenged. "Do you have some kind of fantasy in your mind that you're going to ride off into the sunset with the prince?"

"I have no illusions," she assured the prince's mother.

"I'm pleased to hear that, because although my son might lack sense and discretion in his choice of lovers, he would never tarnish his beloved wife's memory or his daughter's future by marrying someone like you."

One side of Elena's mouth curled in a nasty smile as Hannah's cheeks filled with color. "Did you really think I wouldn't guess the nature of your relationship with my son? I know what a man's thinking when he looks at a woman the way Michael looks at you—and it's not about hearts and flowers, it's about sex, pure and simple."

She forced herself to shrug, as if the princess royal's words hadn't cut to the quick. "Sure," she agreed easily. "But at least it's really great sex. And while this has been a fascinating conversation, I have to get back outside."

"You have not been dismissed," Elena snapped at her.

"I beg your pardon, Your Highness," she said through

clenched teeth. "But the children will be getting hungry and I promised Caridad that I would help serve lunch."

"Well, go on then," the princess royal smirked. "I wouldn't want to keep you from your duties."

And with those words and a dismissive wave of her hand, she quickly and efficiently put the nanny in her place.

Hannah's feelings were in turmoil as she headed up the stairs to her own room. She was angry and frustrated, embarrassed that her own thoughts and feelings had been so transparent, and her heart was aching because she knew that what the princess royal had said was true.

Not that she believed her relationship with the prince was about nothing more than sex. They had fun together and they'd become friends. But she also knew that while Michael had chosen to be with her now, he'd made no mention of a future for them together. And she had to wonder if maybe one of the reasons he'd chosen to get involved with her—aside from the obvious convenience—was because he could be confident that their relationship already had a predetermined expiration date. At the end of the summer, she would be leaving. The time they'd spent together was an interlude, that was all, and she'd been a fool to ever let herself hope it might be more.

Marissa was coming down the stairs as she was going up, and the princess's quick smile faded when she got close enough to see the distress that Hannah knew was likely etched on her face.

"Riley asked me to find you," she said. "She said she's absolutely starving and wanted to know when it would be time to eat."

"Please tell her that I'll be out in just a minute, Your Highness." She was anxious now to move things along and get this party over with, but she needed a few minutes alone to regain her composure before she could face anyone. And especially before she could face Michael.

"Hannah." The princess touched her arm, halting her progress. "I just saw my mother walk out—did she say something to upset you?"

"Of course not."

But it was obvious that Marissa didn't believe her, and that she was disappointed by the obvious lie.

"I thought we were becoming friends," she said gently.

Hannah looked away so that the princess wouldn't see the tears that stung her eyes. "You've been very kind to me, Your Highness, but—"

"Will you stop 'Your Highnessing' me," Marissa demanded, "and tell me what she said to you."

"It wasn't anything that wasn't true," Hannah finally acknowledged.

The princess sighed. "I'm not going to make excuses for her. All I can say is that she's so unhappy, her only pleasure comes from making others feel the same way."

"I'm not unhappy," Hannah assured her. She was simply resigned to the realities of her relationship with the prince, but also determined. If they only had two more weeks together, then she was going to cherish every moment.

"Actually, there is one more thing I'd like to say," Marissa told her.

"What's that?"

"That you're the best thing that has happened to my brother in a long time, so please don't let my mother—or anyone else—make you question what you have together."

Despite Marissa's reassurances, the rest of the day was bittersweet for Hannah, her happiness tempered by the realization that she wouldn't be around to witness the celebration of Riley's fifth birthday. She was only going to be at Cielo del Norte with the prince and his daughter for another two weeks. After that, they would return to their home in Verde Colinas, and she would go back to her apartment in town and her job at the high school, and she knew that she was going to miss them both unbearably.

She tried not to dwell on that fact, and when everyone joined together to sing "Happy Birthday," it was a welcome diversion. Caridad had offered to make the cake, as she had for each of the princess's previous birthdays, and Riley was stunned by the three-dimensional fairy-tale castle confection that she'd created, complete with towers and spires and even a drawbridge.

After everyone had their fill of cake and ice cream, Riley opened her gifts. She enthused over all of them, showing as much appreciation for the Little Miss Tennis visor that Kevin gave her to the elaborate back-to-school wardrobe from her aunt Marissa. Of course, her absolute favorite gift was the *Yo Gabba Gabba* CD collection from Grace, and she insisted on putting on the music for the enjoyment of all her guests.

The prince had given his gift to his daughter at breakfast: a three-story dollhouse, which she had absolutely adored. Partly because it came with dozens of pieces of furniture, but mostly because it was from her beloved daddy.

Hannah had walked the mall in San Pedro three times looking for something special for the little girl. She didn't want it to be anything showy or expensive, just something that might remind Riley of the time they'd spent together after she was gone. She finally found it in a little boutique that sold an indescribable variety of items ranging from handmade lace and estate jewelry to the latest in kitchen gadgets and children's toys. At first, it caught her eye just because it was funky and fun: a three-foot-long stuffed caterpillar with a purple body and high-top running shoes on its dozens of feet. Then when she picked it up, she noted the name on the tag: EMME.

"It's a palindrome!" Riley exclaimed happily.

"It looks like a caterpillar to me," her father said.

Riley just rolled her eyes and shared a secret smile with Hannah.

Several hours later, after the guests had all gone home and the remnants of the party had been cleared away by the rental company, Riley's eyes were closed. Even when Michael touched his lips to her cheek, she didn't stir.

"She's sleeping," he confirmed.

"She had a busy day," Hannah noted.

"A fabulous day—thanks to you."

"I tried not to go too over the top," she said.

His brows rose. "You don't think it was over the top?"

"I nixed the suggested arrival of the birthday girl in the horse-drawn glass carriage," she told him.

"I'm in awe of your restraint," he said dryly. "But truthfully, whatever it costs, it was worth every penny. I've never seen her so happy."

"Now I'm regretting that I didn't get the carriage."

"Then what would we do next year?"

She knew he'd only meant to tease her with the suggestion that this party couldn't be topped, but the words were a reminder to both of them that there was no *we* and Hannah wouldn't be around for the princess's next birthday.

"Brigitte called today," he said, in what seemed to Hannah a deliberate attempt to shift the direction of the conversation. "To wish Riley a happy birthday."

"That was thoughtful," she said. "How is she adjusting to life in Iceland?"

"Not easily."

"Does she want to come back?"

He laughed. "No. As much as she's struggling with culture shock, she is very much in love with her new husband."

"Then what is it that you're not telling me?" Because she was sure that he was holding something back.

"She did ask if I'd found a full-time nanny," he admitted. "And when I said I had not, she suggested that I interview her friend Margaux for the position."

Hannah had to remind herself that this wasn't unexpected. She'd known all along that the prince would be hiring a new nanny because she was leaving at the end of August. "Why do you sound as if that's a problem?" she asked.

"Because I was hoping that I might convince you to stay beyond the summer."

Her heart pounded hard against her ribs. This was what she hadn't even realized she wanted—what she hadn't dared let herself hope for. "You want me to stay?"

"You've been so wonderful with Riley, and she's going to be devastated if you leave."

Disappointment washed the roots of barely blossomed hope from her heart. "She'll be fine," she said, confident that it was true. The child had already proven that she was both adaptable and resilient. It was her own heart that gave Hannah concern, because she knew that when she left Cielo del Norte, she would be leaving the largest part of it behind.

"Okay, maybe the truth is that I'm not yet ready to let you go," Michael acknowledged.

Not yet ready—but he would be. Neither of them had any expectations of anything permanent or even long-term. At least none that she was willing to admit to him now. "We still have two weeks before the end of the summer," she said lightly.

"What if I'm not ready then, either?"

She didn't know what to say, how to answer his question in a way that wouldn't give away the feelings in her own heart. Because the truth was, she didn't want him to ever let her go—she wanted him to love her as much as she loved him, and she knew that wasn't going to happen.

He was still in love with Riley's mother, and even if he wasn't, she knew he wouldn't ever love her. Not enough.

Her father hadn't loved her enough to keep her with him, and Harrison hadn't loved her enough to defy his parents. And if she wasn't good enough for the heir of some obscure earldom, there was no way anyone would ever consider her good enough for a Tesorian prince. The princess royal had made that more than clear.

"Let's not think about that right now," she said, leading the way across the hall.

So long as they had tonight, she wasn't going to think about tomorrow.

Afterward, Hannah would wonder how it happened, because she knew she didn't consciously speak the words aloud. She certainly hadn't intended to tell him of the feelings that filled her heart. But when he pulled her close, tucking her against the warmth of his body so that she felt secure and cherished in his embrace, her emotions overruled reason. And as she started to drift toward slumber, the words slipped from between her lips as if of their own accord.

"I love you, Michael."

His only response was silence. She wanted to believe that he was already asleep and that he probably hadn't heard her impulsive confession, but the sudden tension that filled his body proved otherwise. The muscles in the arm that was wrapped around her grew taut, and she felt the sting of tears in her eyes.

She hadn't intended to confide her feelings. She knew she would be leaving her heart at Cielo del Norte but she'd hoped to at least take her pride. But keeping the feelings to herself certainly hadn't diminished them, and she was through pretending.

She did love him—with her whole heart. And she loved Riley as if the little girl was her own child. But accepting the truth of her feelings forced her to accept the more painful truths that were equally evident: there was no place for her here, and no future for her with the prince and his daughter.

Once again, she was trying to fit in someplace where she could never belong.

Chapter Sixteen

The night after Hannah's whispered declaration of her feelings, Michael didn't go to her room. It was the first time since their first night together that he'd gone directly to his big, empty bed. He didn't sleep well. He wasn't even sure that he'd slept at all.

But he knew he was doing the right thing. To continue to be with Hannah when he didn't—couldn't—feel the same way she did wasn't fair to either of them.

It was on Tuesday, after two restless, sleepless nights, that she knocked on his office door.

"Excuse me for interrupting, Your Highness, but I was wondering if I could have a minute of your time."

He cringed at the formal tone of her voice, hating the distance between them. He wanted to hear her speak his name, not his title. He wanted to take her in his arms and hold her so close that he could feel her heart beating against his. He wanted to touch his mouth to hers, to feel her lips yield to his kiss. But he had no right to want anything from her anymore.

"Of course, Hannah," he responded to her request.

"I got a notice from St. Eugene's that I'll be teaching a new course in the fall, and I was hoping to go back to Port Augustine at the end of this week."

This wasn't at all what he'd expected. He wasn't ready for her to leave, and he had no intention of letting her go. She had agreed to stay until the end of summer, to take care of his daughter.

"What about Riley?" he demanded now. "How can you just abandon her?"

"I'm not going anywhere until you've found someone else to take care of her."

"And what if I don't find anyone else?" he challenged.

He wasn't sure why he was fighting her on this. It was only seven days, and even if he didn't have anyone else by then, he would be happy to spend more time with his daughter during that last week. He didn't need a nanny, but he needed Hannah.

He wasn't sure where that last thought had come from— or how it could simultaneously feel so right and make him break out in a cold sweat.

"Margaux has agreed to come for an interview tomorrow."

"You're so eager to get away from here that you called her to set this up?"

"No," she denied. "Margaux called here, on Brigitte's advice, to set a date and time to meet with you. I just took the message."

"You could have said that I would get in touch with her when I returned to Port Augustine," he countered.

She looked at him oddly, as if she heard the note of desperation he tried to keep out of his voice. But all she said was, "I thought you would want this settled before then—to make sure Riley will be in good hands when you go back."

He couldn't refute the logic in that. Instead, he asked, "Is there nothing I can say to make you stay?"

She hesitated for a moment, as if considering her response, then finally said, "You really don't need me anymore. You and Riley are going to be just fine."

"Have you told her that you're leaving?"

"She won't be surprised. She knows I have to go back to my real job."

Just as he'd known it was only a temporary assignment when he'd hired her, so why was he fighting it now?

"I'll let you know after I meet with Margaux tomorrow," he told her.

"Thank you," she said.

And then she was gone.

Hannah was transferring her clothing from the dresser to her suitcase when Riley came into her room.

"Who's that lady with Daddy?" she demanded. "Is it true that she's going to be my new nanny?"

"That's for your daddy to decide," Hannah told her.

The princess crawled up onto Hannah's bed and hugged her knees to her chest. "Why don't I get to decide?"

"Because you're four."

"That's not my fault."

Hannah tousled her hair and smiled gently. "It's not a question of fault, it's just the way it is."

Riley watched as she continued to fill the suitcase. Hannah forced herself to concentrate on carefully arranging each item, because she knew that if she looked at the little girl right now, she would fall apart.

After a few minutes, Riley spoke in a quiet voice, "I don't want you to go."

Hannah's throat was tight, her eyes burning with unshed

tears. She drew in a deep breath and settled onto the edge of the bed, trying to find the words that would make goodbye easier for both of them.

But as soon as she sat down, Riley scooted over to wrap her arms around her, squeezing her so tight that the dam that was holding back Hannah's tears began to crack.

"I don't want to go, either," she admitted. "But we both knew that I was only going to be here for the summer."

"The summer's not over yet," the princess pointed out.

She rested her chin on top of the little girl's head, so Riley wouldn't see the tears that slid down her cheeks. "No, but it's getting close."

After another few minutes, Riley asked, "Can I come visit you?"

Hannah knew it would be best to make a clean break, to walk away from Cielo del Norte and never look back, but there was no way she could deny the child's request. "That's up to your dad, but if he says yes, it's absolutely okay with me."

"When?" Riley demanded.

The characteristic impatience in her voice made Hannah smile through her tears. "Anytime."

Margaux was everything Brigitte promised she would be. She was compassionate and knowledgeable and professional, and though his daughter kept insisting that she didn't want a new nanny, Michael remembered that she'd been equally resistant to Hannah at first. So he offered her the job, and she accepted. And when she agreed that she could start right away, he released Hannah from her obligation to stay until the end of the month.

It seemed pointless to have Margaux move into the beach house only to have to move back to the city a week later, so he decided that he and Riley might as well return to Verde Colinas early. Maybe his excuses were just that—certainly

Caridad thought so—and maybe it was true that he didn't want anyone else in Hannah's room. Not yet, while the memories were still fresh. By next summer, he was confident that he would be able to think of it as simply the nanny's room again and not think about all the hours that he'd spent in there with Hannah, talking and laughing with her, and making love with her.

Back in the city, Riley seemed to settle into her new routines fairly easily. Since summer was almost over, he'd started some of her lessons again, but on a much more modest scale. His daughter was polite and attentive to her teachers, and she cooperated willingly enough with Margaux, but still, something didn't seem quite right.

It took him almost a week to realize why the house seemed so somber and silent. Because not once in that entire time, not once in the six days since Hannah had been gone, did he hear his daughter laugh.

When she unpacked at home, Riley put the doll that Sam had given her back in its special place on the shelf. The silly stuffed caterpillar that Hannah had given to her as a birthday gift went on the bed, and Riley slept with it hugged close to her chest every night.

He wished that he could comfort his daughter, but he missed Hannah as much as she did. Maybe he hadn't sent her away, but he knew that he was responsible for her leaving just the same. She'd told him that she loved him, and he hadn't dared speak of the feelings that were in his own heart. Because he hadn't been willing to admit them, even to himself.

Now that she was gone, he could no longer deny the truth. Hannah hadn't just shown him how to build a better relationship with his daughter, she'd helped him heal and gave him hope for the future—a future he now knew that he wanted to share with her.

* * *

During the first week after her return from Cielo del Norte, Hannah missed Riley so much that she actually felt a pain in her chest whenever she thought of the little girl. As for the prince—well, she didn't even dare let herself think of the man who had stolen her heart.

She kept herself busy. She washed curtains and scrubbed floors; she repainted the walls and bought new throw rugs and cushions. She knew what she was doing: trying to make a fresh start. She wasn't sure that her plan would actually succeed, but she'd realized that the only way she could sleep at night was to fall into bed completely physically exhausted.

After everything was cleaned and painted and rearranged, she carted all of her boxes out of storage and back into her apartment. As she unpacked her belongings, she was amazed to think that only two months had passed since she'd packed it all away. It really wasn't a lot of time, but so much in her life had changed during that period. She had changed.

But she was doing okay—until she got a letter from Caridad. The housekeeper just wanted to let her know that Loretta had finally had her baby—almost two weeks late— and that she and Estavan were the proud grandparents of another beautiful baby girl.

Hannah was genuinely thrilled for them, and she sent a card and a gift for the baby. She'd considered hand-delivering the items, but decided against it. The memories were still too fresh, her heartache still too raw. She did hope to keep in touch with Caridad, as the housekeeper had become a wonderful friend, but there was no reason for her to ever go back to Cielo del Norte.

No reason except that she'd left her heart with Prince Michael while she'd been there. It didn't seem to matter that he didn't want it; she knew that it would always belong to him.

So many times, she thought back to that last conversation

in his office, when he'd asked, "Is there nothing I can say to make you stay?" And she'd wondered if anything might have been different if she'd had the courage to speak the words that had immediately come to mind: *Tell me you love me.*

But she knew that even if he had actually said those words to her, she wouldn't believe them. Because actions spoke louder than words, and he'd already made his feelings clear. She'd told him that she loved him—and he didn't even give her the lame I-care-about-you-but-I'm-not-ready-for-a-serious-relationship speech. He'd said nothing at all.

Still, she knew the mistake wasn't in speaking of the feelings that were in her heart; the mistake was in letting herself fall in love with a man that she'd known all along could never love her back. But even that knowledge didn't stop her from missing the prince and his little girl.

She was grateful when school started up again in September. She was anxious to get back into the familiar routines, confident that a return to her normal life would help her forget about Michael and Riley and how much she missed both of them.

Still, she thought about contacting him. Every day, she experienced moments of such intense yearning that she was tempted to pick up the phone, not just to hear his voice but to check on Riley. If she did, maybe he would give her permission to visit the little girl, but in the end she decided that wouldn't be a good idea for either of them. Margaux was the princess's nanny now, and she deserved a chance to bond with the child without Hannah in the way.

She was confident that Riley would adjust to these new changes in her life without much difficulty. She truly was an amazing child, and Hannah just hoped that the prince didn't fill her schedule with so many lessons and classes again that she forgot to be a child.

Instead of contacting the prince, Hannah busied herself working on new lesson plans for the current term. She was rereading the first play for her freshman drama class when there was a knock at the door Saturday afternoon. She was feeling desperate enough for a distraction that she responded to the summons. If it was a vacuum cleaner salesman, she might even invite him in to do a demonstration in the hope that it would possibly give her a half-hour reprieve from her thoughts of Michael and Riley.

But when she opened the door, she realized that there wasn't going to be any reprieve—because the prince and his daughter were standing in her hall.

"Hello, Hannah."

She opened her mouth, but no sound came out. She didn't know what to say—whether to invite them inside or send them away. And she was afraid that whatever choice she made would only result in fresh heartache.

"You said I could come visit, remember?" Riley's smile was uncharacteristically tentative, as if she was unsure of her welcome.

Hannah managed a smile, though she felt as if her heart was splitting wide open inside of her chest. "Of course I remember."

"Can we come in?" the prince asked.

She wished she could say no. And if his daughter wasn't standing at his side, she would have refused. But there was no way she could close the door now.

She stepped back so that they could enter, while questions swirled through her mind. Why were they here? Why now? Subconsciously, she touched a hand to her brow. The scar above her eye had started to fade, but the wounds on her heart were still raw and bleeding.

"Hannah?" the princess prompted, her little brow furrowed with concern.

She dropped her hand away, forced a smile. "Can I get you anything?"

She wasn't sure what to offer—her mind had gone blank

when she'd seen them standing outside of her door and she honestly couldn't remember what was in her refrigerator.

"Not for me, thanks," the prince said.

Riley shook her head.

Hannah led them into the living room. As a result of all of the cleaning and painting and redecorating, she knew the apartment looked good. Hardly up to royal standards, but then again, she wasn't a royal.

"So—were you just in the neighborhood?" she asked, attempting a casualness she wasn't feeling.

"No, Riley wanted to see you." Michael tucked his hands into his pockets. "Actually, we both wanted to see you."

"We miss you," the little girl said.

"How is school?" she asked Riley, forcing a note of cheerfulness into her voice even as her heart cracked wide open.

"It's okay," the princess said.

"Have you made lots of new friends?"

"A few."

Hannah swallowed. "And everything's going well...with the new nanny?"

The little girl looked at her daddy, as if deferring the question to him.

"Margaux is...almost perfect," he said.

"That's great," she said, and hoped that she sounded sincere.

"Almost," Riley repeated.

"Is there a problem?" Hannah asked, genuinely concerned.

"The only problem," Michael said, "is that she isn't you."

"We want you to come back," Riley said.

"This isn't fair," Hannah said to the prince, glaring at him through the sheen of tears that filled her eyes. "You can't bring your daughter here to—"

"It was Riley's idea," he told her. "There was no way she was letting me come here without her."

"Please, Hannah." The princess looked at her, those big brown eyes beseeching.

Hannah could barely speak around the lump in her throat. "I'm not really a nanny," she reminded the little girl gently. "I'm a high school teacher."

"We both understand that," Michael assured her. "And the thing is, Riley and I had a long talk about it and agreed that, since she's in school now during the week anyway, she probably doesn't need a nanny."

"Then why are you here?"

"Because I do need a mom," Riley piped up.

"And I need a wife," Michael said. "So—" The prince looked at his daughter, she gave him a quick nod, then they spoke in unison: "Will you marry us, Hannah?"

She could only stare at them both, her eyes filling with tears all over again.

Michael nudged his daughter.

"Oh." The little girl reached into the pocket of her skirt and pulled out a small box. She tried to flip open the lid, but it snapped shut again—catching her finger.

"Ow." Riley shook her hand free, and the box went flying across the floor, disappearing under the sofa.

Hannah had to laugh through her tears.

"This isn't quite how I imagined the scene playing out," Michael admitted.

It was a scene she hadn't dared let herself imagine and still wasn't entirely sure was real.

"Can you trust that I have a ring or do I have to dig the box out from under the furniture before you'll answer the question?" he asked.

"I don't care about the ring," she assured him.

"It's a really pretty ring," Riley said, making Hannah smile.

"But you're not saying anything," he prompted.

"I've got it, Daddy." The princess held up the box she'd

retrieved from beneath the sofa. Then she came over and opened it carefully so that Hannah could see the gorgeous princess-cut diamond solitaire set in a platinum band. "Now you're supposed to say yes."

She wanted to say yes. More than anything, she wanted to say yes, and it had nothing to do with the ring. It had to do with the fact that the prince was offering her everything she'd ever wanted and more than she'd ever dreamed of, but she felt as if they were both forgetting a couple important issues. "I'm a commoner, Michael."

"Which only means you don't carry all of the baggage that goes along with a title," he assured her.

"I realize it's not a big deal to you, but maybe it should be. And your mother—"

"Has absolutely no say in any of this," he said firmly.

"Daddy told Grandmama that if she can't accept you, then she can't be part of our family," Riley told her.

"You talked to your mother…about me?"

"I wanted her to know that I won't tolerate any more interference in my life," he said.

"I don't want to be the cause of any dissension in your relationship," she said, both surprised and humbled that he would take such a stand for her.

"You're not," Michael assured her. "If anything, confronting my mother about her attitude toward you gave me the opportunity to clear the air about a lot of things. I'm not naïve enough to believe that we came to any kind of understanding, but I am confident that she won't cause any problems for us ever again."

He spoke with such certainty, she couldn't help but believe him. But she had other—and even bigger—concerns than the princess royal.

"Needing a wife—and a mother for Riley—aren't the best reasons to get married," she said softly.

He smiled as he took both of her hands in his. "Did I

gloss over the I-love-you-more-than-I-ever-thought-it-was-possible-to-love-somebody part?"

Her heart swelled so much in response to his words that her chest actually ached with the effort to contain it. "Actually, you skipped it altogether."

"It's true," he told her. "I didn't plan to ever fall in love again. Truthfully, I didn't want to ever fall in love again."

"Because you still love Sam," she guessed.

"Sam will always have a place in my heart," he admitted, "because she was the first woman I ever loved and Riley's mother. But the rest of my heart is yours, for now and forever. So now the question I need answered is: do you love me?"

"You know I do."

"Is that a yes?" Riley wanted to know.

Hannah laughed. "That is very definitely a yes."

The princess clapped her hands together. "Now you have to put the ring on her finger, Daddy."

So he did.

"And kiss her."

And he did that, too.

He kissed her very tenderly and very thoroughly, until all of the loneliness and anguish of the past few weeks was forgotten because her heart was too full of love to feel anything else.

And still he continued to kiss her—until Riley pushed her way in between them.

"Are we married now?" she asked.

"Not quite yet," the prince said.

Riley sighed. "Can Hannah come home with us tonight anyway?"

"What do you say?" he asked, drawing her to her feet. "Will you come home with us tonight?"

Home.

She looked around at the apartment that had been her

residence for almost three years and felt absolutely no regret about leaving. It was only a collection of rooms—cold and empty without the man and the little girl she loved.

"There is nowhere else I want to be," she said truthfully.

"Just one more thing," Michael said.

"What's that?"

"If you ever retell the story of my proposal, will you edit out the awkward parts?" he asked.

She shook her head. "Absolutely not. I'm going to remember each tiny detail forever, because this moment—with you and Riley—is my every dream come true."

Epilogue

ROYAL WEDDING BELLS TOLL AGAIN
by Alex Girard

Last summer, Prince Michael Leandres was looking for a nanny for his young daughter and hired a high school teacher instead. At the time, it might have seemed that he'd made an error in judgment, but the lucky guests in attendance when the prince married Hannah Castillo at the Cathedral of Christ the King on Friday night would definitely disagree.

The ceremony began with four-and-a-half-year-old Princess Riley tossing white rose petals as she made her way down the aisle and toward the front of the church where her father, immaculately attired in a classic Armani tuxedo, was waiting. Then came the bride, in a strapless silk crepe sheath by Vera Wang, carrying a bouquet of calla lilies and freesia, proudly escorted by her uncle, Doctor Phillip Marotta.

Despite the more than two hundred people in the church,

the bride and the groom seemed to have eyes only for each other as they spoke traditional vows and exchanged rings. The couple then veered from convention by each reaching a hand to Princess Riley and drawing her into their circle, and the bride made a public promise to the groom's daughter that she would always be there for her, too, to guide her through good times and bad. The little girl chimed in to assert that they would all be good times, now that they were finally a family.

And when the bride and groom and his daughter lit the unity candle together, there wasn't anyone in the church who doubted that the young princess's words were true.

* * * * *

THE NANNY PLAN

SARAH M. ANDERSON

To Maggie Dunne, the founder of Lakota Children's Enrichment. You had a very large check and a whole lot of gumption! While I changed many things, I hope I kept your spirit of charitable action going!

To Maisey Yates and Jules Bennett, who came up with the baby for this book. You guys are the baby experts!

And to Laurel Levy for making sure I got the details of San Francisco right. I'll get back out there to visit you someday!

One

The auditorium was filling up, which was exactly what Trish wanted. Maybe four hundred people had crowded into the lower level and, in addition to the journalists from the college paper, some reporters from the San Francisco television stations were in attendance. Excellent. A good crowd would leverage some social pressure on her target. No billionaire would risk looking heartless by saying no to a charity in front of a big crowd.

Trish had been sitting in her spot—end of the third row, to the left of the podium on the stage—for over an hour. She'd gotten here early enough that no one had seen her smuggle in the check. She wished she could afford a cell phone—then she could at least play with that until the talk started instead of being the only person in the room who wasn't connected.

She was as ready as she was ever going to be. She just had to wait for her moment. Timing an ambush of one of the wealthiest men on the planet required precision.

Trish had planned everything down to her shirt—a great find at Goodwill. It was a distressed blue T-shirt with a vintage-looking Wonder Woman logo emblazoned over her breasts. It was a half size too small, but she had on her black velvet suit jacket, so it looked fine. Polished, with a geeky air.

Exactly like her target, Nate Longmire.

People continued to filter in for another thirty minutes. Everyone was here to see Longmire, the newest billionaire to come out of Silicon Valley's wealth generators. Trish had done her homework. Longmire was twenty-eight, which didn't exactly make him the "Boy Billionaire" that the press made him out to be. As far as Trish could tell, there wasn't anything particularly boyish about him.

He was six foot two, broadly built and according to her internet searches, single. But the plan wasn't to hit on him. The plan was to make him feel like she was a kindred soul in all things nerd—and all things compassionate. The plan was to box him into a corner he could only donate himself out of.

Finally, the lights in the auditorium dimmed and the president of the Student Activities Board came out in a remarkably tight skirt. Trish snorted.

"Welcome to the Speaker Symposium at San Francisco State University. I am your host, Jennifer McElwain…"

Trish tuned the woman out as Jennifer went on about SFSU's "long and proud" history of social programming, other "distinguished guests," blah-blah. Instead of listening, Trish scanned the crowd. Over half of the mostly female crowd looked like they were hoping for a wild ride in a limo to happen within an hour.

The sight of so many young, beautiful women made Trish feel uneasy. This was not her world, this college full of young, beautiful people who could casually hook up and hang out without worrying about an unexpected pregnancy, much less how to feed that baby. Trish's world was one of abject poverty, of never-ending babies that no one planned for and, therefore, no one cared for. No one except her.

Not for the first time, she felt like an interloper. Even though she was in her final year of getting a master's degree in social work—even though she'd been on this campus for five years—she still knew this wasn't her world.

Suck it up, she thought to herself as she counted the number of television cameras rolling. Five. The event was getting great press.

She was a woman with a large check and a secondhand Wonder Woman T-shirt waiting to ambush one of the richest men on the planet. That was her, Trish Hunter, in a nutshell.

"...And so," Jennifer went on, "we are thrilled to have the creator of SnAppShot, Mr. Nate Longmire, here with us tonight to discuss social responsibility and the Giving Pledge!"

The crowd erupted into something that wasn't quite a cheer but came damn close to a catcall as the Boy Billionaire himself walked on stage.

The audience surged to their feet and Trish surged with them. Longmire walked right past her. She had an excellent view of him.

Oh. Oh, *wow*. It's not like she didn't know what Nate Longmire looked like. She'd read up on his public persona—including that ridiculous article naming him one of the Top Ten Bachelors of Silicon Valley, complete with a photo spread.

But none of the pictures—not a single one of them—did the man justice. Attraction spiked through her as she studied him. In person, the tall frame and the broad shoulders weren't just eye-catching, they moved with a rippled grace that left her feeling flushed. He had on hipster jeans and Fluevog boots, but he'd paired them with a white tailored shirt with French cuffs and a purple sweater. A striped purple tie was expertly tied around his neck. He wore a scruffy beard and thick horn-rimmed glasses. They were the nerdiest things about him.

Longmire turned his face to the crowd and Trish swore

she saw him blush as the thunderous noise continued. He did not preen. If anything, he looked almost uncomfortable. Like he didn't quite fit in up there.

"Thank you," he said when the noise did not let up. "Please," he asked, a note of desperation in his voice, motioning for everyone to sit down. That, at least, worked. "There we go. Good evening, San Francisco State University!"

More applause. Trish swore he winced. He sat on a stool in the middle of the stage, gestured and the lights went down. A single spotlight fell on him. Behind him, a screen lowered to the ground and a slideshow began.

"Technology," he started as the screen flashed images of attractive people on tablets and smartphones, "has an enormous transformative power. Instant communication has the power to topple governments and reshape societies at a rate of speed that our forefathers—Steve Jobs and Bill Gates—only dreamed of." The audience laughed at this joke. Longmire gave them a tight smile.

Trish studied him as he spoke. He'd obviously memorized his remarks—not surprising, given that the press had reported his IQ at 145—just above the threshold for a true genius. But when the audience responded in any way, he seemed to draw back, as if he didn't know what to do when he went off script. Excellent. That was exactly the sort of speaker who wouldn't know how to tap-dance out of a blatant donation request.

"And you are on the cusp of this technological revolution. You have that power at your fingertips, twenty-four hours a day, seven days a week." Longmire paused to take a drink from a water bottle and clear his throat. Trish had the distinct impression that he was forcing himself through this. *Interesting*, she thought.

"The problem then becomes one of inequality," Longmire went on. "How can you communicate with the rest of humanity if they don't have those things?" Images of tribal Africans, destitute southern Asians, aboriginals from Australia and—holy crap, had he actually found a picture of…Trish studied the photo hard before it clicked past. No, that hadn't been her reservation out in South Dakota, but it might have been the Rosebud lands.

Well. Yay for him acknowledging the state of the Native American reservations in a five-second picture, even if the montage did irritate her. All the people of color had been relegated to the poor section of the talk.

"We have a responsibility to use that power—that wealth," he went on, "for the betterment of our fellow humans on this planet…"

Longmire talked for another forty-five minutes, calling for the audience members to look beyond their own screens and be conscious consumers of technology. "Be engaged," he told them. "A rising tide lifts all boats. Solar-powered laptops can lift children out of poverty. Make sure the next Big Thing won't be lost to poverty and disease. It all starts with *you*." This time, when he smiled at the crowd, it was far more confident—and far more practiced. "Don't let me down."

The screen behind him shifted to the official Longmire Foundation photo with the Twitter handle and website. The crowd erupted into applause, giving him a six-minute standing ovation while Longmire half sat on his stool, drinking his water and looking like he'd rather be anywhere but here.

The emcee came back out on stage and thanked Longmire for his "absolutely brilliant" talk before she motioned to where the microphones had been set up in the aisles. "Mr. Longmire has agreed to take questions," Jennifer gushed.

Timing was everything. Trish didn't want to go first, but she didn't want to wait until the reporters started to pack up. She needed a lull that was just long enough for her to haul out her check and get to the microphone before anyone could stop her.

About ten students lined up in either aisle. Some questions were about how Longmire had started his company in his dorm room and how a regular student could come up with a billion-dollar idea.

"What's something that people need?" Longmire replied. "I wanted a way to take my digital photos with me. Adapting a simple idea that would make it easier to share photos with my parents—and make it easy for my parents to share those photos with other people—led me to adapting the SnAppShot app to every device, every platform available. It was ten years of hard work. Don't believe what the press says. There are no overnight successes in this business. See a need and fill it."

When he was replying, Trish noted, he had a different style. Maybe it was because he was really only talking to one person? But his words flowed more easily and he spoke with more conviction. The power in his words filled the auditorium. She could listen to that voice all night— he was *mesmerizing*.

This was a problem. Trish rubbed her hands on her jeans, trying to steady her nerves. Okay, so he spoke quite well off the cuff—which he demonstrated when a few people asked antagonistic questions.

Instead of acting trapped, Longmire's face would break into a sly smile—one completely different from the cautious movement of lips he'd used during his prepared remarks. Then he would dissect the question at an astonishing rate and completely undercut the argument, all without getting off the stool.

Ah, yes. This was his other reputation, the businessman who, much like his technological forefathers, would occasionally sue people for fun and profit. Nate Longmire had amassed the reputation of a man who never gave up and never surrendered in the courtroom. He'd completely bankrupted his former college friend, the one he'd started SnAppShot with.

Trish caught herself fidgeting with her earrings. Okay, yes—there was always the chance that her little stunt wouldn't go over well. But she was determined to give it a shot. The only people who lost were the ones who never tried.

Finally, there was only one person in line on her side and Longmire was listening intently to a question from the other aisle. Trish looked back and didn't see anyone else coming forward. This was it. She edged her check out from behind her seat and then stood in line, less than two feet away from the check. She could grab it and hoist it up in seconds. This would work. It had to.

The person in front of her asked some frivolous question about how Longmire felt about his status as a sex symbol. Even as Trish rolled her eyes, Longmire shot beet red. The question had unsettled him. Perfect.

"We have time for one more question," Jennifer announced after the nervous laughter had settled. "Yes? Step forward and say your name, please."

Trish bent over and grabbed her check. It was comically huge—a four-feet long by two-feet tall piece of cardboard. "Mr. Longmire," she said, holding the check in front of her like a shield. "My name is Trish Hunter and I'm the founder of One Child, One World, a charity that gets school supplies in the hands of underprivileged children on American Indian reservations."

Longmire leaned forward, his dark eyes fastened on hers. The world seemed to—well, it didn't fall away, not like it did in stories. But the hum of the audience and the bright lights seemed to fade into the background as Longmire focused all of his attention on her and said, "An admirable cause. Go on, Ms. Hunter. What is your question?"

Trish swallowed nervously. "I recently had the privilege of being named one of *Glamour*'s Top Ten College Women in honor of the work I'm doing." She paused to heft her check over her head. "The recognition came with a ten-thousand dollar reward, which I have pledged to One Child, One World in its entirety. You've spoken eloquently about how technology can change lives. Will you match this award and donate ten thousand dollars to help children get school supplies?"

The silence that crashed over the auditorium was deafening. All Trish could hear was the pounding of blood in her ears. She'd done it. She'd done *exactly* what she'd set out to do—cause a scene and hopefully trap one of the richest men in the world into parting with just a little of his hard-earned money.

"Thank you, Ms. Hunter," the emcee said sharply. "But Mr. Longmire has a process by which people can apply for—"

"Wait," Longmire cut her off. "It's true, the Longmire Foundation does have an application process. However," he said, his gaze never leaving Trish's face. Heat flushed her body. "One must admire a direct approach. Ms. Hunter, perhaps we can discuss your charity's needs after this event is over?"

Trish almost didn't hear the *Ooh*s that came from the rest of the crowd over the rush of blood in her ears. That wasn't a *no*. It wasn't a *yes*, either—it was a very good side step around giving a hard answer one way or the other. But it wasn't a *no* and that was all that mattered. She could still press her case and maybe, just maybe, get enough funding to buy every single kid on her reservation a backpack full of school supplies before school started in five months.

Plus, she'd get to see if Nate was as good-looking up

close as he was at a distance. Not that it mattered. Of course it didn't. "I would be honored," she said into the microphone and even she didn't miss the way her voice shook, just a little.

"Bring your check," he said with a grin that came real close to being wicked. "I'm not sure I've ever seen one that large before."

Laughter rolled through the auditorium as Longmire grinned at her. Behind his glasses, one eyebrow lifted in challenge and then he pointedly looked offstage. The message was clear. Would she meet him backstage?

The emcee was thanking Longmire for his time and everyone was applauding and the rest of the evening was clearly over. Trish managed to snag her small purse—a Coach knockoff—and fight against the rising tide of college kids who had not been invited backstage for a private meeting with the Boy Billionaire. With her small purse and her large check, Trish managed to get up the steps at the side of the stage and duck behind the curtains.

The emcee stood there, glaring at her. "That was some stunt you pulled," she said in a vicious whisper.

"Thanks!" Trish responded brightly. No doubt, Jennifer had had grand plans for her own post-interview "meeting" with Longmire and Trish had usurped that quite nicely.

"Ah, Ms. Hunter. Hello." Suddenly, Nate Longmire was standing before her. Trish was a good five-nine—taller in her boots—but she still had to lean her head up to meet his gaze. "Excellent," he went on, looking down at her as if he was thrilled to see her. "You have the large check. Jennifer, would you take our picture?"

His phone chimed. He looked at it, scowled briefly, and then called up his SnAppShot app. He handed his phone to the emcee, who forced a polite smile. "Hand it up here," Longmire said, taking half of the check in his hand. Then he put his arm around Trish's shoulders and whispered, "Smile."

Trish wasn't sure she pulled off that smile. His arm around her was warm and heavy and she swore to God that she felt his touch in places he wasn't touching.

She would not be attracted to him. She couldn't *afford* to be attracted to him. All she could do was forge ahead with her plan. Phase One—trap the Boy Billionaire—was complete. Now she had to move onto Phase Two—getting a donation out of him.

Forging ahead had absolutely nothing to do with the way his physical touch was sending shimmering waves of awareness through her body. *Nothing.*

Jennifer took two shots and then handed back the phone. Longmire's arm left her and Trish couldn't help it—she shivered at the loss of his warmth.

"Mr. Longmire," Jennifer began in a silky tone. "If you recall, I'd invited you out for a dinner after the program. We should get going."

There was a pause that could only be called awkward. Longmire didn't even move for three blinks of the eye— as if this statement had taken him quite by surprise and, despite his ferocious business skills and dizzying intellect, he had no possible answer for Jennifer.

Jennifer touched his arm. "Ready?" she said, batting her eyes.

Trish rolled hers—just as Longmire looked at her. *Oops.* Busted.

But instead of glaring at her, Longmire looked as if Trish was the answer to all his questions. That look should not do things to her. So, she forcibly decided, it didn't.

"Gosh—I do remember that, but I think I need to address Ms. Hunter's question first." He stepped away from Jennifer much like a crab avoiding a hungry seagull. Jennifer's hand hung in empty space for a moment before she lowered it back to her side. "Call my office," Longmire said, turning on his heel. "We'll try to set something up. Ms. Hunter? Are you coming?"

Trish clutched her check to her chest and hurried after Longmire, trying to match his long strides.

That definitely wasn't a *no*.

Now she just needed to get to a *yes*.

Nate settled into the Apollo Coffee shop. He liked coffee shops. They were usually busy enough that he didn't garner too much attention but quiet enough that he could think. He liked to think. It was a profitable, satisfying experience for him, thinking.

Right now he was thinking about the young woman who'd trucked a comically large check into the hired car and carried it into the coffee shop as if it were the most normal thing ever.

Trish Hunter. She was drinking a small black coffee—easily the cheapest thing on the extensive menu. She'd insisted on buying her own coffee, too. Had absolutely refused to let him plunk down the two dollars and change for hers.

That was something…different. He was intrigued, he had to admit.

The large check was wedged behind her chair, looking slightly worse for wear. "That's not the real check, is it?" he asked over the lip of his grande mocha.

"No. I got a regulation-sized check that went straight into the bank. But this makes for better photos, don't you think?" she replied easily, without that coy tone women had started using around him about the time he made his first million.

"Not a lot of people would have had the guts to try and trap me like that," he noted, watching her face closely. She was lovely—long dark hair that hung most of the way down her back, brown skin that graced high cheekbones. With her strong features and strong body—because there was no missing *that*—she looked like she could *be* Wonder Woman.

She didn't act like the kind of women who tried to trap him with their feminine wiles. Instead, she sat across from him, drinking cheap coffee and no doubt waiting to tell him why he should cut her another check.

For a second—the amount of time it took for her to look up at him through thick lashes—Nate almost panicked. He wasn't particularly good with women, as evidenced by that nagging feeling that he hadn't handled Jennifer's dinner invitation well and the fact that he had flat-out ignored that message from Diana—the third one this month.

Ever since things with Diana had fallen apart—and then really gone to hell—he'd kept things simple by simply not getting involved. Which meant that he was horribly out of practice. But there was no way he would let another woman take advantage of him. And that included Diana. Hence why he would just keep right on ignoring her messages.

Trish Hunter wasn't doing the things that normally made him nervous—treating him like he was a sex god she'd been secretly worshipping for years.

She grinned, a small curve of her lips over the edge of her cup. That grin did something to him—made him feel more sure of himself. Which sounded ridiculous but there it was. "Did it work? The trap, that is."

Nate smiled back. He was terrible about negotiations with members of the opposite sex. Money, however, was something he'd learned to negotiate. And the fact that this lovely young woman wasn't playing coy—wasn't acting like he'd gotten used to women acting around him—only made him more comfortable. Everything was out in the open. He could handle this kind of interaction. "That depends."

Her eyes widened slightly and a flash of surprise crossed her face. It made her look…innocent. Sweet, even. "Upon?"

"Tell me about your charity."

She exhaled in relief. It wasn't a big gesture, but he saw it nonetheless. He wondered what she'd thought he would ask. "Of course. One Child, One World is a registered 501(c) charity. We keep our overhead as low as possible." Nate sighed. He hated the boring part of charity work. It was, for lack of a better word, *boring*. "Approximately $0.93 of every dollar donated goes to school supplies…" her voice trailed off. "Not the right answer?"

He sat up a little straighter. She was paying attention to him. He'd be lying if he said it wasn't flattering. "Those statistics are all required as part of the grant application process," he replied, waving his hand. "The lawyers insisted. But that's not what I wanted to know."

She raised a strong eyebrow and leaned toward him. Yes, he had her full attention—and she had his. "You asked about my charity."

Oh, yeah—her words were nothing but challenge. This was not a woman telling him whatever he wanted to hear. This was a woman who would push back. Even though he had the money and she had a very cheap coffee, she'd still push back.

That made her even more interesting.

And as long as he kept thinking of it in terms of power and money—instead of noting how pretty she was and how she was looking at him and especially how he was no doubt looking at her—he'd be just fine.

"Tell me about why a young woman would start an organization to get school supplies into kids' hands. Tell me about…" *You.* But he didn't say that because that would cross the line of business and go into the personal. The moment he did that, he'd probably start flailing and knock the coffee into her lap. "Tell me about it."

"Ah." She took her time sipping her coffee. "Where did you grow up? Kansas City, right?"

"You've done your homework."

"Any good trap is a well-planned trap," she easily replied, a note of satisfaction in her voice.

He nodded his head in acknowledgment. "Yes, I grew up in Kansas City. Middle-class household. Father was an accountant, mother taught second grade." He left out the part about his brothers. "It was a very comfortable life." He hadn't realized how comfortable until he'd made his money—and started looking at how other people lived.

Trish smiled encouragingly. "And every August, you got a new backpack, new shoes, new school clothes and everything on that list teachers said you had to have, right?"

"Yes." He took a calculated risk. Just because she had black hair and skin the color of copper and was running a charity that helped American Indians on reservations didn't necessarily mean she was a Native American herself. But there was no such thing as coincidence. "I take it you didn't?"

Something in her face changed—her eyes seemed to harden. "My sixth-grade teacher gave me two pencils once. It was all she could afford." She dropped her gaze and began to fiddle with one of her earrings. "It was the best present I ever got."

Nate, being Nate, didn't have a smooth comeback to that. In fact, he didn't know what to say at all. His mom, Susan, had worked as a teacher, and she'd occasionally talked about a student who needed "a little extra help," as she put it. Then she'd fill a backpack with food and some basics and that was that. But that was before she'd had to stay home with Nate's brother Joe full-time.

"I'm sorry to hear that," he said quietly. Once, he hadn't

believed there was a world where a couple of #2 pencils were an amazing gift. But now he knew better.

Her gaze still on her coffee, she gave him a quick, tight smile. He needed to move the conversation forward. "So you're working to change that?"

"Yes. A new backpack full of everything a kid needs in a classroom." She shrugged and looked back at him. The hardness fell away. "I mean, that's the first goal. But it's an important first step."

He nodded thoughtfully. "You have bigger plans?"

Her eyes lit up. "Oh, of course! It's just the beginning."

"Tell me what you'd do."

"For so many kids, school is…it's an oasis in the middle of a desert. The schools need to open earlier, stay open later. They need to serve a bigger breakfast, a bigger lunch and everyone needs an afternoon snack. Too many kids aren't getting regular meals at home and it's so hard to study on an empty stomach." As she said this last point, she dropped her gaze again.

She was speaking from experience, he realized. Two pencils and nothing to eat at home.

"Indians on the rez love basketball and skateboarding," she went on. "Having better courts and parks on the school grounds could keep kids from joining gangs."

"You have gang problems?" He always associated gangs with inner-city drug wars or something.

She gave him a look that walked a fine line between "amused" and "condescending." "Some people have perverted our warrior culture into a gang mentality. We lose kids that way and we rarely get them back."

He thought over her wish list, such as it was. "I haven't heard anything about computers."

She paused, then gave him that tight smile again. "It's the ultimate goal, one that will require far more than ten or even twenty thousand dollars of funding. Most schools don't have the infrastructure to support an internet connection, much less cloud storage. I want kids to have basic supplies and full bellies before I get to that. You understand, don't you?"

He nodded. He'd toured some bad schools—mold growing on the walls, windows taped shut to keep the glass from falling out, ancient textbooks that smelled like rot. But what she was describing…

"What is it you want from me, then? Just ten grand?"

The moment he said it, he realized that maybe he shouldn't have phrased it quite like that. Especially not when Trish leaned back in her chair, one arm on the armrest, the other curled up under her chin—except for her index finger, which she'd extended over her lips as if they were in a library and she was shushing him. She met his gaze full-on, a hint of challenge lurking in her eyes. The air grew tight with tension.

God, she was beautiful and there was something else behind that gaze—an interest in more than just his bank account. He should ask her out. She wasn't intimidated by him and she wasn't throwing herself at him. She was here for the money and all her cards were up front, no hiding funding requests behind manipulative sexual desire. Hell. He didn't meet too many women who could just sit and have a conversation with him.

Except…dating was not his strong suit and he was pretty sure that asking a woman out right after she'd requested a donation would probably cross some ethical line.

Damn.

"Of course, One Child, One World would be delighted with any funding the Longmire Foundation saw fit to disperse," she said, sounding very much like someone who'd written a few grants in her time.

"How'd you get to be a Woman of the Year?"

"One of my professors nominated me," she told him. "I

didn't know she was doing it. One day, I'm trying to organize a bake sale to raise a hundred dollars to cover postage back to the rez and the next, I'm being flown to New York and given a *lot* of money." She blushed. "I mean, a lot of money for me. I'm sure ten grand isn't very much to you."

"I can remember when that much was a lot of money," he admitted. He winced. That was a totally jerky thing to say and he knew it.

He was about to apologize when she said, "Tell me about your charity," turning his question back on him.

He regarded her for a second. "Is that another way of asking why I'm giving money away for free?"

"You *did* go to all that trouble of earning it in the first place," she pointed out.

He shrugged. "Like I said, I had a comfortable childhood. We didn't always get everything we wanted—I didn't get a car for my sixteenth birthday or anything— but we were fine."

How he'd wanted a car. Brad, his older brother, had a half-rusted Jeep he'd bought with lawn-mowing money that he swore made it a breeze to get a date.

Back then, Nate had absolutely no prospect of a date. He was tall and gangly, with dorky glasses and awful skin. They were still trying to integrate Joe into a mainstream classroom at that point and Nate was mercilessly mocked by his peers. The only possible way he could have gotten a girl was if he'd had a sweet ride to pick her up in.

Alas. No car. No date.

"Anyway," he went on, shaking his head, "I made that first million and I felt like I'd made it. But a weird thing happened—that million spawned a second million, then a third. And then the buyout happened and now…" He gave her an apologetic smile. "Honestly, what the hell am I going to do with a billion dollars? Buy a country and rule as a despot?"

It wasn't as if this background was entirely new information—he'd given interviews explaining the rationale for his foundation—but those were formal things with scripted answers, preapproved by his assistant, Stanley.

Right now, sitting here in a coffee shop with Ms. Trish Hunter, it didn't feel like an interview. It felt like a conversation. An honest one.

Nate nodded toward her shirt. "I bought Superman #1— you know?"

A smile quirked at her lips. "I do know. Didn't you pay the highest recorded price for it?"

"I did. It was *wild*—I felt like I was jumping off a cliff, to pay five million for a comic book."

"Did you at least read it? Or did you lock it up?" The way she asked the question made it clear—she would have read it.

"I read it. Carefully." He waggled his eyebrows at her, as if he were saying something salacious. She laughed. It was as close to flirting as he got. "With tongs. In a temperature-controlled room."

Her eyes lit up. "Were you wearing one of those hazmat suits, too?"

"No. Just gloves." She giggled at the image and he laughed with her. It had been totally ridiculous. "But what else am I going to do with this much money besides buy comic books?"

"You donated a lot to mental-health research," she said. She was leaning forward slightly, her body language indicating that she was really listening.

"I have a…personal connection to that." When she waited for more, he added, "I keep my family private. It's the only way to stay sane in this industry."

Yes, he had set up an endowment into schizophrenia, depression and bipolar research. That was the public action. The private one had been setting up a trust fund for the care of Joe. Mom was able to stay home full-time with Joe now, and they had reliable home health aides to assist. Nate had tried to give his parents a million dollars or an all-expenses paid trip around the world, but it turned out that peace of mind about their youngest son was all they really wanted.

And after what had happened with Diana...

Nate's private life stayed private. Period.

"Ah, understood." She tilted her head. "That explains why there's no press on it. I wondered."

He stared at her. Yeah, he expected that she'd done her homework, but it was unusual to have someone admit to digging into his past—and then agree not to discuss it. As the shock of her blunt attitude wore off, he felt himself grinning at her even more. "Thanks. So, you know—I'm rich, I no longer run my own company—what am I going to do with the rest of my life? I set up a fund for my niece, bought my brother a house, took care of—well, I took care of the rest of my family, fended off a few lawsuits. That only left me with about a billion. Giving away the money seemed like something to do. The Longmire Foundation has given away fourteen million dollars and I haven't even made a dent yet."

That was the truth. He was making more in interest than he could give away. The simple truth was that her request for a matching grant of ten thousand dollars was the product of about five minutes for him, if that. He could add two or three zeroes to the end of the check and never even notice the money was gone.

"Is that what makes you happy?"

He looked at her funny. Happy? He was rich. He wasn't the same gangly nerd he'd been in high school. He was a ruthless businessman, a hugely successful one. He owned his own jet, for crying out loud.

But there was something in the way she asked it...

"I'm doing good. That's what counts."

"Of course." She opened her mouth, paused—and then angled her body toward his. Her gaze dropped again, but only for a second. She looked up at him through her lashes. Energy—attraction—seemed to arc between them as he stared at her.

Her eyes were a deep brown, like dark chocolate. Sweet, yes—but much more than that. There was innocence, but now it had an edge to it—an edge that held a hell of a lot of promise.

He leaned forward, eager to hear what she would say—and whether or not it would sound like legal boilerplate or if it would sound like something else.

He leaned right into his coffee and promptly spilled what was left of his grande mocha into her lap.

"Whoa!" she shouted, hopping to her feet. The dark stain spread down her leg.

"Oh, damn—I'm so sorry," he mumbled. What had he been thinking? Of course she wasn't going to say something along the lines of "Maybe we should discuss this over dinner." He grabbed some napkins and thrust them at her. "Here."

This was terrible. He'd been doing just fine when it'd been a business negotiation, but the moment he hoped it'd go past that—it blew up in his face.

"I'm so sorry," he repeated. "I'll pay for the cleaning bill."

She laughed. And after she'd checked her seat for coffee, she sat down, spread a napkin over her lap, and grinned at him. "Don't worry about it."

"But your clothes…" Even now, he could see the droplets of coffee on her shirt.

"I'm used to spills and stains. Don't worry about it."

He wasn't sure if he believed her, but then he met her gaze. It was full of humor, yes—but he didn't get the sense that she was laughing at him. Just the situation. Clumsy billionaire knocks coffee into her lap.

He had to get out of here before he did even worse damage to her clothes or his pride. "Listen, why don't you come by my office in two weeks? I'll have my assistant start the paperwork and we can settle the terms then." He fished out his card, which just said, "Longmire Foundation," with the address and email. "And please—bring the dry-cleaning bill. It hurts me to think that I might have ruined your shirt."

A second too late, he realized he was staring at her chest. The jacket had fallen open a little more. It was a very nice chest.

God, what was he doing? Trying to make this worse? He shook some sense—he hoped—back into his head and handed over the card. "Say, Friday at two?"

"I have to work." She took the card and studied it. "This is in the Filmore area."

"Yes. I keep an office close to where I live." She was still looking at the card. "Is that a problem?"

"No, it's fine. I just thought you'd be down in the Mission or in SOMA. Close to where all the other tech billionaires hang out."

He waved his hand. "I like to walk to the office when it's nice out." She gaped at him, as if she couldn't believe a billionaire would stoop to walking on his own two feet instead of being carried on a gold-plated litter by trained elephants. "Truth be told, we're not some sort of secret billionaire club. And I don't really have much interest in the constant one-upmanship that happens when you get us all together. I like peace and quiet and a nice view. I like to be a little bit not what people expect."

That got her attention. She looked up at him, her dark eyes wide and...encouraging?

If she could still look at him after he dumped his drink all over her, then maybe...

She went back to studying the card. "I won't be able to get there until five. Is that too late?"

"Yeah, that's fine. I'll make sure Stanley knows you're coming."

"Stanley?"

"My assistant." Actually, Stanley was more than that—he picked out Nate's clothes and made sure Nate projected the right amount of geek-cred cool. If only Stanley had been here tonight, no one would have gotten a damp lap.

He'd have Stanley start the due diligence on her charity to make sure her numbers were correct.

She grinned up at him again, as if she wasn't sure how to process an assistant named Stanley. "I look forward to our meeting." She stood, crumpling up the napkins and stuffing them into her empty cup. Then she extended her hand. "Mr. Longmire, it has been an honor. Thank you so much for considering my proposal."

"It's a worthy cause." He took her hand in his and tried to shake it, but the feeling of her slender fingers warming his momentarily froze his brain. He wanted to say something suave and sophisticated that let her know he was interested in more than her charity.

He had nothing.

Maybe their next meeting would go more smoothly—in his office, Stanley would be ready to swoop in and save Nate from himself as needed. "And again—sorry about the coffee."

She waved him off and retrieved her large check from behind the chair. Thankfully, it didn't seem to be too splattered. "I'll see you on Friday in two weeks."

"I'm looking forward to it." That got him a nice smile, warm and friendly and comforting—like she realized exactly how socially awkward he really was and was rewarding him for doing a decent job.

Nate watched her figure retreat from the coffee shop and disappear into the foggy darkness, the check glowing white. Trish Hunter. Yes, Stanley would have to do some due diligence on her charity. And on the woman herself. Nate wanted to know more about her—a lot more.

He sent for a car to take him home and was picking up the coffee cups—his mother had always taught him to pick up after himself and being a self-made billionaire hadn't changed that—when his phone rang. Not the chime that went with a message, but the ring of someone actually calling him.

His mother. She was pretty much the only person who called him, anyway. She was too old to learn to text, she said. That was her story and she was sticking to it.

"Hey, Mom," he said, heading out to the sidewalk.

"Nate? Oh, honey." She was crying. Nate froze halfway out the door. Instantly, all thoughts of Trish Hunter and large checks and coffee were pushed from his mind.

"Mom? What's wrong?"

"Nate—oh, God. There's been an accident."

"Dad?" Panic clawed at him. His parents were only in their fifties. He didn't want to lose either one just yet.

"He's fine. Oh, Nate…we need you to come home. It's Brad and Elena…"

"Are they okay?" But even as he said it, he knew the answer was no. His mother was crying. Something horrible had happened to his older brother and his sister-in-law. "What about Jane?" When his mom didn't answer right away, Nate nearly threw up. "Mom—is Jane okay?"

"The baby is fine. We were watching her so they could go out… Come home, Nate. Come home *now*."

Dear God in heaven. "I'm on my way, Mom. I'll be there as soon as I can." He hung up and called Stanley. This was one of the benefits of being a billionaire. He didn't have to deal with emergency flights. He had an assistant—and a private jet.

"Stanley, get the plane ready. I need to go to Kansas City. Right now."

Two

Trish had spent a good deal of time on this outfit. Wearing the Wonder Woman shirt again would be too obvious, even though it had washed clean. Trish had decided to go a little more formal for this meeting. She had on a coral skirt that came to midcalf. She'd paired it with a white shirt that was as crisp as she could get it in a public Laundromat and a denim jacket from Diesel—another major score from the thrift stores. Her only pair of cowboy boots were on her feet. Once they'd been black, but now they were a faded gray. Which was trendy enough, so she figured she was okay.

She was wearing the one good piece of turquoise she had, a teardrop-shaped pendant that hung on a thin silver chain. She'd twisted her hair up into a professional looking knot and had put in a pair of silver hoops that looked more expensive than they really were.

This was her being a business-professional Lakota woman. This was not her dressing to impress a certain billionaire. Not much, anyway.

She didn't have a cleaning bill to give him and she had the distinctive feeling that he wasn't going to be happy about that. What could she do? Tell him she needed $1.25 in quarters for the Laundromat?

The skirt had necessitated the bus, however. She hadn't wanted it to get tangled up in her bike spokes. So, at 5:08—

after almost an hour and a half—she finally arrived at his address in the Filmore district.

The Longmire Foundation was on the fourth floor of an austere-looking office building. On the ride up, Trish swallowed nervously. Yes, the conversation with Nate at the coffee shop had been pleasant and encouraging—but who knew what might have changed in the past two weeks? Because of how the event had played out in the press, she was worried that he might have changed his mind. The news reports had caught the look he'd given her when he'd asked her to meet him backstage and rumors about something else happening backstage had already started.

Trish had fielded a few phone calls, which was good. Sort of. Yes, any attention she could draw to One Child was good attention—but the quotes reporters had been looking for were much more along the lines of whether or not a romance had sparked.

Which it hadn't. Really.

So Nate Longmire was tall, built and twice as handsome in person as he was in photographs. So there'd been something between them—something that she hadn't been able to stop thinking about since the moment she'd walked out of that coffee shop. It'd almost been like…like she'd belonged there, with him. For just a little bit, he hadn't been some unreachable Boy Billionaire and she hadn't been a dirt-poor American Indian. He'd just been a man and she'd just been a woman and that was—well, it was good. With the potential to be even better.

And that potential? That's what she'd been dreaming about almost every single night for the past two weeks.

Well. They were just dreams. And she needed to stick with reality.

And the reality of the situation was that Nate was not her type. She didn't have a type, but whatever it might be, a Boy Billionaire clearly wasn't it. She would probably never have a total of five million dollars in her entire life—and he was the kind of guy who spent that on a comic book.

At least the Wonder Woman shirt had done its job, she figured. Now, in her fancy clothes, it was time to do hers.

She'd done her best to avoid answering any questions about her supposed involvement with Nate Longmire by throwing out every single stat she could about poverty on Indian reservations and how even a five-dollar donation could make a difference. In the end, unable to get a juicy quote out of her, the press had left her alone.

She'd noticed that, in any report, whether online or on television, Nate Longmire had always been "unavailable for comment." She didn't know if that was a good thing or not.

Trish found the right door—suite 412, *The Longmire Foundation* written in black letters on the glass—and tried the doorknob, but it was locked. A growing sense of dread filled her as she knocked.

A minute passed. Trish didn't know if she should knock again or…what? She had no other options. Nate said he'd be here—that Stanley would be here. He hadn't forgotten, had he?

She knocked again.

This time, a man shouted, "Jeez, I'm coming. I'm coming."

The door was unlocked and thrown open. Instead of Nate Longmire's well-dressed form, a man in a white tank top, oversize corduroy pants held up by bright red suspenders and more tattoos than God glared down at her. "What?"

"Um, hello," Trish said, trying not to be nervous. This guy had spacers in his ears. She could see right through them. She swallowed. "I have an appointment with Mr. Longmire—"

"What are you doing here?" the man all but growled at her.

"I'm sorry?"

The man looked put out. "You're supposed to be at his house for the interview. Didn't they tell you that?"

They? They *who*? "No?"

Mr. Tattoos rolled his eyes to the sky and sighed. "You're in the wrong place. You need to be at 2601 Pacific Street." He looked at her dubiously. "2601 Pacific Street," he repeated in a slower, louder voice, as if she'd suddenly gone deaf. When Trish just stared at him, he pointed again and said, "That way. Okay?"

"Yes, all right." She stood there for a minute, too shocked to do much but not look through the holes in his ears. "Thank you."

"Yeah, good luck—you're gonna need it," he called after her, then she heard the door shut and lock behind her.

Great. Trish was going to be way late. Panic fluttered through her stomach. Was this a sign—Nate had reviewed her case and decided that her charity didn't meet his requirements? Why on earth was she supposed to go to his house—especially if he was going to turn her down? This wasn't about to get weird, was it?

She did the only thing she could do—she started to walk. She loved walking through San Francisco, looking at all the Victorian houses and wondering what it would be like to live in one. To have a view of the bay or the Golden Gate Bridge. To not have to worry about making rent and having enough left over.

Her mother, Pat, had loved the music from the Summer of Love. When she was with a real jerk of a boyfriend—which was often enough—Pat would sometimes get nostalgic and talk about one day coming out to San Francisco to find Trish's father. That was how Trish found out that her father had come to this city when he'd abandoned his family.

Trish did what she always did when she walked the

streets—she looked in the faces of each person she passed by, hoping to recognize a little part of herself. Maybe her father had gotten remarried and had more kids. Maybe Trish would find a half sister walking around. Or maybe the woman her father had settled down with would recognize her husband's face in Trish's and ask if they were related.

Trish had lived here for five years. This on-the-street recognition hadn't happened, not once. But she kept looking.

She walked to Pacific Street and turned. This was such a beautiful place, right across from the park. Nothing like the tiny garret apartment in Ingleside she rented for the subsidized sum of $350 a month.

She found the right house—she hoped. It was a sweeping three-story Victorian home, the exterior painted a soft shade of blue with bright white paint outlining the scrollwork and columns. The curtains on the ground-level windows were closed and a painted garage door was shut. Next to that was a wide, sweeping set of steps that led up to the perfect porch for a summer afternoon, complete with swing.

It was simply lovely. The small part of her brain that wasn't nervous about this whole "interview at his house" thing was doing a little happy dance—she would finally get to see the inside of one of these homes.

But that excitement was buried pretty danged deep. To get inside the home, she had to get through the gate at the bottom of the stairs—and it didn't budge. How was she supposed to be *at* the house if she couldn't even get to the door? Then she saw a buzzer off to the right. She pressed it and waited.

Even standing here felt like she was interloping again. This wasn't right. Nate had been very clear—she was to meet him at the office. Trish had no idea which "they" should have told her about the change, but what could she do? She needed the donation, desperately.

So she rang the bell, again, and waited. Again. She caught herself twisting her earring and forced her hands back by her sides. This was not about to go sideways on her. This was fine. She was a professional. She could handle whatever was on the other side of that door with grace and charm.

Up on the porch, the door opened and a short, stocky woman in a gray dress and a white apron stood before her. "Hello?"

"Hi," Trish said, trying her best to smile warmly. "I have an appointment with Mr. Longmire and—"

"*Ay mia*—you're late," the woman said—but unlike Mr. Tattoo, she looked happy to see Trish. "Come in, come in." A buzzer sounded and the gate swung free. Trish climbed the stairs, schooling her features into a professional smile—warm, welcoming, not at all worried about the lack of communication about any changes to the plan.

"Hello," she said when she was face-to-face with the woman. "I'm Trish Hunter and—"

The woman latched onto Trish's arm and all but hauled her inside. The door shut with a resounding thud behind her.

"Who is it, Rosita?" Trish recognized Nate's voice as the one calling down the stairs.

"The girl," Rosita called back.

"Send her up."

It was only then, with Rosita the maid shooing her up the stairs so fast that she could barely take in the beautiful details of the entry room, that Trish heard it—the plaintive wail of a deeply unhappy baby.

It was pretty safe to say that Trish had absolutely no idea what was going on. But up the stairs she went, bracing herself for what baby-related carnage awaited her.

She was not wrong about that.

Nate Longmire—the same Boy Billionaire who had given an impassioned talk on social responsibility, the same Nate Longmire who had insisted on paying her dry-cleaning bill, the very same Nate Longmire that had looked positively sinful in his hipster glasses and purple tie—stood in front of one of those portable playpens that Trish had coveted for years. Nate was in a pair of jeans and a white T-shirt. That part wasn't surprising.

What was surprising was that Nate was trying to hold a screaming baby. The child was in nothing but a diaper and, unless Trish missed her guess, the diaper was on backwards.

"What on earth?" Trish demanded.

Nate spun at the sound of the exclamation from behind him just as Jane squirmed in his arms. Oh, hell—why were babies so damned hard to hold onto?

"Uh…" he managed to get out as he got his other arm under Jane's bottom and kept her from tumbling. The little girl screamed even louder. Nate would have thought that it was physically impossible for her to find more volume from her tiny little body, but she had.

"Oh, for Pete's sake," the woman said. The next thing he knew, Jane had been lifted out of his arms by a beautiful woman with striking dark eyes and—

Oh, God. "Trish!"

"Yes, hello," she said, slinging the baby onto her hip with a practiced air. "Where are the diapers?"

"Why—what—I mean—you're here?"

Trish paused in her search for diapers and gave him a look. It was a look that he deserved. Never in his entire life had he felt more like an idiot. "Yes. We had an appointment."

He started. "Your appointment?"

"Yes," she said, as she turned a small circle, surveying the complete and total destruction of the room that, until seven days ago, had been a sitting room and now was supposed to be a nursery. Even Nate knew that it wasn't a nursery, not yet. It was a hellhole. He couldn't tell if she was finding what she was looking for or not.

His mind tried to work, but that was like trying to open a bank vault where all the tumblers had rusted shut. He was *so* tired but Trish was here. He'd never been so happy to see a woman in his entire life. "You're here about the nanny position?"

That got him another look—but there was more pity in her eyes this time. "Mr. Longmire," she said in an utterly calm voice. She snagged a blanket and, with the screaming baby still on her hip, managed to smoothly lay the cloth out on the floor. "We had an appointment in your office at five today to discuss a matching grant to my charity, One Child, One World."

Oh, hell. "You're…not here about the nanny position?"

Trish located a diaper and then fell to her knees in an entirely graceful way. She carefully laid Jane out on the blanket. "Oh, dear, yes," she soothed in a soft voice that Nate had to strain to hear over the screaming. "You're so cold, sweetie! And wet, too? Oh, yes, it's so hard to be a baby, isn't it?" Trish changed the diaper and then looked up at him. "Does she have any clothes?"

"Why are you so calm?" he demanded.

"This is not difficult, Mr. Longmire. Does she have any clothes?"

Nate turned and dug into one of the suitcases Stanley had loaded onto his private plane. "Like a dress or something?"

"Like jammies, Mr. Longmire. Oh, I know," she said in that soothing voice again. "I know. I think he's trying his best, but he doesn't know how to speak baby, does he?"

For a blissful second, Jane stopped screaming and instead only made a little burbling noise, as if she really were talking to Trish.

Then the screaming started right back up with renewed vigor.

Nate grabbed something that looked like it could be jammies. Orange terry cloth with pink butterflies and green flowers, it had long sleeves and footies attached to the legs. "This?"

"That's perfect," Trish said in that soothing tone again. Nate handed over the clothes and watched, stunned, as Trish got the wriggling arms and kicking legs into the fabric.

"How do you do that? I couldn't get her into anything. And I couldn't get her to stop screaming."

"I noticed." Trish looked up at him and smiled. "How are you feeding her?"

"Um, my mom sent some formula. Down in the kitchen."

Trish rubbed Jane's little tummy. Then, like it was just that easy, she folded the blanket around Jane and tucked in the ends and suddenly, Nate was looking at a baby burrito.

"One second, baby." Then, to Nate, she said, "Don't pick her up—but watch her while I wash my hands, okay?"

"Okay?" What choice did he have? The baby was still crying but, miraculously, her volume had pitched down for the first time since Nate had seen her.

"Bathroom?" Trish asked.

"Through that door." As he stared at Jane, he tried to think. For a man who had done plenty of thinking while pulling all-nighters, he was stunned at how much his brain felt like the sludge at the bottom of a grease trap.

Trish Hunter. How could he forget her? Not even a funeral or a solid two weeks of sleep deprivation could erase the memory of her talking with him in a coffee shop. She'd been smart and beautiful and he'd—he'd liked her. He'd gotten the distinctive feeling that she'd been interested in him—not just his money.

Crap. He must have forgotten about their appointment entirely when his world fell apart. Which—yes, now he remembered—had occurred moments after his conversation with Trish in the coffee shop.

The woman he'd felt a connection with was the same woman who had just walked into his house and changed his niece's diaper.

Wait.

A woman he'd felt a connection with had just changed his niece's diaper. And gotten her dressed. And wrapped her into a burrito. And, if the indications were to be believed, was about to go down and fix a bottle of formula.

He'd been expecting a candidate for the position of nanny.

Maybe she had arrived.

Trish came out, looking just as elegant as she had before. "There now," she said in that soft voice as she scooped Jane up and cuddled the baby against her chest. "I bet you're hungry and I bet you're sleepy. Let's get some milk, okay?" Jane made a little mewing sound that came close to an agreement.

Trish looked at Nate, who was staring. "Kitchen?"

"This way."

Nate felt like he needed to be doing something better here—but he was at a loss. All he could do was lead the way down stairs and into the back of the house, where Rosita was looking like the last rat on the ship. When his maid saw Trish cuddling the slightly quieter baby, her face lit up. "Oh, miss—we're so glad you've come."

Trish managed a smile, but Nate saw it wasn't a natural thing. "Any clean bottles and nipples?"

Rosita produced the supplies, babbling on in her faint accent the whole time. "I tried, miss, but I never much cared for children." She got out the tub of formula and a gallon of milk and started to mix it.

"Wait—stop." Trish's voice was one of horror. Then she looked at Nate and then around the room again, just like she had in the nursery. When she settled upon the breakfast bar with the stools, she said, "Mr. Longmire—sit."

He sat.

"Hold out your arms like this." She slid Jane down into a cradled position. Nate did as she asked. "Good. Now. Don't drop the baby." Trish set Jane into his arms and then ran her hands over him, pushing his arms tighter here, looser there. Even in his exhausted state, he didn't miss the way her touch lingered on his skin.

He looked up at her. Her face was only inches away from his. If possible, she was even prettier today than she'd been in the coffee shop.

"I'm so glad you're here," he said. It came out quiet and serious.

She paused and met his gaze, her hands still on his bare skin. Heat flashed between them, that attraction he'd felt before.

She didn't say anything, though. She just kept arranging his body until—for the first time—Nate felt like he had a good grasp on his niece.

Although he still didn't have a good grasp on the situation. Well, one thing at a time. Baby first. Attraction second.

"All right," Trish said, sounding very much like a general about to engage in battle. "Dump that out, please. Do you have any other clean bottles?"

"Miss?" Rosita said, hesitantly.

"No milk, not yet. The formula's supposed to be mixed with water."

"Oh," Rosita and Nate said at the same time. Nate went on, "My mom just said she needed her milk every three hours and I thought…damn. I mean dang," he corrected, looking down at Jane.

"I am so sorry, Señor Nate," Rosita said in a low voice. "I…"

"Don't worry about it, Rosita. We both missed it. No harm done." He glanced back at Trish. "Right?"

"Probably not," Trish replied as she fixed a fresh bottle. "Is there somewhere we can go sit? I have a few questions."

"Yeah." She took the baby out of his arms and waited for him to lead the way.

Nate couldn't go back up to the disaster zone that was supposed to be the nursery. That was no image to present to anyone, but especially a lovely young woman who had a way with a baby and hadn't run screaming at the sight of Nate at his worst.

"Rosita, if you could try and make some sense of the nursery while Ms. Hunter and I talk?"

"Yes," Rosita said, sounding relieved to be off the hook. She scurried out of the kitchen faster than Nate had ever seen her move in the three years she'd worked for him.

Nate led Trish to his front parlor. He liked this old house, these old rooms. He kept his technology in a separate room so that this room, where he received visitors, had a timeless feel to it. The front parlor was an excellent room within which to think. No blinking lights or chiming tones to distract him—or disturb an upset infant. "Where do you want to sit?"

"This will be fine." She settled herself in his favorite chair, the plush leather wingback with a matching footstool. She propped her arm on the armrest and got Jane to take the bottle on the second try. Nate watched in surprise. He had hardly been able to get Jane to drink anything.

Of course, if they'd been making it wrong…

"So," she said when he perched on the nearby sofa. "Tell me about it."

Nate didn't like to talk about his family. He liked to keep that part of himself—his past, their present—private. It was better that way for everyone. But he was desperate here. "This doesn't leave this room."

She lifted her eyebrows, but that was the only sign that his statement surprised her. "Agreed."

"I didn't mean to forget our appointment."

"It's pretty obvious that something came up. Didn't it, sweetie?" she cooed at Jane, who was making happy little slurping noises. Nate was thrilled to see her little eyelids already drifting shut.

"I haven't slept more than two hours at a shot in the last two weeks. I don't…I told my parents I couldn't do this. I don't know anything about babies."

"Agreed," Trish repeated with a smile. Nate became aware of a light humming that sounded like…a lullaby?

He took a deep breath. He'd only told two other people about what had happened—Stanley and Rosita. "My brother, my perfect older brother, and his wife left Jane— that's the baby—with my parents to go out to dinner."

The humming stopped and Trish got very still. "And?"

He knew how bad it was to look weak—he'd almost lost his company back at the beginning because he'd been trying to be a nice guy and Diana didn't play by those rules. He'd learned never to show weakness, especially not in the business world.

But the horror of the past two weeks was almost too much for him. He dropped his head into his hands. "And they didn't make it back. A semi lost control, flipped over. They…" The words clogged up in his throat. "They didn't suffer."

"Oh my God, Nate—I'm so sorry." He looked at her and was surprised to see tears gathering in her eyes. "That's— oh, that's just horrible."

"I mean, Brad—that was my brother—you know, it

was hard to grow up in his shadow. He was good-looking and he was the quarterback and he got all the girls. He took—" Nate bit down on the words. He'd made his peace with Brad. Mostly. He'd done his best to put aside the betrayal for the sake of their mother. "We'd…we'd started to become friends, you know? It wasn't a competition anymore because he could never beat me in money and I could never beat him in looks and we were finally even. *Finally*."

In the end, Brad had done him a favor, really. At least, that's how Nate *had* to look at, for his sanity's sake.

There was a somewhat stunned silence as Trish stared at him, punctuated only by the noises of Jane eating. "For what it's worth," she said in a quiet voice, deeper than the one she used on the baby, "you are an incredibly attractive man."

There it was again—that challenge, that something else that seemed to draw the air between them tighter than a bowstring. For a second, he was too stunned to say anything. He didn't feel attractive right now—just as he hadn't felt attractive when he'd been named one of Silicon Valley's Top Ten Bachelors.

But Trish—beautiful and intelligent and obviously much more knowledgeable about babies than he'd ever be—thought he was attractive. *Incredibly* attractive.

He realized he was probably blushing. "Sorry," he said, trying to keep control of himself. "I don't know why I told you that about my brother. I…"

"You've had a long couple of weeks. When did the accident happen?"

"I got the call as I was leaving the coffee shop. I guess that's why I didn't remember you were coming. I'm sorry about that, too."

"Nate," she said in a kind voice and Nate's mind went back to the way she'd touched him in the kitchen. If only he could think straight… "It's all right. I understand. Life happens."

"Yeah, okay." He could do with a little less life happening right now, frankly.

"So your brother and sister had a baby girl?"

"Jane. Yes."

"Jane," Trish said, the name coming off her tongue like a sigh. "Hello, Jane." But then she looked back at Nate. "If you don't mind me asking, why do *you* have Jane? What about your parents?"

Nate dropped his head back into his hands. It was still so hard to talk about. There wasn't the same stigma now, but back when he'd been a kid… "They couldn't take her."

"Not even for a week or so? No offense, but you don't have a baby's room up there. You have a death trap."

"I—" He swallowed. "I have another brother."

There was that stillness again. She was 100 percent focused on him.

"He's severely mentally ill."

"You say that like it's a bad thing."

"It's not. Not anymore. But there were…problems. He was institutionalized for a while until we could get the meds straightened out." He shrugged. "He's my brother and I love him. He loved Brad, too. Brad was his buddy. They'd go out and throw the football around…" His throat seemed to close up on him and he had to swallow a couple of times to get things to work again.

Trish looked at him like she wanted to comfort him. But she said, "No one knows about your brother?"

"In the past, other people have tried to use that against me. Against my family. And I will not stand for it." The last part came out meaner than he meant it to. She wasn't a threat. She wasn't Diana.

"You give to mental illness research."

"Because of Joe, yeah." He sighed. "He needs his routine. My mom takes care of him and I pay for home health workers. But the last few weeks, my parents have been so upset about Brad and Elena... Besides," he added, feeling the weight of the words, "I'm her legal guardian."

"I see," she replied. "Oh, that's a good girl, Jane. Here." She handed Nate the bottle and then casually moved the baby to her shoulder and began patting Jane's back. "So you're trying to hire a nanny?"

"Yeah. You want the job?"

Trish paused in midpat, and then laughed a little too forcefully. "That's not why I'm here."

He wasn't about to take *no* as an answer. So he didn't always know what to do around members of the opposite sex. He knew how to negotiate a business deal. He needed a nanny. She needed money.

"What do you mean? You obviously know what you're doing." The more he thought about it, the better he liked this idea. He'd already sort of interviewed her, after all. He liked her. Okay, maybe that wasn't a good enough reason to offer her a job changing diapers and burping a baby, but he was comfortable with her and she knew what she was doing and *that* counted for something.

She sighed. "Of course I do. My mom had nine kids with...four different men. Then she married my current stepfather, who had four kids of his own with two other women. I'm the oldest."

Nate tried to process that information. "Your mom had ten kids?"

"Not that she took care of them," Trish replied and for the first time, he heard a distinctive note of bitterness in her voice.

"You?"

Her smile was tight. "Me."

"Perfect."

"Excuse me?"

"Look, I need a nanny. More than that, I need *you*. I've had three people come to the door and no one's made it past five minutes, whereas you've gotten Jane to calm down and stop screaming. I swear this is the first time in two weeks I've been able to hear myself think."

And all of that had nothing to do with the way Trish had touched him, so he was still acting aboveboard here.

"Mr. Longmire," she said in a deeply regretful tone, "I can't. I'm due to graduate with my master's degree in a month and a half. I need to finish my studies and—"

"You can study here. When she sleeps."

Trish's eyes flashed in defiance, which made him smile. "I work two jobs," she went on, in a stronger voice. "I do research for the professor who nominated me for the *Glamour* award and I answer phones in the department."

This was much better. She was negotiating. And God knew that, despite the fact that he was so tired he was on the verge of seeing two Trishes cuddling two babies, he could negotiate a business deal. "For, what? Ten dollars an hour?"

Her back stiffened. "Twelve-fifty, if you must know, but that's not the point."

He felt himself grinning. This was what he'd liked in the coffee shop. She wasn't afraid to push back. She wasn't afraid to challenge him. "What is the point?"

"I have a plan. I have school obligations and employment obligations and charitable obligations that I *will* meet. I have to start organizing the back-to-school drive now. I can't drop everything just to nanny your niece. You'll find a perfectly qualified nanny, I'm sure."

"I already have."

"*No*, Mr. Longmire."

He did some quick calculations in his head. He had to keep her here with him. He needed her in a way he'd never needed any other woman. Everyone had a breaking point. Where was hers?

"I will personally call your professor and explain that you've been selected for a unique opportunity."

Her eyes flew wide in disbelief. "You wouldn't."

"Obviously you'll finish your degree, but you'll need to stay here during the month. Sleep here."

"Excuse me?" She looked indignant. The baby, who had actually stopped crying and was possibly asleep, startled and began to make mewing noises.

"I'll pay you five thousand dollars for one month."

Whatever biting rejection she'd been about to say died in a gurgling noise in the back of her throat. "What?"

"One month. I can probably find another nanny in that amount of time, but I need you now."

"Mr. Longmire—"

"Nate."

"Mister Longmire," she went on with whispered emphasis. The baby mewed again. Without appearing to think about it, Trish stood and began rocking from side to side.

Yeah, he was looking at his nanny. "One month. A temporary nanny position."

"I'll lose my lease. I'm—I can't afford much. My landlord wants me out so she can triple the rent."

"Ten thousand."

All the blood drained out of her face, but she didn't answer.

"Come on, Ms. Hunter. Ten grand could get you set up in a nice apartment. For one month of teaching me how to care for my niece and helping me find a more permanent nanny. I'd hazard a guess that you'd be moving out of that apartment after graduation, anyway. This can be the nanny plan. Just a slight change to your original plan."

Her mouth opened. "A *slight* change?"

Which was not a *no*, but also wasn't an agreement to

his terms. Where was her breaking point? Then it hit him. The charity.

"Twenty thousand," he said, impulsively doubling the salary. *Let's see her say no to that*, he thought. "In addition to that salary, I'm prepared to make a donation to the One Child, One...whatever it was. One hundred thousand dollars."

Trish collapsed back into the seat, which jostled the baby. She quickly stood again, but instead of rocking from side to side, she turned and walked to the window. "You wouldn't do that."

"I can and I will." She didn't reply. He realized she wasn't necessarily playing hardball with him, but what the hell did a couple hundred grand mean to him? Nothing. He'd never even miss it, but he might change her life. "Fine. Two-fifty. My final offer."

"Two...fifty?" She sounded like she was being strangled.

"Two hundred and fifty thousand dollars to your very worthy charity, to be paid half now, half at the end of the month, provided you stay here, handle the night feedings and whatever else has Jane up every two hours, and teach me how to do some of the basics."

"And...hire a permanent replacement?"

He had her then. She couldn't say no to that kind of cash and they both knew it. "That's the plan, yes."

She didn't reply and he let the silence stretch. Final offers and all that.

He watched her as she thought it over. She was gently rocking from side to side and he could see the top of Jane's fuzzy little head over Trish's shoulder. It looked...something in his chest clenched. It was probably just the sleep deprivation but, Trish standing at the window, soothing the baby—it looked *right*, somehow.

Was he really doing this—convincing this beautiful

woman to stay here, with him? To sleep under the same roof with him? What the hell? He'd wanted to ask her out, not move her in. Still, if she were living in his house…

Stay, he thought. *Stay here. With me.*

"This…" She took an exceptionally deep breath. "This *generous* donation—it's not contingent upon anything else?"

"Such as?"

"I can't sleep with you."

He let out a bark of a laugh, which caused her to half turn and *shush* him. "Do I look that bad?"

"I didn't mean to offend." Her gaze flicked over him again and he simultaneously remembered the sad state of his shirt and that earlier she'd decreed he was attractive. *Incredibly* attractive. He sat up a little straighter. "It's just that…I don't sleep with anyone."

That seems a crying shame.

The words waltzed right up to the tip of his tongue, but even in his sleep-deprived state, he knew better than to say them out loud.

She looked down at Jane's head. "I've raised *so* many babies already. Whatever money doesn't go to the charity directly goes to support my siblings. My youngest sister is nine. And I…" She sighed and looked out the window. The fog was starting to roll in. "I want her to have more than two pencils."

She turned back to him, determination blazing in her eyes. "It's not that I don't appreciate your generous offer, but there's more that I can do than change diapers and make bottles. I know exactly what sacrifices it takes to raise a child and I…" She glanced down at the baby in her arms and sighed heavily. "I'm not ready to make those sacrifices again. Not just yet."

"One month. That's all I need, Trish. And it's not contingent upon you sleeping with me." She raised her eyebrow at him, as if she doubted his resolve. "I give you my word of honor. Sex is not a part of the plan." He wasn't terribly good at seduction, anyway.

However, there was nothing in their bargain that ruled out him asking for a date after the month was up.

She got a weird look on her face, like she was trying not to smile and not quite making it.

"I just—look," he stammered, trying to recover. "I just need...you. You're perfect."

From this angle—the warming light coming through the window, her face half-turned to him—he couldn't tell if she was blushing or not. But she dropped her gaze and said, "One month. No sex."

"Twenty grand payment for you and two hundred fifty thousand dollars to your charity. Agreed."

She exhaled. "I want it in writing."

"Done. By tomorrow. But..."

"But what?"

"Will you stay tonight?" The words felt foreign on his tongue. He didn't ask women to stay over, not since the thing with Diana had wound up in court.

Her mouth—her deep pink lips—opened and shut before they opened again. "I have to get my things."

A spike of panic hammered into Nate's head. "What if she wakes up? While you're gone?"

"I won't be long. Here. Sit in the chair." She motioned toward the seat she'd just left. "I'll put her on your chest and she'll probably sleep for a few hours. Maybe you can get some sleep, too." She gave him a sly grin. "You look like you need it."

Was that flirting? Sex might not be part of the plan, but flirting was still on the table?

The power had shifted between them again. He held the money, but she had all the know-how. He did as she said, kicking his feet up onto the footstool and settling back into the chair.

She carefully placed Jane on his chest and again guided his arms around the baby until he was holding Jane tightly. Trish's touch—her fingers moving over his muscles—was warm, strong, *soft*.

He was *not* going to sleep with her. But it would be helpful in accomplishing that noble goal if she didn't touch him. "What if I drop her?" he whispered as Trish's fingers trailed off his forearms, searing him with her warmth.

"You won't." She was close to him then, almost close enough to kiss. But he'd just promised—no funny business. She patted the baby's head. "I'll be back. If she wakes up, just sing to her, okay?"

"Hurry," he told her, trying to sound as if this were all no big deal. "Take a cab. I'll pay for it."

There was a moment when their gazes met—a moment when something shifted between them. She looked down at him with a mixture of confusion and...tenderness?

Then she was gone, walking out the door and hurrying away.

He prayed she'd come back.

He couldn't do this without her.

Three

"What the *hell* am I doing?"

"Sorry?" the cabbie asked in a heavily accented voice.

"Oh—nothing," Trish mumbled, turning her attention back out the window. She had only been in cabs a few times, when going to a symposium with a professor or something. Single travelers probably didn't randomly mutter to themselves.

But, seriously—what the hell was she doing? Moving in with a hot, sweet, *rich* man to take care of his niece? During the last month of her collegiate career? While she was supposed to be organizing the back-to-school drive?

For how much money?

Trish realized she was looking at her fingers, which were slowly counting off the twenty thousand dollars she was going to earn. She ran out of fingers and started over. That was five thousand dollars a week. A week! She didn't earn that much in five months with two jobs.

Twenty grand. That was more than she made in a year, if she didn't count the scholarships—which she tended not to do, since the scholarships didn't buy food or keep the lights on.

And Longmire—Nate—had just thrown that number out.

Along with that *other* number. Two hundred fifty thousand dollars.

Trish stared at her fingers, trying to process the magnitude of that number. Good lord, what her charity could do with that kind of money! New backpacks, shoes and winter coats for every kid on the rez and possibly a few other rezs as well. She could get new sports equipment and fund the afternoon snack in the schools and maybe even get some computers.

It was like a dream come true. Even the part where the hot, rich man was asking her to basically live with him. That was definitely the stuff of dreams. Her dreams, to be specific.

She pinched herself, just to be sure.

The cab pulled up in front of her apartment. "Wait, please," she requested as she got out. The landlady was sitting on her porch, making her disgust for Trish obvious. "Hello, Mrs. Chan," Trish said.

"You leaving?" Mrs. Chan demanded. It was her usual greeting. "You not leaving, you pay more rent. I get $1,900 a month for such nice place, but you only pay me $350."

"Yes, that was the lease we signed," Trish replied. "You get another $450 from the government." Mrs. Chan's "nice place" was a five-hundred-square-foot "garden apartment," which was another way of saying "one step above a root cellar"—only mustier. It'd been furnished, which was helpful when a girl couldn't afford even thrift-store furniture and had no way to get it home, anyway, but it was a combo living-bedroom and bathroom-kitchen. Two rooms in a hole in the ground. Not exactly the lap of luxury and nothing like Nate's elegant Victorian.

But, thanks to the subsidies, it'd been a place Trish could afford and it'd been her own. For the first time in her life, she hadn't had to wait for a bathroom and hadn't had at least two other kids in her bed with her. It hadn't been freezing in the winter and the water always worked. For the past five glorious years, she'd been able to breathe.

"You should pay more," Mrs. Chan sniffed. "My daughter—a *lawyer*—says so." This conversation happened on autopilot.

"Mrs. Chan, you get your wish today."

"What?" The older lady sat up straight and suddenly a bright smile graced her face. "You leaving?"

"I'm leaving. I have a…" She didn't know how to describe the situation. "I have a new place."

"You leave now?"

Trish turned back to where the cab was waiting. It felt too decadent, letting the meter run. "Yup. Right now. I just came back for my things."

"Oh, my." Honest to God, Mrs. Chan batted her eyelashes at Trish. "You such a sweet girl. I always like you."

Trish managed not to roll her eyes, but it took a lot of effort. "Can I get my deposit?"

Some of the sweetness bled out of Mrs. Chan's face. It wasn't like Trish needed the money right now—how weird was it to think *that*?—but she couldn't not get it. It was her $350. Getting the deposit money scraped together had practically taken an act of God—and a favor from her stepfather. She could pay him back now.

"I mail to you," Mrs. Chan finally said.

"Fine. I'll leave my address. I have to go pack."

She unlocked her door as Mrs. Chan rhapsodized about how Trish was "such a sweet girl." This wouldn't take long. She had no furniture to move—even the coffeepot that was possibly as old as she was had come with the apartment.

She started shoving clothes into laundry bags. The books took several trips and then the only thing left was her one true luxury—a laptop. True, it was an old laptop. She didn't particularly like to pull it out when there were people around because the last thing she needed were more funny looks.

But it was a computer and she owned it free and clear and that was what counted.

Forty minutes was all it took to erase the signs of her five years in this dank little apartment. The cabbie helped her load the last bag into his trunk and then they were off, back to the historical Victorian that contained a billionaire and a baby.

There was no going back. Mrs. Chan wouldn't let her come back, not without another grand in rent money every month. Trish was committed now.

The enormity of what she was doing hit her again. Oh, God. She was moving in. With Nate Longmire. Who was out of her league and yet also adorably clueless about small children.

Instead of panicking, she forced herself to make a list. She had so much to do. Explain what had happened to her bosses. Call home and make sure her mom had her new address. Finish her degree.

Live under the same roof as Nate Longmire. He who promised not to sleep with her.

Which was just fine. She did not want to be seduced. Not in the least. Seduction always came with the risk of pregnancy and that was a risk she was not willing to take.

Except...

She had the feeling that if she'd had her wits about her, she could have gotten a million dollars out of him, he was so desperate. But that felt wrong, too.

She'd gone in there for the money, but she didn't want to take advantage of him. Not after watching him struggle to keep his composure as he talked about his family.

Damn her helpful nature. As bad an idea as this was, she couldn't say no and leave him and that poor girl in such obvious distress. Mixing milk in with the formula? Good lord. That baby had probably only been a day or two away from a visit to the emergency room.

Rosita was waiting for the cab. She hurried down the wide stairs and rushed through the gate as Trish unloaded all of her worldly possessions. "Oh, good—you've come back," she said as she handed over a credit card to the cabbie.

"I promised I would."

"They're still sleeping," Rosita went on. "*Ay mia*, this is the most quiet we've had in weeks."

"Will you help me unload? I don't even know where I'm going to be sleeping."

"I made you up a bed. This way, please."

Hefting one of her duffels over her shoulder, Trish followed the maid inside. She paused to peek into the parlor. The man and the baby hadn't moved. Nate still had a firm hold of Jane. The little girl was curled against him, breathing regularly. And Nate?

God, it wasn't fair that he should look so good, so sweet, sleeping like that. It almost made Trish's heart hurt. She'd helped raise nine other babies—and she couldn't remember seeing any father in her house holding his child. She liked to think that, once upon a time, her father had held her before he pulled up stakes and came to San Francisco.

She knew that many men cared for their children. But Jane wasn't even Nate's child—and he was still trying his hardest.

No. She was not going to crush on him. This was not about her attraction to Nate Longmire, no matter how wealthy and good-looking and easy to talk to he was. This was about funding her charity for the foreseeable future and making sure that little girl was well cared for. Trish had too much to do to allow an infatuation to creep into her life and that was final. They'd both agreed to the plan and she would stick by that plan come hell or high water.

She followed Rosita up the stairs. This time, she was able to actually look around. The staircase was a magnificent creation that, at the landing, broke into two sets of stairs, one on each side of the wall. The whole place was so clean it almost glowed in the early evening light. Expensive-looking art—some of it old-looking oil paintings, some of it framed movie posters from schlocky old movies she'd never heard of—decorated the walls in coordinating frames. The walls were a pale green, cool and refreshing, with coordinating chairs in the landing.

Oh, yeah, this was much fancier than anything she'd ever lived in before. This was even fancier than the hotel she'd stayed in for the *Glamour* award in New York. That'd been a very nice hotel—a Marriott—but this? This was officially the lap of luxury. And it was Nate's.

Rosita took the staircase to the right and Trish followed. She wondered if she might go up to the attic—she'd be out of the way there—but Rosita led her down the hall on the second floor.

"That is Señor Nate's room," Rosita said, pointing to the other side of the hallway. "It runs the length of the house. The nursery and the guest room are on this side. Here we are." Rosita opened the first door on her right.

Wait—what? She was going to be right across the hall from him? That felt…close. Too close. He would be too accessible.

But that flash of panic was quickly overridden by the room Rosita led her into. "Oh, my," Trish breathed. A huge, beautiful room awaited her. She'd never had a beautiful room before. The wallpaper was a deep blue-and-cream floral pattern. An actual chandelier hung in the middle. The room had a small bay window that held two sitting chairs and a small table. To one side was a fireplace with deep blue glazed tiles. A flat-screen television hung over the mantel, which was decorated with small vases and figurines. And on the other… "That's an amazing bed."

"Yes. Señor Nate's mother prefers this room when she is able to visit."

The bed was huge. At least a queen-size with four posts that reached up almost to the level of the chandelier, the whole thing was draped with gauzy fabric. The bed was made up with color-coordinating pillows and a down comforter that looked so light and fluffy Trish couldn't wait until she could sleep in it.

Alone. She would be sleeping in that bed *alone*. That was the plan.

Except all the dreams she'd been having for the past two weeks came crashing back down on her head. Nate would be right across the hall, no longer a fantasy, but a flesh-and-blood man who had, in no uncertain terms, said he needed her.

Oh, this was going to be a long, hard month.

"The bathroom, miss," Rosita said. "It connects with the nursery."

"Okay, good." That way, she wouldn't have to walk into the hall in the middle of the night in her T-shirt and boxer shorts and run the risk of stumbling into Nate Longmire. Because that would be terrible. Awful. She was just sure of it.

Her head began to spin. This was too much. Too much money. Not her life. She didn't get paid this kind of cash to watch a billionaire's baby while sleeping in a guest room that was far bigger and cleaner than any other place she'd ever lived.

Her knees wobbled and she sat heavily on the bed. Of course it was soft and comfortable. And it was hers. Hers for the month.

"Tell me about him," she said to Rosita. The maid's eyebrows jumped. "I just agreed to move into his house and I really don't know…anything." She'd done her homework a few weeks ago and yes, he'd shared that little moment down in the parlor. But suddenly that wasn't enough.

Because there'd been huge holes in his biography online. The lawsuits he'd filed—and won. He'd sued a woman named Diana Carter because she'd claimed that half of SnAppShot was hers and had tried to sell it. They'd been old college friends, according to the filings. There were rumors that they'd been more, but that was it—just rumors. And Nate had run her into the ground.

But those were dry legal texts. Anything else that might have provided context about what went on between "old college friends" was simply not there. The information was conspicuous in its absence.

"Señor Nate? He is a good man. Quiet, not messy. Does not make me uncomfortable. Very polite."

"Okay, good." That was mostly how he'd come across during their meeting at the coffee shop. Well, maybe except the messy part.

"He likes to sleep late and he drinks maybe too much coffee," Rosita added in an entirely motherly sounding voice. "But I do not mind. He pays me very well and the work is not too hard. Mostly cooking, cleaning and laundry. It is a very good job."

"Does he…I mean to say, will there be other guests? Who spend the night?" She didn't know why she'd asked that question, but it was out there and there was nothing she could do about it now. She felt her cheeks flush.

It was a matter of self-preservation, that was all. If other people were going to be in and out of this house, that was something she needed to know for Jane's sake. She'd have to lock both her and Jane's doors to make sure no "guests" accidentally wandered into the wrong room. It had nothing to do with not wanting to see Nate going into his bedroom with someone else and closing the door behind them.

"Ay, no! Señor Nate keeps to himself. His helper—

Stanley," she said, drawing the name out in an unflattering way, "he will sleep on the couch sometimes, down in the media room. That is only when they are working on a project. But no. No other guests."

"Stanley—does he have a lot of tattoos, a horrible sense of fashion and big holes in his ears?"

Rosita nodded. "I do not like him. He is loud and messy and rude. But Señor Nate says he is a good man, so I cook for him when he comes over."

Yeah, that pretty much summed up the man Trish had talked to at the office. Loud, messy and rude. "Anything else you think I should know?"

Rosita stepped back and gave Trish the once-over. "No, miss. Just that I'm glad you've taken the position. I…" her voice dropped to a whisper. "I do not care for children. Never had one of my own. They make me nervous," she admitted with an awkward laugh. "That is why this was such a good job. Other people, they want you to look after the children and I…I am no good at it. And it is far too late for me to suddenly become good at it. You understand? It would be hard to find another position as good as this one and I am getting too old to start over."

Trish patted Rosita's arm. Being a woman who currently had no desire to have children, she understood. Some people just didn't like babies. Oftentimes, Trish had to wonder if that included her own mother. Why else would she have left her oldest to care for each new infant?

"No worries. I'm going to unpack a little and then check on them." She looked at the clock beside the bed. Even the clock was fancy—a built-in dock for smartphones and more plugs than she recognized. If only she had a smartphone to dock there. "They've probably got another forty minutes or so before they wake up."

Rosita started to leave but paused at the door. "Miss? I do all the cooking. Anything special you like?"

Trish blinked at her. She was not a gourmet cook. She existed on the cheapest groceries she could afford, and those usually came from corner markets and little shops that carried ethnic foods. Her big splurge was, once a week, buying a nice cup of coffee. If she got really wild, she might eat two whole packets of ramen noodles for dinner. She did not dine at nice restaurants. She didn't even dine at bad ones.

The prospect of this nice woman cooking her food was beyond Trish's comprehension. "I'll eat anything."

Rosita nodded and closed the door behind her.

Trish flopped back onto the bed and stared up at the gauzy canopy. This was, hands down, the craziest thing she'd ever done. Moving in with a billionaire. What the hell?

But already it was hard to think of Nate as just the Boy Billionaire, not when she'd seen him so upset over his family and napping with his niece. She hadn't just moved in with a billionaire. She'd moved in with *Nate*.

She forced herself to stop thinking about the way his very nice arm muscles had tightened under her touch and the way certain parts of her own body had tightened in response. *If* she allowed herself to dwell on those moments—and that was a pretty darned big *if*—well, those thoughts were best kept for after everyone had gone to bed in their separate bedrooms, with all doors safely shut.

Right now, she had things to do. Moving quickly, she unpacked her meager wardrobe. The room had a closet that was almost as big as her kitchen/bathroom in the basement of Mrs. Chan's house, and all the hangers were those fancy padded ones wrapped in satin. Her second-hand clothes looked jarringly out of place on them.

She put her laptop on the table in the window—the little nook would be a wonderful place to do her work—and lined up her books on a built-in bookshelf on the far side of the canopy bed. Finally, she was unpacked.

Time to get down to business. She pulled off her boots and considered her options. Baby duty required wash-and-wear clothes and her professional outfit wasn't it.

As she stripped down to her underwear, she thought about what Rosita had said. Nate was quiet, kept to himself.

He didn't bring women home with him. And, aside from Stanley, who slept on the couch, he didn't bring men home with him, either.

Trish threw on the Wonder Woman T-shirt and a pair of jeans, and then removed her earrings and braided her hair back so that it couldn't be yanked by small hands. She was not going to think about Nate and whom he did or did not bring home with him. It was none of her business whom he slept with, as long as he didn't—what had Rosita said? As long as Nate didn't make Trish "uncomfortable."

He'd promised. No sex.

During the month.

Which left what might happen after the month as something of an open question.

Trish shook her head and forced herself to think about the real reason she was here—Jane, the baby. The poor girl.

God, Trish didn't want to be a mother again so soon, not to someone else's child, but...Jane needed her and Nate needed her. And Trish—she needed a well-funded charity that could make a huge difference in her people's lives.

Just a month. She was a temporary nanny. That was the plan.

She opened her door and, barefoot, peeked into the nursery. Rosita had done an admirable job in the hour and a half since Trish had last seen the nursery, but the place was still a mess. Boxes and suitcases were stacked against the walls, baby things spilling out of them. The playpen was almost in the middle of the room and—wait. She stepped around it. A pair of formal sitting chairs—much like the ones in her room, only in a deep rose color—sat in the bay window. That, in itself, wasn't that remarkable.

But one of the chairs had a suitcase that had clearly been used as a footstool. A used coffee cup sat on the little table and a phone—she assumed it was Nate's—was next to it. The whole area looked rumpled, much like Nate had when she'd showed up.

Oh, dear God—no wonder that man was so tired. He'd been sleeping in the chair to be closer to Jane.

She shook her head. He had *no* idea what he was doing, but he was doing his best. She'd work on the nursery tomorrow. There wasn't even a changing table. She'd have to ask if Nate could afford to get a crib, a table and another dresser...

She caught herself. Of course Nate could afford that. Hello, Boy Billionaire who'd just thrown close to three hundred thousand dollars at her. A couple of thousand on some furniture wasn't anything to him.

She left the mess behind and went downstairs to the parlor. She studied the room. For being a tech billionaire, there was very little actual tech in this room. Instead, old toys were artfully arranged on the built-in bookcases around a fireplace with an elegant floral pattern done in bright blue tiles. The mantel that went over it was hand-carved and polished to a high shine. And there, in a place of honor, was Superman #1 in a glass case.

Earlier, when she'd seen the distress Jane was in, Trish had acted without thinking. Her instincts were to get the baby changed and clothed and fed and napping in quick succession.

There was a distinctive possibility that she *might* have been bossing a billionaire around.

But now the situation was not as dire. The baby was resting. Nate was asleep. She didn't know if she could walk in there and pluck Jane off his chest or if that would be crossing a line she shouldn't cross. She really shouldn't touch him. Not like she'd already touched him. No more touching. Touching was not part of the plan.

As she was debating doing that or going back and showing Rosita how to make the formula properly, Nate's eyes fluttered open. He saw her standing there and blinked a few times.

"Hey, Wonder Woman," he mumbled as his long legs stretched out.

"I'm not really a superhero," she felt obligated to remind him.

That got her a sleepy grin. Oh, my. Yes, Nate Longmire could be quite attractive. "You came back."

"I keep my word." She paused. "Listen, about the money…"

His eyes widened. "What about it? Not enough?"

"No—no—it's just—that's an insane amount of money. You don't have to pay me that much. Really. I hadn't even considered the room and board as part of the agreement. And the room—it's really nice. I mean, that alone is worth—"

"Don't worry about it," he sighed as his eyelids drifted shut again. "We agreed. I keep my word, too."

He couldn't be serious. She hadn't been negotiating, not really. She'd just been too stunned to tell him no earlier. "But—"

"The deal is done." His voice was harder now—the same voice he'd used when he had refused to take *no* for an answer. "Not open to renegotiation, Trish."

She tried very hard not to glare at him. "Fine. I have a favor to ask."

One eyelid opened back up. She could almost see him thinking, *another favor?* "Yes?"

"I need to borrow a phone so I can call my family and

tell them where I'm at and I haven't seen a landline in here."

"I don't have a landline," he said as if she'd observed that he didn't have any woolly mammoths in the closets. Both lids swung up in a look of total confusion. "You don't have a phone?"

"Nope." Shame burned her cheeks. She lived in the most technologically advanced city in quite possibly the entire world—and didn't even own a cell phone. "I have a laptop," she said, desperate not to sound pathetic. "I assume you have Wi-Fi or something I can log into, to finish my classwork?"

He regarded her for a minute. She got the feeling he was fully awake now.

"You need a phone."

"I'm fine, it's just that—"

"No, you need a phone," he said with more force. "In case of an emergency. I'll have Stanley get you one. I've cleared most of my schedule, but I have a few events I need to attend and you need to be able to get ahold of me."

"Nate…"

She was going to tell him he absolutely could not buy her a phone. She had existed for twenty-five years without a mobile device just fine. He was already giving her too much.

But when she said his name, something in his eyes changed—deepened. And all those things she was going to tell him floated away like the fog.

"You are too generous," she said, unable to make her voice sound like a normal version of herself. She could never pay him back, not in a million years. "You're giving me too much. I'm not…" *worth it.*

She almost said it out loud but managed not to.

His eyebrows lifted and he opened his mouth and she was suddenly very interested in what he was about to say, but Jane awoke with a start and a cry. Her head lifted up and crashed back into Nate's shoulder. "Ow," he said. "You've got a hard head, Janie girl."

"Here." Trish strode into the room and lifted Jane out of his arms. "I told you that you wouldn't drop her."

"I bow to your superior knowledge," he said working his head from side to side.

She caught a whiff of stale milk. *Old* stale milk. Nate Longmire was on the verge of curdling before her very eyes. "I don't want to tell you what to do…"

He looked up at her, a curious grin on his face. "Don't let that stop you. What?"

"You might consider a shower."

An adorable blush turned his cheeks pink, then red. "That bad?"

She wrinkled her nose at him. "Go. I've got Jane."

He got to his feet and leaned in. For a blistering second, she thought he was going to kiss her. He was going to kiss her and she was going to let him and that was the stupidest thing she'd ever thought because she did not let people kiss her. She just didn't.

He pressed his lips to the top of Jane's head, nestled against Trish's shoulder. Then he straightened up. "Thank you."

This was the closest she'd been to him. Close enough to feel the warmth of his body radiating in the space between them. Close enough to see the deep golden flecks in his brown eyes, no longer hidden behind the hipster glasses. "I haven't done anything yet."

"You're here. Right now, that's everything."

Even though Jane was waking up and starting to fuss at still being swaddled in the blanket, Trish couldn't pull away from the way his eyes held hers.

"You don't have to buy me a phone." It came out as a whisper.

The very corner of his mouth curved up and he suddenly looked very much like a man who would seduce his temporary nanny just because he could. "And yet, I'm going to, anyway."

Trish swallowed down the tingling sensation in the back of her throat. This was Nate after a nap? What would he be like after a solid night's sleep?

And how the hell was she going to resist him?

The baby saved her. Jane made an awful noise and Nate reeled back in horror. "Um…yeah. I'll just go shower now." He stepped around her and all but ran toward the door.

"Coward," she called out after him. "You're going to have to learn sometime!"

"Can't talk, in the shower!" he called back. It sounded like he was laughing.

Trish sighed. "Come on, sweetie," she said to the baby. "It's you and me for the month."

She needed this baby—needed the constant reminder of why she didn't sleep with anyone and especially not with the man who was paying her a salary. She was not going to get caught up in Nate Longmire being an atypical billionaire who looked at her like she was the answer to his prayers, even if she was—in a strictly nanny-based sort of way, of course.

Thank God for dirty diapers.

Four

Nate stood under the waterfall showerhead with his forehead slowly banging against the tiled wall.

When had an easy plan, such as to not sleep with a nanny, suddenly become something that seemed so insurmountably difficult? He didn't seduce people. And when people tried to seduce him—like that woman at the last talk he'd given, the one where he'd met Trish—he managed to sidestep around it.

What was it about Trish Hunter that had him struggling to keep his control in his own home?

It's not like he was a prude. Okay, he sort of was, but it wasn't because he didn't like sex. He did. A lot. But sex was…it was opening yourself up to another person. And that he didn't like. Not anymore.

He didn't pick up women and he didn't get picked up. It was a holdover from a long, painful adolescence, where he'd learned to take care of himself because he sure as hell wasn't going to get much help from anyone else. And yes, it was the fallout from Diana. He wasn't going to put himself in that kind of position again if he could help it. Better to stick it out alone than open himself to that kind of inside attack again.

He turned the cold knob up another three notches.

It didn't help.

He wasn't innocent. College had been good for him on

a couple of different levels. He'd started this company. Started dating. He'd gone to MIT, where no one knew about Brad Longmire or his football championships. Nate had no longer been Brad's little brother. He'd been Nate.

And what was more, he wasn't the biggest geek on campus, not at MIT. He'd blended. For the first time in his life, he'd belonged. He'd filled out, started growing facial hair and gotten lucky a few times. He'd met Diana...

No. He wasn't going to think about that mess. All the paperwork was signed, sealed and approved by the judge. He didn't care if she was trying to get ahold of him again. He was *done* with her.

But Trish...

His hand closed around his dick as Trish's face appeared behind his closed eyes, smiling down at him from where she'd stood in the doorway. She'd looked like an angel as he'd blinked the nap out of his eyes. He'd swear there was a glow around her. And then? She'd tried to give the money back. She could ask him for a million dollars and he'd happily sign the check tomorrow, as long as she stayed and kept Jane happy and healthy.

She hadn't. She'd tried to give some back.

As he stroked himself, he thought of the way she'd been looking at him when he woke up—one arm leaned against the doorjamb, her Wonder Woman–clad breasts no longer hidden behind a respectable jacket. She'd looked soft and happy and glad to see him.

He. Would. Not. Sleep with. Her. He'd given his word. Not for the month, anyway. After that...

After that, he'd ask her out. Ask her to stay—not for the baby, but for him. They'd talk and he'd kiss her and then he'd lead her up to his room and they'd fall into bed together, hands everywhere. Lips everywhere. He wouldn't be able to keep his hands off her.

She'd be on top of him, stripping that superhero shirt off, her thighs gripping him as he thrust up—

Groaning, he reached a shuddering conclusion. *Hell.* It was going to be a long month.

He let the water run on cold for a few more minutes until he was sure he had the situation under control. He'd been in control for years now. He could handle a beautiful young woman living under his roof, no problem.

He was drying off when he heard something—a high, trilling sound that seemed different from all the screaming that Jane had been doing in the past week but was just as loud.

Oh, no. The baby—he shouldn't have taken a shower, not while she was awake. What had he been thinking? Nate wrapped the towel around his waist and shot out of his bathroom, running across the hall toward the sound.

He slipped around the corner to find Trish sitting on the floor with Jane—bouncing the baby on her knee?

"What's wrong?" he demanded.

"What?" Trish looked up and her eyes went wide. "Oh! Um…"

Jane made that noise again and a sick dread filled him. He'd told his mom he couldn't do this. But what choice did he have, really? "What's wrong with her?"

"She's fine," Trish said in a reassuring voice. "We're playing. That's a happy noise." Her gaze cut to his chest— then to the towel—and then back up.

"It…is?" He was wearing a *towel*. And nothing else. He grabbed at it so fast that he almost knocked it loose and suddenly he was very aware that flashing his new nanny probably invalidated any promise, written or spoken, not to have sex with her.

He did the only thing he could do—he stepped to the side, so that his body was on the other side of the doorway.

"It is," Trish replied. "She's had a good nap and a clean

diaper and I bet this is the best she's felt in a little while.
Isn't it, sweetie?" she said to the baby. Then she leaned
forward and blew a raspberry on Jane's tummy.

The baby squealed in delight and Trish laughed. It was
a warm, confident noise.

Then she looked up at him, her full lips still curved up
with happiness. "We're fine, if you want to—you know—
put on clothes."

"Right, right." Feeling like a first-class idiot, he ran
back to his room and threw on some shorts. What the hell
was wrong with him? Seriously. That had bordered on totally disastrous—much worse than knocking a coffee into
her lap. He absolutely could not afford to do anything to
drive her away.

He dug out some clean clothes. In any other situation, he
might have called Stanley for advice on what to wear—but
what the hell. She'd already seen him at his worst.

Oh, Lord—what had he done? He should have held out.
He should have hired a grandmother who was as wide as a
bus and had whiskers or something. Not a beautiful young
woman who was going to drive him mad with lust. Who
was going to challenge him.

He forced himself to run a few lines of code through his
mind as he gathered up his very dirty clothes and dumped
them in the hamper. The original code to SnAppShot. He
knew it by heart. That code was like a security blanket.
Whenever he couldn't sleep—which was often—he'd mentally scroll through that code.

Then he got a clean pair of jeans and, after a moment's
consideration, his Superman T-shirt. Superman and Wonder Woman, saving the universe one baby at a time. Stanley wouldn't approve, but what the hell.

This time, Nate walked with a purpose back to the nursery. Trish now had the baby on the floor and appeared to
be tickling her feet. Whatever she was doing, Jane was

kicking and wriggling and making that loud, not-crying noise again.

This was okay, this noise. If Trish said it was okay, it was okay. Loud and unsettling, but okay.

She looked up at him from the floor, where she was lying on her side and had her head propped up on one hand. "You look…good. Nice shirt."

He felt his cheeks get hot. "Couldn't have been much worse, I suppose?"

"It can always be worse," Trish replied. Her eyes darted back down to his chest. Almost unconsciously, he stood up straighter. It'd been one thing for her to stare while he'd been wet and basically naked. But was she checking him out?

She dropped her gaze and he swore the color of her cheeks deepened. "So…"

He leaned forward. "Yes?"

"Jane's going to need a few more things," Trish said in a rush.

"Like what?"

Trish stood and lifted Jane onto her hip with that practiced air. "Everything. This room is a disaster, you know. Were you sleeping in the chair?"

Nate looked over the nursery. The place was still a wreck—and that got his mind firmly back into the here and now and far away from whether or not Trish might have liked what she'd seen a few minutes ago. "Well, yeah. Rosita doesn't live here. She goes home at six most days and comes in at ten because I sleep late. And I was just afraid…"

"That you wouldn't hear her?"

"Or SIDS or something," he agreed. "Elena—Jane's mother—was worried about SIDS, I remember that." God, it was almost too much to bear. He'd liked Elena. She kept Brad grounded and had told Nate to keep the beard because it made him look a little like Ben Affleck and that couldn't be a bad thing, Nate had figured.

But Elena and Brad were gone and Nate was suddenly the guardian of their daughter.

He leaned against the playpen for support.

"You okay?" Trish asked.

"I just…I can't believe they're not coming back, you know? To just have them up and disappear out of my life like *that*?" He snapped his fingers.

"I know." Trish stepped into him and put her free hand on his shoulder. The same fingers that just a few hours ago had skimmed over his skin, making sure he could hold his niece, were now a reassuring hold on him. Without thinking about it, he reached up and covered her hand with his.

"Do you?" He had no business asking—and even less business asking while she was touching him—while he was touching her back. Even if that touch was a reassuring touch, full of comfort and concern and almost no lust at all.

"I do." Then, mercifully, she released her hold on him. She switched Jane to her other hip—the one closer to him—and leaned so the little girl's head was touching him.

Weirdly, that was what he needed. He didn't have his brother or sister-in-law anymore, but he had Jane. And it was his duty to take care of this little girl. He wasn't married and he hadn't foreseen having children anytime soon, but…she was his flesh and blood.

He was a father now. He had to stand tall for her. For them both.

He tilted his head to the side and looked at Trish out of the corner of his eye. She was watching him with concern. Jane made a squealing noise and Nate jumped. "Yeah, that's why I was sleeping in here," he said, getting himself back together. "She makes all these weird noises that don't seem normal…"

"They are," Trish said calmly. "How old is she?"

"Almost six months."

Trish stepped back from him and twirled around. Her mouth open wide, Jane let out a squeal of delight. Trish stopped spinning and looked in her mouth. "Hmm. No teeth yet. But if she's having trouble sleeping, that might be part of it."

"Oh. Okay." Teething. Yet another thing he didn't have a clue about. "That's normal, right?"

Trish grinned at him, then unexpectedly spun again, making Jane giggle. Yes—definitely a giggle. "Right. We've got to get this room whipped into shape."

"One moment." He pulled out his phone and video-messaged Stanley.

Stanley's face appeared. "What? It's after seven."

"And hello to you, too. I need you to go shopping. Start a list," Nate said. "Company phone for Ms. Trish Hunter."

Off to his side, Trish sighed heavily, but she didn't protest.

"And?" Stanley said.

Nate looked at Trish. "And?"

"A crib, changing table, dresser drawers, a rocker-glider chair, stroller, car seat, high chair, size two diapers, more formula."

"Did you get all that?" Nate asked.

"Is that the girl? She came here first. I had to send her your way," Stanley said in that absent-minded way of his that meant he was taking notes.

"Yes," Nate said. "She took the position. Also, I need you to do the due diligence on One Child, One…" he could not remember the last part of her charity's name. It just wasn't there.

"World. One Child, One World," Trish helpfully supplied. Her eyes had gotten big and round again.

"One Child, One World," Nate told Stanley. "I'm going

to be making a donation for two hundred fifty thousand dollars. Also, please put Ms. Hunter on the payroll."

"Salary?" Stanley said.

"Twenty thousand for one month."

There was a moment's pause in which Stanley's eyebrows jumped up. "Can I have a raise?"

This time, Nate did snort. For as much as he paid Stanley, the man was constantly haranguing him for more. "No."

"She must be *highly* qualified," he said in that distracted way again. "Good body, too."

Nate cringed. "She's also listening."

After a frozen pause—his eyes wide in horror—Stanley cleared his throat. When he spoke again, he did so in his most professional voice. "When do you need this by?"

Nate looked at Trish and was surprised to see that she was trying not to laugh. "As soon as possible," she managed to get out.

"Right. Got it." Stanley ended the call.

Nate stood there, staring down at his screen. He really didn't know what to do next. Trish did have a good body. And an excellent sense of humor about it, too.

"Well. That wasn't awkward at all."

He grinned. "The least awkward conversation ever, possibly."

They stood there. There was tension in the room, but it wasn't the kind that normally had him tripping over his words or his feet. He was comfortable with her. And, despite all the not-awkwardness, she seemed pretty okay with him. Enough to send him to the shower because he reeked.

"Señor Nate?" Rosita called up from downstairs. "Dinner is on the table. Do you need me for anything else? It is after seven o'clock…"

Nate glanced at Trish, who shook her head. The past few nights, when Rosita had fled from the house at exactly six—leaving Nate all alone with Jane—he'd been filled with a sense of dread that was far heavier than anything else he'd ever had to overcome.

But not tonight. A sense of calm brushed away the nagging conviction that he couldn't do this. And that calm was named Trish.

"I think we're going to make it," he called back. "See you on Monday?"

"Yes," Rosita called back, sounding relieved.

The sound of the front door shutting echoed through the house. "She's a very good cook," he felt like he had to explain, "but she doesn't really like kids."

"So she said. And Stanley?"

"Don't feel too sorry for him. He gets fifty bucks an hour." Her face paled a bit—no doubt, she was thinking about the twelve fifty an hour she'd earned as of this morning. "I know he's a little rough around the edges, but he's the height of discretion. They both are."

"You value your privacy."

"Doesn't everyone?" Which was a true enough statement, but he knew that wasn't what she was asking.

She'd as much as admitted that she'd dug into his history. But he didn't want to go down that path right now. Just because she was someone he'd like to get to know better and who was technically living under his roof at this very moment didn't mean he had to just open up and share his deepest secrets with her.

So he did the only thing he could do. He changed the subject. "Shall we have dinner? Then I can show you the rest of the house and you can teach me how to make the formula." Because he was going to have to learn it sometime and that was a concrete task that probably wouldn't involve lingering touches or long looks. Hopefully.

Like the long look she gave him right then, punctuated only when she shifted Jane to her other hip. There was something in her eyes, as if she didn't believe what he'd just suggested. "Yes," she said after that measured gaze, "We shall."

Five

Trish lay in bed, not sleeping. This house sounded different. She was used to the shuffling of Mrs. Chan over her head and the blaring of the evening news. But Nate's house?

This place was quiet. Nearly silent. In the distance, a foghorn sounded.

She'd never had so much quiet. Funny how it felt loud. Was this why Nate lived here—he could hear himself think?

They'd gone up to the dining room, where the best danged chicken enchilada dinner she'd ever eaten had been waiting for them in a dining room that was not rated for kids. The table had ten chairs and was set upon a thick white shag rug. Trish had suggested that Nate remove the carpeting before Jane started eating solid foods.

And then there'd been the view. Not that she'd been able to see much in the fog, but Nate had said that the floor-to-ceiling glass windows that separated the dining room from the patio had an excellent view of the Golden Gate Bridge. Trish hadn't had a view of anything but the sidewalk in five years. There was even a fenced-in yard with trees and grass. Nate had asked her if he should get a swing set or something for Jane. After that, Nate had showed her the media room and the home gym in the basement.

Trish didn't belong here. This house, the food, everything about Nate was out of her league. Had she really felt like an interloper at San Francisco State University? Good lord. That was nothing compared to finding herself suddenly living in the absolute lap of luxury with a man who took such a vital interest in his niece's welfare.

Trish's current stepfather was a pretty good guy. He supported Pat and the kids still living at home and that counted for a hell of a lot. He'd even loaned Trish the $350 for her security deposit five years ago—and that had only been two years after he'd hooked up with Pat.

But there'd been so many men who'd passed through Pat's and Trish's lives and not one of them had ever taken an interest in the kids. Not someone else's kids, not their own kids. Trish's own father had abandoned them, for crying out loud.

To watch Nate try so hard—care so much—well, it spun her head around. One of the reasons she'd gone out of her way to avoid a relationship, and men in general, was because she didn't want to be saddled raising a child on her own. She knew exactly what kind of sacrifices a baby would require and she was done making them for other people.

But Nate… He'd stood shoulder-to-shoulder with her in the kitchen and made up three bottles of formula until he'd gotten it right and he hadn't complained at all. In fact, they'd wound up laughing together after his first attempt had resulted in something closer to a pancake batter than formula. He'd taken another crack at changing a diaper, too. Willingly.

Not like the man who'd come into her life when Trish had been nine. That year had made her tougher than she knew she could be. She'd decided then that she would protect her little brothers and sisters. She would get her education even if it took her two years longer to graduate and then she would get the hell off that rez. And when she'd made it, she'd do everything she could to make sure that no other kid went hungry.

She would never again be at the mercy of a man.

Which did not explain why she was living in Nate Longmire's home, caring for his niece, completely dependent on him for her meals and money. Taking this position was something so impulsive, so not thought-out, that even her mother, Pat, would be surprised.

She was completely at Nate's mercy right now and all she had to go on was that his maid said he was a good man and he'd promised sex wasn't part of the plan. That was it. She tried to reason that at least Nate had a reference—her mother had hooked up on far less—but it didn't change the fact that, for the first time in her life, Trish had followed in her mother's footsteps. When a good-looking man had said jump, she'd asked how high and tossed everything to the side to take care of another baby.

Trish didn't know what to think anymore. The certainty with which she'd lived her life for the past ten, fifteen years—suddenly, she wasn't so certain that she was absolutely doing the right thing.

Trish went around and around with herself. Then she heard a soft *whump* and she sat up, her ears straining. The clock said one-thirty. She must have drifted off at some point.

Then she heard it, the building whine of a baby who was not quite awake yet. She threw off her covers and hurried through the adjoining bathroom door. She turned on the bathroom light and let the door open enough that she could see her way to the playpen.

Jane had gotten herself loose from her swaddling and was flailing about. "Shh, shh, it's okay, sweetie," Trish said as she picked up the baby. "I'm here. Let's go get a bottle, okay? Let's let Nate sleep."

The moment the words left her mouth, the overhead lights flipped on. Jane flinched and began to cry in earnest.

Blinking hard, Trish spun to see Nate standing in the doorway in a T-shirt and a pair of boxers—not all that different from what she was wearing.

"Everything okay?" he asked in a bleary voice.

"The light—turn it off."

"What?"

"Nate," she hissed in a whisper. "Turn the light off. Please. You're upsetting Jane."

"Oh." He flipped the light off and Jane quieted back down to a pleading whimper. "Was that bad?"

"We should keep it as quiet and as dark as possible during the night." She could see what had happened now. Every time the baby had made a noise, Nate had hopped up and turned on the overhead lights, which had woken Jane up even more. No wonder he hadn't slept.

She realized she was aware of Nate standing there in his boxers—and she didn't like being that aware of him, all sleepy and rumpled and still very attractive. Like a man who'd feel just right curled up against her in bed. Her nipples tightened under her tank top.

No, no—bad. Bad thoughts. She could only hope that, in the dim light, he hadn't noticed. She shifted Jane so the baby covered her breasts and headed toward the door. She kept her voice low. "I've got this. You go back to bed."

He yawned. "Anything I can do to help?"

"Nope. Just going to get her a bottle, get her changed and lay her back down."

Nate scratched the back of his head. "You want me to get the bottle for you?"

She stopped then, not three feet from him. "You're paying me to do night duty, you know." Besides, the odds of him doing something not conducive to getting a baby back to sleep were pretty high.

He looked as if he was going to argue with her, but then he yawned again. "Okay. But you'll let me know if you need me, right?"

"Right." She started walking again, but Nate didn't get out of her way. She was forced to squeeze her body past his in the door frame.

Unexpectedly, he leaned forward and kissed the top of Jane's head. "Be a good girl," he murmured. Then he looked up. He was close enough to touch, except for the infant between them. "You're sure you don't need me?"

An unfamiliar sensation fluttered across Trish's lower back, like static electricity right at the base of her spine. It tightened muscles in unfamiliar areas, sending a dull ache through her body.

"No," she whispered so softly that he was forced to lean forward a bit just to hear her. For some insane reason, she wanted to run her fingers over his beard. She clutched the baby tighter. "I'm...I'm fine. We're fine."

"Good night, Trish." He pushed off and walked back to his room.

It was only when his door was safely shut that Trish sagged against the door frame. "Good night, Nate."

Oh, heavens. One night down.

Twenty-nine nights to go.

Through the fog of the first decent night's sleep in two weeks, Nate heard Jane fuss twice more during the night. Both times, he woke up with a start, his heart pounding in terror. The baby—

But then, both times, he heard the soft footsteps moving around his house and he remembered—Trish. The woman who was taking care of Jane. The beautiful woman who made him think about things he had long ago learned not to think about. Like sex.

And he lay there both times, fighting the urge to get up

and check on Jane—and Trish—because, after all, he *was* paying her to get up in the middle of the night.

He shouldn't have gotten up the first time, but he was still a tad jumpy about the whole situation. And then Trish had been there, her body silhouetted against the dim light from the bathroom like an angel of mercy, come to save him from himself. Her bare shoulders had been haloed with the light and her curves—

He'd almost kissed her. He'd promised he wouldn't and he almost had, anyway. It'd been the sleep deprivation, that was all. He must be too tired to think straight because he knew he could control himself better than that.

So, in a monumental effort of self-control, he stayed in bed, drifting between true sleep and awareness. The first time, the house eventually became quiet again and he slept. But the second time—even though Trish was not being loud—he still heard her moving around downstairs.

He rolled over and looked at the clock. Six-fifty in the morning. Ugh. He normally slept much later than this, until nine or ten. He tried to bury his head in a pillow, but it didn't work.

He pictured Trish moving through his house, Jane on her hip, looking like she belonged here. He remembered the way she'd looked at him when he'd tried to make the bottle of formula—a smile she was trying to hide and a warmth in her eyes that couldn't be hidden.

That warmth—that had to be why he'd not-so-subtly hit on her last night. He was out of practice. He wanted to think that she looked at him like that because there was some interest on her end—the same interest he thought he'd seen in the coffee shop.

Of course, if she knew about what had happened with Diana…maybe she wouldn't look at him like that anymore. It's not like he had to worry about Brad swooping in and charming the pants off Trish, though.

The moment he had that thought, enormous guilt swamped him.

God, he was a mess and because he was such a mess, he'd almost broken his promise to Trish. That wasn't like him.

What if, after last night, she'd changed her mind about staying? What if he'd crossed a line he couldn't uncross? Then he'd be little better than Brad had been, unable to keep it zipped around a woman who should be hands-off. And he'd be on his own with a baby again, trying not to screw things up and probably screwing up, anyway.

Panicked, he dragged his tired butt out of bed and threw on a clean pair of jeans. He'd apologize, that was all. He'd do a much better job of keeping a mental wall between Trish Hunter, his nanny, and Trish Hunter, woman of his fantasies. He was not ruled by his baser urges. He was better than that. He was better than Brad, God rest his soul.

Nate hurried downstairs, trying to come up with a mature, responsible way to apologize for his behavior and failing pretty badly.

He looked in the parlor, but they weren't there. The kitchen was also empty, but there were more used bottles in the sink. It wasn't until he got to the dining room and saw the open doors that he found them.

The fog from the night before had mostly burned off, leaving the world with a hazy glow similar to the most-used filter on SnAppShot. And in the middle of the patio sat Trish. Her hair was long and loose, spilling down over the back of the padded patio chair she occupied. Her feet were bare and kicked up against the railing. She had on a long-sleeved flannel top to ward off the morning chill, so her shoulders were covered, thank God. She'd also added a pair of jeans. Jane was on her lap, a small blanket tucked around her and both were facing out to bay, where the outline of the Golden Gate Bridge was just emerging from the mist. The scene was one of complete and total peace. Trish was rubbing Jane's little tummy and humming again—a tune Nate didn't recognize.

He hesitated. The scene was almost too perfect—there was no way he wanted to kill the moment by stumbling out and opening his mouth. He just wanted to feel the serenity in this moment a little longer. All his anxiety seemed to ease.

"Good morning," she said in that sweet voice of hers.

Nate stepped out onto the patio. Jane rolled in Trish's arm and, grinning a particularly drooly grin, stretched out a hand for him.

This was something new. The baby was actually glad to see him. "Good morning. Long night?"

Trish twisted to look at him over her shoulder, her long hair rippling like silk in water. Her face lit up as she looked at him, as if not only was she not going to hold his midnight madness against him, but she might just welcome a little bit more madness. "I've had longer. God, this is an amazing view."

No more madness. That was the deal. Nate offered his finger to Jane, whose smile got even wider. "She's happy," he said. "I mean—well, you know what I mean. I hadn't seen her happy until you came."

Trish dropped her gaze to the baby's head and smoothed the fine hairs. "A decent night's sleep and a full tummy will do that."

He *had* to make sure Trish stayed. He needed her in a very concrete way that had nothing to do with his attraction to her. "Look, about last night…"

"There's coffee, if you want some. It's not good coffee," she interrupted, turning her gaze back to the bay. "But it *is* coffee. You'll have to show me how to use that machine."

Jane made a cooing noise and turned back to the view, too. But she didn't let go of Nate's finger.

Well. This was awkward. He decided the manly thing to do was to set the record straight. Time to suck up his pride. "I'm sorry that I crossed a line last night. I wasn't all the way awake and—"

She looked up at him again and this time, there was confusion in her eyes. "What line did you cross?"

"I…" he swallowed and dropped his gaze. "I…"

"You wanted to kiss me?"

So. After all these years of being a geek and a klutz and failing at a majority of social interactions involving the opposite sex, he was *finally* going to die of embarrassment. Fitting. "Well, yeah."

She tilted her head, as if she were pondering this admission. "But you didn't."

"Because that was the plan. I don't want to break our deal. You're making Jane happy. I want you to stay the whole month." The words fell out of his mouth in a rush.

"You didn't kiss me. You didn't come into my room in the middle of the night. You aren't trying to force me to do anything I don't choose to do of my own free will."

The way she said it hit him like a slow-swung sledgehammer because no matter how clueless he could sometimes be, even he heard the truth behind those words.

He hadn't done any of those things.

But someone else had.

"I would *never*," he got out, his voice shaking. White hot fury poured through his body at the thought of someone doing any of that to her.

She nodded. "Then I'll stay. A deal's a deal. There's nothing wrong with attraction if we don't act on it."

"Okay. Good." Then what she'd said sunk in. Did she mean his attraction? Or did she mean she was attracted to him, too?

It didn't matter. Because even if she was attracted, she

wasn't going to act on it. Because that was the deal. For the month.

After the month was up…

He looked down and saw a mostly empty coffee cup on the patio table. "I'll get you some more coffee."

"Thanks."

Nate was gone so long that Trish was on the verge of going to look for him. But the early-morning sun had burned off the rest of the fog and the view was simply amazing and this chair was very comfortable and…

And he'd wanted to kiss her. But hadn't.

So she stayed in her chair and played with Jane. The little girl's personality had done a complete 180 in twenty-four hours. Jane was a happy, smiley baby who was definitely teething. "You're a sweetheart, you know that?" Trish cooed to her as the baby bit down on one of her fingers. "I bet you were the apple of your mommy's eye."

A pang of sadness hit her. Jane would never know her mother—and would never remember Trish, either. Trish would be long gone before that could happen. All she could do was make sure that Nate was set up to care for the girl.

And then…

No. She wasn't going to get ahead of herself. Just because Nate was attracted to her didn't mean a damn thing in the long term. The short term was why she was here. She needed to start Jane on solid foods and get some teething rings. But first, Trish was going to make sure the baby stayed up until after the lunch feeding. What this girl needed was a regular sleep schedule, the faster the better.

Finally, Nate re-emerged, a tray in his hands. "Breakfast?" he said, setting the tray down on the small table.

Trish leaned over and saw that he'd assembled bacon, scrambled eggs and toast, in addition to a carafe of coffee—and a fresh bottle of formula. "Oh," she breathed at the sight of all that glorious food. "I wondered what was taking so long."

"It turns out that you make really bad coffee," he said, settling into the other chair. "So while it was brewing, I decided to make breakfast. And I didn't know if Janie needed another bottle or not, so I brought one just the same."

"You cook? I thought that was why you had Rosita." She selected a piece of toast and took a bite. He'd buttered it and everything.

"She's only been with me since I bought the house. Before I sold the company, I couldn't bring myself to spend the money on a cook. It's that frugal Midwestern upbringing. And a man's got to eat. Her cooking is better, but I can get by." He speared a couple of pieces of bacon and said, "Eggs?"

"Yes, please." Trish had another moment of the surreal. Was one of the most eligible bachelors in all of Silicon Valley really making her *breakfast*? How was she supposed to stand strong against this? "This is really good. Thank you."

He nodded in acknowldgment, because his mouth was full of food. They ate in comfortable silence as sunlight bathed the Golden Gate. The neighborhood was waking up. Trish could hear more traffic on the street, and the muffled sounds of voices from the surrounding houses. But the noise still felt distant. "It's so quiet here."

"I worked with a landscape architect to dampen outside noise." He pointed to the trees and shrubs and then at the trailing vines that surrounded the patio. "There are fences on the other side that you can't see—that keep prying eyes out, too. You can't be too careful. You never know what people will try to turn up."

There it was again—another allusion to something that he wanted to keep buried. "Where did you live before you moved here?"

"I had an apartment in the Mission District," he admitted. "Predictable, huh?"

"Very," she agreed. Even the eggs were good. Jane tried to grab a piece of toast, but Trish handed her the bottle instead. She wanted to have a better understanding of the girl before she started feeding Jane things like bread.

"What about you?"

"A 'garden' apartment in Ingleside. I lived there for almost five years—the whole time I've been in the city."

He chewed that over. "So you came here from where, again?"

"Standing Rock reservation. It straddles the line between North and South Dakota. We lived on the South Dakota side." She tried to call up the mental picture of the never-ending grass, but it didn't mesh with the view of the San Francisco Bay she was looking at. "It's a whole bunch of nothing and a few Indians. Our school was one of those portable trailers that someone parked there about twenty years ago." She sighed.

"Wait. You said you were twenty-five."

"I am."

"You didn't go to college until you were twenty?" She must have given him a sharp look because he added, "I mean, I'm just surprised. You're obviously intelligent. I would be less surprised if you'd graduated a year early or something."

She set her plate aside. Her appetite was gone and Jane was getting squirmy. She pulled the baby back into her arms and held the bottle for her. "I suppose if I'd gone to a normal school or had a normal family, I might have. But I didn't."

"No?"

She debated telling him about this part of her life. He was going to be funding her charity for the foreseeable future, after all. Maybe if she could make him understand how bad it really was, he'd be interested in more than just cutting her a check. He might take an active advisory role in One Child, One World. It could be a smart strategic move.

Except…except then he'd know. He'd know everything and when people knew everything, they had a hard time looking at her as Trish Hunter, regular woman. Instead, they looked at her with pity in their eyes or worse—horror. She didn't want his pity. She didn't want anyone's pity. She wanted respect and nothing less.

She considered lying. She could tell him that she'd gotten two years into a mathematics program and decided she just didn't like sines and cosines that much.

But she didn't want to lie to him. He'd been nothing but honest and upfront with his situation. So she decided to gloss over the harsh realities of her life, just a little. Not a lie, but not the painful truth.

"Life's not always fair. For various reasons, I had to miss a couple of years to help out at home." That was the understatement of the century, she thought with a mental snort. Raising her siblings—and burying one—wasn't "helping." It was taking care of *everything*.

He appeared to weigh that statement. "No, life's not always fair. If it were…we wouldn't be here."

"Exactly." She'd still be back in her underground cavern of an apartment, listening to Mrs. Chan berate her for paying such a low rent and counting down the days until she got her master's degree. "Although having a billionaire serve me breakfast on his private patio isn't really all that bad, is it?" She managed a grin. At least her mouth had managed not to add "hot" to "billionaire." Score one for really bad coffee.

"Just making the best of a lousy situation," he agreed. "Better than it was yesterday, I'll say that much."

"Agreed." Yesterday, she'd eaten dry cereal out of the

box—but not too much, because that box had to last her another week.

"What about tomorrow?"

"It's Sunday?"

"Okay," he said, rolling his eyes in a very dramatic way. "Next week, then. We should probably get a schedule set out. You need to finish your degree and I can probably handle Janie on my own for a while…right?"

"You will be fine. You're a quick study."

She swore he blushed at the compliment and danged if it didn't make him look even better. "If you say so. When do you have classes?"

"I managed to get them all on Tuesdays and Thursdays. I worked the other three days, but I guess I'm not doing that anymore right now?"

He shot her a look that could only be described as commandeering and she remembered that, even if he had made her breakfast, he was still a billionaire who had a reputation as being ruthless in business—and that he basically controlled her time. "Right."

"Well, SFSU isn't exactly within walking distance. It'll take me an hour or so to get there by bus, but if I follow the schedule right, I won't—"

"You're not taking the bus," he informed her.

She physically flinched at his harsh tone. "Excuse me?"

"I mean," he said, "it's not a good use of your time to take the bus. Losing you for a couple of extra hours each day just so you can take the bus is unacceptable. I do own a car. You're free to use it."

A car she could use. There was only one problem. "I couldn't do that."

He waved her hands. "You are, at this exact moment, working for me. Your time is valuable to me. I'm not going to let you waste that time because you don't want to borrow my car."

She glared at him. She couldn't help it. "I don't have a license." His eyebrows jumped up, as if that was the last thing he'd expected her to say. "I mean. I've driven, of course. But I…"

He leaned forward, all of his attention focused on her. "Yes?"

"I couldn't afford to take the driving test and there was no hope of being able to afford a car, so what was the point?"

"Then we'll call for a car," he decided. "That's how I travel a lot, anyway."

"No."

"Because it's too expensive?"

"Well, yes," she said her cheeks shooting red. "I can afford the bus." Even with the overwhelmingly generous salary he was paying her, she couldn't start spending money like she had it. She had to make that twenty grand last for as long as possible.

"And I can afford a car service."

She glared at him openly then. "You're not going to make this easy, are you?"

"Are you kidding? This *is* the easy part. I'm paying the tab. I'm the boss. You'll take a car. I'll drive you myself if I have to." She raised an eyebrow. "Once you install the car seat, that is."

"This is ridiculous," she muttered, turning her attention to the meal.

"No, ridiculous is a five million–dollar comic book. This is a wise use of your time."

"You're already paying me too much—housing me, feeding me," she said quietly. "And the phone." She was going deeper into his debt and that feeling left her… unsettled.

He scoffed. "It's not like I'm going to have my private jet fly you the five miles." Then he turned on the most stunning smile she'd ever seen. "The jet is only for trips over ten miles."

She laughed at him, but that smile did some mighty funny things to her—things that spread a warmth through her body that warded off the last of the early-morning chill.

He'd almost kissed her. And she'd almost let him.

"What about you? What's your schedule?"

"I can be home this week, but I have a gala charity function I really should attend next Saturday night. I think the next two Saturdays are also booked. If that works with your schedule."

"That's fine." That'd be three less nights that she had to be around him, because it was becoming very clear that being around Nate Longmire was a dangerous place for her to be.

Because, after less than twenty-four hours, she was already becoming too attached. She'd lived in that hole in the ground for five years and had walked away without a second thought because it was nothing more than a hellhole with a bed in it. But this place? With the feather beds and beautiful decorating and amazing views and every comfort she'd ever dreamed of growing up?

This place where Nate lived, where Nate slept with a baby on his chest, where Nate made her breakfast and insisted on taking care of her?

It'd be hard to walk away from this, to go back to living in cheap and crappy apartments. To being alone all the time.

To having no one care if she was an hour later on the bus or not.

Trish was in *so* much trouble.

Six

Nate found himself on the phone with the Chair of the School of Social Work at San Francisco State University first thing Monday morning, explaining how he'd poached the chairwoman's best student worker for a nanny position. And then pledging some money to the Social Work program to ease the strain he'd put on the chairwoman's department.

A complete baby's room showed up Monday morning, along with Trish's phone and a passable legal contract codifying their agreement. They both signed with Stanley serving as witness.

Then Nate and Stanley put the furniture together under Trish's increasingly amused direction. Nate let her arrange the room as she saw fit and Stanley followed his lead.

It was only when Trish took Jane downstairs to get her a bottle and try to nap in the quiet of the parlor that Stanley dared open his big mouth. "Dude, she is *hot*."

"It's not like that."

Stanley snorted. "It never is with you. Man, when was the last time you got laid?"

Against his will, Nate felt himself blush. "That's not relevant to the discussion."

"Like hell it's not. And don't try to tell me it's not because you're not into her." Stanley punched him in the arm, which made Nate almost drop the side of the crib he was holding. "I've seen you stick your foot into your mouth around every species of female known to mankind and I've yet to see you actually talk to a woman like you talk to *her*. It's almost like aliens have taken over your body and made you *not* lame or something. And what's even more unbelievable is that she totally seems to be digging you." Stanley shook his head in true shock.

Nate glared at him. He didn't want to particularly own up to the conversation he'd had with Trish at breakfast the other morning, where she'd easily identified how interested he was and conveniently sidestepped whether or not she felt anywhere near the same. "I've stuck my foot in my mouth enough already."

"Yeah?" Stanley looked impressed as they tried to get the crib to lock together like it did in the instructions. "What went wrong? Tell me you didn't stick your tongue down her throat on the first kiss."

"I didn't kiss her," Nate got out. His brain oh-so-helpfully added, *yet*. Yeah, right. "She made her position very clear. No sex."

Stanley whistled. *"Dude."*

"And may I just take this moment to remind you—again—that if I ever hear a word of this conversation even whispered by the press that I'll—"

"Personally turn my ass into grass, yeah, yeah, I got it. You know I can keep my mouth shut." But he looked at Nate expectantly.

If it were anyone other than Stanley...but the man was the closest thing to a confidant that Nate had. "Look, she's an amazing woman. You have no idea."

Stanley chuckled. "No, but I'm getting one."

"But," Nate went on, "we had a deal and you know I won't break a deal."

"Yeah," Stanley said in a pitiable voice, as if this was

the saddest thing he'd ever heard, "I know. You're very reliable like that."

"What about her charity? Did you finish the due diligence?"

"Gosh, gee, I was a little busy freaking out the workers at Babies 'R' Us," he said in an innocent voice. "Apparently, single men who look like I do rarely go shopping for baby things by themselves. So no, not yet. I'll get started after we get this damn crib together. You still going to the event on Saturday?"

"Yeah."

"Remember, I have a family thing. If I set your tux out now, can you get your tie on by yourself?"

Nate debated the odds of that. He didn't think so, but Stanley rarely asked for time off. "Probably."

Stanley nodded, but Nate didn't miss the look of doubt. "You going to take *her*? You know that Finklestein's going to try and set you up with his granddaughter again."

"Oh, God," Nate moaned. He'd forgotten about Martin Finklestein, a pillar of San Francisco's high society who'd become convinced, upon Nate's entry into the billionaires' club, that he and Lola Finklestein were perfect for each other. "I had forgotten. Is it too late to cancel?" He debated telling Stanley about the most recent message he'd gotten from Diana, but decided against it. He was just ignoring her at this point. He didn't need help to pull that off.

Stanley snorted. "Just take Trish."

"And do *what* with the baby? We haven't even gotten to the point where I'm ready to start interviewing other nannies yet and there's no way in *hell* we're going to use that service again."

"Mental note made," Stanley said. "There!" He slid the panel in and the crib stood on its own. "Man, babies are a hassle."

That made Nate laugh. "Dude, you have no idea."

* * *

Trish was trying to get Jane on a sleep schedule, which meant that the baby was supposed to stay awake from whenever she got up until at least one, so, for a couple of hours around lunchtime, Jane was a tad fussy.

And by "a tad fussy," Nate really meant that Jane reverted back to her pre-Trish state of near-constant screaming. He found the noise to be almost unbearable, but Trish would just smile and power through as if baby wailing was music to her ears.

Nate was forced to admit that the payoff was pretty nice. Jane started sleeping from one to three in the afternoon within a matter of days and went from getting Trish up three times a night to two, which meant that everyone—even Nate—was sleeping better.

He even did okay when Trish went to school on Tuesday and Thursday—in a hired car. She only left after she was confident that both Nate and Rosita could fix the formula and Nate could change the diapers. "Call me if you have a problem," she said. "But you can do this."

That she'd said it when Nate was so clearly about to panic was nice enough. But what was even nicer was the way she'd laid her hand on his biceps and given his arm a light squeeze. Then, after kissing Jane's little head, she'd gathered up her bag and headed out to the hired car.

"What do you think?" Nate had asked the little girl.

Jane made a gurgling noise.

"Yeah," Nate had agreed. "I feel the same way."

The day was long. The screaming wasn't too bad and he'd gotten Jane to go down for her nap. That was something he hadn't even gotten close to in the week before Trish showed up.

Still, Nate was waiting for her when the hired car pulled up in front of the house at five-fifteen and Trish got out.

Jane had woken up at two-fifteen and had not been exactly a happy camper without Trish.

"I'm so glad you're back," he said when she walked into the house.

"Rough day? Come here, sweetie." She took Jane from him. "It looks like you're doing okay. She's dressed and everything this time."

Nate blushed. "She's just fussy. I don't know if she's teething or if she just wanted you?"

"Oh, sweetie," Trish said in that soothing voice as she rubbed Jane's back.

Jane buried her tear-streaked face into Trish's neck. Nate was once again struck by the feeling of how *right* the two of them looked together. Trish would never be Elena and God knew that Nate would never be Brad, but life wasn't fair and they were doing the best they could.

Suddenly, he wanted to ask her to go to the gala with him. She'd look amazing in a gown, her arm linked through his as they strode up the steps of the Opera House. That would get Finklestein to back off about Nate settling down with his granddaughter.

Except...Nate was reasonably confident that Trish didn't own a ball gown and that she wouldn't let him buy her one without one hell of a fight.

And there was the problem of Jane. Rosita was back to her happy self now that she was not responsible for Jane's well-being. There was no way Nate could ask his maid to babysit and who else did he trust? Stanley? That wasn't going to happen, either.

So he resigned himself to fending off Finklestein's advances—again.

Once Trish had Jane, Nate called his parents. He knew Joe would be down for a nap, thanks to the meds he was on. Nate resisted the urge to put them on video chat—some things were just beyond his parents. His mom answered.

"Hey, Mom. How are you?"

His mother sniffed. "We're getting by. How are you? How is Jane?"

"Good. Really good. She's teething, but I think she's doing as well as could be expected. I hired the perfect nanny and she's just done wonderfully with Jane. She got the nursery all set up and Jane's even started sleeping better."

"Oh, thank God," Mom said, the relief obvious in her voice. "We've been just worried sick about you two together. Honey, we're so sorry we had to ask you to take Jane, but you know Joe hasn't been dealing with any of this very well and—"

"I know, Mom. But it's going to be okay. Trish is here—that's the nanny. Trish Hunter. She knows what she's doing. I'll send you a couple of pictures later, okay?"

"That would be wonderful, dear."

They talked a bit more about how Joe was doing and how the town was reacting to the loss of one of its golden boys. Then Mom said, "Oh, Joe's up. Honey, we'll talk later and maybe after things calm down here a bit, I'll see about coming out, okay?"

"That'd be good, Mom. I know Jane will be happy to see you again."

"We're so proud of you, Nate," Mom said. It was her usual closing statement, but it hit Nate differently this time.

"I love you, too. Tell Joe I said howdy." He ended the call.

If only he knew what was going to happen next. Obviously, he was going to be a father. But was he going to find love and get married? Would he settle down with Lola Finklestein? Okay, he knew the answer to that one—no.

But…Stanley had been right. Nate didn't talk to a lot of women. Would he just have nannies who helped raise

Jane until she was old enough that he could handle her by himself?

The thought of Lola and other nannies bothered him. Then he thought of how Trish looked in the morning, watching the sunrise with Jane tucked on her lap.

She was only here for a month—less than a month, now. That was the plan.

But after the month was up?

He didn't know.

It wasn't until Thursday afternoon, from the cushy backseat of a hired car on her way back to Nate's house after her classes that Trish used her brand new smartphone to call home. Even with the hired car, it was going to take about forty minutes to navigate all the rush-hour traffic. Trish had time to call.

"Hello?" Patsy's thin voice answered on the fourth ring.

"Hey, baby girl," Trish said. She'd always wondered why her mother had named two of her daughters after her—Trish and Patsy. They were all Patricia.

"Trisha!" Patsy squealed. "I miss you. When are you going to come back? Are you going to send me any more presents? I really liked the cool notebooks you sent me last time."

"Whoa, whoa—slow down, girl." Trish couldn't help but grin at her youngest sibling. The Hello Kitty notebooks had been on super clearance here because no one wanted them, but out on the rez? They were a prized possession. "Are you still going to school? I expect to see a good third-grade report card before any more presents show up."

Patsy sighed heavily and Trish was sure she could hear the accompanying eye roll. "Yes. I'm going every single day. Mrs. Iron Horse says I'm her best reader."

"Good."

"When are you coming back?"

"Not for another couple of months," Trish replied gently.

"What? Why not?" Patsy pouted. "I thought you were going to come back after you finished your school."

"Something came up. I got a new job and I have to stay here for a while."

Patsy was silent as she thought this over. "Do you like it? The new job?"

"Yes," Trish said without hesitating. The good food, the nice house, the amazing view—even without the huge paycheck, this was something of a dream job. That didn't even count Nate Longmire. And Nate? He counted for quite a lot. "I'll be home after the job is over. Is Mom home?"

"No, she got a new job, too. But Dad's here—you want to talk to him?"

"Sure. Put Tim on." As far as Patsy was concerned, Tim was her father. He'd come into their lives when Patsy had been only two. But Trish couldn't think of Tim as her father. He was a good guy, but she just couldn't do it.

"Daddy!" Patsy yelled in Trish's ear. She jerked the phone away from her head and winced. For such a little girl, Patsy had a heck of a set of lungs. "It's Trish!" Then she said in a normal voice, "I hope you can come home this summer. Then I can show you the award I got for writing an essay in Lakota!"

Homesickness hit Trish hard. She'd been there for all the other kids' awards and honors. She'd spent her entire adolescence making sure that the other kids got to basketball practice or assemblies or awards ceremonies. But she'd missed the past five years of that. "That's *so* awesome, baby girl. I can't wait to see it."

"Here's Daddy. Bye, Trish!"

"Bye, Patsy."

"Hey, Trish," Tim said in his gruff voice.

"Hi, Tim. How's it going?"

"Not bad. Your mom got a new job. Your sister Millie

got her a job at the state trooper's office. She's typing up the police reports at night."

"Really? Does she like it?" Because the Pat that Trish remembered couldn't hold down anything—a man, a job, a house. Nothing. It'd all been on Trish.

"Eh," Tim said. "You know how she is. But she gets to find out a lot of gossip as it's happening and she likes that, so I think she'll stay with this for a while."

"Yeah," Trish said. "I know how she is. Hey, the reason I'm calling is that I got a new job and I wanted to give you the address I'll be at for the next month."

"Gimme a sec," Tim said. She heard him rustling through papers and pens. "Okay, shoot."

Trish recited the address and then the new phone number. "I got a huge signing bonus," she went on. "I can pay you back that $350 you loaned me for my security deposit."

There was a moment of silence on the line that Trish wasn't sure how to interpret. "Trish, that was a gift."

"Well, I can pay you back. This is a really good job and—"

"Trish." It was as sharp as she'd ever heard Tim speak. "It was a gift. I've tried to help out all your brothers and sisters here, but you were so independent. The best I could do for you was to front you a little traveling money and give you a chance."

"You really don't have to do that," Trish said. Her throat was in danger of closing up and she wasn't sure why. "I mean, if you hadn't come along, I wouldn't have been able to leave. I'd have had to stay home and…" and continue being a mother to Pat's babies.

Trish never would have made it to San Francisco, never would have gotten one degree and almost completed a second one—never would have started her charity. She'd be stuck on that rez, no prospects and no hope. Nothing but doing her best to make sure that all of her siblings had the best chance *she* could give *them*.

"You don't have to give me anything more than what you've already given me," she finished in a low whisper, her voice shaking. "At least use it to get the kids something."

Tim had the nerve to laugh. "You always were the hardest of hard-headed kids. Toughest girl I ever did meet. I guess you had to be, what with Pat being Pat."

Then, before she quite realized it, she asked, "Why do you stay with her?"

She'd always wanted to know. She got why men would hook up with Pat—she was beautiful and liked to have a good time. Despite the ten kids, she still had a good figure. But looks weren't everything and no one else had lasted anywhere near as long as Tim. Sooner or later, Pat's drama would cancel out whatever good grace her face bought her and men would walk. Sometimes that was a good thing and sometimes it wasn't.

Tim kind of chuckled. "Love does funny things to a man, I guess." He sounded wistful. "I know she's not perfect and I'm not, either. I got the failed marriages to prove it. But there's something about being with her that makes me feel right with the world. And when you've seen as much of the world as I have, you know that's no small thing."

"Yeah, I guess…"

Tim laughed. "You're an old soul, Trish. You had to grow up early and quick. But take it from an old man— you're still young. You'll know what I mean one of these days. Keep the $350 and do something nice for yourself or run it through your charity or whatever. It's your money. I don't want it back."

"Thank you, Tim. I…" She swallowed, trying to get her voice under control. "It means a lot to me."

"Don't mention it. You want me to tell your mom you called?"

"That'd be great. Tell her I'm glad she's liking her new job, too."

"Will do. Take care, Trish."

The call ended. Trish sat in the back of a very nice car being driven by a very nice man, taking her back to a very nice house with a home-cooked meal and an attractive, interesting billionaire who liked *her*.

There was nothing about this that made her feel right with the world.

Seven

He couldn't tie the tie. This was why he paid Stanley money—to tie his damn ties for him.

Every time Nate tried to loop the ends around and under, just like the how-to video on YouTube, it came out… not tie-like. More like a four-year-old's attempt to tie his shoes than a polished, James Bond–like piece of neckwear.

"Hell," he mumbled as he undid the mess again. Maybe he wouldn't wear the bow tie. Maybe he'd go tieless and proclaim it was the latest fashion trend. It might even be a fun sociological experiment—how many people would follow suit because the richest man in the room said so?

Or he could still just cancel. That was an option, too. Sure, it was a gala sponsored in part by the Longmire Foundation and yes, people were probably starting to wonder if he'd died, since he hadn't been seen in public in three weeks. But he was Nate Longmire. He could do whatever he wanted.

"Knock, knock," Trish said from the doorway. "We came to say good-night."

Nate turned and saw Trish silhouetted from the light in the hallway. Jane was in her arms, her little head tucked against Trish's neck.

Mental correction—he could do *almost* whatever he wanted.

"Ready for bed?" he asked.

Jane turned her head away from him, which Trish had explained meant not that she didn't like him, but that the little girl was too tired to process.

Still, it stung in an entirely childish way. Nate crossed the room and kissed the back of Jane's head. "Good night, Janie. Sleep well."

He straightened up. Trish was looking at him, her large brown eyes taking in everything.

They stood like this a lot—so close together he could see the way her eyes shifted from a lighter brown to a deeper chocolate color. Close enough to kiss, except for the baby in between them. And, of course, there was no kissing.

In theory, he was getting better at not thinking about it. It was a nice theory, too. But right now…

She blinked, which pulled him out of his thoughts and back into reality. "You need some help with your tie?"

"You know how to tie a tie?"

The corners of her mouth quirked up. "I can't do much worse, I suppose. Can you wait until Jane's down?"

"Sure." He watched as she turned and walked across the hall. She settled into the glider chair and told Jane a story about Goldilocks and the Three Bears while the baby had her bedtime bottle.

Nate knew he should stay in his room, finish getting ready, maybe try the tie one more time. That was the safe thing to do—the legally advisable thing to do. But he was drawn across the hall, watching Trish rock Jane to sleep.

There it was again—that feeling of absolute peace as he watched Trish nurture the baby. She looked up at him, her eyebrows raised as if she were expecting him to ask a question or something, but he just shrugged a shoulder and watched.

Yeah, it could be that the serenity was simply because he was so damned relieved that Jane was being well cared for—that he wasn't solely responsible for her tiny person. But there was something more to this, something he didn't quite recognize.

Something Stanley had said came back to him—"I've yet to see you actually talk to a woman like you talk to *her*."

Comfort? Familiarity? No, that wasn't quite it, either. They'd only been coexisting for the past week, really. They'd had some good chemistry at a coffee shop and then he'd hired her in a moment of true desperation.

Jane finished her bottle and Trish gently patted her back before laying her out in the crib. She touched her fingertips to her lips and then brushed them over Jane's head as she murmured, "Good night, sweetie."

Then she turned and, slowly, walked toward him. He knew he needed to move—at the very least, he needed to get out of the way so they could shut the door and let Jane sleep.

But as she approached him, a knowing smile tugging on the corners of her mouth, he couldn't move. She was beautiful, yes, but there was so much more to her than that. She was kind and thoughtful and, perhaps most importantly, she didn't make him feel like an idiot.

She didn't hesitate. She walked right up to him and took hold of the ends of his tie. "Here," she said in a breathy whisper, gently pushing him back and out of the doorway. His hands lifted themselves up and settled around her waist—for balance, he justified after the fact. "Let me."

Without releasing her grip on his tie, she turned and pulled Jane's door shut. Then they were moving again as she backed him toward his bedroom.

He let her. He'd let her do whatever the hell she wanted right now. If she wanted to tie his tie, that'd be fine. If she wanted to rip his shirt off his chest, well, that'd be fine, too. He had other tuxedo shirts.

"Ah," she breathed, stopping well short of the bed. *Damn.* "I think I can do this."

"I'm sure it'll be better than what I was coming up with."

She grinned as she started looping the tie. "You look good in a tux. Very..."

He stood a little straighter. Her body underneath his hands was so hot he was practically sweating. "Yes?"

"Very grown-up. Not like a Boy Billionaire at all." He felt the tie tightening around his neck.

"I suppose that's a good thing?" Was that the same as "incredibly attractive"? That's what she'd told him once, when he was having a very bad day.

"It is. Damn." The tie loosened. "Let me try again."

He grinned down at her. "I think that's the first cuss word I've heard you say."

"Is it? I guess I've trained myself not to say bad words around kids." The necktie tightened again. "Where are you going tonight?"

"The Opera House for the gala charity function for ARTification, a big fund-raiser. The Longmire Foundation is a sponsoring partner." Her eyebrows jumped. "Well, that just means I gave them money and didn't do any of the planning."

She grinned, but it faltered. "Okay, I think I know what to do this time." One of her fingers touched the underside of his chin and lifted. "Look up, please."

Her touch took his theoretical mastery of his desire for her and pretty much reset it at zero. It took all of his concentration not to dig the pads of his fingertips into her glorious hips.

"I wanted to take you to this," he said before he knew what he was doing.

Her hands stilled for a moment. "You did?"

"Yes."

"You didn't ask me."

"I didn't think you'd say yes." He was careful to keep his chin up. "I don't know if you know who Martin Finklestein is, but he's pretty much decided that I should marry his granddaughter."

"And that's a problem?"

"Lola Finklestein makes me nervous." He forced a small smile. "Don't tell anyone I said that."

She didn't respond as she adjusted the tie. He felt her hands smoothing the bow. The tips of her fingers fluttered over his neck, right above his collar. Blood began to pound in his ear. "Is that why you wanted me to go with you? To run interference with Lola?"

He should say yes. He should back away. He should do *anything* but look down at her, so close. So damn close and not a single baby in between them.

But then her hands were smoothing over the shoulders of his tuxedo shirt, running down the front of the shirt. *She* was touching *him*.

"No." His hands moved without his explicit permission, tightening around her waist and then sliding toward her back. Pulling her in. He wanted to fill his hands with her skin, to know how she'd feel under him. Or over him. He wasn't picky. "I wanted…"

He swallowed and looked down. She was staring up at him, her lips parted and her cheeks flushed. She looked… like a woman who wanted to be kissed. He didn't know if she stepped into him or if he stepped into her, but suddenly what space had existed between them was gone and her arms were around his neck and he was lifting her toward his lips.

"You," he whispered. And then her lips were against his and he was kissing her back and it was good. *So* good. His hands kept right on moving of their own accord, sliding down until he'd cupped her bottom, the pads of his fingertips digging in as he pushed her higher. Her mouth opened for him and he tasted her, dipping his tongue into her honeyed sweetness. He went hard in an instant, pressing against the soft warmth of her stomach. Her nipples seemed to respond, growing hard and hot against his chest—so hot he could feel them through his shirt.

God, her mouth—this kiss—it was right. She was *right*, tucked in his arms where he could taste her and feel her body pressed against his and—and—

She pulled away. Not very far, but far enough that he had to stop kissing her, which was harder to do than he expected.

Her arms unlinked from around his neck and then, as coolly as if the kiss had never happened, she was smoothing the shirt over his shoulders. "You're going to be late."

"Um…yeah." That was not exactly the kind of thing a man liked to hear after the kind of kiss that left said man practically unable to walk. "I should—I should go."

She stepped away from him and it was only then that he saw how the kiss had affected her. Her eyes were glazed and her chest was heaving with what he hoped was desire. As he watched, the tip of her tongue darted out and ran over her top lip as if she were tasting his kiss and he almost lost it. Almost fell to his knees to beg her forgiveness but he was *going* to sleep with her, contractual language be damned. All that mattered was him and her and absolutely no bow ties.

She took another step back. "Don't—" She took a deep breath, which did some interesting things to her chest. "Don't let Lola steamroll you, okay?"

He managed a perfectly serviceable grin, as if her body in his arms was not a big deal at all. "Don't worry. I won't."

Nate didn't want to do this. He did not want to walk into one of the premiere high-society events of the social season. He did not want women to look at him like he was a lamb being led to sacrifice on the altar of Eligible Billionaire Bachelors. He didn't want to sit through a dinner on a dais in front of the room and know that people were watching him to see if he would do something of note.

"Mr. Longmire," an older gentleman who looked vaguely familiar said as he hurried forth and shook Nate's hand vigorously. "We weren't sure if you were actually going to make it."

"Yes," Nate said, feeling the wall go up between him and his surroundings. He hated social events in general and formal ones in particular. The only way to get through this was to pretend that he was somehow above the proceedings. That's how he'd gotten through the lawsuits and it probably had contributed to his reputation as being ruthless.

He'd be much happier back home—even if Trish had locked herself in her room and he spent the night in the media room, staring at code.

He'd kissed her.

At the very least, he'd kissed her back.

But hot on the heels of that delicious memory of her tasting him and him tasting her, a terrible thought occurred to him.

He'd broken the deal.

Oh, *no*. How could he have done that? A deal was a deal and he *always* kept a deal.

Except for this. Except for Trish.

Worst-case scenarios—each more terrible than the last—flipped through his mind. They all ended in basically the same way—Trish packing up her things and being gone by morning, all because he couldn't resist her.

The older gentleman's welcoming smile faltered. "Yes, well, this way, please. Mr. Martin Finklestein has been asking after you."

"I bet he has." The older man's smile faltered so much that he lost his grip on it entirely, which made Nate feel bad. He was sure the rumor mill was working overtime as it was. "Lead on, please."

The older man—Nate could *not* remember his name—turned and all but scurried off toward the bar. Alcohol was already flowing, all the better to get people to crack open their wallets.

Nate followed. He was aware of people pausing in their conversations and watching him as he passed, but he was too worried about what Trish might be doing at this very moment to give a damn.

"Ah, Nate." The bright—some might say grating—voice of Lola Finklestein snaked through the hushed conversations and assaulted his ears. "There you are!"

He turned toward the voice. It was a shame, really. Her voice notwithstanding, Lola was a beautiful woman. She had a mass of thick black curls that were always artfully arranged. She had a swan's graceful neck and a slim figure. She was a beloved patron of the arts and of course she was heiress to the Finklestein fortune. By all objective measures, she was one hell of a catch.

Despite it all, Nate couldn't stand her. Her voice rubbed his nerve endings raw and she always had an odd scent, like…peaches and onions. He couldn't imagine spending the rest of his life stuffing cotton balls in his ears and lighting scented candles to cover the smell of her perfume.

Especially not after that kiss. Not after having Trish in his arms.

"Here I am," he agreed, feeling like a condemned man standing before the gallows.

"We've been worried sick about you. Where on earth have you been keeping yourself for the last three weeks? You know that the Celebration of the Zoo last week was just no fun without you."

"Couldn't be helped," Nate said. Which was a lame excuse—but still much better than being subjected to all kinds of condolences from this crowd. That was one of the reasons he kept Brad and Elena's deaths out of the press. He simply couldn't bear the thought of Lola hugging him and crying for his family.

He kept his back straight and what he hoped was a polite smile on his face. Of course, he'd seen photos of his "polite smile." It barely broke the threshold of "impolite snarl," but it was the best he could do.

He just wanted to be back at home. With Trish.

Was there a chance, however small, that the kiss had been the start of something else? Something more?

"Well, you're here now," Lola said, leaning in to brush kisses across both of his cheeks. "Oh, I have someone I want you to meet." She turned. "Diana?"

The name barely had a moment to register before a blonde woman in a blue dress separated from the others. Nate's brain crashed so fast, it felt like someone had tripped the surge protector in his mind.

She looked different now. Her face was tighter, her breasts larger—and was her nose slimmer, too?

Diana *Carter*.

The woman who'd nearly ruined him.

"Oh," she said in the breathy voice that he'd only heard on a few occasions—like when he'd told her about the first big round of investing he'd managed to secure for SnAppShot. And when he'd introduced her to Brad. "Nate and I do know each other. We go way back."

"Diana. You're looking…lovely." He realized he'd forgotten his polite smile, but this was possibly the worst thing that could have happened tonight.

Well, not the worst. Trish could have slapped him after that kiss. She could still leave.

But this was a close second.

Diana batted her eyes at him.

Damn it all. A *very* close second.

"I need to talk to you. Privately," he added as Lola stepped forward. Lola frowned.

Diana's demure face froze before she purred, "Of course."

"This way." Nate stalked off to a corner, chasing a lingering waiter away with a glare. "What are you doing here?" he demanded when they could speak without being overheard.

She gave him a reproachful look, as if he'd wounded her pride. "Is that any way to greet your fiancée?"

His teeth ground together. "*Former* fiancée. And yes, it is."

"About that." She sighed, her new and improved chest rising dramatically. "I was actually hoping to talk to you."

Nate's mouth opened to tell her where she could go but he slammed the brakes on and got his mouth shut just in time. If he looked hard enough, he could see the woman he'd once thought he'd loved. The Diana he'd known had been pretty enough, but with glasses and a habit of smiling nervously. She'd been shy and a little geeky and intelligent—exactly the kind of woman he'd thought he'd needed.

Until he'd taken her home to meet his family. And then she'd revealed that she was something more than all that.

"Why?"

Diana dropped her gaze and then looked up at him through her thick lashes. It felt entirely calculated. "I thought...we could let bygones be bygones." She exhaled through slightly parted lips. "I thought we might start over."

His mental circuitry overloaded and suddenly he was back at a single blinking cursor on an otherwise blank screen. The woman who'd broken his heart *and* tried to claim half of his company as her own because they'd just started dating when Nate thought it up— "You want to *start over*?"

She had the nerve to look hopeful. "Yes."

No. *No.*

"Brad's dead."

This time, Diana's reaction wasn't schooled or calculated. The blood drained out of her face and she took a shocked step backwards. "What?"

"You remember Brad? My older brother, the one you slept with because—and stop me if I'm not remembering this part correctly—you told me it was because he was 'like me' but better? He's dead."

Diana fell back another step. Her hand dropped to her side and what was left of her champagne spilled onto the floor. "What—when?"

"After we settled in court, he married an old girlfriend and they had a baby. They were very happy." He didn't know why he was telling her this. Only that, on some level, he felt like she deserved to know. "Until three weeks ago. A car accident. And now they're both dead."

Diana covered her mouth with her hands, her eyes painfully wide. "I didn't—I hadn't heard. I didn't know."

"No, of course not. After you cheated on me—after you tried to cheat me out of my company—I learned to keep things close to the vest. I learned how to avoid giving people anything they might use against me. I learned how to keep things out of the media."

Diana shook her head from side to side, as if she could deny that she'd changed him. That he'd let her change him. She took another step back and Nate matched it with a step forward. "I have you to thank for that. So, to answer your question, no. We can't start over. We can't go back. I can't trust you. Not now, not ever. You said it yourself, didn't you? 'I can do better.' That's the justification you had for falling into Brad's bed. He was better than me in everything but brains. That's the justification you used to try and take half of SnAppShot. And now that I'm the richest damn man in the room, you realize you can't do better, can you?"

"No—that's—I'm—"

He couldn't stop. He couldn't lock it down and bury all of this behind his wall of distance. In a moment of panic, he even tried to recall the original code to give him some measure of control over himself, but all he had was a flash of white-hot anger. Because she'd changed him. She'd made him afraid to be himself because being Nate Longmire hadn't been good enough. And he was tired of only being good enough because he was a billionaire.

That's not how Trish saw him. He was not a bank account to be conquered. He was a man who hadn't figured out all the mechanics of changing a diaper, who wasn't afraid to ask for help. He was not a meal ticket to be exploited until there was nothing left.

"It is. And I'm not the same naive nerd anymore, grateful for a pretty girl who didn't think I was a total loser."

"I never said that about you." She seemed to be regaining her balance. "I *cared* for you."

"But you didn't care enough." All of his anger bled out of him.

She had changed him. She'd made him tougher, smarter. He knew how to play the game now. It wasn't all bad. Just a broken heart. Everyone had one, once. He couldn't hold a grudge. "I wish you luck, Diana. I hope you find the man who's good enough for you. But it's not me. It never was me and we both know it. Now, if you'll excuse me."

He turned and walked off, pushing through the crowd like they were just so many sheep in Armani tuxedos. He couldn't bear to be here for another moment. He needed to breathe again and he couldn't do that with this stupid tie around his neck.

"Nate? Wait!"

He didn't know why he slowed. He'd said what he needed to say. But he slowed, anyway.

Diana Carter—the woman who had held so much sway over his life—caught up to him. "Nate," she said, her perfectly made-up eyes wet with unshed tears. "I'm sorry. I'm sorry for what I did. I'm sorry about your brother and his wife. Please—" Her chest hiccupped a little. She reached over and touched his shoulder. "Please accept my condolences on your loss."

"Thank you." He patted her hand where she was touching him and then, on impulse, lifted her hand to his lips.

She nodded in acceptance. "She's a lucky woman."

"Who?"

Diana gave him a watery smile, then she leaned up on her toes and brushed a kiss on his cheek. "Whoever she is. Goodbye, Nate."

"Goodbye, Diana." Their hands touched for another moment and then, by unspoken agreement, they separated. Nate had to bail. He couldn't do this, he couldn't sit in the front of this crowded room and pretend he was above the dinner and the speeches and all the people trying to figure out how to get closer to him. He couldn't put up his walls. Hell, he couldn't find his walls. Even his original code, which always kept him calm, failed him.

"Nate?" The voice was unmistakable. *Lola.* "Nate! Where are you going? You just got here!" Honestly, it was like fingernails down a chalkboard.

Nate kept going. He'd had things to say to Diana. He'd been close to marrying her, after all. But Lola? No, he didn't have things to say to her.

He dug out his phone and called for a hired car as he stalked out of the Opera House.

He had things he wanted to say to Trish.

He hoped like hell she'd listen.

Eight

Trish had her laptop on her lap, her thesis document open.

She wasn't looking at it.

She wasn't looking at anything, really. Her eyes were focused out the big curved picture window in Nate's front parlor, but the darkness was not what she was seeing.

No, what she was seeing was the way Nate's pulse had jumped in his throat when she'd grabbed the ends of his tie. She was feeling the way his hands had settled around her waist.

She was tasting the kiss on her lips. *His* kiss.

This was a fine how-do-you-do, wasn't it? She'd kissed him. She didn't kiss people. She didn't sleep with people. She kept anyone who might even be remotely interested in her at twenty paces. Technically, that made her a twenty-five-year-old virgin, although she'd never thought about it in those terms. Not often, anyway. Sure, sex was probably a lot of fun—why else did her mother keep having it?—but she wasn't going to pay for twenty minutes of pleasure with the rest of her life.

She was not her mother's daughter, damn it all. At least, she hadn't been until one week ago. She was only four months from being twenty-six. By the time Pat Hunter was twenty-six, she had three kids, was pregnant with her fourth and had six more yet to come. She couldn't hold a job or a man. She was barely getting by.

That's not what Trish was. Trish was educated. She had
a plan. She had things to do, things that would be derailed
by something so grand as falling in love and so base as
getting laid. She kept her eyes on the prize and her pants
firmly zipped.

Until Nate. Until the very moment when he'd walked
out on stage, if she was going to be honest about it. She
hadn't had a single intention of doing anything remotely
sexual with, about, or to Nate Longmire when she'd re-
searched him. She'd noted he was attractive in the same
way she might admire a well-carved statue, but there'd
been no attraction. No desire.

There sure as hell was now. Because she'd kissed him.
Prim, proper—some would say prudish—Patricia Hunter
had kissed Nate Longmire.

What was she doing?

Wondering what sex with Nate would be like, that's
what. Wondering if she'd actually go through with it, or
if her healthy respect for the consequences would slam
her legs shut again.

She could do it, after all. She was smart enough to use
protection. She could enjoy safe sex with a man she was
attracted to without losing herself in him, like Pat always
had.

Couldn't she?

Dimly, she was aware of traffic outside, but it wasn't
until the front door slammed shut that she became aware
of her surroundings.

Then he was there. Nate Longmire filled the parlor
doorway, each hand on the door frame as if he was physically holding himself back.

"Nate! Is everything all right?" She glanced at the clock.
It was only 8:45. "I wasn't expecting you home for hours."

"I want you to know something," he said, his voice
low and from somewhere deep in the back of his throat.

A shiver raced down her back at his commanding tone. "I want you to understand—I do *not* break a deal."

He bit the words out as if he were furious with them— or with her. She sat there for moment in a state of shock. This was, by far and away, the most enraged she'd ever seen him. "Oh?"

"I keep my word. My word is my bond. That's how my father raised me." She saw his fingers flex around the door-jamb. Would he rip the wood right off the wall? "When I say I'm going to do something—or not do something— then that's how it is. Canceling those two events because of Brad and Elena—it drove me nuts. But it couldn't be helped."

She closed her laptop and set it aside. She couldn't tell if he was going to fire her for kissing him or rip her clothes off. And worse—she didn't know what she wanted to happen. "I see."

"It's when people break their word to me, that's when the trouble starts. People make promises to me and then they break them and I won't stand for it."

He spoke with such conviction. Surely he wasn't try-ing to sound erotic, but heat spiked through her. He was barely holding himself back. She should probably be afraid of this display of anger—of power.

She was *totally* turned on. "You can be ruthless. That's your reputation."

"I have to be." It came out anguished, as if it wounded him to sue people back to the Stone Age. "Kill or be killed." Even from twenty feet away, she could see the white-knuckled grip he had on the frame. But he didn't take another step into the room. "I was engaged. To be married."

"You were?"

"To Diana Carter." The admission seemed to hollow him out a bit.

The name rang a bell. Nate Longmire v. Diana Carter. The court case. The rumors that maybe there'd been something else between them, rumors that could be neither confirmed nor denied because the court records were sealed. "Wait. Isn't that the woman you sued over the right to the SnAppShot code?"

He nodded, a short crisp movement of his head that did nothing to dislodge his grip on the door frame. "She was there tonight. I try not to think about her, but I realized tonight that because of what she did, she's affected *everything* that I do."

This time, Trish stood. When she did—when she took a step toward him—his head jerked up and he got that ferocious look on his face again. "What did she do?"

"We were engaged. I took her home to meet my family and she slept with my brother."

Her mouth dropped open in surprise. Not what she was expecting to hear. "She broke her promise."

"And then claimed half the company was hers, since we'd been together when I started it."

"And tonight?" She took another step toward him. And another.

"She wanted to start over. But I can't trust her." He swallowed, his Adam's apple bobbing above his bow tie. "Not like I trust you."

She considered this. "Do you? I mean, we haven't known each other very long."

"I trust you with my niece's life. That's far more important than a stupid piece of code."

She took a few more steps toward him, closing the distance between them. His head snapped up. "Don't come any closer."

"Why not?"

"Because I keep my promises. And I promised you that I would not have sex with you. That I would not take advantage of you just because you're beautiful and intelligent and I'm as comfortable with you as I've ever been with any woman, including Diana. Just because I trust you." She took another step forward and he actually backed up. He didn't let go of the door frame, but his feet were now in the hall. "And if you come any closer, I'm not going to keep my promise."

The words ripped out of his chest and seemed to hit her in the dead center of hers. She put her hand over her heart to make sure it was still beating.

"All those women tonight, trying to catch my eye," he went on. "Lola and Diana and the rest of them, looking at me and seeing a prize they could win. And all I could see—all I could think about—was *you*. I wanted to take you because I wanted you there with me. And since that couldn't happen—since Jane is upstairs—I came home."

"Will you keep your promise to me?"

He swallowed again, looking haunted. "I *have* to. Three more weeks, right? I'll hire a new nanny and you'll move out and then…then I'll ask you to dinner. That's how it has to be. I can't kiss you. Not like I did earlier. Not like I wanted to since I met you. I gave you my word." He sounded like he was ripping his heart out with that last bit.

A promise. A promise he intended to keep, no matter how much it hurt him. She didn't know too many men who kept their promises like that. Hell, she didn't know too many women. People lied and cheated and did all sorts of horrible things to each other in the name of love all the time with very little thought to how it might affect others. Just like her mother had.

Just like her father had.

But not Nate. He'd given her his word and he'd keep it, even if it killed him.

That made all the difference in the world.

She didn't give him the chance to back away any farther. She closed the remaining distance between them so fast that he didn't have time to react. She stepped into him and put her arms around his neck and refused to let him go.

He tensed at her touch. "Don't." It was half order, half plea.

"Because you'll break your promise?"

He closed his eyes. He was back to his white-knuckle grip on the door frame, doing everything in his power to not touch her. "Yes."

She loosened her arms from around his neck and trailed her fingertips until she had the ends of her best bow tie in her hands. "I made no such promise, did I?"

Nate jolted against her—hard. She swore she heard the crack of wood giving way. "You don't sleep with people. You said so yourself."

She pulled on the ends of the tie, slowly loosening it until it hung down against his tuxedo shirt. "People in general, no." She slipped the top button free. He had a nice neck. The next button came loose.

"Trish," he groaned. His eyes were still closed but his head had started to tilt forward—toward her. "What are you doing?"

She undid another button. "Making sure you keep your promise."

His eyes flew open and he stared down at her in true shock. *"How?"*

"By seducing you." As the third button gave, she leaned up on her tiptoes and placed a kiss against the exposed skin of his neck, right under his Adam's apple. She could hear his pulse pounding through his veins. "If you want me to."

Then—and only then—did he relinquish his hold on the poor door frame. His arms swung down and surrounded her with his strength. She wanted to melt against him, but she didn't. Not yet. There'd be time for that later.

She toyed with the pointed tips of his collar. "Do you want me to?"

"This doesn't have anything to do with money or charities or anything, right?"

She leaned forward and kissed his neck again as she worked another button free. His pulse jumped under her lips, a wild beating that matched her own heart's rhythm. She was doing this, seducing Nate Longmire, the Boy Billionaire.

Except, she wasn't, not really. She wasn't seducing one of the most eligible Billionaire Bachelors. She was just seducing Nate. Beautiful, geeky Nate, who *always* kept his promises.

"No." Then she skimmed her teeth over his skin and felt him shudder. His body's response did things to her. Sweet, glorious heat flushed her breasts and spread farther. She was doing this to him. And he was letting her. "This is between you and me. That's all I want. Me and you."

"Trish," he groaned.

"I take that as a yes, then." She pushed him back, but only so far that she could slide his tuxedo jacket off his shoulders. It hit the ground with a whoosh and then she was working at his buttons again.

He didn't touch her, didn't try to lift her T-shirt over her head. He just stood there as she undid the rest of his buttons, his chest heaving with the effort of *not* touching her.

He had on a white undershirt, which was irritating. Formal clothing had so many layers. She slid her hands under his tuxedo shirt and stepped in again. This time, she kissed him proper.

And this time? He kissed her back. His arms folded around her again and she was pressed against his massive chest.

Oh, *yes*. Trish didn't actually know much about the art of seduction, but even she knew that was a good thing.

The heat focused in that spot between her legs and the only way she could think to ease the pressure was to lift one leg and wrap it around Nate.

But it didn't ease the pulsing heat. Instead, when Nate grabbed her under her thigh and lifted her higher, it brought her core in contact with something else—something long and thick and—

"Upstairs," she demanded, her back arching into that thick length.

She wasn't sure what she'd expected him to do. Turn and race up the stairs, maybe. That's what she would have done.

But she wasn't Nate. He hefted her up and leaned her back against the poor, misused door frame and kissed the hell out of her. She really had no choice but to put her legs around his waist, did she? And when she did, his erection ground against her. "Oh. *Oh!*"

"Mmm," he hummed against her mouth as he devoured her lips. Then he shifted his hips and heat exploded between them. Her body shimmied under his.

She could have stayed like that forever, except the door frame was exacting its revenge on her back. "Take me to bed, Nate. *Now.*"

"Yes, ma'am," he said.

And then Trish was floating through the air as Nate carried her up the stairs as if she weighed nothing, as if each step weren't driving his erection against her, as if she weren't on the verge of climaxing when he bit down on her shoulder.

Oh, yes.

Then they were in his room and he was kicking his door shut—quietly—and he'd laid her out on the bed. He started to strip off his shirt, but she sat up and said, "No, stop. That's my job."

His hand froze on his cuff links. "It is?"

"I'm doing the seducing around here," she replied,

pushing his hand away and undoing the offending cuff link herself. "That was the deal, right?"

"Absolutely," he agreed.

So Trish got to her knees on the bed and undid his other cuff so that she could push the very nice shirt off his shoulders and then strip the undershirt off him and then *finally* she could see the massive chest.

"You are built," she whispered as she ran her fingers over his muscles.

She skimmed her fingertips over his nipples and was rewarded with another low groan. His only other reaction was to clench his hands into fists, but he held them by his side. He didn't say anything. The last of his self-control, hanging by a thread.

He had a smattering of dark brown hairs in the space between two nicely defined pecs and a treasure trail that ended in the waistband of his pants. She followed it with her fingertips, then hooked her fingers into his waistband and pulled him into her so she could kiss him.

"Trish," he moaned into her mouth. "You're going to kill me."

She responded by running her hands over the huge bulge in his trousers. The heat pouring off him was electric. *He* was electric, setting her nerves on fire and threatening to overwhelm her. He shuddered under her touch.

"Oh, my, Nate," she whispered as she stroked his length through the fine wool of his trousers. He was built in *so* many ways. "Oh, *my*."

"Please," he begged.

"You have condoms?"

"Yeah. Somewhere."

"Go get them. Right now." Because once those pants got unbuttoned, there'd be no stopping, no turning back.

She might be doing the wild and crazy thing of seducing Nate Longmire, but that didn't mean she wanted to get carried away. She wanted to enjoy this night, this time, with him without having to deal with the consequences.

He pulled away from her so fast she almost toppled off the bed. She caught herself and sat back on her heels, watching him. She hadn't spent much time in his room. She'd seen it only when she'd tied his now-crumpled tie. It was the whole side of the house, with the bathroom in the back. The room was done in cool grays and blues, with a more modern touch than her room.

And the bed itself? She had no idea how they'd gotten a California King into this house but they had. And she was going to make good use of such a large bed.

He checked a drawer in the bedside table, then went around to the other side. "Got them," he muttered.

He came back to where she was waiting and stood there, an unopened box of condoms in his hand, like he wasn't sure what should happen next.

"Okay?" she asked. She had him shirtless and he was definitely interested, but now that he'd had a moment to think, a hint of doubt had crept into his eyes.

"Yeah. Yes," he repeated with more force. He closed his eyes and took a deep breath. "It's just…been a while." Then he opened his eyes and cupped her face and kissed her, soft and sweet and full of promise. "You?"

"You could say that." He lifted an eyebrow, but she didn't elaborate. She had no room in her life for antiquated notions of virginity, anyway. She'd already raised nine kids—ten, if she counted Jane. Her virginity was completely irrelevant to the situation.

But she could tell he was trying to figure out the best way to ask that question, so she went back on the offensive. She pulled him down into another kiss as she let her hands move over all those muscles.

"Shoes," she murmured. "Take them off."

He kicked off his shoes and peeled off his socks, but

when he went for his waistband, she grabbed his hands. "Wait," she told him. "Watch."

Then, because it seemed like the thing to do, she stood on the bed. Slowly, she peeled her T-shirt over her head. Nate made a noise in the back of his throat that was part groan, part animalistic growl as he stared at her simple beige bra.

Then she undid the button and slid down the zipper on her jeans. As the jeans slipped past her hips, she wished she had a pretty matching set of underwear instead of ones of cheap cotton. She wanted to be sexier for him.

Not that he seemed to mind her mismatched set. As the jeans slid free of her legs and she kicked them off, his mouth fell open. "Trish," he groaned again, his arms held tight at his side, his hands fisted. "Look at you. You're *stunning.*" His voice shook with raw desire.

And just like that, she felt desirable in spite of her under things. She walked over to where he stood. The added height of the bed meant that, instead of having to crane her neck up to look at him, she was a few inches taller than he was. She draped her arms around his neck again.

Stunning. She hadn't often felt beautiful. She'd had some people try to compliment her, but the best she usually got was "striking."

"And you, as I believe I noted before, are incredibly attractive."

He grinned up at her, the doubt gone from his eyes. "Can I touch you now or are you still seducing me?"

"I didn't say you couldn't touch me, did I?"

In response, his hands skimmed up the back of her thighs, over her bottom. He moved deliberately, trailing his fingertips along the waistband of her serviceable panties, over her hips, and along the elastic of her leg bands.

She couldn't help it. She closed her eyes and let her skin take in his every movement. She tingled under his touch, little shocks of pleasure wherever his fingertips caressed her.

"You are so beautiful, Trish," he whispered against her chest. Then he pressed his lips against the inner curve of her breast, right above the bra cup. "Let me show you how beautiful you are."

He turned his head and kissed the other breast as he began to unhook her bra. A moment of panic flashed over her—what was she doing? Having sex with Nate? Was she *crazy*?—but then the bra gave and he pulled it off her shoulders and she moved her arms to let it fall helplessly between them and he—and he—

He licked her left nipple like he was licking an ice cream cone. As his tongue worked her into a hard, stiff peak, he glanced up at her. "Watch me," he ordered and then he closed his lips around her nipple and sucked.

"Nate!" she exclaimed in a whisper at the sudden pressure. She wanted to cry out and scream his name, but she didn't want to wake the baby. She laced her hands through his hair. "Oh…"

"Good?" he asked, his voice muffled against her skin.

"Yes," she said. In response, he sucked again, harder. *"Oh…"* she managed to say again. Her legs started to shake.

One of his hands slid down her back again, tracing her bottom before coming between her legs from behind. The position locked her body to his. Softly—so softly—his fingertips rubbed over the thin fabric of her panties. The sensation of someone that wasn't her touching her there was so overwhelming that she couldn't even make a noise.

"Open your legs for me," he whispered. "Let me show you how beautiful you are."

Despite the way he had her legs pinned with his arm, she managed to scoot her knees a little farther apart without losing her balance.

"Mmm," Nate hummed as he licked her other nipple. His fingers rubbed in longer strokes, so close to hitting that hot, heavy weight in the front.

So close—but not quite. He was going to drive her mad with lust. Her! Trish Hunter, who had always been above such base things. With Nate's mouth on her, his fingers against her—

She ground against his fingers as she held his head to her breast. "Nate," she moaned when his teeth scraped over her nipple. "Oh, *Nate…*"

"Like that. Just like that, Trish." His voice was low and deep and sent a shiver up her back. "Oh, babe."

She wasn't doing the seducing anymore. He'd taken the reins from her and she was only too happy to hand them over. She really didn't know what she was doing, after all. But Nate?

He knew. He knew *exactly* what he was doing to her.

Then his mouth left her nipples and he kissed his way down her stomach. He hooked his thumbs into the waistband of her panties and slid them down. And then she was nude before him, nothing between them but a pair of tuxedo pants.

She had a moment of panic—she hadn't exactly prepped for this encounter. As Nate drifted south and she lost her grip on his hair, she fought the urge to cover herself.

"Let me see you—all of you," Nate said, catching her hands and lifting them away. "You're so beautiful, Trish."

"Nate…" Now that he wasn't holding her up, her knees were practically knocking.

But that was as far as she got before he pressed a kiss against the top of her thigh, then the other. And then?

Then he gripped her by the hips, tilting her back ever-so-gently, and ran his tongue over the little button that he hadn't quite managed to hit earlier.

Her body seized up with pleasure. She'd touched herself, of course. But this? This was something else. Something entirely different.

"I—I can't stand," she gasped as his tongue stroked her again and again. Light heat shimmered along her limbs, making her muscles tighten and weaken at the same time. *So different*, she thought. "I can't take it, Nate."

He looked up at her and for the first time, she saw something wicked in his eyes. "Babe, we're only just getting started."

Nine

This was really happening. Nate wondered if he might be dreaming, but then he'd tasted her sweetness on his tongue. None of his dreams had been this good.

Trish, in the bare flesh, was so much better than any fantasy he'd had.

Her eyes went wide at his words. "What?"

If he were a suave kind of guy, he'd figure out how to sweep her off her feet and lay her out on the bed without causing bodily harm to either of them, but he wasn't going to risk that right now. So he took her by the hands and guided her down to her knees on the bed, which meant that they were almost eye-to-eye.

"When I'm done with you, you *won't* be able to stand," he promised, tilting her back in the bed. The look of shock on her face told him pretty much everything he needed to know.

She didn't have a whole lot of experience. Maybe none. And yet, she'd still worked him into a lather.

It was time to return the favor.

He hooked his elbows under her knees and pulled her to him. She made a little squeaking sound, so he said, "Let me love on you, Trish." Then he lowered his mouth to her again.

She really did have a honeyed sweetness to her and he couldn't get enough of it—of her.

Years of sexual frustration—of avoiding hookups and dodging would-be brides, all because he didn't want anyone to break a promise they never intended to keep—seemed to surge up within his chest and he poured all of that energy into every action of his mouth, his tongue, his teeth. Trish's hips shifted from side to side as he worked on her and her hands found their way back to his hair again.

"That's it, babe. Show me how you want it."

"We can't wake the baby," she panted in a forced whisper.

"I'll be quiet, I promise." Then he slipped a finger inside of her.

Her tight muscles clamped around him with such force that he almost lost it right then. He licked her again and was rewarded with a noise that went past a groan into almost a howl.

"Come for me, Trish. Show me what you can do." He flicked his tongue back and forth over her, so hard and hot for his touch.

"Nate," she gasped out. "Nate—oh, Nate!"

His name on her lips, his body inside of hers—this was worth it. Years of self-denial—all worth the way they fit together.

He reached up to grasp her dark pink nipple between his thumb and forefinger and pulled. Not hard, but enough that she gasped again and came up off the bed a couple of inches.

Then he felt it—her inner muscles clamped down on him and her head thrashed from side to side and her mouth opened, but nothing came out. She came silently, her gaze locked onto his.

He couldn't remember being this excited. He was probably going to lose it the moment he plunged into her wet heat, but it didn't matter. He'd done this for her, given her this climax.

But he couldn't waste time patting himself on the back. Trish propped herself up on her elbows, her eyes glazed with satisfaction. "Boy," she said weakly. "I'm sure glad I did the seducing here."

"Me, too." He forced himself to pull away from her. He needed to be rid of his pants right now. He was so hard he was going to break the damned zipper. That's what she did to him.

But she sat up and swatted his hands away from his trousers. "Mine," she said as she jerked the button free and ripped the zipper down. "I can return the favor." The pants fell down and there he was, straining his boxer-briefs to the point of failure. She ran her hands over his length again. "If you want."

There it was again—that hint of innocence. "I consider myself well and truly seduced." As he said it, she rubbed her thumb over his tip.

He jerked under her hands, so close already. He couldn't withstand the pressure of her mouth on him and he didn't want to disappoint her.

"Condoms," he got out through gritted teeth.

She snagged the box and haphazardly tore it open. He took a condom from her and held as still as he could while she yanked his underwear down.

He ripped open the foil packet but before he could sheath himself, she'd taken him back in hand. *"Built,"* she murmured, encircling his width with her hand and stroking up, then back down.

"Trish," he hissed. "I need to be inside you. *Right now.*"

She looked up at him with big eyes. She was panting now, the haze of desire edging back. "I love it when you're all ruthless like that."

He paused halfway through rolling on the condom, then finished the task at hand. "You do?"

"Very powerful." Her gaze darted down to where he was sheathed. "That'll…that'll work, right?"

"Right." He climbed onto the bed, scooting her back so that she was against the pillows as he went. "Tell me if it's not working, okay?"

"Okay," she said as she looped her legs around his waist.

He kissed her as he fit himself against her. "Beautiful," he murmured as he tried a preliminary thrust.

Her body took him in, but she still sucked in air.

"Okay?"

"I think—just a second—"

"Take your time. I've got all night." Which was not, in the strict sense of the word, true. He could feel her hips shifting beneath his as she adjusted to his width and it about killed him.

Then she shifted again, her hips rising toward him and, without being conscious of the motion, he pushed in deeper. "Oh!" she said, but he didn't hear any pain in her voice. Just surprise.

"Okay?"

"Yes. I think so…" Her hips flexed and her tightness eased back just enough that he was able to go deeper. And deeper. Until finally he was fully joined to her.

"Oh, babe," he groaned as he pushed back against the climax that already threatened to swamp him. "You feel so *good.*"

"Um…okay."

He kissed her eyelids. Yeah, she'd never done this before. He had to make this count. "Ready?"

She looked worried, as if she were expecting a marching band to show up. "For?"

"This, babe." He withdrew and thrust back in, focusing on keeping his breath even and his climax firmly under control. *"This."*

"Oh. *Oh!*" As he pulled out and thrust in again, everything about her changed. Her hips rose up to meet him and her eyelids drifted shut as she felt him move inside of her. "Oh, *Nate*."

"Yeah, babe." They fell into a good rhythm, the give-and-take between his body and hers something different than he remembered. He wasn't as experienced as some, but he'd learned a lot during the two years he and Diana had been together.

He put that experience to good use now. He and Trish— they fit. Her warmth, wet and tight, took everything he had and then some, until she was arching her back and thrashing her head around and opening her mouth but not making a single noise as everything about her tightened down on him.

"So beautiful," he managed to get out again as her shockwaves pushed him faster and harder until he gave up the fight with himself and surrendered to her.

Then they lay still. He remembered to pull out so he didn't compromise the condom. But after that, he just lay on her chest.

"Oh, my," she finally breathed as she stroked his head.

"Is that a good 'oh, my' or a bad one?"

"Good. Very good." She sighed dreamily. "I didn't…" the words trailed off and she looked worried again.

He hefted himself up onto his forearms so he could look at her. "Thank you."

A wary look clouded her eyes. "For?"

He grinned down at her. "For not making me break my promise. Not at first, anyway."

"Oh." She exhaled. "I thought you were going to say something foolish, like thanking me for my virginity or something archaic like that."

He started to laugh in spite of himself. *Must be the euphoric high*, he thought, because he did not remember being this happy after sex. "Archaic?" He slid off to her side, but he didn't let go of her. One hand around her waist, pinning him to her chest. "You really hadn't done that before?"

After a moment where her body tensed up, she relaxed in his arms. "I didn't want to. I mean, I did, but…"

"You weren't ready to be a mother." That's what she'd said. He just hadn't realized how deeply that commitment went.

"No." She laced her fingers with his. "I didn't know it was going to be like that."

As the words trailed off, the keening wail of Jane crying cut across the hallway. "Oh," Trish said, visibly shaking off the last of her desire. She sat up and looked around as if coming out of a dream. "I've got to go."

He sat up and reached for her. "Trish—"

But she was out of bed, gathering up her clothes and all but sprinting out of his room. "I've got her," she called back over her shoulder, right before she pulled the door shut.

What had just happened here? One moment, she was sated and happy in his arms and the next?

Basically running away from him.

A sinking pit of worry began to form in his stomach. He tried to push it aside—she'd seduced him, not the other way around—but it didn't work. They might have followed the letter of their agreement, but not the real spirit of it.

He'd slept with her.

What had he done?

Trish used the bathroom and dressed quickly, making soothing noises to Jane the whole time.

She'd slept with Nate. Her first.

She needed to get Jane quieted back down so that Nate would go to sleep because she couldn't bear to talk to him right now, couldn't bear to lay in his arms and feel his body pressed against hers.

"Shh, shh, I'm here, sweetie," she hummed to Jane as she picked up the baby. She glanced at the clock. The little girl was up two hours before she should be. "Is it your teeth? Poor baby." For once in her life, she hoped it really was Jane's teeth—and not that Trish and Nate had been too loud.

She carried the baby downstairs and got one of the wet washcloths she'd stashed in the freezer. "Let's try this and see if we can go back to sleep, okay?" She headed back up to the nursery and sat in the glider, rocking Jane and humming softly as the little girl soothed her sore gums.

Trish wished she could soothe herself, but alas that didn't look like it was going to happen anytime soon. She kept a close eye on the door to the nursery, wanting Nate's shirtless form to appear and hoping like hell it didn't.

She'd slept with him. There was nothing wrong with that, per se. But...

She'd liked it. His mouth on her body, his body inside of hers? The way he'd made her feel?

God, how she'd liked it.

In the moment when he'd pulled free of her, she'd almost cried out to lose that connection with him. And when he'd tucked her against his chest, his arms tight around her waist?

She'd been on the verge of taking him in her hand—on the verge of seducing him a second time, just because she wanted that connection back. Because she wanted that feeling of clarity when his body pushed hers over the edge.

And she knew that, if he appeared in the doorway and said, "Come back to bed, Trish," she'd be helpless to say no, helpless to do anything but march right back into his bedroom and strip off her clothing again and explore his body over and over until they were both spent and dazed and the only thing in the world was Nate and Trish and a very big bed.

She would be his. Body, mind and soul. There'd be no turning back.

She'd be just like her mother.

This realization made her start, which jolted poor Jane. The baby started to fuss again. "Shh, shh," Trish whispered, finding a still-cold corner of the washcloth for Jane to chew on.

Of course Trish knew that sex had to be fun. That's why people did it so much, right? That's why her mother couldn't stay single—why she'd pick up a man at a bar and screw him in the parking lot and then, when he turned out to be an asshole, she couldn't kick him out of her life.

Trish had asked her once why she kept going with men who didn't even seem to like her. And Pat had replied with tears in her eyes, "Oh, Trish, honey, I know that the bad times can seem pretty bad. But when it's good…" and she'd gotten this far-away look in her eyes, a satisfied smile curling her lip up. "When it's good, it's *so* good."

Which hadn't made any sense to Trish at the ripe old age of ten because, as far as she could tell, there was nothing good about the men her mother picked.

As she'd grown up and come to understand the mechanics of sex—and as she'd explored her own body—she still hadn't understood what the big deal was. She could bring herself to a quick, quiet little orgasm, but that wasn't enough to make her want to throw away everything she'd worked for.

Except now she knew. She knew how a man could make her feel, make her body do things that Trish couldn't do to herself. Oh, Nate…with his big hands and bigger muscles and his damned principles about keeping his promises.

Jane had fallen asleep at some point in the past twenty minutes, but Trish was in no hurry to put the baby back in her crib. She needed this small child—needed the physical barrier Jane provided. Hadn't that been the problem tonight? Trish had tied Nate's tie without a baby between them and she'd kissed him because a man had no business looking as handsome as he did in that tux.

And then he'd come home early just because he wanted to see her. Her! She was nothing—a poor Indian woman who didn't even know who her father was. Tonight, Nate had walked away from heiresses and self-made women— women who matched his social standing and his love of modern technology—for her. There was no way she could keep up with him.

What a mess. Easily the biggest mess she'd ever gotten herself into, all because she liked him. Because she *let* herself like him instead of holding him at an arm's length.

What could she do? Quit? She looked down at the baby sleeping in her arms. She'd gotten Jane calmed down and mostly on a schedule. It'd be easier for Nate to hire a nanny now because he knew what to expect from a nanny and he knew what Jane needed.

But. Of course there was a "but."

If she quit, would he withhold the funding he'd promised? He'd signed a contract; so had she. She didn't think he would. He was a decent man—possibly the best man she'd ever met. But rejection did nasty things to people. She'd watched her mother curse and cry and throw their few dishes against the wall when she'd found out her current man was seeing someone on the side and Trish had huddled in her room with her siblings when the breakups happened.

But if Trish stayed…she'd want Nate again. And again. She'd want to spend the night trying different positions, different ways to make him cry out her name in that hoarse voice. She'd want to sleep in his bed, his strong arms firmly around her waist, his chest warming her back. She'd want to wake up with him and have breakfast with him out on the patio of this house and count the hours until

Jane went down for her nap so that Trish could pull Nate into his room and do it all over again.

She could stay here with him, raise his niece for him. She could do whatever he wanted, as long as he kept making love to her.

The intensity of this need scared her. For once in her life, she understood her mother, how she could overlook the health and safety of her children in favor of a man who might make her feel like Nate had made Trish feel.

Because if she stayed here with Nate and raised Jane—became a permanent nanny during the day and his lover at night—well, then what would happen to One Child, One World?

How was Trish supposed to look her baby sister in the eyes and say, "Yes, I know I said you should put your education and career ahead of any man, but he's a *really* great guy!"

Because that's what her mother would say. That's what her mother would do.

Trish was *not* her mother.

And that was final.

Ten

Nate drifted in and out of consciousness as he waited for Trish to come back. He heard her go downstairs and then, sometime later, he heard her go down again, which didn't make any sense. When had she come back up?

His head was heavy with sleep. He'd sort of forgotten how much really awesome sex took out of him. But when he heard her come back upstairs again and yet she still didn't come back into his room, he forced himself to roll over and check the time on his phone.

Three-thirty.

He blinked at the red numbers again, but they didn't change. That wasn't right, was it? She'd left the first time around eleven and he knew she hadn't come back to him.

He sat up and rubbed his eyes. Where was she? He hadn't heard Jane crying.

He slipped his briefs back on and silently opened his door. Both Jane's door and Trish's were shut.

Maybe she'd fallen asleep in the glider, he reasoned. Both she and the baby had passed out and that's why she hadn't come back.

He tiptoed across the hall and opened Jane's door. The glider was empty and the little girl was in her crib, making those noises that Trish had promised him were perfectly normal for babies to make.

Which meant only one thing. Trish had gone to bed.
Alone.

He backed out of the nursery and closed the door. Then
he looked at Trish's door. He could knock but the hint was
not-so-subtle. She'd gone back to her own room instead
of his.

He ran through the evening's events. He hadn't cornered
her, hadn't pressured her. She'd come to him of her own
accord. She'd started it—he'd finished it, though.

Foreplay? *Check*. Orgasms? *Double check*. Cuddling? A
little, right until the baby cried. All good things—unless…

Unless she'd changed her mind—about him, about sex,
about sex with him.

Well, he wasn't going to figure out this puzzle standing in the hallway in nothing but a pair of shorts in the
middle of the night.

But tomorrow, he and Trish were going to talk.

Trish heard Nate's door open, heard Jane's door open.
Oh, God—he was looking for her. Would he come to her
door, begging her to come back to his bed?

She curled herself around her pillow, willing him not
to. She had to be stronger than this. She had to hold herself back from him and that was going to be damnably
hard at—she checked the clock—three thirty-seven in the
morning.

Go back to bed, she mentally screamed into the night.
Don't come in here.

Jane's door whispered shut. Trish heard Nate take a
footstep toward her room, then another. She tensed with
fear—or need. Her brain was shouting, *no*! while her body,
her traitorous body, was already clamoring for his touch.
Trish was this close to throwing the covers off and fling-
ing open her door and rushing into his arms.

She had to be stronger. She *was* stronger, by God.

The footsteps stopped. The house was silent. She pictured Nate standing on the other side of her bedroom door—so close, yet so very far away.

Then, just when she couldn't stand it another second—she *had* to go to him—she heard him walking again. His footsteps grew more distant, and then his door shut.

She should have been relieved.

Why did she feel like crying?

Trish felt like hell. She supposed that was to be expected. Her body was punishing her for her late-night activities in ways that made regular old sleep deprivation look like a cakewalk.

Somehow, Trish got the bottle made and the coffee started. She didn't even bother to attempt breakfast. Her stomach was so nervous at the thought of Nate coming downstairs and—well, even looking at her would be bad enough. Talking would be sheer torture. Yeah, there was no way she could handle breakfast at this point.

The morning was hazy with fog, but Trish decided to sit out on the patio with Jane, anyway. Fresh air and all that.

Plus, it put a little more space between her and Nate. And maybe she could come up with a way to *not* throw everything she'd ever worked for away because of him.

Jane was fussy, which helped. Trish focused on the girl with everything she had. Jane was why Trish was here. Jane was why she needed to stay. Not because of Nate.

She really did need to finish the month, she thought as she held Jane's bottle for her. For one thing, the poor girl had been through a lot and was just getting settled into her routine. It would be another setback for her if Trish just up and left.

And for another, there was the money. The other reason she was doing this. Nate was going to fund One Child,

One World for the foreseeable future. She could not tuck tail and run just because she could fall in love with him.

She could *not* fall in love with him.

The idea was so crazy that she started laughing. Would it be possible to *not* fall for him? That was where her mother always screwed up. If she'd just wanted the sex, that would have been one thing. The trouble came when she fell in love with whatever man she had and refused to let him go, no matter what common sense dictated.

Maybe Trish could take the sex and leave the love. After all, she'd spent the past few decades not allowing herself to get close to anyone. And, up until the moment she met Nate, she'd been very good at it.

She could enjoy Nate, safely, and not love him. She could refuse to give into the madness that had ruled her mother. It would be—well, it'd be physical. Short-term and very physical. But nothing more.

Could she *do* that?

Behind her, she heard him in the kitchen. Unconsciously, she tensed, which made Jane pop off her bottle and start to whimper. "Oh, now," she soothed, getting Jane to take her bottle again. "None of that. That's my good girl."

Pots and pans rattled. He was making breakfast. He was just too damn nice, that was the problem. Too damn perfect. This would be so much easier if he'd been a royal ass, or a really lousy lover or just a horrible person all the way around. Was that too much to ask, for him to be awful? Because that was the kind of man who didn't interest her at all. That was the kind of man she'd never tumble into bed with.

How was she supposed to even *look* at him this morning? After what she'd done to him? And especially after what he'd done to her?

This was the awkward part of being a twenty-five-year-old virgin. Everyone else in the world had figured out how to handle the post-hookup interactions back in college. They either left afterward or slipped out of bed in the morning or…or she didn't know what. They probably never had to sit around, playing with a baby while their lovers made them breakfast.

Life was so much easier without sex in it.

But what could she do? Nothing. It's not like she could wander off into the fog with a baby in her arms to avoid talking to him. She had to sit here and deal with this like a grown-up, because that's what she was.

Finally, after what felt like a small eternity, she heard the patio door slide open and felt Nate walk out. "Good morning," he said as he set his coffee cup on the table. No tray—no breakfast.

"Hi," she got out. It sounded weaker than she wanted it to, damn it all.

He leaned over and kissed Jane's head, then turned and made eye contact with her. He held it for just a beat too long and panic flared up in her stomach. Was he going to kiss her? Yell at her? What was happening here?

Then he turned back and shut the patio door. "Not much of a view this morning," he said in a casual voice.

"The fresh air feels good." Were they going to pretend it hadn't happened? "Um, thank you for making breakfast."

"Rosita left homemade pecan rolls in the fridge. They're still baking. And you made the coffee. It was the least I could do." He settled into his chair and, thankfully, turned his gaze toward the wall of fog, his mug clutched between his hands as if it were a shield. "You didn't come back to bed last night," he said in a quiet voice.

Trish swallowed. She didn't know why this was so hard. She'd been a practicing grown-up since she'd been—what, five? She'd stared down hard men and defended her siblings and done everything in her power to escape the life her mother had. She could do this. She could have a completely rational conversation with a man she really, really liked who'd seen her naked. No sweat.

"Jane's teething. I got up several times. I didn't want to wake you up. One of us should sleep," she added weakly. Then she mentally kicked herself. Stop sounding weak! She was not weak!

"Ah," he said, in that same quiet voice. "I thought...I thought it might have been something to do with me. With something I did. Or didn't do."

She blinked at him. "No, it's not that. It's just..."

Words would be great. If only she had some.

"If I did something that you didn't like," he went on, "you can tell me. I promise, my ego can handle it."

But I don't know if I can handle it, she thought.

He sipped his coffee, patiently waiting for a reply from her. But then Jane pushed her bottle away and stretched her plump little arms over her head and began to whine and Trish was thankful for the distraction.

"Here," Nate said as Trish started to maneuver Jane onto her shoulder. "I've got her."

He got up and lifted Jane into his arms and began to rhythmically pat her on the back. He didn't sit back down, though. He went and stood at the edge of the patio, a few feet farther away from Trish.

He was over there thinking he'd been a lousy lover when the truth was, he'd been amazing. Trish stared into the fog, trying to pretend she wasn't about to say this out loud. "Actually, it was amazing. I didn't think it'd be that good."

Out of the corner of her eye, she saw him pause before he continued patting and rocking Jane. "Oh? Well. Good to know." He was trying to sound casual, but she could tell he was smiling, just by the tone of his voice.

Last weekend, she'd sat on this porch and decided not to tell him why she was so good with kids and why she wouldn't sleep with him. He hadn't needed to know, she'd rationalized then.

But now? After what they'd shared? "You want to hear the whole story?"

"I want to understand you."

Heat flooded her body and that tingling sensation tightened across her lower back again. This man seriously needed some flaws and fast.

"My father—or the man I think of as my father—left when I was four. My brothers Johnny and Danny were two and one, so I suppose that he might not have been my real father. But he's who I remember." She did manage to look at him. "They both joined the army the moment they were eligible. Johnny's down at Fort Hood and Danny's done a tour of Afghanistan."

"Then what happened?"

Trish closed her eyes. She could still feel the weight of Jane's small body against hers. Just like all the other small bodies that had lain in her arms. "There was a gap of about three years. I think my mom was trying, I really do. I remember being home alone a lot with Johnny and Danny. I got pretty good at opening cans and heating them up so we'd all have something to eat. Then, when I was seven, Clint happened."

"I take it that was not a good thing."

"Nope. Mom got pregnant again and…" she sighed, pushing back on the memory. "Mom had Millie but then Mom was never home so I got used to taking care of the baby. The boys started sleeping on the floor and Millie and I took the bed. Then Mom had Jeremiah. And there just wasn't enough food. Not for five of us."

"How old were you?"

"I was nine. Then Mom got pregnant again. And Hailey was not a healthy baby. I wound up skipping most of my sixth-grade year to take care of her."

"Your mom wouldn't take care of a sick baby? My mom quit her job teaching elementary school when we couldn't get Joe into a stable routine at school. My grandmother thought it'd be better for all of us if we put him in an institution, but Mom wouldn't hear of it. He was her son. It was her job to take care of him. It was all of our jobs."

She studied him. He really did seem pissed off at her mother. "Well, she did have a job. That helped. For a while, anyway. But no, she couldn't take care of Hailey. She couldn't really take care of any of us. But I could." She looked at Jane, who was falling into a milk coma on her uncle's shoulder. "I graduated with honors when I was twenty because of Hailey and Keith, who was born when I was fourteen. Keith…"

"Was he okay?"

"There was something wrong with him, with his heart. He died. When he was fourteen months old. I couldn't save him. And I always thought, you know—if we'd been able to get to a doctor, maybe…"

That *maybe* had haunted her for years. Just because, every single time her mother got knocked up by yet another man, Trish wanted to scream and cry and ask her what the hell she thought she was doing—it didn't mean she didn't do everything in her power to save that baby when he'd gotten here. But she'd only been fifteen. She had very little power to do anything. Including saving her little brother.

"I'm so sorry," Nate said. He'd grown quiet. "That must have been so hard on you."

Trish sniffed. "And that doesn't count Lenny, Ricky or Patsy. I left home when Patsy was five. It was the hardest thing I've ever done because I knew…" her words trailed off as her throat closed off. "Because I knew she'd be on her own. That I wouldn't be there to make sure she went to school or did her homework or had a real dinner every night."

"And your mom?"

"Oh, she's fine. She got her tubes tied after Patsy because the doctors said she couldn't have any more kids. She's…it's like she's my older sister, you know? Not my mom. My flighty older sister that's always screwing up. But the guy she's with now, Tim, he's a good guy. Good job, not rough. Helps take care of the kids. I hope he sticks around."

"Why did she do it? Why did she have so many kids when she couldn't take care of them? Because it wasn't fair of her to assume that you'd do it. It wasn't fair to you."

"Life is not fair. It never has been and it never will be. If it was, your mom wouldn't have had to quit to take care of your brother and Jane's parents would be on their way to pick her up right now and…" She almost said, "Diana wouldn't have cheated on you." But she didn't.

Nate sat down in his chair, Jane cuddled against his chest. "You don't—didn't—sleep with people because of your mom?"

"Yeah. She'd fall head over heels in love with some guy, have a couple of his babies, and then it'd all fall apart. I guess she thought the kids would help her hold onto a man, but it never worked that way. The funny thing is, she can't have kids with Tim and he's the one that's stuck around the longest. Seven years and counting."

The silence settled over them. She wondered how long his folks had been together. If he'd had an older brother… maybe thirty years? Maybe more?

"I don't want to be like her," Trish admitted, letting her words drift into the fog. "I don't want to be so in love with a man, so in love with sex with a man, that it becomes my whole world. I don't want to forget who I am. I don't want to have to be someone else to keep a man. I can do *so* much good in this world, more than just changing diapers."

"And to do that, you didn't get involved?"

"No." She swallowed, feeling unsure of herself. "It was easier that way. No distractions. I got off the rez, I got to college, I started the charity. And I...I can't give that up." *Not even for you*, she thought.

He turned Jane around so that the little girl was sitting on his lap, facing out into the fog. Trish saw that Jane was only half-awake, her eyelids fluttering with heaviness.

"So why didn't you come back to bed last night?" he asked softly.

"Because."

He snorted and finally turned to look at her. "That's not much of an answer."

She took a deep breath, but she didn't break his gaze. "Because I'm just the temporary nanny. I can't stay here with you forever. I can't give up my goals, my whole life, to play house with you. I can't turn into my mother and—I can't fall in love with you, Nate. I just *can't*."

"Ah," he exhaled, his eyebrows jumping up. "And you think that by sharing my bed you...might?"

She thought back to the way their bodies had fit together, how he'd made her feel alive and vibrant and perfect. How she'd wanted him again and again, how she'd felt like she was standing on the edge of a very tall cliff and all he'd have to do to get her to jump was ask.

"I might," she admitted.

If I haven't already.

Eleven

"So," Nate said in a voice that sounded remarkably calm, all things considered. "How would you like to proceed?"

"What do you mean?" Trish had turned her beautiful eyes back to the fog.

"With your remaining time here, assuming you'd like to finish out the three weeks."

She dropped her chin. "I don't want to break our deal," she said in a quiet voice. "I gave you my word just as much as you gave me yours."

Yeah, and part of his word had been *not* sleeping with her. That had lasted all of a week. Barely eight whole days.

He tried to think rationally, but that wasn't working. Because, rationally, not only should he have been able to stay away from her, but he should have been able to *keep* staying away from her.

He had to smile. How many other women in the world would take him to their beds and then tell him they couldn't come back because they couldn't risk falling for him and his billions in the bank? How many would keep their word to him?

Not that many. Maybe not any, except for Trish.

He ran his code as his tired brain tried to come up with a solution that didn't involve her leaving before the rolls were done in the oven.

"I can't leave," she said. "It'd be bad for Jane to go

through so many caretakers so fast. She's teething and we're just getting into a rhythm and you don't have anyone else lined up."

Can't wasn't the same as *won't*. *Can't* made it sound like he was forcing her and that was the last thing he wanted. "This is all true, but I don't want that to be the only reason you stay."

"You're paying me," she reminded him.

That was better, he thought. She sounded a little more like herself—more confident, more willing to push back. Trish sounding vulnerable only made him want to fold her into his arms and tell her he'd take care of everything, just so long as she stayed with him.

"Insane amounts of money," she added. "Both in salary and in donations. That was the deal. I won't take your money and run."

"The deal was we didn't sleep together. And now we have. The deal is open for renegotiation."

A wary look crossed her face. "How do you mean?"

"Look, I'm going to be honest. I like you. A lot. And I really enjoyed last night. You were amazing and it's going to be hard to look at you every day and not want to take you to bed every night."

She didn't immediately respond, which made him pretty sure those weren't the right words. The fact that he was making even a little bit of sense was a minor miracle, when all he really wanted to do was deposit this sleepy baby back in her crib and curl his body around Trish's and sleep for another five or six hours.

He probably should tell her that hey, one-night stands were fine and she knew where he was if she wanted another fun night in the sack—he should keep himself walled off, above the situation, just like he always did when he was out of his league.

But instead, no—he was laying it all on the line because, damn it, he liked her, he trusted her and, by God, she was someone he could fall for, too. For the first time in five years, waking up alone had bothered him. He'd wanted to see her face when he opened his eyes, to kiss her mouth awake.

He didn't want a casual one-night stand or even a casual one-week stand. It wasn't like he wanted to marry her or anything. He wasn't that old-fashioned. But he wanted something…in between.

He wanted a relationship.

From behind them, a buzzer sounded. "That's the rolls." He stood up, jostling Jane back from her semistupor as he handed the baby to Trish. "I'll be right back."

The rolls were slightly underdone, but that was good enough. He didn't want to stand in this kitchen for five more minutes while she was out there, talking herself out of another night of passionate sex with him. So he plated up the food and loaded everything onto the tray and tried his damnedest not to run right back to her.

If it came down to it, could he not touch her for another three weeks? He'd made it five years without taking a lover. Surely he could keep his hands—and other parts—occupied for another measly twenty-one days?

Jane had perked up a bit and Trish was singing and using the baby's chubby little legs to act out the song. It was a perfect image of what a family—his family—could be. Was it wrong to want more mornings like this? Breakfast on the patio, just the three of them?

He set the tray down and ate his breakfast while he waited. He'd respect her decision. He had no choice, because she was right. It would be hard on the baby if she left. It'd be hard on him, too, but he was a grown-ass man. He'd deal. Jane just needed more stability at this point in her life.

So this was parenthood, he realized as he burned the

roof of his mouth on a roll. Putting the baby's needs ahead of his own.

Stupid maturity.

Finally, after what seemed like ninety-nine verses, the song ended. Nate watched the two of them together. Jane clearly adored Trish—he hoped that, wherever she was, Elena would approve of his choice for a nanny.

And Trish was smiling down into Jane's face as if she really did care for the girl. Was it wrong to be attracted to a woman who would care so much for a child that had no connection to her?

Trish lifted her head and caught him staring. Her warm smile faded beneath a look of pensiveness. "How are the rolls?"

"Hot."

She managed a smirk so small, he almost missed it. "Shocking, that."

He forced himself to grin. "Come to any decisions over there?"

Jane squealed and tried to grab a roll. "I think," Trish said, capturing Jane's little fingers before they could get burned, "that we should finish this conversation during naptime."

That was a perfectly reasonable thing to say—after all, there was something a little weird about discussing sex with a baby around—but it still left him disappointed.

Jane trilled again.

"Right. Naptime. Looking forward to it."

Trish hesitated in the doorway of the parlor long enough that Nate looked up from the book he was reading. "She go to sleep okay?"

"Yes."

Nate was sitting on one end of the couch, close to the

leather chair. She could either sit in the leather chair or next to him.

He closed his book and waited for her to make her choice.

So she stood. "I feel like I owe you an apology," she said. "I've never had an affair before. I don't feel like I'm handling myself very well."

"An affair. Is that what this is?"

"Isn't it?"

"Right now it's closer to a one-night stand. Without the standing," he added as her cheeks heated. "An affair implies more than one night together."

"Oh, okay." Right. She couldn't even get her terminology right. Yeah, she was pretty bad at this. "About that." She forced herself to take another step into the room.

"Yes?" He sat up and, putting the book aside, leaned forward. But he didn't come toward her, he didn't sweep her into his arms and say the kinds of things that might weaken her resolve. He just waited for her to choose.

"I'd like—I mean, I think I'd like to, you know, maybe have an affair." Calling it an affair made it sound sophisticated and glamorous—nothing like the wild, indiscriminate coupling her mother engaged in. Trish was a responsible woman who could have an affair with a handsome, wealthy, powerful man *without* losing her head—or her heart.

She hoped.

The corner of his mouth crooked up. "You don't sound certain."

"I just want to make sure things don't get complicated. Messy," she explained.

"You don't want to fall," he clarified for her. The way he said it made her feel like she'd rejected him, which didn't make a lot of sense.

Wasn't she agreeing to the affair? How was that rejecting him? He didn't expect her to fawn over him, did he? "I don't want to fall," she said firmly. She could do this—indulge in a little passion without losing herself. She would *not* fall.

Falling in love with Nate Longmire was not a part of the plan.

"I've been thinking about that."

"You have?"

He nodded and stood. "Just you and me and a casual affair."

Casual. That was both the right word and not at all. "How would we do that?"

"We could have some…rules. Guidelines, if you will. No spending the night, no funny business when Jane is awake—"

"Right. Guidelines." She liked the sound of that. Boundaries. Like the three weeks they had left. That was a boundary that would keep her from falling in a very real way. Nate would hire another nanny and Trish would move out and that space—*that* would keep her from falling. It had to. "Nothing in front of Rosita or Stanley or anyone. And no seeing other people while we're being casual, right?"

"Sure." He grinned at her. "I doubt either of us would have, anyway."

"I suppose not." She felt herself exhale a little. She knew she wasn't doing a bang-up job at this, but it didn't appear she was botching it beyond all hope. "What else?"

"Just this." Suddenly, Nate was moving, his long legs closing the distance between them and his hands cupping her cheeks. He was kissing her so hard that her knees didn't entirely hold her up. "Just that I'm glad you said yes," he whispered against her mouth.

"Oh, Nate," she breathed as his lips trailed down her neck. This desire she felt—this need—surely this wasn't a bad thing, right? This wasn't the kind of thing that was going to push everything she'd ever worked for aside. Right?

They had guidelines to help keep everything from spiraling out of control. She could have an affair with Nate, enjoy being with him and sleeping with him.

And she would do it without falling.

They settled into a routine after that. Trish couldn't bring herself to sleep with Nate when Jane was down for a nap, but that didn't stop her from kissing him. She'd never even made out before, so just tangling up with Nate on the couch or against the counter in the kitchen, or when they caught each other on the stairs—anywhere, really, where Rosita wouldn't walk in on them—was a gift. A gift that left her in a near-constant state of arousal.

So by the time she closed Jane's door for the night, Trish could hardly wait to get her hands on him.

And he was ready for her. Instead of the leisurely kissing and touching that happened during the day, they would rip off each other's clothes and fall into bed as fast as they could.

Nate did not disappoint. The more they made love, the better it got. After the first week, when he'd introduced her to most of the basics, he started asking her what she wanted—what she'd always wanted to try, what she was curious about. For so long, Trish hadn't even acknowledged that she *had* sexual desires—if she didn't cop to them, then she didn't really have them. So suddenly to have a man who not only was interested in her, but also interested in making sure her fantasies were fulfilled was sometimes more than she could handle. It took her three days to admit that she wanted to go down on him—in the shower. Which he was more than happy to help her try out.

Nate didn't push her, though. And he didn't complain

when, after they were panting and sated, she gathered up her clothes and went back to her own bedroom.

Which got harder every night. The more time they spent in each other's arms, the more she wanted to wake up in his arms.

And the more she wanted to do that, the more she *had* to go back to her side of the hallway. Because she knew what was happening.

Despite the guidelines, despite the routine—despite it all—she was falling for him. And that scared the hell out of her.

Because there was only a week to go until her time was up.

She had no idea how she was going to leave.

Twelve

Trish turned to him as the door shut behind the third and final nanny candidate, a squat Polish grandmother with impeccable references. The first candidate was a middle-aged former receptionist who'd been laid off in the Great Recession and the second was a young woman about Trish's age who just "loved kids!"—as she so enthusiastically phrased it.

"Well?" Trish said, leaning against the closed door with her hands behind her back. "What did you think?"

"I think I should hire you to do all my interviews," Nate said, moving in on her and pinning her to the door with a kiss. She'd grilled each woman on schedules, sleeping philosophies and life-saving qualifications. All Nate had had to do was watch. "You're ruthless."

"I just want the best for Jane." She pushed him back, but she was smiling as she did it. "Rosita will see us," she scolded quietly.

"I don't care." And he didn't. It was Friday. He only had Trish here for another three days. Monday morning, the new nanny would start. Trish would move out. She'd come back to help settle the new nanny into the routine on Wednesday, if needed, but that was it.

He kissed her again, feeling her body respond to his. Three more days of feeling her tongue tracing his lips, her body molding itself to his. And then…

She pushed him back again. "Nate," she said in her most disapproving voice, even as her fingers fluttered over his shoulders. "Focus. You need to pick a new nanny from the three candidates."

"Do I have to?"

She gave him a look. He knew he sounded childish, but picking a new nanny put him that much closer to not having Trish around anymore. If there were any way to stall hiring her replacement, she'd have to stay, right?

Because he wanted her to stay.

He and Trish had not spent a great deal of time talking about what happened next. He wanted to keep seeing her, obviously. The past month had been something he hadn't even allowed himself to dream of. The sex was amazing, sure, but what he felt for her went beyond the physical. He connected with her in a way that he hadn't connected with another woman—another person—since he'd fallen for Diana almost ten years ago. This time, he was older, smarter—more ready for it. This wasn't a casual affair, not anymore. This was a relationship—the one he wanted.

Yes, they'd had these guidelines that were supposed to keep her from falling for him. Unfortunately, nothing had prevented *him* from falling for *her*.

Because he'd fallen, hard. Unlike when he'd met Diana, Nate knew he wasn't with Trish just because she was the best he thought he could do. He wasn't the same insecure geek he'd been back in college. He could have his pick of women, if he really wanted to. They'd line up for him, starting with Lola Finklestein.

That wasn't what he wanted. He just wanted Trish. He missed her like hell when she was in class every Tuesday and Thursday and it no longer had to do with his panic over Jane. He could take care of Jane now. He'd learned her different noises and her likes and dislikes and he was doing a passable job at changing diapers—all because

Trish had patiently walked him through the ins and outs of basic fatherhood.

He wanted to be a better man for her. Every night he tried to show her how much he cared for her, how much he wanted her to stay with him. And every night, she slipped away from him again.

When he tried to bring up the prospect of dating, she kept shutting down on him. He knew that she had made arrangements to crash with a friend for the remaining week and a half until she graduated, and then she planned to go home and see her family for a while. But beyond that...

"You pick," he told her as he traced his fingertips down her cheek. "I trust your opinion."

"Nate. You *have* to pick. I'm—"

"Señor Nate?" Rosita called from the kitchen. "I am going to do the shopping." Nate stepped clear of Trish just as Rosita walked out of the kitchen, her purse on her arm. "Is there anything that..." Her eyes darted between Trish and Nate. "Ah, anything you want?" she finished in a suspicious voice.

"No. You?" he asked Trish.

"Maybe another box of those teething biscuits Jane likes?" Trish suggested. She managed to sound perfectly normal, but she couldn't stop the blush.

"Sí," Rosita said, a look Nate couldn't quite make out on her face.

Trish stepped away from the door so Rosita could pass. Nate caught the small smile Rosita threw to Trish, and then the housekeeper was out the door. "What was that about?"

"I think we've been busted." Trish frowned at the closed door.

"Does that mean we don't have to sneak around anymore?" As he said it, he moved back to her, wrapping his arms around her waist and resting his chin on the top of her head. They stood like that for a while, just enjoying each other's warmth. They had time. Jane was still down for her nap. And later, they'd load her into the stroller and go for a walk. Then, tonight, she'd come to his bed again.

It was a damn good life. One he didn't want to end. Not in three days, not in three months. Maybe not in forever.

He had to find a way to make her stay. The sooner, the better.

"Nate." She looked up at him and rested the tips of her fingers just above the line of his stubble. "You have to decide. Not me, not Stanley and not Rosita. *You.* It's your choice."

Suddenly, he didn't know if they were talking about the three nanny candidates or if she was talking about them.

"I already found the perfect woman," he told her, tightening his arms around her. "You." He took a deep breath. This was the moment. He wasn't going to let her slip away from him. He *needed* her. "You should stay."

She tensed in his arms. "That's not what I mean."

"Why not?" She started to slip out of his grasp, but this time, he didn't let her go. He put his hands on her shoulders and turned her to face him. "Trish. Look at me."

Almost as if she was doing so against her will, she raised her gaze to meet his. He was surprised to see that she looked…afraid?

He was all in. "I want you to stay."

"I can't," she said in such a quiet whisper that he barely heard her. "Oh, Nate—don't ask me this. I can't."

"Why not?" he demanded. "Jane loves you," She sucked in a hard breath and her eyes began to shine with wetness. "I'm falling in love with you," he went on. "You fit here."

"No, I don't. Can't you see?" She laughed, a sharp thing that cut him. "I grew up in a three-room house with mold growing up the walls and electricity that only worked some of the time. I slept in a bed with two or three little kids my entire life. We didn't have food. We didn't have things."

She waved her hands around her, at all the nice things he had. "And now? I'm still so poor that I buy all my clothes from a thrift store and before I moved in here, I lived on ramen noodles and generic cereal—that I ate dry because I couldn't afford milk. I do *not* fit here." Her voice dropped. "I don't fit *you*, Nate. Not really. This was…an affair. A casual affair between two people living in forced proximity. That's—" Her voice caught. "That's all this was."

"No, it wasn't. You fit me," he said, beginning to feel desperate. "You fit *me*, Trish. We can change everything else. Anything you want. Name it. I won't let you go back to living on the edge like that. Not when I can take care of you. Not when I need you." He cupped her face in his hands. "I need you, Trish."

"You need—" She gulped. "You need a nanny."

"Stop it, Trish. You know that's not true. I need *you*. You're not some interchangeable woman. I can't just swap you out and carry on as if nothing has changed. I'm different when I'm with you. I'm not nervous or geeky or nothing but a bank account. You make me *me*. You make me feel like everything's finally right in the world."

She closed her eyes and shook her head. "Oh, Nate. Don't make this harder than it has to be. We had a deal, you and I. A temporary nanny. A casual affair. That was the plan. No falling."

The desperation turned and suddenly he was mad. Why was she being so stubborn? She had feelings for him, he knew she did. He gripped her by the arms. "I want a new deal. I want a different plan."

"Don't do this," she whispered again, trying to back away from him, but he held tight. "*Don't*. I can't fall."

"What's it going to take, Trish? To get you to stay. Twenty thousand a month? Two hundred and fifty thousand for your charity? That was our deal, right? I want an extension on our contract."

"Nate."

She was trying to cut him off, trying to stop him, but what did billions in the bank mean if he couldn't take care of her? If he couldn't make sure that she never felt poor ever again?

If he couldn't get her to stay?

She was worth more than that to him. She was worth more than all of it. All that cash was pointless if it couldn't get him what he really wanted—her. "Anything you want, name it. Just…stay with me, Trish."

Too late, he realized he'd gone too far.

"Oh, Nate." She shook free of his grasp and looked up at him. Tears streamed out of the corners of her eyes. "I—I can't. I can't give up everything I've ever been, everything I've ever wanted to accomplish, to raise another baby that's not mine. There's so much more I need to do in this world right now and I can't sacrifice all of that, not yet." Her eyes filled with tears. "I'm not ready to be a mother. Not even a mother. A nanny."

"You're more than that to me, babe. You know that."

She shook her head. Why couldn't he make her see reason? "I can't turn my back on my own family, my tribe, just to play house with you."

"This isn't playing house. I want you to live with me. I want you to sleep in my bed with me." Why was that a bad thing? He didn't understand. "I want more than casual. I want more than an affair. I want *you.*"

"On your terms, Nate. We aren't equals. We can *never* be equals." Her voice broke.

Where had he gone wrong? Since when had telling a woman he loved her become such a mess? Panic bubbled just beneath his surface, threatening to break free. He'd never been that good with women, never known what to say to them. That'd been what he loved about Trish—he could talk to her. But not right now. His words were failing him.

"I would always be dependent on you," she went on, her face pale. "I would always need you more than you needed me."

"That's not true."

She smiled at him, a weak and sad smile that hurt to see. "Just because you can't see that doesn't mean it's not true." She touched his face but pulled her hand away quickly, as if she'd been burned. "I…I can't need you as much as this."

"Why not?" He said louder than he meant to, but was she being serious? "I need you, too. That doesn't make me weak and it doesn't make you weak, for God's sake. It makes me want to take care of *you*. So let me."

She stood before him, her face creased with pain. Then, unexpectedly, she leaned up on her toes and kissed him. For a moment, he thought that was her giving in, her agreeing to stay. He tried to wrap his arms around her to hold her tight. *Thank God*, he thought.

Then she was away from him. "Of *course* I care for you," she said, skirting around him. "I could love you for the rest of my days."

"Could?" he asked incredulously as she started up the stairs.

"But I can't lose myself in you. I can't…" A sob broke free of her chest and she stopped, four steps up. "I can't forget who I am."

"I'm not asking you to do that. Damn it, Trish—I'm asking you to stay!"

She turned, looking down on him with a face full of pain. He started up the stairs to reach for her, but she backed away from him. "If I agree to your new terms—if I agree to stay—then what? Another month passes, we fall more in love, you extend the contract again, one month at a time."

"Don't you want to stay with us?" he demanded. "Isn't that what you want?"

"Oh, God, of course I do. But this isn't real, don't you see? All of this," she said as she swept her arms around, "and...you—God, Nate." Her voice caught in another sob. "People are depending on me. I have things I *have* to do."

"So do them from here!"

She shook her head. "I can't. I can't be your kept woman. I—I have to go."

Before he could do anything else, she spun and raced up the stairs, her shoulders shaking under the strain of her sobs.

What the hell? Okay, so he shouldn't have brought money into the conversation. That was a mistake, one he wouldn't make again. But...

A kept woman? That wasn't what was happening here! He was in love with her, for God's sake! And she might be in love with him, too—wasn't that what she'd said when she'd said she could love him the rest of her life?

So what was the problem here?

Overhead, he heard her door shut—and the lock click. He could go after her, go in through Jane's room. He could make her see reason—

And what? Argue with her until she agreed just to keep the peace? Force her to stay?

He sat heavily on the steps, pulled down by a weight in the center of his chest. For some reason, his brain decided that this would be the perfect time to revisit Diana's betrayal. To remember walking into the house that was supposed to be empty and hearing the distinctive noises of sex. To remember reasoning that it was just Brad with his latest girl. To remember calling Diana's phone to see where she was—and hearing it ring from the coat stand right at his elbow.

To remember walking up the stairs in his parents' home,

each footstep heavier than the last. Opening the door to his brother's room and seeing Diana, naked and bouncing on top of Brad.

Realizing with crushing certainty that he'd screwed up somewhere along the line—that he hadn't been enough for her. He'd been good enough until someone better came along.

He'd closed himself off after that. He didn't let himself get close to people, to women, because he couldn't be sure they weren't after something else—his company, his money.

He'd let himself get close to Trish. He'd trusted her with a part of himself he'd held back from every other person. He'd let himself be more real with her than he'd been in... years. Maybe in forever. He'd let himself think that he was enough for her. Him, Nate Longmire. Not the Boy Billionaire, not the philanthropist who cut the checks. Just him.

And what had she done?

She'd decided he wasn't enough. He wasn't enough; Jane wasn't enough. The two of them could never be more important to Trish than a bunch of backpacks.

He wasn't more important than two new pencils. Not to her.

Damn, but that hurt.

Trish packed quickly. Anything to not think about what had just happened. What was still happening.

Nate...

The moment she felt herself waver, she pushed back. Her mother would do anything to keep a man happy. Her mother would quit her job, ignore her children—anything, as long as it kept her man coming back for more.

And Trish? She could do it. She could agree to what Nate wanted, when he wanted it, as long as he kept on loving her. Even that last kiss—it'd almost broken her resolve.

She couldn't do it. She couldn't give herself over to him and cast everything that she'd held dear to the wind.

So she packed as fast as she could. She couldn't stay, not a moment longer. Every second she was around Nate was another second of temptation. Another second she would break.

It didn't take that long. Since she'd completed her schoolwork, she'd sold most of her books back already. She only had a few that were worth keeping more than they were worth the few dollars she'd get at the bookstore.

Her clothes fit into the duffel. She packed up her laptop, her shoes and the phone.

No, the phone was his. She didn't need it, didn't need the constant reminder of how Nate wanted to take care of her. If she kept his phone... Besides, they didn't get a lot of cell-phone reception on the rez, anyway. Who would she call, except him? She put it back on the dock.

What was she doing? This whole thing was ridiculous. It'd been ridiculous since she'd first agreed to his contract. She had no business being in this nice house, surrounded by nice people and things and food. But more than the material comforts, she had no business being in Nate's bed, having a casual affair. She had absolutely no business being with a man who was going to break her heart.

She couldn't stay. She couldn't give herself over to him, mind, body and soul. She could not lose who she was to become the woman he loved. That was what her mother did.

That's not what Trish did. She shared a name and a physical resemblance with her mother, but that's where it ended. Trish was a strong woman with a plan.

A plan that had never included falling in love with Nate.

Except she had. She *had*.

She buried her head in her hands, trying not to sob. She'd been wondering if maybe it wouldn't be such a bad thing to stay for another two weeks—finish out the school year living here, taking the comfort of Nate's bed—until she went home for a couple of months. She'd been sorely tempted. It was just another twelve, fourteen days at the most. Where was the harm in that? And then, after she'd spent some time away from Nate, she'd be in a better position to figure out how she wanted to proceed with him. Because she hadn't been done. She'd just…needed to get some perspective to make sure she didn't lose herself in him.

How had this happened? That was the problem. Somewhere, the attraction she'd felt at their first meeting had blossomed into something else, something infinitely more. Watching Nate cuddle Jane? Eating breakfasts out on his patio? Talking about comic books and charities?

Lying in his arms at night? All those stolen moments during the day?

A month ago, she hadn't loved him. A month ago, the little girl still sleeping in the next room had been in dire straits, only days from a trip to the emergency room.

A month ago, everything had been different.

Including Trish.

She was not her mother's daughter. No matter how much she wanted to open that door and run down to him and tell him that she was sorry and he was right and she'd do anything he wanted, just so long as he said he loved her and he kept on loving her. She wouldn't.

She had to walk away. Before she lost herself completely.

Her things packed up into two sad bags, Trish forced herself to go through the bathroom to Jane's room. The little girl was restless, although her eyes were still closed. She'd probably picked up on the sudden tension in the house, Trish thought.

"You're a good girl," she told the drowsy baby as she stroked the fine hairs on her little head for the last time.

"You take good care of your uncle Nate, okay? Make sure to smile at him and make him laugh like you do, okay?"

Jane shook her head from side to side, as if she was trying to tell Trish to stay, too.

"He's going to be a great daddy for you," Trish went on. "He loves you and he'll take good care of you." She thought back to all the times Nate had cuddled Jane or changed her or fed her—all the times he'd been a father.

All the times she'd been so surprised that he would be a father to someone else's child only because she didn't know men would do such things.

She leaned down and kissed Jane's head. "Goodbye, Jane. I love you. I won't forget you." The thought made her start to cry again because she knew that Jane would never remember her.

She hurried back to her room—no, it wasn't hers. It was merely the room she'd slept in for a month. Nothing here was hers, except for the sad duffels. She hefted them onto her shoulders and, with one last look, headed out.

As she trudged down the stairs, part of her brain was screaming at her that she was being stubborn—she didn't have to go! So Nate had been less than smooth. He wasn't always, she knew that. She was overreacting and she should let him take care of her.

But she was so much more than a temporary nanny with benefits. She ran a charity that hundreds, maybe thousands of children depended on for food and school supplies and the chance at a life better than the ones they'd been born into. She owed it to those kids—the ones who would never have a billionaire uncle to suddenly show up and make everything better—to do her best for them. For Patsy, her littlest sister. Trish was defined by her actions, not by the man she was sleeping with. She'd told him she would not fall for him and, at least on the surface, she had to hold that line.

She was a temporary nanny who'd had a casual affair and now it was time to go back to her real life. That's all there was to it.

Nate was waiting for her at the bottom of the stairs, hands on his hips. Just the sight of him nearly broke her resolve. *Be strong*, she told herself. Her mother would cave. She was not her mother.

But this was Nate. Her Nate. The man who'd said he was falling for her...

"I want you to stay, Trish," he said in a voice that was almost mean.

In that moment, she buckled. He was everything she wanted but... *Be strong*, she told herself. "You'll be all right? You and Jane? For the weekend?"

He stared at her as if she were speaking Lakota instead of English. "Don't we mean *anything* to you? How can you just walk away from her? From *me*?"

"I...I have to do this." Her own excuses rang hollow because he was right. Jane meant something to her. She wasn't just a baby that Trish had to take care of because no one else would.

And Nate? He wasn't just a man—any man, like her mother would have settled for. He was a man who stepped up when he had to. He took an active role in his niece's care. He didn't just take from Trish—he listened to her, he made her feel important.

"And that's it?" He made a sweeping gesture with his hands, as if he could clear everything away. "That's *that*?"

He was breaking her heart. For so long, she'd guarded herself against just this—the pain that went with the end. That's what her mother had taught her. It always ended and when it did, it always hurt. Every single time.

"I don't know," she admitted. "We just—I need some space. This has been a *great* month," she hurried to add, "but everything's happened so fast and I need to step back and make sure that I'm not losing myself. I've got to graduate and go home for a while. Maybe for the summer, I don't know. And after that…"

"Will you call me? At least let me know where you wind up tonight, so I won't worry about you."

Oh, God. Somehow, admitting this was almost as hard as leaving because it felt so *final*. No calls, no texts. A definitive break. "I left the phone upstairs."

All the blood drained out of his face. He knew it, too. "Oh. Okay. I see."

"Nate…"

"I, uh, I called for a car. It'll take you wherever you want to go."

"Thank you." She didn't know what else to say. She'd never broken up with anyone before. She'd only seen the screaming, crying fights her mother had had. He was being polite and respectful and, well, Nate.

Then, unexpectedly, he stepped up the few stairs separating them and cupped her face in his palms and touched his forehead to hers. She was powerless to stop him. "You probably don't want me to say this, but I don't care. I love you, Trish. Think about that when you go home. *I love you.* It doesn't make me less to love you. It makes me want to be someone *more* than who I was before I met you."

She gasped and closed her eyes against the tears. She couldn't do this, couldn't break his heart and hers—

Outside, a car horn honked.

Nate moved again, but instead of kissing her, he grabbed one of her bags and carried it down the rest of the way. He opened the door for her.

Struggling to breathe, Trish picked up the other bag and walked out into the weak afternoon sunshine.

It'd always been easy to stick to her principles, to keep herself safe from the messy entanglements that had ruled her childhood and all the children that they'd produced.

But putting her few belongings in the back of the trunk of some hired car? Silently standing there as Nate opened the backseat door for her? *Not* telling him she'd changed her mind when he leaned down and said, "I'll wait for you," right before he closed the door?

"Where to?" the driver said.

No, nothing about this was easy.

But she did it, anyway. She would not live month to month, at the mercy of this deal or that. She would *not* be ruled by love.

"San Francisco State University," she told the driver in a raw voice.

And that was that.

Thirteen

The day of graduation dawned bright and hot. Trish was already sweating in her cap and gown. Underneath she had on a pair of cutoffs and her Wonder Woman shirt. It was foolish to hope that the shirt would imbue her with enough power to make it through all the speeches and waiting to finally cross that damn stage and get her master's degree without dying of heatstroke, but it was the best she had.

"Who's the speaker, again?" Trish asked her neighbor after she took her seat in Cox Stadium.

"I don't know," the woman replied. "It was supposed to be Nancy Pelosi, but they said she canceled at the last minute."

"Great." Trish pulled out the water bottle she'd hidden in the sleeves of her master's gown and took a long drink.

As the university president and student body president made remarks about everyone's dedication in achieving their chosen master's degrees—the undergraduates were graduating tomorrow—and how their true potential could now be unlocked and so on and so on and *so on*, Trish only paid the bare minimum of attention. She was running through her plans.

Somehow, Stanley had tracked her down in the library. He'd brought her three checks—one for twenty grand and another for two hundred and fifty thousand, made out to

One Child, One World. The last one had been her security deposit from Mrs. Chan. All he'd said when he found her was, "You doing okay?"

"Yes, I'm fine. Nate, is he okay?" she'd asked in a rush. "Is Jane okay?"

"She's fine." Stanley had given her a look that she couldn't interpret before saying, "And Nate, well, he's been better." Stanley handed her a padded envelope. Then the tattooed, pierced man was off again, leaving Trish alone with a vague sense of guilt as she looked at the hundreds of thousands of dollars in her hands.

She'd opened the padded envelope to find her phone and the charger. The phone was charged and she had a waiting text message.

Just in case. Nate.

She'd sat staring at the phone for a good twenty minutes. Just in case.

Just in case she wanted to call him. Just in case she changed her mind.

That was almost as unbelievable as the rest of it. All those men her mother had "loved"? All of them had had someone on the side. None of them had ever kept their promises, except for Tim.

Except for Nate.

Then she'd all but sprinted to her bank. Because she was now rich, comparatively, she was going to buy an actual plane ticket to Rapid City, South Dakota, instead of taking the bus. From there, she'd figure out a way to get home. It might take her a few days, but she'd make it there one way or another.

And after she'd been home for a few days...well, she

had to see how it went. She didn't plan on staying on the rez, but she had no apartment in San Francisco to come back to. After today, she had nothing to tie her to this city except Nate. If her father still lived here, she hadn't found him and he hadn't found her. She could make a fresh start somewhere new—somewhere with cheaper rents—or...or she could come back to Nate. If he'd still have her.

"I'll wait for you," he'd said when he'd closed her car door. She desperately wanted to believe him but at the same time, she was afraid to get her hopes up, afraid to think that there really was a future between them.

Because how would it work? She didn't even have a proper job lined up. If—and that was a big *if*—she went back to him, she wanted to walk up to that door on her own merits, not because she was crawling back.

But she had no idea how to level the playing field—the huge, gaping playing field—that existed between them.

She was getting ahead of herself. Before she could even think about that, she had to get through the next few days. The idea of getting on a plane was a terrifying one— so terrifying that, when the commencement speaker was announced, she didn't hear the name. But someone behind her whooped and then the crowd was cheering. Trish looked up to see...

Nate.

Nate Longmire, wearing a fancy cap and gown, strode out onto the stage and shook the university president's hands.

Oh, God, was all she could think before he stepped up to the microphone. What was he doing here? This couldn't be a coincidence—could it? No. This was intentional. This was because of her.

"Congratulations, graduates!" he said with one of those

tight smiles that she recognized as him being nervous. "I know you're all disappointed that Congresswoman Pelosi was unable to make it—" There were a variety of muffled groans from the audience. "But," Nate went on, ignoring the noise, "I had such a great time here about two months ago that I jumped at the chance to talk to you one more time."

Sporadic applause erupted. Someone wolf-whistled.

"Today I want to talk about the power each and every one of you possess," Nate continued. Even she could see him blushing at this distance. "You may be sitting there, asking yourselves, 'now what?' You may have student debt. You may not have a job. Maybe you've got someone, maybe you broke up."

"Oh, hell."

She didn't realize she'd spoken out loud until the woman sitting on her left said, "What?"

"Oh. Sorry. Nothing." Nothing except that her last—her only—lover was up on stage, slowly circling his way through a commencement speech that was all about her.

"You may not think you have any power to change things—to get a job in this economy, to find the 'right' person, to affect change in your surroundings. I'm here to tell you that's not true."

"You okay?" the woman on her left asked. "You don't look so good."

"I'm—fine. I'm fine." Trish forced herself to look away from Nate and smile at her neighbor. "I just can't believe Nate Longmire is up there, that's all."

The woman smiled. "He's even better-looking in person."

"Yes," Trish agreed weakly. "Better in person."

"I recently spent some time with a SFSU graduate by

the name of Trish Hunter," Nate was saying. As he talked, he searched the crowd until his gaze fell upon hers. The corner of his mouth moved and she knew he was glad to see her.

She wasn't sure if she was breathing or not—she was definitely light-headed. What was he *doing*?

"I was impressed with her education but more than that, I was impressed with her dedication. Despite a limited amount of funds, Ms. Hunter has single-handedly run a charity called One Child, One World, which provides school supplies and meals to Native American children living in poverty on reservations in South Dakota."

The audience settled back into their heat-induced stupor as he went on about her charity, her awards and, yes, her dedication. Trish couldn't do anything but gape at him. This wasn't happening, was it? Maybe she'd just had a heatstroke and was hallucinating this whole thing.

He was really here. He was—well, he was fighting for her. No one had ever fought for her before, not like this. She'd known he wasn't the same kind of man her mother had always chased—but this?

He wasn't going to run away. He wasn't going to hide behind lies.

Something Tim, her stepfather, had said to her the last time they'd talked floated back into her consciousness— "There's something about being with her that makes me feel right with the world. And when you've seen as much of the world as I have, you know that's no small thing."

The epiphany hit her so hard she jolted in her chair. Her mother—her flighty, careless mother who chased after any man she could catch—had been happily married for almost seven years to a decent guy who wouldn't even let Trish give him back a security deposit. She'd stayed married to him because they made each other feel right with the world.

Nate had said it himself. "You make me feel like everything's finally right in the world," he'd told her during the last few moments she'd stood before him and wavered.

And Tim was right—it was no small thing. It was something huge. It might be everything.

Would she really keep pushing herself away from Nate just because her mother had a long, scarred history of making bad choices? Or was Trish forcing herself to make a bad choice, just because it was the opposite of what her mother would have done?

Did Nate make everything right in her world, too?

"And so," Nate finally said, "I am happy to announce that the Longmire Foundation will be awarding two endowments. The first is to establish a scholarship for Native American students who enroll in San Francisco State University. The other is an endowment of ten million dollars to One Child, One World to help prepare those Native students for college and beyond."

Trish shot to her feet and tried to ask him what the *hell* he was doing, but all that came out of her mouth was a gurgling noise.

"Ah, yes, there she is, ladies and gentlemen. Please give Ms. Hunter a round of applause for all her hard work."

The crowd broke out into what could only be called a standing ovation as people cheered for her. She barely heard it. All she heard was Nate leaning forward and saying, "Ms. Hunter, if I could speak to you after you graduate?"

"That's you?" the woman on her left said. "Girl, you better move."

But Trish couldn't because she was trapped in the hell

of having a last name that started with an *H*. All she could do was go through the motions. The rest of the graduation passed in an absolute blur. Trish didn't remember hearing her name called, barely remembered walking across the stage to get her diploma. She did, however, have full recall of when some university higher-up pulled her out of the line that was moving back toward the seats and ushered her off the stage. "...Very exciting," he was saying as he led Trish to where Nate was waiting. "An endowment! This is excellent news..."

Nate was waiting for her in the shadows under the stands of the stadium, cap in hand and gown unzipped. He had on a button-up shirt and a tie and he looked *so* good.

Suddenly, Trish was very conscious of the fact that she was in cutoffs and a T-shirt. Just another way they didn't match up.

"What did you do?" she demanded the moment Nate was in earshot.

He grinned at her as if he'd expected her to say that, but then he turned to the official. "If I could have a moment with Ms. Hunter..."

"Oh, yes. Yes, of course!" The man hurried back into the sunlight, still muttering, "Excellent news!" as he departed.

And then she and Nate were alone. "What did you *do*, Nate?"

"I removed the money from the equation."

"By giving me ten freaking million dollars? Are you *insane*? That's not removing it—that's putting it front and center!"

"No, I didn't. I gave your charity the money, free and clear. No strings attached. You'll be able to draw a salary as the head of the charity and do all those things you wanted to do—basketball courts and after-school snacks and computer labs. All of it."

He hadn't forgotten her wish list. Why did that make her feel so good? "What do you mean, no strings? You just *gave* me ten million dollars!" Her voice echoed off the bottoms of the stands.

"No, I didn't," he repeated with more force. "I divested myself of some of my money to a worthy charity. I do that all the time."

"But—but—"

He touched her then, pulling her deeper into the shadows. "I gave *you* a choice."

"What?"

"I want you to come back to me," he said, dropping his voice down. "But I don't ever want you to feel that you're not my equal, that you're not good enough for me. And I sure as hell don't ever want you to feel that I hold all the cards. So, here we are. I give your charity money that I'll never miss and you'll do so much good with it—and you'll be able to pay yourself a salary." He grinned. "Knowing you, it won't be very much, but still."

"I don't see what this has to do with you giving me a *choice*, Nate. How is this not the same deal as before?"

In the safety of the shadows, he trailed his fingers down the side of her face. "This money is for your charity. It's not contingent on you moving back in with me. That's what no-strings-attached means. I won't take this money back—in fact, I believe certain government regulations would frown upon that. No matter what happens next, the charity gets the money. *That's* the deal."

"But—"

"If you want to come back to me—or if you want me to come to wherever you are—then you and I will both know that it's not because you couldn't say no to the money. You won't have to rely on me. You will be your own woman. That's what you want, isn't it?"

"I want…" She had to lean away from his touch. "But it won't change the fact that the money came from you."

"I doubt that any of those kids on the rez will give a damn where the money came from," he said in a matter-of-fact voice. "And you're missing the *if. If* you come back to me. It's your choice. It always has been."

"Nate…"

"I messed up the negotiations last time," he went on. "A good negotiator always knows what the other side wants and the first time, you wanted funding. It was easy to give it to you because all I needed was a nanny. But the second time, that's not what you wanted and I should have known it because I didn't want you as a nanny anymore. The situation had changed."

"You…didn't?"

"You wanted something else—you told me yourself. You didn't want to lose yourself in me. I didn't figure out what that meant at first." He grinned and despite the fact that she'd been yelling at him, he still looked thrilled to see her. "But I think I've got it now."

"What?" Her words failed her. She knew she was repeating herself, but she couldn't get a grasp on this situation.

"I think you wanted a promise," he said, going down on one knee in the shadows under the stadium bleachers. "A promise that I would honor your wishes—that I would honor *you*—with no strings attached. I didn't give that to you then. But I'd like to try again." He reached into his pocket and pulled out a small, bright blue box. The size that usually held a ring.

The air stopped moving in her lungs as he opened the box. "What are you doing, Nate?"

"Making you a promise," he said. A splendid pear-shaped diamond was nestled on a silver band. "Trish Hunter, will you marry me?"

Her mouth opened, but no sound came out as she looked from the ring—the promise—back to him.

"I want to marry you. I hope you want to marry me." He cracked a nervous little grin. "It usually works better that way."

"But I was going to go home!"

"I want you to go." He stood and, taking her hand in his, slipped the ring on her finger. "I want you to think about this, about us. I don't want you to come back to me because you're worried about Jane or you think you owe me. I don't want you to lose yourself. I want you as you've been. You push back when I do something dumb, you teach me how to do things. You make me a real person, Trish—not some caricature of a billionaire geek with too much money. You give me a purpose. You make everything feel right in my world and that's something I honestly wouldn't ever get back."

"You're not that—not to me," she told him, her words getting caught in the back of her throat. "You're just Nate and you're a wonderful man. I'm—I'm afraid, Nate. I'm *afraid*. I don't have any great role models for how to make a relationship work. I spent so long not being in one that to suddenly fall in love with you? You were my first. And when I was with you, I didn't feel like the same person I'd always defined myself as—the poor American Indian woman, the responsible daughter of an irresponsible woman. You—you make me feel right, too. And I felt it *so* much it scared me. It still scares me because I could love you so much. *So* much."

He grinned down at her. "There's that word again—*could*."

"I…" she took a deep breath. "I do love you. You've shown me what a man can be—not someone cruel, not someone who comes and goes. A man who'll stay, who'll do the right thing even if it's hard. Even if…"

"Even if it scares me. Like taking a baby home with me." He took a step in and touched his forehead to hers. "I hired the Polish grandmother, by the way. She's very efficient. Just so we're clear—I'm not asking you to be a nanny. I'm asking you to be my wife." He grinned. "My *permanent* wife."

"Oh, Nate." She kissed him then, a light touching of the lips.

He wrapped his arms around her and held her tight. Suddenly, everything that had been wrong about the past few days was right again because Nate was here and she was here and they were together. "I missed you," she whispered. "I was already thinking about calling you after I made it home."

He squeezed her tighter. "I couldn't wait that long. I couldn't let you go without knowing exactly how much I need you. I want you to come back to us because you know that you belong with me."

"Yes," she whispered. "You're right. Loving you doesn't mean I lose myself. I feel like, for the first time, I've *found* myself."

He tilted her head back and stared into her eyes. "I'm already yours, Trish Hunter. Will you be mine?"

This was what she wanted. To know that love wouldn't destroy her like it always had her mother, to know that Nate would fight for her. For them. "I'm yours, too. You're the only man I ever want."

He kissed her then, full of passion and promises. "Come home," he said when the kiss ended. "Sleep in my bed with me. And tomorrow we'll work on getting you out to the rez, okay? That's the plan."

"Tomorrow," she agreed. "But tonight…"

He kissed her again. "Tonight is ours."

That was a promise she knew he'd keep.

* * * * *

LET'S TALK
Romance

For exclusive extracts, competitions
and special offers, find us online:

f facebook.com/millsandboon

🐦 @MillsandBoon

📷 @MillsandBoonUK

Get in touch on 01413 063232

For all the latest titles coming soon, visit
millsandboon.co.uk/nextmonth